Dark Rising Through the Looking Glass

LOOKING GLASS SERIES
BOOK THREE

J.G. SAUER

OLIVERHEBERBOOKS

Acknowledgments

As children, we've all spent our fair share of time playing pretend and making believe. There are so many scenarios to choose from when we're young—fantasy worlds to inhabit—and our creativity runs wild in our early years. Though I'm a firm believer that our childlike wonder, our penchant for make-believe never really leaves us, it does, unfortunately, tend to slip into the background as adulthood takes shape and form...and life gets in the way.

For me, writing is a form of "adult" make-believe. I love all things "fairy tale"—from Carroll to Baum to the Brothers Grimm, from light to dark. This Looking Glass series is a tribute to those brilliant tales of fantasy, wonder, and yes, even darkness. I am so grateful that I'm surrounded by folks that are as enamored with these stories as I am. With regards to **Dark Rising Through the Looking Glass**, I would like to thank a few of those kindred spirits here...

First and foremost was—and always will be—my agent extraordinaire & incredible mentor, Christine Witthohn. Though you've entered a well-earned retirement, I know that when needed, you're only a phone call away. You made me a better writer in so many ways. You are a blessing, my friend.

A huge thank you goes to Liz Lipperman for being my CP. You've also made me a better writer, and even though you're retiring (or so you say...again), having you as my critique partner has been and continues to be a delight. I love you, my friend.

Natalie Bellissimo—I've said it before but it bears repeating. You are family and a sister of my heart.

Much love and gratitude to you, my friend, and not just for your editing and grammar skills (which are legendary at this point), but for your support for every book that I write. You say you aren't a fantasy reader, but I beg to differ. Your childlike wonder and penchant for make-believe is still firmly in place, pal!

Val "Valine" Braun, and Kelli McMellon—you guys really ROCKED the beta-reads...again. You are both amazing. And my special thanks to my fantasy muse, Melissa Jenck. You keep me on track, inspire me, push me. You are a jewel, and I am grateful.

And finally, another huge shout out to Tanya Anne Crosby and her entire team at Oliver Heber Books. Thank you for the support, hard work and, as always, providing a healthy space for what we do.

Blessings to you all...

REALM of ARTEMYSIA
ARCTIC OCEAN
NORTHERN WASTELANDS
CANTILEY MNT RANGE
THE UNWELCOMING RISE
WILLOW GLEN WOOD
EASTERN GLADE
WESTERN SEA
ROSELAND WOOD
TARKINGTON FOREST
EASTERN BARRENS
LARKSPUR MEADOW
ROSELAND
CHESHIRE WOOD
WYSTERIA
SOUTHERN OCEAN HORN
N E S W
COURTS
EVENING
TWILIGHT
STARLIGHT
DAYLIGHT
DAWN
WINTER
SPRING
AUTUMN
SUMMER
KALEB'S CABIN
WHITE PALACE
RED PALACE
TEMPLE OF ORACLES

Prologue

Light snowflakes drifted like fine crystals through the ashen light of mid-morning. Field Marshal Alexi Tovin pulled the collar of his heavy, wool duster closer as he surveyed the landscape before him, his breath fogging the crisp, frosty air. Though they hadn't gotten much in the way of sticking snow over the last few weeks, fall had definitely begun its slow drift into winter. It had been spitting snow for the last fifteen minutes and was just beginning to accumulate in a thin, pristine layer, making his tracking, such as it was, more difficult.

The realm of Artemysia was Alexi's homeland. A wild and magnificent land full of magick and wonder. Split into two separate kingdoms centuries ago, Wysteria and Roseland, each had their own unique beauty. And their own unique dangers.

Alexi loved the whole of it with his entire being.

Since both kingdoms had just been reunited under one rule within the last year, the persistent unrest that had plagued the land for the last decade or so had diminished to a certain degree. But what had Alexi and the rest of the leadership cautious over the last few months were the dangerous rumbles just beneath the surface that still remained. Adding to Alexi's concern, had been the odd sporadic deaths within the various dryad communities, the bulk of which were here in the northland in the vicinity of Willow Glen Wood.

Alexi reined in his destrier and scanned the northeast treeline of the Wood.

The deaths occurring here were still a mystery, as most dryads—or tree fae—were normally a peaceful group. Inhabiting the old growth trees of both kingdoms, dryads posed no threat to anyone. Yet, several extremely violent deaths had been discovered over the last eight months, pointing to a disturbing trend with no obvious cause or perpetrators. There were also the vague rumors of outside threats that persisted, which was one of the reasons he'd been recently making these early morning treks.

War had taken its toll yet again as it had centuries ago, and Queen Beatrice, the White Queen, had made it clear that they were to be vigilant. They would need to put an end to those rumors—as well as any actual threats—to soothe the fears of those who lived within the boundaries of both kingdoms. To that end, Alexi, along with the Queen's son, Prince Graydon, and Alexi's cousin, Chancellor Valian Winchester, had been working day and night to discover the origins of the rumors or any true threats found. They would deal with the situations in either case as they came up. The Queen wished for the realm to get back to a peaceful existence, and they were all intent on granting that wish as soon as possible.

Alexi's destrier, Solas, stamped and pawed at the hardened ground before snorting his displeasure.

"Yes, yes, I'm fully aware of your impatience, old friend," Alexi murmured. "We've both missed our breakfasts, which I'll admit makes one a bit testy. It won't be much longer. I want to follow this unfamiliar scent just a little farther. And these odd tracks that keep disappearing and then reappearing are starting to piss me off."

The warhorse, white as the snow beginning to accumulate on the ground, snorted again and shook his massive head.

Alexi laughed out loud. "Oh no. Don't worry, pal. Believe me, we aren't getting any closer to the eastern tip of the Barrens than absolutely necessary, especially this far north and so near to the Barrens-Wastelands boundary. The wards have been strengthened all around and, so far, are doing their job of securing our borders." He blew out a breath in resignation, watched the fog of it drift in the frigid air. "But if that's where these weird tracks eventually lead, we'll not follow; at least not without a legion of soldiers with us."

"You talk to that horse like a fellow warrior."

Alexi had immediately reached for his sword, but then relaxed his grip when he recognized the voice. "That's because Solas *is* a fellow warrior." He turned with a smirk as he watched Finvar, the High Lord of Wysteria's Winter Court, ride out of the tree line to the left, leading a handful of his fae warriors. "It sounds as if perhaps you've forgotten how to relate to an immortal partner, High Lord."

"Not likely." Finvar grunted, giving his own massive gray and black warhorse a pat. "Rolim and I have been together for over a century and understand each other perfectly." The charger pawed the ground and nodded his head up and down vigorously as if agreeing with his High Lord.

Finvar smirked, but then his icy-blue eyes narrowed above his wild, silvery beard. "And what, pray tell, are you doing this far north so early in the morning, Field Marshal?"

"I could ask you the same. You're just as far from your Winter Court as I am from the White Palace." Alexi grinned. "I would imagine I'm doing much the same thing as you, Fin."

Finvar urged his enormous steed a bit closer. "Where is your entourage?" he asked in a low voice edged with concern.

Alexi laughed out loud again. "Come now, Fin. You know better than to ask me that. I don't need a squad of men for an early morning ride."

"That would be true enough if that was all that this is. But this is far more than an early morning ride, Alexi, for either of us, and you know it. With all that's been happening in the realm over the last few months, the mysterious tree fae deaths? You should not be out here on your own. 'Tis not safe these days. Especially, as you said, so close to the Barrens-Wastelands border."

"Oh, trust me, I'm aware. Our last trip into the Barrens was one trip too many for me. I don't even want to think about what exists farther north in the Wastelands. However, I caught a scent on the morning air as we entered the Eastern Glade that unsettled me, so we followed it to Willow Glen Wood." Alexi gestured to the strange tracks now barely visible beneath the thin, white layer of the recent precipitation. "Then we found these weird disappearing tracks, and Solas and I followed those as well. At least as well as we could."

"Oh, aye. I know of what you speak as I have had the same experience on several occasions recently, have caught that scent, seen those tracks."

"It's strange. The tracks seem to disappear and then reappear farther along. Perhaps whatever made them is fading in jumps like we did in the Barrens this last summer." Alexi squinted at the High Lord. "Do you know their origins, Fin?"

The High Lord stroked the icy flakes from his long, silvery beard. Then he slowly tilted his head. "Seems that something which doesn't belong has been making treks into Wysteria and possibly Roseland as well. That is why you should not be out on your own, Field Marshal." He shook his head. "Whatever it is, it could be dangerous, Alexi."

Alexi frowned. "We've had no reports of the wards failing along any border in Wysteria or Roseland. How could anything or anyone be crossing into either kingdom? After our last trek into the Barrens to rescue the descendant from the Red King, Old Minerva made sure to strengthen the wards."

Minerva, the Witch of the Eastern Glade, lived not far from Willow Glen Wood where they now stood. She was ancient and formidable, the most powerful witch in the realm and had created the wards with her mysterious magicks centuries ago.

"The witch assured the Queen that the wards were secure," Alexi added.

"I am aware."

"Yet you know something, don't you, Fin? I can see the knowledge of it in your face. You've seen these strange tracks before, know the scent."

The High Lord glanced around the clearing, and then urged his steed still closer. Leaning over the destrier's withers, he patted Rolim's muscular neck before speaking in a low voice. "The tracks may be familiar to me, aye. And the scent...well, it's not something you'd forget, and something I've not run across for a very long time; and definitely not in Wysteria or Roseland." Finvar's eyes took on a faraway look as he scoured the landscape before murmuring to himself, "Indeed, I'd not thought it possible after all this time."

"What, Fin? What is this?"

Finvar shook his head as if coming out of a daydream. "The High Lord of Twilight Court and I have discussed this possible threat at length, as he's concerned and has seen the signs in Roseland as well."

"You and Niall have discussed it?" Alexi frowned. "Well, don't keep me in suspense. What the hell is this? And whatever it is, where is it coming from? How is it entering the kingdom through the security wards?"

Finvar looked off toward the tall wards in the distance, the security that stood between Wysteria and the eastern tip of the Barrens. Then he sighed. "I'd rather not say just yet, Alexi." He put up a hand when Alexi would have argued. "At least, not until I'm completely certain. If this is what I think it may be, it would be a stunning revelation. I do not wish to cause panic."

Alexi's apprehension deepened. During the search for the Red King in the Barrens, and the subsequent rescue the previous summer of the descendant, Alyssa Montague, Finvar and Niall, the High Lord of Roseland's Twilight Court, had not held back. They'd had no restraint in stoking Alexi's fears of the nasties that lived in that terrible place. Though the Wastelands were immeasurably worse than the Barrens, it wasn't like Finvar to be so cryptic or to hold back pertinent information, whether certain or not.

Another thing that did not bode well.

Alexi frowned. "Okay, now you're starting to piss me off. And spreading the panic fairly efficiently, I might add, considering what we experienced last summer in the Barrens." Leaning forward, he pressed the High Lord. "Spill it, Fin. What have you seen? What do you know? Or what do you *think* you know?"

"Not here, Alexi." The High Lord sighed and then shook his head. "Here, the trees have ears. I had planned to come to the White Palace this evening to meet with the Queen. However, we'll follow you back to the palace now. You're right, this is something that needs to be shared and discussed with her and the Chancellor. And the sooner the better."

One

The air was frigid and seemed to eagerly sink its teeth into her like a hungry animal, spearing its icy fingers into her flesh in spite of the heavy overcoat she wore. Isabella Christensen kept moving, trying desperately to find her way through this murky forest with its covering of snow on every bush and tree branch.

Where the hell was she? Roseland? Wysteria? She hadn't remembered coming through a portal. She looked both ways on the path she'd taken but the forest gave no clues and continued to be dark and silent. At least here in its midst, the path was clear with only a light dusting of snow. So, that was a plus. However, nothing looked familiar in any way, and she wished for a compass but had none. Which meant that there was no way to even know which direction she was walking. She could only hope that she would run across something to show her the way soon, as the cold was beginning to weigh on her.

Fortunately, it didn't take too much longer until the forest opened up onto a wide, snow-covered meadow. The only problem was that the deep snowy layer obscured any path forward. She stood for a moment, frowning, before movement across the wide expanse caught her eye. Oh, thank goodness, she thought, as a tall figure dressed in ebony robes emerged from the forest at the treeline directly across the meadow from where she stood. At least I'm not alone, she thought. But then she didn't *recognize him, and as she watched, two more figures in similar garb joined him.*

In spite of their imposing dress, she was just about to lift a hand and wave at them when a voice to her right said, "No, do not engage. You should not be here, Isabella Doyle. This is a dangerous place. Go. Go quickly."

Isabella Doyle?

Turning toward the voice, a tall, lean woman dressed in leaf-green pants, a tunic embellished with gold that glittered in the dim light of the day, and leather boots that topped her knees stood a few yards away. A long bow and quiver were strapped to her back. Though the woman faced the meadow and the figures standing on the other side, and Isabella had only a side view, this woman was a faerie or an elf. Maybe some kind of hunter or warrior. Her long red hair—much like Isabella's own—was intricately braided back at the sides of her head, revealing her delicately pointed ears, which were adorned with sparkling jewels and hoops of different sizes and shapes.

"Where am I?" Isabella asked. "I don't remember how I got here."

The woman turned then, and her deep emerald eyes held a touch of concern. "This is the far northland, Isabella. They call it the Wastelands. There are dangerous secrets buried here along with powerful entities not seen for centuries. But they are coming. Go back and tell the others...and prepare."

At that, the woman's image began to shimmer.

"No, wait!" Isabella called. "I don't even know what that means."

But it wasn't just the woman's image that began to blur but everything else around her.

"Wait!"

Isabella yelled and sat bolt-straight up in her bed, covered in sweat with her pulse racing. Putting a hand to her chest, she took several deep breaths, trying to slow the rapid beat of her heart. Though she wasn't quite awake, the disturbing dream or nightmare and its contents—like so many she'd been having of late—was already beginning to fade as she flopped back down, and mumbling, turned over and was asleep again in minutes.

The next thing she knew, her alarm was blaring. Glancing at the digital readout, she groaned, a string of expletives filling the air. She'd just pried her eyes open, and she was already twenty minutes behind. She'd scheduled a staff meeting at her event company, Party Poppers, for nine a.m., and then had several client meetings over the course of the day. And all of that before a new artist's showing at the Montague Art Gallery this evening.

How on God's green earth am I going to get through this day? she thought with a sigh. Feeling like someone had drained her blood while she slept, Isabella crawled out of bed and went looking for coffee.

SHE WASN'T QUITE SURE HOW SHE DID IT, AND IT TOOK every bit of determination she'd possessed, but Isabella *had* made it through the day, and without any kind of major calamity. Even so, there was a nasty bite to the light wind when she stepped to the curb, hand in the air, to hail a cab. She grimaced and then sighed. New York City in late October as the weather began its crossover between fall and winter. October was typically a mild month in the city with the requisite rain showers, and then getting cooler as the month progressed. However, though the temperature was in the upper fifties this evening, with the windchill Isabella felt it all the way to her toes like a bad omen. They were probably going to be in for it this winter, which was only a handful of weeks away. Her nose warned of an early snow, but she put those thoughts aside.

She had other things on her mind.

Pulling her wool coat close around her, she scrambled into the first taxi that pulled up in front of her building almost before it came to a stop. She blurted out an address and then glanced at her watch as they pulled away from the curb. There was little traffic this evening, but if the cabbie didn't move it, she was going to be late.

And she was never late.

Well, normally that was true, yet, over the last few weeks she couldn't seem to stay on schedule to save her life, which was beginning to be problematic. She could blame it on the sleepless nights she'd been having, yet that wasn't exactly true either. She *had* slept every night, and soundly for the most part. At least, as far as she remembered.

More like the dead, she thought.

And that was the issue. No, it wasn't the lack of sleep, but rather the damned dreams intruding on her sleep. Bits and pieces of another realm, a magickal storybook world. There was a niggling feeling in the back of her mind that she couldn't quite shake. Something was coming and more disturbing than the impending winter weather.

"Hey, lady, you okay?" The cabbie's voice shook her out of her dark thoughts.

"What?" Isabella blinked up at him.

"This is the address you gave me, right?"

Looking around, she realized that he'd pulled up in front of the Montague Art Gallery. *Geez, I have got to get a grip*, she thought. These lapses were getting more frequent, and she had no idea why or what was wrong with her.

"Sorry, yes. This is the correct address," she muttered as she handed him a twenty for an eight-dollar fare. "Keep the change."

"Thanks, lady," she heard him say as she climbed out of the cab and turned to close the car door, stepping back up onto the sidewalk.

However, before she could turn toward the gallery she was struck by the oddest sensation—an unfamiliar prickling that had a shiver running down her spine, and it had nothing to do with the cold.

Someone was watching her.

She didn't know how she knew that. In a city of over 1.6 million people, she supposed that someone was always watching. But her specifically? What were the odds? But she knew it in her bones. Someone *was* watching her. As the cab pulled away, her eyes were drawn across the avenue to a woman staring directly at her. When their eyes met, Isabella felt the strangest sense of déjà vu and could hardly breathe as the woman smiled, her lips beginning to move. Isabella froze as she heard the woman's voice in her head say, *Yes, there you are, Isabella Doyle. I see you...the time is coming, you know.*

Another chill ran through her. Isabella Doyle? Where had she heard that before, and recently? It was on the tip of her tongue but she couldn't quite get a hold of it. Why on earth would this woman refer to her by her mother's maiden name, and how did she even know that name? A better question would probably be how it was possible that Isabella had just clearly heard the woman's voice as if she was standing next to her? Yet, she was all the way across the street. Then a large delivery box truck drove by and blocked Isabella's field of vision, and when the truck finally passed a few seconds later, the woman was gone—had simply vanished. Isabella looked up and down the avenue but she was nowhere to be seen.

"What the..." With that chill still running through her, Isabella turned toward the gallery. "I just may be losing my marbles," she muttered to herself, and with a shaking hand, she opened the door and entered the gallery.

"Izzy! There you are," Alyssa Montague called over the surprising crowd of people as she made her way through the throng. "Sorry, we were really slammed today, and then with this new artist's showing, it's turning out to be a monster. I mean, it's been like this all day." Alyssa stopped and searched Isabella's face. "What's up with you? You're usually twenty minutes early for everything. Not that you're late, but I was starting to worry."

Alyssa was the owner of the gallery and Isabella's best and oldest friend. Her family was also the direct descendants of the little Alice celebrated in Lewis Carroll's books. Alyssa was the great-granddaughter of the great-granddaughter of the original Alice, and her family history was tied to little Alice's wonderland. Indeed, they were the custodians of the history of a real world alongside their own, a world woven into a children's book centuries ago; Artemysia—with the kingdoms of Wysteria and Roseland.

Wonderland.

Alyssa herself had only found out about this world, this history, at the first of the year as well.

Isabella removed her knit cap and shook out her curly red hair, before shoving the heavy mop of it out of her face.

"Hey. Izzy? What's wrong?" Alyssa asked with a look of concern. She took Isabella's arm and led her through the crowded gallery back toward the office. "What's happened?" she whispered urgently. "You look like you've had a bad scare or something. I mean, there's literally no color in your face."

"That's probably because I *have* had a scare," Isabella said, taking a deep breath and releasing it in a huff.

"Is it Alexi? Has something happened in Artemysia? Niall hasn't said anything."

Alexi Tovin was the Field Marshal in charge of Artemysia's security forces and a handsome Elven soldier. He and Isabella had been together since the summer after she'd had an amicable split with his cousin, Valian Winchester, a celebrated author in this realm and Chancellor of Artemysia in the other.

"No, Alexi's fine. At least, I think he is. I haven't seen or spoken to him since last week."

"Then what?" Alyssa asked gently when they'd settled in her office on the sofa.

Isabella hesitated, and then scrubbed her hands over her face. "Aly, I seriously think that I'm losing my mind."

Alyssa rolled her eyes. "What? Don't be ridiculous. Why would you say that?"

Unable to sit, Isabella got up and began to pace. She rubbed her forehead where she could feel a headache brewing, then stopped suddenly and spun around, pointing a finger at Alyssa. "After the whole New Year's Eve deal, when we first found out about Artemysia...when we got home...you had disturbing dreams, right?"

Alyssa leaned forward, elbows on her knees, and spoke quietly. "I did. You know that I did. It took me a long time to work through it all. Learning about my family's true history and that I was the descendant was pretty unbelievable. But then having to use a weapon of mass destruction like the Scepter of Fire to save a magickal realm that I'd never heard of from annihilation by the evil Red King and learning that I was the only one who could? It was a lot to come to grips with, and it plagued me for months. The more I obsessed over it, the worse it seemed to get. That realm is full of magick and wonder, but as you well know, there are terrible things that live in the Barrens, as well as the Wastelands." Alyssa tilted her head. "Why do you ask, Izzy? Is that what this is about? Are you having dreams?"

Isabella's pulse sped up just a bit. Yes, Artemysia was a place of magick and wonder, both kingdoms were beautiful and exciting and filled with elves, and faeries, and all manner of interesting creatures.

Truly a wonderland.

But that realm also held incredible dangers, which was why these recent dreams—or what she could remember of them—were so disconcerting. Though Isabella had experienced little of those dangers, Alyssa, being the great-granddaughter of the great-granddaughter of the original Alice, certainly had. Considering that most of Isabella's experiences in that other realm were pleasant enough, she could only imagine what Alyssa had gone through, and what her friend's dreams—or rather nightmares—had held.

"Izzy? Talk to me."

Isabella shook her head. "I don't even know where to begin or how to explain about the dreams that I've been having, Aly."

"Are they about Wysteria and Roseland?"

"Yes...no...well, sort of." Isabella shook her head again. "Sometimes I'm there in a familiar place like the White Palace, and it's eerily quiet, like, maybe I'm the only one there. Other times I'm in a glade or a forest, but I don't recognize it. It could be in Artemysia somewhere but it's unfamiliar. It's never Cheshire Wood or Tarkington Forest, or any place that I've been while there."

Alyssa tilted her head. "Okay, so the White Palace, yes, obviously Wysteria, but how do you know that the glade or the forest are in Wysteria or Roseland? Could they be here, maybe in Central Park? I mean, there is the old portal there."

"No. I know these dreams are all taking place in Artemysia... *somewhere*. I just know, like you sometimes do with dreams, but it's very disorienting."

"Boy, do I know what you're talking about. Unfortunately, for me, it wasn't a dream. It was the real thing," Alyssa murmured. "Scary, right?"

"Oh, Lord, so scary," Isabella nodded. "I've had a variation of the same dream over and over. I don't know where I am but Valian is there, and he's pointing toward something in the distance that I can't see and saying something that I can't make out." She shrugged in frustration. "Other times, it's Alexi, and he's also pointing and shaking his head, but in his case, it feels more like a warning, but about what, I have no idea. Then there is this latest dream...last night."

"Was it the same?"

"Again, sort of, but I don't remember much of it. Yes, I was in another forest, and it was so, so cold. Bitter cold, you know? But neither Alexi nor Valian were in this one. At least, I don't think they were." She shook her head. "It all gets so jumbled. I do remember coming to a snow-covered meadow and looking across to the other side where the forested area continued. Because the snow was so deep, I was trying to see where the path would be to cross the meadow. That's when I saw a man—or maybe it was a couple of men —all dressed in black robes on the other side. I remember thinking that I should wave, talk to them, ask them if they could show me the way home. But...something stopped me. Anyway, I don't remember much else."

"Sounds like you're not getting much sleep, either," Alyssa said. "And that can be a factor in repetitive dreams like this."

Isabella went back over and plopped down onto the sofa next to Alyssa. "But that's just it, Aly. Sleep is not the problem. I'm sleeping like a coma patient. Seriously," she insisted when Alyssa chuckled. "I'm sleeping through my damned *alarm*, Aly. I can't stay on schedule, and I'm exhausted most of the time." She leaned toward Alyssa and whispered, "And I've been late for appointments."

Alyssa frowned. "Yeah, now that sounds serious."

"Ya *think*? It's why I was later than normal today. You know me. You said it yourself. I'm normally early for literally everything." Isabella rubbed her eyes and then gave Alyssa a miserable look. "It's starting to affect my work, Aly, and that's unacceptable. I've also been having...lapses."

"Lapses? What kind of lapses?"

"Oh, nothing serious, at least I don't think they are. I mean, it's not like blackouts or anything. It's more like my mind wanders at the oddest moments. It happened in the cab coming over here tonight. Between pick-up in front of my building and arriving here...I lost time. The cabbie was like, *Hey, lady. Are you okay?* And I realized that we were here." She rolled her eyes. "It's embarrassing. I don't even remember what I was thinking about. Then there was the weird encounter I had when I got out of the cab."

"What weird encounter?"

Isabella sighed and explained about the woman across the avenue. "I gotta say, it freaked me out pretty good."

"No doubt. That is concerning."

"I know! I would think that maybe I imagined the whole episode but she called me Isabella Doyle. I mean, how would she know that was my mom's maiden name? Plus, there was the weirdest sense of déjà vu when our eyes met. Like maybe I should know her but I couldn't put my finger on it. And then she just disappeared. I mean, a truck went by, and she'd literally vanished."

"Yeah, weird, for sure, but we've seen this kind of thing in Artemysia, right? So, I'd say that it has to be connected, but why you?"

"What do you mean?"

"Well, I'm the great-granddaughter of the great-granddaughter of the original Alice, remember? I've learned to expect these kinds of things happening." Alyssa gave her a quizzical look. "But why you, Izzy?"

"I never thought about it that way. It's a good point."

"Alright. How about we start with this. How long has this been going on? How long have you been having these dreams?"

Isabella sighed. "Several weeks, I guess. Maybe a month and a half."

"Okay." Alyssa paused for a moment. "Can you think of anything else odd that's happened recently, either here or in Artemysia? You'd been going over with Alexi more often about that time, right? You and I hadn't gone through the portal together for a while."

"I know." Isabella nodded. "Seems like our work has gotten in the way more often since we came back from the debacle during the summer. But no, I can't think of anything out of the ordinary."

Before they could get much further, Lenore, Alyssa's gallery manager, rapped on the door and stuck her head into the office.

"Hey, you two, I hate to bother you, but there are a couple of clients out here who want to talk with you, Aly. I think they're looking to spend a boatload on several pieces in the collection and want to talk to the gallery owner first."

Alyssa gave Isabella a sympathetic look. "Guess I better go make an appearance."

"It's okay," Isabella said. "I'll be out in a minute."

As Alyssa started for the door, Lenore held out an envelope. "Oh, and I found this on the front counter."

Alyssa took the envelope, and Isabella could see that it was made of heavy parchment and it looked very old, or had been made to look that way.

Alyssa flipped it over and studied the writing on the front, then looked up at the manager. "Who left this, Lenore?"

The manager shrugged. "I don't know. It wasn't there earlier. I just found it when I started back to get you."

"Okay, I'll be out in a minute. Thanks." As the manager left the room, Alyssa closed the door behind her, and then turned to give Isabella a weird look.

"What's the matter, Aly?" Isabella asked. "Who's that from?"

Shaking her head, Alyssa held the envelope out to her. "I don't know. It's addressed to you."

Isabella slowly reached out and took the envelope, staring down at the old-style script. Her name was obviously written with a calligraphy pen or quill, and done with a beautiful flourish.

Isabella Doyle Christensen

She glanced up at Alyssa with a stunned look, and her mouth had suddenly gone very dry.

"What the hell is going on here, Aly?"

Alyssa shook her head again. "Heck if I know. Open it already!"

Two

By the time Alexi and Finvar had arrived at the White Palace to speak with the Queen, Alexi was itching to get any and all of the details that Finvar had been reluctant to share. They needed a plan if this really was a significant threat to either kingdom. That meant that Alexi needed to know who or what had made the unfamiliar tracks that he'd run across earlier in the morning, and where this unknown entity had come from.

However, after hearing that both Finvar and Niall had experienced similar sightings in both kingdoms over the past month, Queen Beatrice was disinclined to discuss the matter until all the pertinent attendees were present. To that end, she'd delayed the conference for two hours until all could arrive for the important security meeting that was now taking place in the war room.

The Queen sat at the head of the conference table with Prince Graydon to her right. Also present was Alexi's cousin, Chancellor Valian Winchester; Niall, High Lord of Roseland's Twilight Court; and Finvar, High Lord of Wysteria's Winter Court and the Prince's biological father.

Alexi had just finished explaining about his early morning ride and the strange tracks he'd found along with the scent that he'd followed before meeting Finvar north of the Eastern Glade in Willow

Glen Wood. "Fin informed me at the time that he'd seen similar tracks and was familiar with the scent that I'd discovered and followed," he told the Queen before turning to Finvar with a nod. "I'll defer to him, as he was hesitant to give any details until he could do so in your presence, Majesty."

"High Lord," Queen Beatrice addressed Finvar. "I am anxious to hear what you have to say. What is this possible new threat to our realm?"

The High Lord took a deep breath and ran a hand down his snowy-white beard before clearing his throat. "First and foremost, I will say that I'm not confident that it is a threat as of yet, but from what I have seen and sensed...it is definitely something that I haven't seen in..." He paused and took another deep breath. "Well, it's been a very long time."

Alexi studied his face. Whatever Fin was thinking, whatever he suspected, it had the High Lord anxious. And Finvar was never anxious. That alone gave Alexi pause.

"Though I cannot be completely certain, you understand," Finvar continued, "but if it's what I suspect, then it would be quite a shocking revelation for those of us who fought in the Great War."

"What in the name of the Oracles are you talking about, Fin?" Alexi blurted, eager to hear the details and unable to contain himself any longer. "Spit it out, man. Not all of us had the pleasure of fighting in the Great War."

"Field Marshal," Valian murmured in warning tone. "Have some respect. Give him a minute."

"Okay, okay." Sighing, Alexi sat back and put up his hands, palms out, before turning to look at Finvar. "But do get on with it, please. You're escalating the panic inside me that we talked about earlier."

Niall made a show of clearing his throat. "Unfortunately, disrespectful or not, I tend to agree with the Field Marshal, Fin," he muttered with a disdainful look in Alexi's direction before giving Finvar a side-eye. "For my sake, give everyone the good news."

Finvar frowned but nodded and then turned to the Queen. "My apologies, Majesty. It's just that this is difficult, as I'm referring to the ancient race known as the Caemmeirth."

The silence which followed that statement, as well as the stunned look on the faces around the table—with the exception of Gray and Niall—spoke volumes. Niall probably wasn't surprised because, having fought in the war, he knew exactly what Fin was talking about. Alexi figured that he and Gray were the only ones in the dark.

He leaned forward with another heavy sigh. "And these Caemmeirth were who exactly?"

"Only a few of us at this table will remember, but the Caemmeirth were—"

"An ancient race of shapeshifting, fire-breathing dragons," Valian finished for the High Lord.

Alexi's mouth dropped open, and he gaped wide-eyed at his cousin. "Say what now? Shape-shifting, fire-breathing *dragons*? Are you kidding me? You can't be serious."

Valian smirked. "Oh, but I am."

Turning, Alexi skewered Finvar with an incredulous stare. "You and Juppar told me last summer in the Barrens that dragons were extinct."

Finvar shook his head. "Obviously your memory is faulty or you heard what you wanted to hear, boy-o, as that's not what we said at all. We *said* that they hadn't been seen for centuries and were thought to have been mostly driven to the far north. Possibly back into the Wastelands."

"I thought that you were *joking*! Just winding me up like you and Twilight boy here take so much pleasure in doing," Alexi snarled, jabbing a finger in Niall's direction.

"Well, we were...in part," Finvar said with a grin. "As you really couldn't *drive* a dragon to do anything they didn't want to do."

Alexi threw up his hands in frustration. "Okay. Now, you're saying that they're real and they've come down from the damn Wastelands? If that's the case, how the hell would they get through the security wards?" He closed his eyes and shook his head. "And I can't believe we're even discussing *dragons!*"

"Gentlemen," the Queen said quietly, interrupting their back and forth. "Let's just step back a few paces for a moment, shall we. Lord Niall? Finvar said that you've also seen these signs in the north country of Roseland. Are you in agreement with his assessment?"

Niall glanced at Finvar and then back at the Queen. "I am. He and I have discussed this at length. I know what I've seen and scented in the air on several occasions. Lord Finvar is correct. It's been a very long time, and this is not something that I'd ever thought to run across again, but neither is it something one forgets."

The Queen nodded and then leaned toward Valian. "And you, Chancellor? I, myself, remember talk of the dragon race, but I'm assuming that you're 'one of the few' people in the room to whom Finvar is referring who's had experience with—or at least remembers—the Caemmeirth."

"Yes, Majesty." Valian nodded. "As both high lords have stated, the war was a long time ago, but the great dragons are something I'll not soon forget, either. Though I've not seen the signs with my own eyes, if Fin and Niall are in agreement, I would stand by their assessment as well."

"All right, then." Queen Beatrice sat up tall in her chair and folded her hands on the tabletop before skewering each participant around the table. "Since we'd all assumed that the Caemmeirth had died out long ago—much like my ancestors, the Ellurians—this will require some intensive research and discussion. Well, gentlemen, threat or no threat, I suggest this small council get to it and give me some sort of plan going forward as soon as you can."

With that, they all stood as the White Queen rose, and turning, left the room without a backward glance.

"Well, isn't this gonna be fun." Alexi sat down, muttering into the silence of the room, and then shaking his head. "First the insanity of Wolvataurs and now dragons, for fuck's sake. I'd like to know what the hell's next." Then he thought better of that. "You know what? Scratch that. This is plenty."

"I agree, Alexi," the Prince replied and studied the others. "Since Alexi and I have no experience with dragons, we're at a loss. So, where do we begin? Who wants to flesh out this dragon race for us and give us a baseline? I think my first questions would be which side of the war were they on? And did you fight with them or against them?"

When Niall chuckled under his breath, Gray narrowed his eyes at the High Lord. "Do you have something to say, Niall? You find my questions funny, perhaps?"

Niall took his time responding and the smile never really left his face, but he met Gray's gaze without apology. "I suppose I do. The ancient dragons were protectors of life, of the innocent. So, in that sense, I would say that one could assume we were fighting alongside them against Qadira–the Dark Fae, and the hordes of goblins, trolls, Red Caps, and the like that she'd recruited for the destruction of life as we know it. On the other hand, the dragons could be incredibly mercurial...and unpredictable."

Finvar grinned and held up a finger. "Now, that's not really fair, Niall. Not all the breeds were so inclined."

"Yes, my recollection is that the Nyrilio were the worst in that vein," Valian added with a nod.

"Oh, aye," Finvar replied. "Those red bastards were definitely the ones to step lightly around. They may have been fighting alongside us, but they tended to be, shall we say, less than mindful with their blasts of fire."

Niall's shout of laughter filled the room. "Less than mindful? That is a more than diplomatic way to put it, Fin. I would say it was more like they didn't give a digger troll's arse who got in the way as long as their target was fried to a bloody crisp."

"Okay, okay, point taken," Gray said, shaking his head.

"And just how many of these dragon 'breeds' are there?" Alexi asked, still not sure he was believing any of the conversation they were having.

Valian leaned forward, elbows on the table, and glanced at Alexi. "The Caemmeirth included four separate breeds or clans, each with their own special gift or powers. They all could breathe fire in some fashion, as well as shape-shift into a human form."

"And they were all quite beautiful, each unique in their own way," Finvar mused. "However, the four breeds did have very different behavioral traits."

Niall laughed again. "Ha! Very different traits and different personalities."

"So, what were these four breeds or clans?" Gray asked. "Valian, you mentioned the Nyrilio."

"Yes. The Nyrilio were a deep red color with an almost lumines-cent sheen. In human form, they had dark red hair and radiant red eyes. And as Fin said, they didn't so much breathe fire as blast it out like fucking bombs. However, though they could be unpredictable, and I use that word lightly, they were fierce warriors, males and females alike. I will give them that."

"Okay, note to self, be careful around a Nyrilio if I ever run into one," Alexi rolled his eyes. "What about the other three breeds?"

"The Gheori clan was a decent breed," Finvar murmured. "All the breeds were intelligent, incredibly so with their battle strategies and such. But the Gheori were very calm, thoughtful, and confident. They were silver in color, like a newly minted coin, as was the fire they breathed. In dragon form, they could completely blend into their surroundings like a chameleon. At times you would never even know you were standing right next to one if it wasn't for the heat they generated."

"A lot of them looked like old men or women in human form with gray hair and polished gray eyes," Niall added with a grin. "I always found that quite amusing."

"Oh, now, there were a couple that we both met that were actu-ally really beautiful in human form, Niall," Valian pointed out. "Do you remember Azzertha?"

Niall nodded. "I do, vaguely. It was a long time ago. Anyway, the Gheori could blend into a crowd in human form as well, and no one would even take a second look." He shook his head and chuckled. "It was great for surveillance."

"Okay, that's two breeds," Gray said. "Next?"

"I guess that would be the somewhat rare Issai," Valian replied in a respectful tone.

"Ah, yes," Finvar smiled. "The blue armor-plated warrior breed. They were something to watch in the air, remember?"

Valian nodded. "I do indeed, old friend. Glossy blue scales of armor, azure-blue eyes that you could see at a distance, their blue flame. Incredibly gifted on the ground or in the air, but definitely something to see."

"Harder for them to blend in when in human form, though," Niall put in. "All that blue."

"Maybe that was why they were usually a rare sight in human form," Valian agreed.

"And our last addition to the list?" Alexi asked. "Let me guess. A black dragon?" He wiggled his eyebrows for emphasis.

Valian, Finvar, and Niall exchanged looks, looks that Alexi couldn't quite decipher, but he could have sworn they leaned toward awe.

"Guys?" he prodded.

Niall hesitated a moment and then cleared his throat before speaking with quiet admiration. "The fourth breed was the Airsayrth. The golden dragon, and the rarest of the breeds."

"Their scales were so bright that they almost hurt your eyes the way they shimmered in the sunlight," Valian murmured in a voice filled with that awe Alexi had thought he'd detected.

Finvar shook his head. "I never got the chance to actually see an Airsayrth, but I heard from others who had."

"They were quite impressive," Niall spoke up. "I saw only one or two during the whole of the war campaign. They were massive in dragon form—much larger than all of the other breeds—with an enormous wingspan."

"I saw only a couple as well," Valian said softly. "But I actually spoke with one—a male—while he was in human form. Long hair like mine or Alexi's, only golden, not silver or white. Golden eyes and warm, burnished skin tone. I watched him transform and take to the air after the meeting. I must say, I have seen some incredible things over the centuries, but that's something that I will never forget as long as I live. It was...majestic."

Alexi looked back and forth between Valian, Finvar, and Niall. "Well, what happened to these dragon clans? I mean, after the war? Where did they go?"

Valian shrugged. "I guess it was assumed that they went home, because they just disappeared."

"Went home?" Gray looked confused. "Where did they live?"

"They originated in the Antiley mountain range in the far north-east of the Northern Wastelands," Niall murmured, then grinned at Alexi. "That was their homeland."

"Wait— What?" Alexi glared at the High Lord. "Okay, we're

going to skip right over that and go directly to the part about these mountains. So, you're saying that there are real mountains and not just dry mesas in the Northern Wastelands? I thought the Wastelands were just that, like the Barrens, all desert and scrub."

Finvar shook his head. "Oh, no, Alexi. The mesas of the Barrens get steeper and more mountainous the farther north you go. By the time you cross into the Wastelands, the Unwelcoming Rise divides the Northern Wastelands into two regions. The west side of the Rise is very much like the Barrens, as you said, desert and scrub."

"Yes, but if you dare to cross the Rise, the terrain is much different on the other side," Valian added. "There, the landscape is green and lush, much like the northern terrain of Roseland or Wysteria. However, though quite beautiful, the Antileys are a rugged mountain range—snow-covered most of the time—in the far northeast. Legend has it that they are not only the homeland for the Caemmeirth, but also the birthplace of the race." He leaned back in his chair. "Add to it, and a much more interesting theory, it was also thought that the Antileys were the origin of much of the magick that we all know and use today. There was even speculation that the Caemmeirth themselves had magick that no one has ever seen." He shrugged. "There are all sorts of legends about those mountains and the different races and species that inhabited that land."

"Like my ancestors the Ellurians?" Gray asked.

Valian nodded. "Yes. The legend of the Ancients say that they ruled that region for centuries. There were also Elven clans that lived in the far northeast back then, distantly related to the Ellurians, as you know."

"As well as the many distant fae courts who fought with us in the war against Qadira," Niall added. "They disappeared at the end of the war as well, so it was assumed that somewhere in the Northern Wastelands was where they all went."

"But nobody knows for certain, correct?" Gray asked.

"Correct," Valian said.

"Well, if nobody knows any of this for sure, and it's all just legend in the first place, then how can you be positive that the landscape differs on the other side of this *Rise*, or that the Antileys even exist?" Alexi asked with a frown.

Valian gave him a bland stare. "Because I can read, cousin. Books, maps, all sorts of things, really. I'm gifted in that way."

Both Finvar and Niall snickered at that, which irritated Alexi to no end.

"Yeah, yeah, you're all terribly funny. And you can bite me, *cousin*."

Gray shook his head. "Don't feel bad, Alexi. I didn't know any of this either, so if they are making fun of you, they are making fun of the Prince of the realm." He gave Finvar a pointed look. "As well as the heir to Wysteria's Winter Court's throne."

"Oooh, snap!" Alexi cried. "Sick burn, Gray. You old codgers better get your shit in order. The Prince of the realm will tell his mum, the queen. Then you'll be in deep doo-doo."

"Oh, brother," Valian snorted, then grinned. "You are such an idiot."

"Okay, okay, come on, back to business," Gray said, putting an end to the inane patter.

Valian's grin faded then. "Look, Alexi, all kidding aside, there are maps that have been created by explorers who've ventured into that territory and lived to tell the tale. Some of those maps are right over there in that tall cabinet, should you wish to enlighten yourself. And I would highly encourage both you and Gray to do so as soon as you can to get up to speed and get a clear understanding of that distant region."

"Good suggestion, Val. We'll get on that as soon as we can so that we're prepared going forward. But if the signs are correct, and it is one of these dragons that has entered our realm, would you say friend or foe?" Gray asked, looking from Valian, to Finvar, and then to Niall.

"That would be impossible to say at this early stage," Niall replied. "It would depend on the 'why' of it, which we have no way of knowing."

"And is there any way to tell which breed has come visiting from what you've seen?"

Niall and Finvar exchanged a look, then Finvar shook his head. "Unfortunately, not from what we've seen so far."

"So, how the hell do we move forward with any kind of a plan?"

Alexi asked in frustration. "I mean, we don't know the breed. We have no idea why they've come." He gestured toward Finvar and Niall. "For that matter, no offense to either of you, but we don't really know for certain that we're even talking about the Caemmeirth. At this point, it's all just speculation based on the signs that you've seen."

"Alexi brings up a good point," Gray said. "Despite what you both have witnessed, we have little tangible evidence so far."

Alexi shook his head. "Again, what do we do? The Queen wants some kind of plan. Do we post lookouts all over the damn realm in case they come back? That's just not feasible, even if we had the help of every one of the nine fae courts in both Wysteria and Roseland, plus the dwarf clans to boot. And then there's the possibility that this entity, whatever it is, may not come back at all."

"Also, a good point." Gray nodded.

"If both Niall and Finvar have found signs on several occasions, I have to surmise that whatever this is, they'll be back. Therefore, I don't think that's an issue," Valian disagreed. "However, the lookout theory could hold a feasibility problem."

"And like you said to me in Willow Glen Wood, Fin," Alexi added. "We don't want to start a panic, either. I can't imagine that there are too many left in the realm who even know about the dragon race's existence."

Finvar frowned. "Niall and I have discussed the issue of surveillance, as well. Maybe we can't post lookouts all over the realm, but we can raise awareness with specific groups. Get that awareness high in pockets around the two kingdoms. Then we're more likely to get wind of sightings."

"Those eighteen fae courts, nine in each kingdom, are a start," Niall said. "All it would take is for squads to go out and patrol their court lands regularly, which most courts already do. Maybe if there are enough sightings or signs, we could discern some kind of pattern, or at least get an indication of where they are coming from, and then follow the trail."

Valian nodded. "I guess that's as good a starting place as any. Let's look at the map of the realm and at least get a jump on it."

As the group began to divide up areas in both kingdoms for

routine patrols and those courts that would need to be informed of the rollout, Alexi couldn't help but wonder if they would just be chasing their own tails. But the thought of having to possibly head out into the Barrens again or even into the Wastelands, for that matter, wasn't something he was eager to contemplate any time soon.

It would all depend on the next sightings...if there were any at all.

Three

Isabella stared down at the fine parchment envelope in her hand—her name written so beautifully in an elaborate old-world script—and concentrated on just breathing in and out. She could feel Alyssa's eyes on her and sense her friend's anticipation yet couldn't quite bring herself to open the envelope. It felt like a heavy weight in her palm, consequential, life-changing. And with everything that had been happening lately, she wasn't sure that she even wanted to know what it contained. Which was ridiculous, she admitted to herself.

Yet...

"Izzy?" Alyssa's voice cut into her thoughts.

Looking up at her friend, Isabella shook her head. "I know it's absurd. I mean, it's just an envelope...but I'm scared to open it, Aly," she almost whispered as if someone might hear the dread rising up inside of her. "I'm afraid of what it might contain. How stupid is that?"

Alyssa gave her a sympathetic look. "Honey, it's not stupid at all. You've had some very strange dreams lately that have unnerved you, to say the least. Then there's the encounter earlier with the 'disappearing woman' who talked to you in your head. And she called you by your mother's maiden name, for the love of mud, just like the faerie did in your dream, and now this?" Alyssa took her by the shoulders and gave her a sympathetic look. "Trust me, I can relate to experiencing this kind of weirdness and how it can freak you out."

"Yes, but your experience happened after being thrown into an alternate realm," Isabella countered in a grumpy tone. "Everything was weird there. This is happening to me here, right here...in our world."

"True. But Izz, there's always been bleed-over. We just didn't know it. And we don't know for sure that this has anything to do with Artemysia yet, or any other realm, for that matter."

Alyssa put up a hand when Isabella opened her mouth to reply.

"Now listen, you and I had no idea that any other realms even existed until New Year's Eve. And remember that Valian Winchester had been living right here in New York City as an acclaimed author for decades before we actually found out that he was an elf, the Chancellor of Wysteria, and that he knew who *we* were all along."

"Who's we, pal? He knew who *you* were."

Alyssa gave her an annoyed look. "Come on, you know what I mean. There's also Niall, who came to see me at the gallery out of the blue, and there's no telling how many times he'd been here wearing a glamour before that. There have been a ton of fae and elves and who knows what else coming and going through the portals for eons."

Isabella took a deep breath and nodded. "You're right. Of course, you're right. But what if it's not related to Artemysia but another realm altogether? Or what if I'm just losing my mind?"

Alyssa scoffed. "You're not losing your mind. But Izzy, we're not going to know if it's all related until you open that envelope." She narrowed her eyes. "You are my best friend and one of the strongest women I know, and you also have something that I didn't have."

"Oh, really? And what's that? A prescription of Valium?" Isabella asked with a large helping of snark. "I think this situation may take a bit more than that, don't you?"

"Don't be a smart-ass. What I mean is, this is happening here in our world, and you're surrounded by friends and family. I had none of that. And if we find out that it is connected to Artemysia, we now have friends in that realm as well to help you though whatever this is. So, be bold, my friend. Step up and stare down your fear. You can do this, Izz. I know you can."

"Well, since you put it that way." Isabella smirked and then rolled her eyes. "And nice pep talk by the way." Looking down at the envelope, she slipped her thumbnail underneath the wax seal closure and lifted up on the flap. "Okay, here goes nothing."

As she took hold of the note inside and pulled it from the envelope, a startling burst of sparkling pink dust exploded into the air around them both.

Isabella blinked and then sneezed. A spicy, pleasing scent engulfed her in a cloud of such an amazing fragrance that it nearly took her breath away. "Oh! Well...that was...something," she said with a chuckle, and then took a deep breath. "Pretty pink sparkles, anyway."

"That was something all right," Alyssa agreed with a worrisome look. "Pretty, but a bit of a shock and kinda bizarre."

"Maybe a little, but it's not only pretty, it smells yummy, too," Isabella said with a grin.

"What do you mean?"

Isabella looked at Alyssa with wide eyes. A soft glow flooded her senses, and a strange sensation of well-being was taking over. "Can't you smell that?"

"Smell what?" Alyssa asked with a frown.

Isabella fought for the right words to explain the scent, the sweet aroma that seemed to fill her head. "It's like a garden of the most fragrant flowers all blooming at the same time. Seriously? You can't smell that?"

Alyssa shook her head. "No, Izz, I can't. Are you all right?"

Isabella couldn't seem to wipe the grin from her face. "Absolutely. In fact, I suddenly feel great."

"Okay," Alyssa said slowly. "Well, what does the sparkly, scented note say?"

"Note? Oh— Yeah, right." Unfolding the note, Isabella scanned the elaborate writing. "This first part looks like a poem."

"A poem? Read it out loud."

"It says, '*Can you feel it in your blood, the sparkle in your soul? That's the faerie essence, there to make you whole. When you find your center, you'll find that magick tone. Breathe deep the faerie flower, and find you're not alone.'"* She turned to Alyssa with a bemused look. "Huh. What do you make of that?"

Obviously confused, Alyssa shook her head again. "No clue. That's...so odd."

"Yeah, but kinda sweet, don't you think?"

Alyssa raised an eyebrow. "I guess. What else does the note say? That can't be it."

Isabella looked down at the note—this time with its kaleidoscope of colors now swirling on the page—and giggled. "I don't know. I can't read it." She shoved the note at Alyssa. "Here, you read it out loud. I have to sit down now. I'm feeling a little bit dizzy."

"Isabella, are you sure you're okay? You're starting to look and sound like you're high." Leaning in, Alyssa frowned. "And your pupils are enormous." Easing Isabella down onto the sofa, Alyssa took the note and regarded her with a doubtful look.

"Don't look at me like that. I'm fine...I think. I feel fine, just a little light-headed is all. Well, maybe with a heap of euphoria added into the mix." She giggled again and waved her hand at Alyssa to sit down, then followed the colors trailing from her fingertips with another giggle. "Would you look at that. So pretty."

"Would I look at what?" Alyssa asked in frustration. "You're starting to scare me, Isabella."

"Just read the note already," she murmured in a distracted tone as she watched the colors swirl.

SOMETHING IS DEFINITELY GOING SIDEWAYS HERE, ALYSSA thought.

With another concerned look at Isabella, Alyssa sat down next to her and scanned the note. "Okay, after the poem, there's only a couple of sentences, which seems to be an invitation of some sort to meet...um...someone named Tempest. Do you know who that is?"

"Nope." Isabella waved a hand in the air again and snickered. "Check this out, Aly. How is this happening?"

"Izzy, look at me." Alyssa took Isabella's chin in her hand, attempting to gain her friend's attention. "Are you listening to me? Did you hear what I just said?"

"Sure. Someone named Tempest sent me an invitation for something. Is it a party? Because Party Poppers could handle it, if it is."

At the glazed look in her friend's eyes, the alarm bells already ringing in Alyssa's head ascended to a whole new level. Isabella had seemed fine when she'd first arrived, though she'd been a bit anxious and troubled over recent events. Now, she was giggling like a five-year-old—with all her troubles apparently forgotten—and acting like she'd taken some kind of hallucinogen.

Just what the hell was going on here? Was there some kind of drug mixed into the pink dust that had burst out of the envelope along with the note? If so, why hadn't she herself been affected? Why just Isabella?

"No, Izz, the invitation isn't for a party. It says, *Follow the sparkle to the Old Portal in the Great Park at the witching hour. See the swirling colors, feel the pull & find your center. Best, Tempest.*' So, it sounds to me like this whole thing—the dreams, the lapses you've been having, the disappearing woman—may actually *be* connected to Artemysia in some way."

"That's good to know, right?" Isabella murmured in a distracted tone. "I wonder who this Tempest is and what they want."

"I don't know, but the way he or she talks about the portal is very familiar." Alyssa re-read the two sentences. "I mean, it's exactly what I remember when that evil fae wench, Kasandra Delacourt, sent me through the portal on New Year's Eve."

Isabella jabbed a finger at Alyssa. "I did *not* like that evil bitch."

Alyssa laughed at the look on her friend's face. "Yeah, well, join the club, pal." She glanced back down at the note. "That curious pull, the swirling colors of the vortex. In this sentence, they describe it perfectly," she murmured, thinking back to her first trip through the portal.

"Swirling colors...yes indeedy. They seem to be everywhere tonight, right?" Isabella sighed and then with wide eyes, suddenly grabbed Alyssa's arm. "You know what we should do? We should go to the Central Park portal like the invite says."

Alyssa stared at Isabella for a few seconds. "That's a terrible idea.

We have no clue who this Tempest is or what kind of situation we could be walking into. And if you were in your right mind, you'd know that. You, my friend, are starting to worry me big time. I'm beginning to think that you've been drugged somehow."

Isabella's looked up at her with raised eyebrows. "I've been drugged? With what?" She trailed her fingers in front of Alyssa, watching them with almost a childlike delight. "Other than all the crazy colors in the air, I feel fine. Wait...not just fine...I feel *great*."

"Yeah, that's the problem. I'm gonna call Valian. And I mean, right now. In your state you probably can't feel it, but something is really off here, Isabella." Alyssa shook her head. "I'm sorry, but I also have to go out and meet with these clients in the gallery. You are going to stay right here and not move from this sofa. Got it?"

"Yep," Isabella said, continuing to watch her wiggling fingers as she waved them around in the air.

Alyssa took out her cell phone and punched in Valian's number, then cursed when it went directly to voicemail. She left an urgent message with the pertinent details of what was happening with Isabella and a request for an immediate callback. Hanging up, she glanced at Isabella who seemed to be enjoying a world that only she could see, and Alyssa hoped and prayed that Valian would get the message as soon as possible. Because she was getting more and more concerned and at a loss as to how to deal with the situation on her own.

"Alright, Izzy. I'm going out to the gallery now. I won't be long, I promise. There's bottled water right there in the little fridge by the desk if you get thirsty. Hopefully, Valian will call back in a bit, and we can get your situation all sorted out. Okay?"

"Okay."

"Now, you stay right here in this office until I get back." When Isabella didn't acknowledge her, Alyssa tried again. "Isabella? Did you hear me?"

"Yep. I'll be here."

The dreamy smile on her friend's face was worrying Alyssa more and more. What if this got worse before they heard from Valian? It was obvious that something was really wrong with Isabella, and Alyssa had no idea what to do. She could take her to an emergency room, but would that be a help or a hinder? And if this was a drug or poisonous compound from another realm, would they even know what it was or how to deal with it?

Alyssa crossed the room and then turned back from the open doorway. She hated to leave Isabella alone in this state, but she was needed in the gallery. It would be dicey, but maybe she could send Lenore back for a bit just to make sure Isabella didn't go wandering around. Mulling over some kind of explanation that she could give to her gallery manager, Alyssa left the room, closing the door firmly behind her.

THE LIGHT-HEADED WHIRLING SENSATION HAD diminished into a soft humming sound in Isabella's head as she stood up on unsteady legs and made her way across the room to the small fridge next to the desk. The trailing colors continued to accompany her movements, but had faded somewhat into soft pastels, which were still distracting but lovely. However, she'd found herself quite thirsty all of a sudden after Alyssa's suggestion, so thought a bottle of water would be just the ticket. Just as she'd grabbed a bottle and closed the fridge door, she turned to find that she was not alone in the room. A woman sat on the sofa where Isabella herself had just been sitting.

"Hey, where did you come from? I didn't even hear you come in."

The woman smiled, her emerald-green eyes sparkling as she ran a hand through her long, red hair.

A quick sense of déjà vu washed over Isabella, and she realized that this was not just any woman.

"Wait a minute. I know you," she said, pointing at the woman with the unopened bottle of water. "I saw you earlier out on the street, didn't I? You spoke to me...in my head."

When the woman only continued to smile, Isabella gave her a closer look, and another image slowly surfaced from her memory. The snapshot of a tall, lean woman dressed in a warrior's garb with long, red hair braided back from the sides of her head revealing the pointed ears of a faerie. Though this woman was dressed in an elegant floral dress, and her long red hair was worn loose around her shoulders concealing her ears, Isabella suddenly knew where else she'd seen her.

"Oh my gosh. You're also the faerie from my dream last night."

The woman nodded then and stood. "Yes, Isabella Doyle, that is correct," she said with the music of Ireland in her voice.

"No, but that's not right." Isabella shook her head, a move that had the bright colors swirling across her vision again. "My last name is Christensen. Doyle was my mom's maiden name. You called me that before." Isabella frowned at the woman. "But how would you know that?"

"How? Because I knew your grandmother—your Mamó—well when she was young. I remember your mum, too." The woman nodded. "And though we've never met, I've known all about you from the time you were born, *mo linbh milis.*"

My sweet child? Isabella's eyes widened, and she blinked in surprise. She was certain that's what the phrase meant, but how in the world would she know that? She didn't even know what language it was.

Did she?

She held up a hand. "Wait, are you saying that you know my family?"

The woman's smile was engaging, compelling. "Indeed I do, as if they were my own."

"My grandmother lives in Ireland. You sound a bit like her when you speak. Is that where you're from?"

The woman shook her head, setting the numerous earrings she wore fluttering, and Isabella could now see clearly her delicately pointed ears. "No, I'm not from Ireland but I have visited your Mamó there on numerous occasions. You could say that my home-land is...similar."

"What's your name?"

"I'm called Tempest."

Isabella grinned. "Hey, you're the one that sent me the note."

"I did."

"It smelled so, so good. How did you do that?"

"I'm glad you liked it. It was done with faerie magick." Tempest came closer and reached out a hand. "Would you like to see where your ancestors come from, Isabella? You'd like to find your center, wouldn't you? Come with me. I can show you."

Isabella's grin faded as she stared at Tempest's outstretched hand, and another memory surfaced, a memory not of her own. "I don't think that's such a good idea. I'm not supposed to leave the office until Aly gets back. She thinks that I've been drugged."

Tempest tilted her head and smiled. "Really? Do you feel drugged?"

Isabella thought for a moment. Did she? "No," she said slowly. "At least, I don't think so. I feel...really good. Happy."

"Well then, that can't be bad, now can it? And what would a quick trip hurt? It won't take long. Besides, the descendant would want you to know your history, your ancestry, as she now knows hers, right?"

Isabella gasped.

"You know about Aly," she whispered. "About her being the descendant?"

Tempest gave a throaty laugh. "Of course, *mo linbh milis.* Everyone knows of the descendant in my homeland."

"So, where is this place? I mean, what's it like?"

"Why, it's a beautiful land full of magick and wonder."

Isabella took a deep breath. "Like Wysteria or Roseland?"

"Very much so." Tempest took another step closer. "In fact, it's in the very same realm. Take my hand, Isabella. We'll go through the portal in the Great Park, and you can see it for yourself."

ALYSSA FINALLY FINISHED UP WITH THE CLIENTS WHO'D spent an obscene amount of money on the new artist the gallery was showing this evening. She'd just walked them to the front door and waved them goodbye when Lenore sidled up beside her.

"Aly, you need to come back to the office," the gallery manager urged quietly. "Right now."

Alyssa took in the frantic look on Lenore's face and felt her stomach lurch. "What is it, Lenore? Is Isabella okay? Has something happened?"

Lenore took her by the arm and began to pull her toward the back hallway, threading their way through the still crowded gallery. "Come on."

"Lenore, talk to me. What's going on?"

"That's the problem. I don't know."

"What do you mean, you don't know?"

At the office door, Lenore turned to her. "Just what I said." She opened the door wide and inclined her head toward the interior of the office. "When I got back here, she wasn't here."

"What? Where could she have gone?" Alyssa asked as she stepped into the room. "I told her to stay right here and not to move until I got back, that I wouldn't be long. But I was afraid that I'd get caught up with the clients, which I did. That's why I sent you back, because I was worried that in the state she was in, she would wander."

Looking around the office, Alyssa stopped at the desk, picking up an unopened bottle of water. "Okay, she must have pulled this out of the little fridge. It's still cold. And look, her handbag is right here where she left it. Plus, her coat is still draped over the chair. She has to be somewhere in the gallery, right?"

Lenore nodded. "That's just what I thought. Unfortunately, I got waylaid a couple of times before I could get back here, so I thought maybe she went to the ladies room or just went out into the gallery to stretch her legs. So, I spent fifteen minutes looking everywhere I could think of and scanning the crowds. She's not here, Aly."

"That can't be." But even as Alyssa spoke those words, a sinking feeling was beginning to take hold. However, before her panic could really ramp up, her cell phone rang. Looking down, she saw Valian's name on the readout and turned to Lenore. "Okay, go round up a few people, and we'll take another look around the gallery, just to be thorough," she told the office manager. "I have to take this, it's Valian returning my call."

"You got it."

As Lenore left the office, Alyssa answered the call. "Valian, thank God."

"Alyssa? What's happened? Is Isabella all right? Your message said you thought she'd been drugged, but you didn't say how."

"I know. I'm sorry. I was on my way out to the gallery to speak with some clients, so I had to be quick. I told Isabella to stay here in the office, but when Lenore came to check on her she was gone. Now, she's missing, Valian."

"What? Missing? Have you searched the gallery?"

"Yes, of course, and we're just about to do it again. Look, it's a long story and too much to get into over the phone. Can you come? I'm afraid for her, Valian. Something's not right, and after what happened to me on New Year's Eve..."

There was a pause on the other end of the line, and then relief poured through her at Valian's response.

"Just breathe. I'm on my way. I'll be there as soon as I can. We'll find her, Alyssa. In the meantime, close up the office, nobody goes in until I'm there, okay?"

"Please hurry," she said before hanging up. "Valian will know what to do," she whispered to herself as she headed out to join the search.

He had to know what to do. Because something told her that Isabella was in trouble, and that time was of the essence.

Four

By the time Valian got to the gallery, the crowd for the showing had thinned out considerably. He stood for a moment, searching the remaining customers for Alyssa's face. Luckily, that didn't take long. They spotted each other about the same time, and she hurried over to meet him.

"Oh, Valian. I'm so glad you're here," she said with obvious alarm. "I didn't know what to do when I realized that something was really wrong with Isabella. I mean, she was fine when she got here and then thirty minutes later she was...well...acting weird. It was like she was drunk or something. And now she's gone."

"Okay, okay," he said, taking her hand. "Again, just breathe. We'll figure this out. First things, first. Can Lenore and your crew take care of closing down the showing so that we can decide on a plan? I'm gonna need to take a look at your office, so can you to take me there first and give me a rundown of what happened from start to finish?"

Alyssa nodded. "I told Lenore that when you got here I'd let her know. Just give me a minute."

He watched her walk away and then scanned the people still milling about in the front gallery area. After Alyssa's comment on the phone referencing her ordeal on New Year's Eve when Kasandra Delacourt—Fae Queen Mabry's lieutenant from Roseland's Evening Court—had abducted Alyssa from her own New

Year's Eve party at just after midnight, Valian was not taking any chances on a repeat occurrence. The fae lieutenant had come in search of the Scepter of Fire that night. Alyssa, being the descendant—the great-granddaughter of the great-granddaughter of the original Alice—was the only one who could wield the scepter to protect the Kingdom of Wysteria from a Roseland invasion that Aramond, the Red King, had been planning. With war on the horizon, it had been a terrible time for all involved, but especially for Alyssa who'd spent several days in Aramond's dungeon before escaping. Fortunately, Niall had found her more or less unscathed by the ordeal and had escorted her to the White Palace in time to protect the kingdom.

Valian had been Chancellor of Wysteria back then, and he, Alexi, and Prince Graydon had all been in attendance the night of the party. Alyssa's abduction had taken place on his watch, which was not his finest hour, and he still berated himself for not being more vigilant that night. But in the end they'd been victorious after Alyssa's use of the scepter, and since the Red King's defeat, Queen Beatrice had reunited the kingdoms making Valian Chancellor over all of Artemysia. He was determined that what had happened to Alyssa on New Year's Eve would not happen again...ever. He scanned the crowd carefully one last time, but didn't see anything or anyone that concerned him at the moment.

Still, he would keep a close eye for anything out of the ordinary... or anything magickal.

When Alyssa came hurrying back, she grabbed his hand and said, "Come on. I'll explain everything."

They hurried down the back hallway and when they'd reached the office door, she stopped and turned to him. "Okay, I closed this door right after I spoke with you on the phone, and nobody has been in here since. What is it you're expecting to find in the office?"

Valian shook his head. "I'm not entirely certain of that yet. However, I am going to ask you to wait out here in the hallway for a few minutes while I...get a feel for the room. Okay?"

"Sure." Alyssa nodded but he could clearly see the fear in her eyes in the dim light of the hallway.

He took her by the shoulders and smiled. "Hey, no worries,

okay? Don't borrow trouble just yet. We're going to find her. I promise. Just give me a minute in here, all right?"

As she nodded again, he turned and went into the office, closing the door behind him.

He could smell it in the air the minute he'd walked through the door, could almost taste the cloyingly sweet scent of it on his tongue.

Faerie magick. It was the one thing he'd hoped not to find.

Crossing to the desk, he recognized Isabella's handbag and the attractive winter coat he himself had given her for Valentine's Day earlier in the year. Then he noticed the envelope on the floor next to the desk. Picking it up, he found that it reeked of fae magick as well.

But the envelope was empty.

He took a turn around the office, looking carefully for signs that would give him some idea of where Isabella had gone and if it was by choice or by magick. When he was finished, he opened the door and beckoned Alyssa in.

"Let's sit over here on the sofa," he suggested.

"Did you find anything?"

"Unfortunately, yes. I did," he replied as they both sat down.

Alyssa grabbed his hand and held onto him in her panic. "Oh, my God, Valian. Tell me."

"I could smell faerie magick the moment I came into the room, Alyssa, which is not necessarily bad—"

"But it's not good either, right?" she interrupted him. "I mean, considering what happened to me on New Year's Eve."

"True, but again, let's not get ahead of ourselves. There was a specific reason for what happened to you that night. Kasandra Delacourt was looking for the Scepter of Fire, which Gray and Alexi had already taken from your library. Because you were the only one to wield it, when Kasandra found that the scepter was gone, she abducted you instead." He shook his head. "This is different, Alyssa, which means that we have to consider other possibilities. The first of those being, if this was an abduction, why Isabella? There's no reason that I can think of, can you?"

"Before tonight, I would've said no, but there have been some really weird things happening with Izzy over the last few weeks that I only found out about tonight."

Valian frowned. "What do you mean? What kind of weird things?"

He listened with mounting concern as Alyssa explained about the dreams Isabella had been having in the recent weeks, the lapses in attention, the "disappearing woman" from earlier in the evening, and finishing up with the invitation that had arrived after Isabella did.

"I see," he said when she'd finished, then held up the envelope he'd found. "I'm assuming this is the envelope from the invitation you're talking about, because like the room, it also smells strongly of fae magick."

Alyssa nodded. "Yes, but it didn't just hold the invitation, Valian. When Isabella opened it and pulled out the note, a cloud of pink, sparkly dust literally burst over both of us."

"Pink dust?"

"Yeah. It was peculiar how it just kind of exploded out with the note, but other than that, I didn't think much of it until Isabella commented on how *yummy* it smelled."

Valian smiled. "She used the word 'yummy'?"

Alyssa grinned back at him. "Yeah. She did."

"Well, what did it smell like?"

"That's just it. I don't know because I couldn't smell anything. She said it was like a bunch of really fragrant flowers blooming all at once. That's when her weird behavior started, and it got worse from there on. Within fifteen minutes or so she was giggling like a child and waving her hands around, talking about all the colors in the air." Alyssa sighed. "I thought maybe she'd been drugged somehow, you know? I didn't know what to do."

Valian instantly sobered. This was a very strange and unnerving turn of events. Pink, sparkly faerie dust that smelled of flowers could mean only one thing that he could think of, and something he'd seen in action recently in liquid form.

Faerie Bomb.

"Tell me about this invitation," he asked slowly. "What exactly did it say?"

"It started with a poem of sorts, but rather than tell you about it, I can do you one better. I put it into my pocket when I left the room because I wanted you to see it, and I didn't want it to get misplaced."

She pulled it out of her jacket pocket and handed it to him.

It was made of heavy parchment like the envelope with the same elaborate script. Scanning the poem and then the sentences that followed, he became more and more uneasy until he got to the end. There he froze.

Best, Tempest...

"This can't be," he murmured.

"What is it, Valian? You know something, don't you? What?"

Valian shook his head. "I don't know anything for sure, yet," he said, waving the note in his hand. "But this, this can't be."

"I don't understand. What can't be?"

"Listen, I'll explain what I can but not here. We need to go to the palace immediately. I need to talk to Niall and Finvar as soon as possible. Can you have the staff finish up here and close the gallery without you?"

"Yes. Of course, but—"

"Good. We'll hit your place on the way to the portal so you can pick up whatever you may need for a few days."

"Okay, but Valian—"

"Alyssa, I'll explain what I can on the way, but right now I need you to tell me everything that happened in as much detail as you can remember from the time Isabella got here to the time you left her in the office and went out into the gallery. Even the smallest thing could be crucial. Do you understand?"

Alyssa quickly nodded and then began to explain.

"WHAT ARE YOU *TALKING* ABOUT, VAL?" ALEXI BLURTED. "What do you mean Bella's missing? Since when?"

Valian and Alyssa had arrived at the palace just before midnight and had gone directly to Alexi's rooms wanting to apprise him first of the situation.

"She's been missing since earlier this evening, Alexi," Alyssa answered. "She disappeared from the gallery office when I went out to speak with a buyer."

"Maybe she just went home," Alexi suggested. "Did you check there?"

"Alexi, her handbag and coat were still in the office. We searched the gallery before Valian even got there and didn't find any trace of her. But to answer your question, yes, Valian and I made a stop at her condo on the way to the portal. She wasn't there, either." She shook her head. "She's just...gone."

"However, the circumstances do lead to a very disturbing conclusion," Valian added.

Alexi frowned. "What circumstances?"

Valian hesitated but began to describe Isabella's recent dreams, the lapses, and all the rest, but his cousin interrupted him before Valian could get to the note.

"Bella has been having dreams about Artemysia, about us? How long has that been going on? I talked to her this last week, and she didn't say anything. And besides, what's so weird about that, anyway?"

"Normally, I would agree with you, Alexi," Alyssa replied, nodding, "but she only told me about her dreams tonight when she got to the gallery, and I can tell you, she was scared. While she could only remember bits and pieces of the dreams, coupling them with the lapses in attention, it's been taking a toll on her. The event tonight outside of the gallery with the 'disappearing woman' talking to her in her head kind of sent her over the edge. Then the invitation came."

"What invitation?"

Valian cleared his throat. "I was just going to tell you about it when you interrupted me."

"Well, for the love of the Oracles! Tell me now," Alexi muttered, sitting forward on the edge of his chair.

Valian pulled the envelope containing the invitation out of his coat pocket and handed it across to his cousin. "Open it. Read it. There are other elements to this that I'll explain when you're done. However, I think just reading it you'll begin to see why I'm so concerned and why we came back to the palace so quickly."

Alexi sniffed the envelope and looked up at Valian in surprise. "Fae magick?"

"Indeed. But like I said, that's not the only problem with this invitation. Read it and then I'll tell you what the disturbing issues are and explain why I need to speak with Niall and Finvar."

It took his cousin only moments, but when he looked up in confusion, Valian could see that Alexi was beginning to worry in earnest. "Do you think this may be a situation like..." He paused and glanced at Alyssa.

"Go ahead and say it, Alexi. Valian and I have already talked about it," she said. "You're thinking a situation like my ordeal with Kasandra Delacourt on New Year's Eve?"

Alexi gave a reluctant nod. "Yes. But why? I mean, why Bella?"

"That was my question as well," Valian agreed. "But there are a couple of extra points to this quandary. One of those that I alluded to earlier is that the invitation wasn't the only thing that popped out of the envelope, so to speak."

"What do you mean?"

"When Izzy pulled the note out of the envelope, a cloud of pink, sparkly dust burst out with it. It basically exploded over both of us," Alyssa told him.

Alexi frowned. "Pink dust?"

"Yes," Valian said quietly, giving him a knowing stare. "Now, ask why Isabella said that it smelled—and I quote— yummy?"

Alexi's frown deepened. "What did it smell like?"

"I can't tell you that, Alexi," Alyssa murmured. "Because I couldn't smell it, but Izzy said it smelled like a bunch of fragrant flowers all blooming at once. She said it was strong and was baffled that I couldn't smell it. Do you know what that means?" She glanced briefly at Valian, and then back at him. "Because I don't, but Valian obviously does and expects that you will as well."

Alexi's pale skin lost color and his gaze flew to Valian. "No. That can't be."

"Mmm, yes, it's definitely a dilemma," Valian mused. "However, it's the only thing that makes sense to me. Can you think of anything else to explain it?"

"Uh, gentlemen, do you want to lay it out for the cheap seats?" Alyssa asked, giving them both a narrowed look. "This is one of the *issues* that has not been explained to me."

"Faerie Bomb in powdered form?" Alexi asked, his stunned gaze on Valian.

"That is my theory, yes." Valian nodded. "I'll need to confirm with Áine, but that seems to be indicated with Isabella's state after opening the envelope."

"But that can't be, Val," Alexi got up and began to pace. "Only someone with fae blood can be affected by Faerie Bomb, can even smell it, for that matter. It's *made* for the fae."

Valian nodded again. "As you know, I am aware, cousin."

"Okay, enough!" Alyssa yelled, jumping up from her seat next to Valian on the sofa. "You both are discussing this as if I'm not even in the room. And I am *not* aware, as you put it, Valian. So, somebody better start explaining...right...now, or there will be others—and by others I mean Gray and the Queen—joining this conversation pronto!"

Alexi stopped pacing and put up his hands. "Okay, okay, calm down. You're right. Sorry. This is just so unbelievable." He looked at Valian. "You want to explain?"

Valian blew out a breath and reached out a hand to Alyssa. "Come and sit down, Alyssa. This may be difficult to hear but I'll tell you what you want to know."

With obvious temper rising, Alyssa avoided his outstretched hand and sat back down next to him. Alexi returned to his seat as well, though Valian could tell that his cousin was having a hard time with the explanation so far.

"Faerie Bomb is a...concoction made specifically for the fae. It's made from essence of Aquaro root. It would account for what you've described as Isabella's reactions and behavior."

"This Faerie Bomb is some kind of drug made for the fae?"

"Sort of. It causes euphoria, a sense of well-being, as well as light hallucinations." He held up a hand at the frightened look that crossed Alyssa's face. "Don't panic. Faerie Bomb isn't dangerous and the worst that can happen is that the recipient awakes maybe days later with a raging hangover-like malaise." Valian took her hand. "I know this because Gray inadvertently took a whiff of liquid Faerie Bomb in Old Minerva's casting room this last summer, which was how the secret that he was a Halfling came to light. He had a similar reaction."

"That was a surprise to most of us, I can tell you," Alexi added. "Only a handful of people knew the truth, and it had been kept under wraps for decades."

"*Anyway*," Valian said, shooting his talkative cousin a shut-the-hell-up look. "It is the only theory that matches the scenario you described to me."

Alyssa looked at Alexi. "But you said that only someone with fae blood can be affected by it, can smell it. If that was the case, it would mean that Izzy...has fae blood. That can't be. I've known Isabella Christensen almost all of my life. I would've known."

"Like you both knew about *your* ancestry?" Valian asked quietly.

"That's not the same th—" Alyssa stopped and sighed. "Okay, point taken. I just...don't know how to take this whole thing in. Isabella? A possible Halfling? It just seems...impossible."

"Alyssa, you said that Isabella told you the 'disappearing woman' outside the gallery spoke to her in her head and called her by the name Isabella Doyle," Valian said. "And the envelope is addressed to Isabella *Doyle* Christensen."

"Yes. Doyle is Izzy's mother's maiden name, and her grandmother lives in Ireland. Why? What are you thinking?"

"Well, I think that may be significant, but I can't quite decide how. That may be another question for Áine. Her home is in Ireland. She may have some insight, as she knows most of the fae living there."

"Okay, so we've sent word to Niall and to Fin to come to the palace at first light," Alexi said. "Do you want to tell me why, Val? What's the hurry to talk to them? And how does Bella's disappearance play into it?"

Valian stared at his cousin for a moment. He'd rather wait for Niall and Finvar, but he figured Alexi should be given a bit of a heads up. "That is the other point to the quandary that has me concerned. Did you look at the closing on the invitation?"

Alexi picked up the note where he'd laid it with the envelope and opened it up.

"Read the whole thing from start to finish aloud for us," Valian suggested.

"Okay," Alexi said slowly. "It says, '*Can you feel it in your blood, the sparkle in your soul? That's the faerie essence, there to make you whole. When you find your center, you'll find that magick tone. Breathe deep the faerie flower, and find you're not alone.*'" He looked up briefly and nodded. "Having all the info now, that seems like it's obviously indicating Bella should find her heritage, which is possibly fae. Then the last two sentences, the invitation, '*Follow the sparkle to the Old Portal in the Great Park at the witching hour. See the swirling colors, feel the pull and find your center.*' That's clearly alluding to going through the portal in Central Park at midnight. So, what am I supposed to be looking at?"

"There is something else there, is there not?"

"Well, yeah, it's signed, *Best, Tempest.*'"

Valian nodded. "And there it is. Another 'this can't be' moment. That's what I need to talk to Niall and Finvar about."

"This Tempest is who, Val? I mean, obviously a faerie, but why is this significant?"

"Because, if I'm right, it's a voice from a very long time ago that I thought to never hear again, but I'd rather not say anything more until Niall and Finvar arrive. I'm hoping to get confirmation from them, but I think it will be as much of a shock to them as it was for me."

Five

Gray had just finished his coffee after an early morning breakfast meeting with the Queen when their conversation was interrupted by Gryphon, the Queen's chamber elf.

"Pardon me, Your Majesty, so sorry to interrupt your breakfast," the diminutive elf said with a deep bow.

"It's fine, Gryphon," the Queen replied with a smile. "The Prince and I have just finished with our meeting. What is it?"

"It's Chancellor Winchester and Field Marshal Tovin, ma'am. They've requested the presence of Your Majesty and Prince Graydon, if you both are available."

"Wait— Val's back?" Gray looked at his mother. "I thought he said he wouldn't be back from the New York realm for a couple days. He did say Saturday or Sunday, right?"

The Queen nodded. "I do believe so. Of course, he did add that he'd be back sooner if there were any developments pertaining to what we discussed yesterday."

Gray turned to Gryphon. "Are there developments?"

Gryphon gave a slight nod. "I do believe there has been something new, my lord, but what that entails, I do not know. Both the Chancellor and the Field Marshal are waiting in the war room with Lords Niall and Finvar, along with the descendant."

Gray sat up at that. "What the...Alyssa's here, too? Did she come with Niall?"

"No, my lord. She arrived with the Chancellor just before midnight."

"She came with Val last night? Why? Do these new developments pertain to her as well?"

Gryphon gave him a bland look. "I'm sure I wouldn't know, my lord."

When Gray narrowed his eyes and opened his mouth to respond, the Queen put up a hand.

"Well then, I suppose we shouldn't keep them waiting." She stood.

Gray followed suit, giving the obstinate Gryphon a hard stare as they passed. He found it impossible to believe that the eavesdropping little elf was unaware of anything that happened within or without the palace walls.

However, as they left the dining room and started for the war room one level down, his thoughts were only on Alyssa. With the Red King turned over to the Oracles for banishment and the kingdoms reunited, the danger had been neutralized, which meant that the descendant should be out of any significant danger. But could these new tracks that they were now monitoring be a threat, not to only the kingdoms but also to her? And if so, how, and why?

The meeting was evidently in full swing as Gray followed his mother into the room. All conversation paused as the attendees rose at the Queen's presence.

Valian cleared his throat. "Good morning, Your Majesty. Sorry to interrupt you so early but something new—and I believe urgent—has come up."

The Queen shook her head as she sat at the head of the table and waved to the others to resume their places. "No worries, Chancellor. The Prince and I had just finished our morning meeting when Gryphon came in with your request, so it was perfect timing, it seems. Now, what is this all about?"

"We were just about to get down to it, Majesty," Alexi said.

The Queen nodded. "I see both high lords are here, along with Alyssa. Does this involve the descendant in some way?"

"That is unclear at this time, ma'am," Valian answered. "So far, Alyssa's involvement is only peripheral."

"Peripheral? Explain," Niall demanded with a frown.

Gray smiled inwardly as Alyssa put a hand on Niall's arm and shook her head. The High Lord sighed and then nodded at Valian. "Explain...*please*."

Valian smirked but did as Niall asked. "Alyssa called and left an urgent message for me yesterday late afternoon before I'd gotten back to New York from Wysteria. Something disturbing had happened. It seems that Isabella Christensen is now missing."

Finvar sat forward. "What do you mean missing?"

"Just what I said, Fin. Between the time that Alyssa left me that message and when I finally was able to call her back, Isabella had vanished. There's been no trace of her...yet. I'm going to ask Alyssa to give you the rundown that she gave me when I got to her gallery." Valian turned to Alyssa. "Would you do that now, please? Just tell them what you told me from the time Isabella got to the gallery until you went back to the office to find her gone. I'll take it from there with the reason that I've asked both the high lords to be here this morning."

Alyssa nodded. "Of course." She looked around the table. "My gallery was having a showing for a new artist last night from six to ten, and I'd invited Isabella to come by. We hadn't seen each other in over a week, which wasn't all that unusual, but I hadn't even talked with her. So, I'd reached out and just about begged her to attend the showing so that we could also touch base." She sighed and waved a hand in the air. "Anyway, it all started when she got to the gallery. She was...in quite a state. Anxious, upset, and she was almost late. And that was the first sign for me that there was something wrong. Isabella is never late. She's usually twenty minutes early...for everything."

Valian smiled. "I will attest to that."

As Alyssa continued to describe the evening's events, Gray became more and more disturbed, especially when she described the strange dreams Isabella had been having with the men dressed in ebony robes. He himself had been experiencing similar odd dreams for the last three or four weeks, and at least a few of them that he could remember included men in black robes. However, when Alyssa got to the invitation, the pink dust, and Isabella's odd behavior, warning bells began to peal in his head.

He looked over at Valian. "Is this what I think it is?"

Valian nodded. "Unfortunately, I do believe so."

Gray frowned. "But that would mean—"

"That Isabella Doyle Christensen has fae blood running through her veins," Alexi said quietly.

Gray stared at him. "But Alexi, that can't—"

"That can't be?" Alexi snorted. "Yeah, that's a phrase that's been going around a lot since last night."

"What did this note say...exactly?" Finvar asked with concern.

Valian sighed and took an envelope out of his pocket. He handed it across the table to Finvar. "Here. Read it for yourself and then pass it on to Niall. Both of you pay special attention to the closing signature and tell me what you see. Other than Isabella's disappearance, the presence of Faerie Bomb, and the revelation that she may be a Halfling, this is the most disturbing part of this whole thing where the kingdoms are concerned, in my opinion."

They didn't have to wait long for a reaction from either of the high lords.

Finvar uttered several expletives in his shock and then went silent as he continued to stare down at the note as he passed it on to Niall.

After giving the note a quick scan, Niall sat back, a stunned look on his face. However, he was not silent. "I will repeat the current phrase. This cannot be."

"May I see the note, please?" Gray asked, holding out a hand as Niall passed it to him. Reading it over, he shook his head and then looked up at Valian. "I'm assuming the problem is with the signature, so who's going to explain the issue? Let's start with who this Tempest is and why her signature is the most disturbing part?"

He watched Valian, Niall, and Finvar exchange looks, before Valian nodded to Niall.

"Tempest was a lieutenant from one of the fae clans from the northeastern Wastelands during the Great War," Niall murmured. "A fierce warrior in her own right and well-known by many. You think my twin is impressive on the battlefield? Tempest rivaled her in every way, and more. Tisharu would tell you the same."

"So, you fought with this Tempest against the Dark Fae?" Alexi asked.

"Aye." Finvar nodded. "We all did on several occasions. I'll agree with Niall, she was something to behold on the field. I would say that she probably had few equals, male or female. The word quietly spread was that—though she was fae—she also had Ellurian blood running through her veins."

"What?" Gray asked, leaning forward. "That's...well, astonishing."

"Of course, that was never confirmed, that I know of," Valian added. "But yes, her warrior prowess could very well have been put down to her being half fae and half Ellurian. It would be a lethal and close to unparalleled combination."

Gray nodded. "Half fae and half Elven, which is what the Ellurians actually were, a powerful immortal race related to an ancient Elven line, correct?"

"Indeed, for a start," Valian murmured. "Yet they were much, much more than that."

"Okay, but if Tempest, this powerful Halfling, was on our side during the war, then why are you three looking like her appearance here and the possibility that she may have taken Bella with her somewhere, is not such a good thing?" Alexi asked, his worry showing clearly on his face. "Get to the point. There's something none of you are saying. So, somebody spit it out, already."

"Alexi, it's not so much that Tempest taking Isabella with her for some reason would be a bad thing," Valian began and then paused for a moment. He looked up at his cousin and sighed. "The something no one is saying is that it's a documented fact that Tempest died toward the end of the Great War in a battle with Qadira, the Dark Fae herself."

"It's a documented fact?" Gray asked. "Did any of you see her death? Do you know anyone who did?"

"No," Niall admitted, quietly. "But there were those who said they had, and she was widely mourned for weeks by all who'd fought with her."

"She was never seen nor heard from again." Finvar shook his head. "Tempest was a warrior with a strong warrior's spirit. If she'd not been dead, if she'd survived that battle, she would've returned to the fight at some point. Yet, she did not."

"However, the good news—if there can be any in her story—is that Tempest also mortally wounded Qadira during the fight. It was the turning point of the war," Valian said.

Niall nodded in agreement. "It cut off the head of the serpent, so to speak. The dark army's forces began to falter and flee."

"Well, this history lesson is very interesting and incredibly sad, but where does this leave us?" the Queen asked. "This would be the second reference to the Great War with Qadira to come to light in recent weeks. The first, the signs of the Caemmeirth, the great dragons, possibly entering both of our kingdoms. And now, this famous Halfling warrior. What do you think this is indicative of, gentlemen? An ancient threat resurfacing? Reborn somehow?" She looked around the table, skewering each with a steely look. "Was Qadira actually vanquished as history tells us? Or is this some new threat from a bygone era? It's hard for me to believe that something dire is now surfacing from the Great War after all this time."

"Those are all good questions, Majesty," Valian said. "And I agree with your summation. However, the stories of Tempest's battle with Qadira have been passed down through the years. They've been immortalized in song, in poems. As it was told by those who saw it all happen, neither body was ever recovered, and after the passage of so much time with no word or sightings, it would be hard to say if the stories are true or fabricated."

"Then how do we pursue this?" Gray asked. "If there's no way to confirm these points one way or another, we're just back to square one, right?"

"I would suggest that the immediate concern here is that we must find Isabella as soon as possible. That would be essential." The Queen turned to Alexi. "Field Marshal, you've coordinated with the fae clans, the dwarf clans, and others to all begin patrols keeping an eye out for more possible signs of the Caemmeirth, correct?"

"Absolutely, Your Majesty. We've been ramping up as fast as we can over the last few days, but we do have a ways to go. However, I agree that finding Bella is crucial."

The Queen gave a satisfied nodded. "Then I would say that you at least have your starting point." She stood, as did everyone seated at the table. "Keep me informed with your progress, and let me know the moment you find Isabella." She turned to Alyssa. "My dear, would you join me in the sitting room upstairs for a cup of tea. I know you'll need to stay involved with the search, but I would I'd like a word."

"Of course, Your Majesty."

The four others sat back down at the table as soon as Alyssa and the Queen had left the room, and Gray looked over at Valian. "Our first priority is finding Isabella, so I'm thinking that you and Alyssa go back to New York later today and re-check the gallery, Isabella's condo, and any other place you can think of. Do a thorough search."

"Why Val?" Alexi exclaimed. "I could take a couple of my best warriors and be there within the hour."

Gray sighed. "Look, Alexi, I know how worried you are about Isabella, but I need you here staying on top of the Caemmeirth issue. You said it yourself, we've started the rollout of the patrols but we've got a ways to go." He put up a hand when Alexi opened his mouth to object. "Plus, Val has already scoped out the gallery, was on the scene within an hour or so of Isabella's disappearance. He lives in the New York realm most of the time, Alexi. He'll know places to search and people to call for assistance that you won't. I'm sorry, but between him and Alyssa, they have the best chance of tracking her down if they can."

"But Bella—"

"Alexi, you want Isabella back as soon as possible, don't you?"

"Of course, but—"

"Well, I think that this is the best course of action to that end, and if you look at the situation objectively, so will you."

Alexi didn't look happy but he finally nodded. "I guess you're right." He turned to Valian. "You'll let me know the minute you find her, right?"

"Absolutely, cousin," Valian confirmed with a hand on Alexi's shoulder. "You know that I will."

"I'll also be going along to the New York realm," Niall spoke up, a contemplative look on his face. "A few of my warriors are always watching Alyssa's townhouse and the gallery. I'll speak to them. Perhaps they've seen something that might fill in some gaps."

"Yes, that would definitely be helpful," Gray said.

"It may also be a good idea to talk to some of the other elders," Finvar murmured. "Some of the other fae queens and high lords who were around for the Great War. Not all were, but enough to make it worthwhile to check, I think. They may have some insight into this issue, may remember something that could give us some direction as to what to do next."

"That's a good thought, Fin," Valian replied. "The more information we can dig up regarding Tempest, the war, Qadira, and anything or anyone associated, the better. I've also sent word to Áine Ó Mordha about the Faerie Bomb and Isabella's grandmother who lives in Ireland, since the invitation included Isabella's mother's maiden name. That may have some connection as well." He grinned. "Having said that, perhaps it would be prudent to also speak with Old Minerva, since she was around for the war...when she felt like it."

Finvar made a strangled sound and looked up at the ceiling.

Alexi blanched. "Uh, yeah, I'm with Fin. Pass." But then he turned to Niall with a snicker. "Maybe you could swing by and have a chat with her, Niall. You know, like you did in the Barrens last summer and lived to tell about it?"

Gray watched the High Lord roll his eyes, but a smile touched his lips. "I'll not be doing that again anytime soon. Thank you, Field Marshal."

"Alright, well, as the Queen said, it seems like we have a good start." Turning to Gray, Valian nodded. "Anything else you can think of now?"

"Actually, yes. On another subject that may or may not be connected to any of this," Gray began. "I have something that I should probably share. It's regarding the dreams that Isabella described to Alyssa."

"Her dreams? What about them?" Valian asked.

"Well, funny thing, that. As it turns out, I've been having some of the same kinds of dreams in recent weeks."

Alexi frowned and looked at Valian. "Didn't Alyssa say that Isabella had been having the dreams for four or five weeks? Sounds like the same timeline."

"She did, yes." Valian swiveled toward Gray in his chair. "How much of these dreams do you remember, Gray? Isabella told Alyssa that she couldn't remember a lot of her dreams, just bits and pieces. Were yours the same as she'd described? Just disjointed odds and ends? Or did they include more detail?"

Gray nodded. "I remember most of them, though neither you nor Alexi made an appearance in my dreams as you did in hers." He grinned briefly but continued on in a more serious tone. "However, I did see something else that Isabella mentioned to Alyssa."

"And what was that?" Finvar asked.

Leaning forward, Gray shot a glance at the High Lord. "I've seen the men in ebony robes on more than one occasion—and in a forested area that is unfamiliar to me."

"Ah, now that seems significant," Niall said.

Gray held up a finger. "Okay, to be fair, it could be just my mind messing with me, making shit up," he added with another quick grin, but then sobered. "But it didn't *feel* that way. Every time I'm there in the dream, it feels like I should know the place, know the men, but I'm damned if I do." He shook his head. "The more I think about it, the more it feels important, linked in some way, but to what, I have no idea. It's been bothering me since the dreams started. It's like the answer is right there in front of me but just out of reach."

"And now that Alyssa has shared Isabella's dreams, it seems that you may be right," Niall murmured. "You're certain that you don't know these men? Don't know the forest?"

"Hell no, I'm not sure of anything!" Gray ran a hand through his hair. "I've been thinking about it for a couple of weeks but kinda just blew it off as my mind conjuring stuff up. Then I hear about Isabella's dreams, and it's like, maybe not. Maybe this is as important as I've been thinking it might be."

"Okay, here's a suggestion," Alexi said with a grin. "And I know this is going to be a shocker coming from me, considering my feelings on the subject, but why don't you give the Oracles a shout, Gray? I'd think they could give you some insight into what it all means. Hell, they may even tell you who these guys in the black robes actually are."

When they all stared at Alexi with stunned expressions, he burst into laughter. "I told you it would be a shocker, my dudes. Deal with it, okay?"

Six

"Have a seat here on the settee with me, child," the Queen said as Alyssa followed her upstairs and into the main salon. "Gryphon will be in shortly with refreshments."

Alyssa wasn't sure why Queen Beatrice wanted to speak with her, but she figured she'd get to it eventually. She only hoped that the Queen wouldn't take too long to do so because, though Alyssa didn't want to be rude, finding Isabella was the only thing she had on her mind at the moment.

Her worries must have shown on her face because the Queen smiled and patted her hand. "Don't look so anxious, Alyssa. I won't keep you long," she murmured as Gryphon came into the room carrying a silver tray containing a pot of tea, two cups with matching saucers, and a basket of fresh scones.

"Ah, and here's Gryphon now." The Queen nodded at the chamber elf. "This is lovely, Gryphon. Just what we needed. Thank you."

"Ring if you wish anything else, Majesty." The chamber elf bowed deeply, and backing toward the side door from which he'd entered, he disappeared.

"Now, Graydon and I had just finished our breakfast meeting this morning when Gryphon came in with the news that you and

Valian were here. Getting in so late last evening, I'm sure you're tired. And I know you must be filled with all sorts of fears for Isabella, but did you get enough sleep, my dear?"

Alyssa nodded slowly. "I slept some, but though the bed was comfortable, it probably wasn't the best night I've had in a while, considering."

"No. Of course not. I can only imagine. Did you have any breakfast? I could have Gryphon bring you whatever you'd like."

"No, no, I'm fine, Majesty. A cup of tea and one of these delicious-looking scones will hold me over for now. Thank you." Alyssa watched Queen Beatrice pour out two cups of tea, and then tilted her head as the Queen handed one to her. Taking the cup, Alyssa hesitated. "Your Majesty, what is it you wanted to talk to me about?"

Queen Beatrice took a small sip of her tea and then nodded at Alyssa over the rim. "Yes, I understand that you're worried for your friend, and you'll definitely want to get back to the search as soon as possible, I imagine."

"No...well, yes, but I am curious about what's on your mind."

The Queen put down her cup and turned to Alyssa. "Valian has probably already asked you about Isabella, about her ancestry, but I just wanted to touch base as well. You see, my dear, neither you nor Isabella were here when Gray found out about his heritage. It was... quite a shock for him."

"You mean, about his fae lineage?"

The Queen nodded. "Yes, in part. However, as you now know, with Gray there was much more to it than that."

"Sure, finding out about the Ellurian side of him, too. Right?"

"Mmm, learning that he's a Halfling, that Lord Finvar is his biological father, and that he also has Ellurian ancestry? Well, it was incredibly complicated to explain and a lot for him to absorb in a short period of time. And I can freely admit now that I was weak. I waited far too long to tell my son about his heritage, to set the record straight, so to speak." She sighed. "Unfortunately, the longer I waited, the harder it became and the easier it was to put it off. I told myself that I was protecting him, but in the end, I was protecting myself."

"Oh, Majesty—"

"No, no, it's true," the Queen said, putting up a hand. "You see, Sir Edward and I had agreed to tell Graydon the truth once he was older, but then Edward was killed in the war before we ever got that opportunity. Gray adored his father and missed him terribly in those years following Edward's death. I simply couldn't bring myself to approach the subject with him while he was mourning, struggling so with the loss. Against the advice of the few who knew the truth, I decided to wait."

"I don't have children but can certainly understand that instinct to protect your child," Alyssa murmured. "Seems to me that you were just giving Gray some time to find a place for the sorrow of losing his father."

"Yes, just a few years longer, I thought. What could a bit more time hurt?" The Queen paused and shook her head. "But before I knew it, a few more years had turned into decades. And at some point, I told myself that it really wouldn't matter that Edward wasn't Graydon's biological father, that surely his cherished memories of Edward were enough. It just took my son's accidental dosing with Faerie Bomb to make me see that I'd denied my son his right to understand where he came from, to understand the power that was waking inside of him."

Alyssa's heart went out to the Queen. "It must have been a very difficult decision to tell him the truth after all that time."

"Oh, unquestionably, but you see, I had no choice, difficult or not. It was all unraveling, Alyssa. His power was growing, and he'd started to question everything. Oh, there had been many signs of his magickal abilities early on, but he always seemed to accept them as natural. After all, his closest friends were Elven and had numerous magickal powers themselves. Yet, in the months leading up to the Faerie Bomb event, he'd been asking pointed questions, wondering why he had magick in his blood when his parents had none."

"Forgive me, Majesty, but don't you have magickal abilities because of your Ellurian lineage?"

"I do, yes, but I rarely use them."

"Then I can see how that must have been pretty confusing for

Gray," Alyssa replied. "And I understand now how the situation could spiral out of your control in an instant."

Queen Beatrice nodded with a sad smile. "Indeed. Valian had been keeping a close eye on Gray, anticipating an inevitable situation like the one that ultimately occurred that night in Old Minerva's casting room. He'd been urging me to tell my son the truth for many years. Valian was one of those who'd been against my decision to wait to tell Gray the truth from the very start, but I thought I knew best. I didn't want to harm Gray's memories of the only father he'd ever known. However, Valian had been right all along, but my Chancellor is loyal to his queen, and he had kept my secret throughout the years. A secret that came close to ruining my relationship with my only son."

"No, Majesty, I'm sure that's not true. Gray adores you."

The Queen chuckled. "Yes, and there I am most definitely blessed, but it was touch and go for several weeks, and I feared that I had lost him for good at one point. You see, when Graydon finally learned the truth, it was devastating for him. He felt betrayed, deceived, and I could not blame him for feeling that way. His whole world as he'd known it was upended with that single conversation. This was an outcome that I'd never taken into account with my decision to wait. The way my son found out about his true ancestry was the worst possible scenario."

Alyssa tried not to squirm in her seat, but hearing such personal things from the Queen made her so sad and a bit uncomfortable. "Majesty, why are you telling me all of this?"

The Queen picked up her cup and took a sip. "Alyssa, you have to understand that Gray knew deep down that there was something...different about him, but he just couldn't put a finger on it because he didn't know the entire truth. I wanted to talk to you about Isabella. This is something that she will also grapple with, as I assume that she has no idea of her actual heritage. However, you've known her for a very long time."

Alyssa frowned. "Yes, most of my life. Our parents have been friends for decades."

The Queen nodded, took another sip of tea, and then set her cup down. "Let me start by saying that I don't believe in coincidences. I'm a firm believer that there is a purpose for everything that happens. I trust in the power of the universe, the wisdom of the Oracles, and the truth that all things happen for a reason. That you are the descendant and your best friend is now found to have fae blood is more than a coincidence, in my mind." She put up a hand when Alyssa opened her mouth to deny the thought. "Please, just hear me out. I'm going to ask you something now that Valian probably has not, and I want you to think very carefully before you answer. Will you do that for me?"

"Okay." Alyssa took a deep breath and let it out slowly. She didn't know where this was going but she was willing to give it some time to find out. "What's your question, Majesty?"

"I want you to think back over the years. Were there any abilities that Isabella exhibited that seemed...somehow out of the ordinary for a human being?"

Out of the ordinary for a human? Alyssa thought, stunned by the question. This was certainly a twist and so not what she was expecting. "Do you mean, like powers that could be traced to a fae lineage?"

The Queen shook her head. "Not necessarily powers or something that obvious. Let's call them gifts. Maybe something quirky that she could do that seemed unusual, uncanny. Something that no one else—certainly no human—could do."

Alyssa opened her mouth to tell the Queen how ridiculous the thought was, that there was nothing, but then thought better of it. That was a knee-jerk reaction, she realized. The Queen had asked her to really think about it, so she would, at the very least, give her that courtesy and do just that. *Were* there "gifts" that Isabella had possessed that Alyssa had just accepted as part of her friend's natural abilities, gifts that were possibly more than just natural? It took her a bit of time, but as the minutes ticked by, a few things began to slowly emerge in her mind. Things that seemed perfectly fine at the time... but now...looking more closely?

"Alyssa? What is it, child? I can see it in your eyes. You've thought of something, haven't you?"

Alyssa frowned and set her cup down. "Well, yes and no. I mean, they seem like such small things on the surface, but when you really look at them, maybe they aren't so small after all."

"Like what? Give me an example."

"Well, for one thing, even when we were kids, whenever I would misplace something, no matter what it was...a favorite book, favorite sweater, favorite toy, Isabella was the one person who could always tell me precisely where I'd left whatever it was...always."

"Was that only in your childhood?" the Queen asked with an intrigued look.

"No." Alyssa shook her head. "No, it wasn't. When we became adults it was no different, maybe even more frequent...a set of keys here, a watch there, a phone, where the car was parked in a garage. And it wasn't just random or generic, either. She could tell me exactly where I had left the item I was looking for. It was, as you said, uncanny. I did ask her once how she knew where to find these things, how she could be so accurate."

"And what was her answer?"

"She just shrugged and said that she could always see it in her mind." Alyssa took a sip of her tea, her mouth suddenly dry. "I remember laughing at that, but she was so serious. I guess I just put it down to one of Isabella's quirks, but looking back, it was...very surreal. Every time."

"I see." The Queen seemed to digest this information for a moment and then nodded. "What else?"

"I beg your pardon?"

"You said 'they' seemed like such small things. What else did you remember?"

"Oh. Well, it's going to sound silly, but when we were little, we would play games like hide and seek all the time. Isabella was great at it, or at least that's what I always thought."

"What do you mean?"

"She was always the last one standing. No one could ever find her. I used to think, wow, Izzy really knows how to hide, you know? I mean, there were times that I watched her hide, knew exactly where she was, but when whoever was 'it' would look in that spot, Isabella wouldn't be there."

"Are you saying that she disappeared?"

"I don't know what I'm saying." Alyssa sighed. "All I know is that at the end of the game when the call went out 'all free,' Izzy would pop up from that precise spot."

"Did you ask her about how she did that?"

"Yes, on several occasions. She'd just roll her eyes and ask me what I was talking about, that she'd been right there in that spot the whole time."

The Queen nodded again. "Anything else?"

"Well, again, it's a bit ridiculous, and I don't know that it's weird, but Isabella has incredible senses."

"Senses?"

"Yeah, like, she has the keenest hearing, which has always amazed me, but comes in handy for eavesdropping." Alyssa laughed. "Anyway, she also has the unusually accurate senses of taste and smell. And I'm not kidding. She can tell you every ingredient of any drink concoction or recipe just by smelling or tasting it. And she has an unerring sense of direction, too. She's adventurous. Always goes boldly off to do things that I'm just gobsmacked by." Alyssa paused with a frown. "Except that seemed to change this last summer. Not the accurate sense of direction but her adventurous confidence."

"Change? How so?"

"Well, you remember when she and I first came to the realm this summer, when we got separated in the vortex and I ended up in Roseland. Then I got abducted as Niall and his men were bringing me to the palace."

"Yes, of course. Isabella found her way to Cheshire Wood where she ran into Alexi." The Queen smiled. "I'm assuming by way of her accurate sense of direction?"

Alyssa laughed. "Well, I think she had the help of her little compass, but yes. Anyhow, here's the thing. When we set out for the park and got to the old portal, she suddenly froze and the color just drained from her face. She seemed terrified and backed away from it, even though she'd been through it numerous times. She was *afraid* of the portal, of the vortex. So much so that I thought that I was going to have to come through by myself. She kept saying that maybe we should wait for Valian, but he'd been so secretive—which was why we'd made the decision to come in the first place—

that I was intent on coming here to find out why. It was very weird."

"Did she give a reason for her sudden fear?"

"Not really. Just that she'd always gone through the portal with Valian and never alone, and also that she wasn't really sure how it all worked, which gave her pause, but I don't think that was all of it."

"What else could it have been, do you think?"

Alyssa shrugged. "Not a clue. So, I don't know if these are the kinds of things you were looking for with your question, but that's all I can think of for now."

"Those will do for a start. Thank you for indulging me." The Queen put a scone on a plate and handed it to Alyssa. "Here. I'll feel a bit better if you at least eat something before heading off to search with the others."

❧

POUNDING.

Isabella surfaced slowly, wondering vaguely where the distant pounding sound was coming from. Rolling over on the bed, she realized with a heap of hazy annoyance that there seemed to be somebody between her ears with a mallet that was making the persistent racket. And that racket was developing at a rather astonishing rate into the beginnings of what quite possibly would become a monster headache.

However, that didn't seem to be where her malaise ended if the fact that her eyelids felt like someone—perhaps the little bastard in her head with the mallet—had glued them shut was any indication.

And my God!, she thought through her haze, *what died in my mouth?*

Carefully, very carefully, Isabella pried one gummy eyelid open to a slit only to have her retina blasted by a spear of light coming from a nearby window and almost blinding her. Laying perfectly still for a moment, she tried not to panic. What on earth had happened to her? Had she been in an accident? Hit by a bus? Which she had to admit that by the way she was feeling was a perfectly logical explanation. If so, why was she not in a hospital? Wait— *Was* she in a hospital?

In a moment of uncontrolled alarm, she pried both eyes open and jackknifed up, sweeping the room with her burning orbs. Which was a critical error because it felt like her head just about split down the middle with the sudden movement. Whimpering and gingerly laying back into the pillows for several minutes, she made a conscious effort not to move in hopes that the damn pounding would subside enough for her to get up and go in search of aspirin and at least a gallon of water.

In the meantime, she'd confirmed several things with her brief sweep of the room. She was at home, she was *on* her bed and not *in* her bed, and she was fully clothed. What the hell was going on? And why couldn't she remember anything?

"Okay, think, Isabella," she mumbled and then winced at the rusty sound of her own voice as it reverberated around the back of her skull. Clearing her throat, she took in several deep breaths, letting them out slowly. Then, she silently began retracing a memory that seemed to be a jumbled mess of images and sound. She clearly remembered going to the gallery for the showing and vaguely having a conversation with Aly when she got there about the dreams that had been plaguing her sleep. She remembered getting an invitation for...something...but from there on it was mostly a collage of fragrance and color, which, for some reason, was disturbing in itself.

Finally steeling herself to push up into a sitting position, Isabella dangled her legs over the side of the bed, and though said legs felt like rubber, she contemplated standing and making her way downstairs. However, before attempting that feat, there was water and pain relief in her bathroom, so that would be the first step.

It was a tentative first step, to be sure. In the bathroom mirror, her pale face stared back at her through red-rimmed eyes and haloed by her red curls going in every direction. *This is gonna take some work*, she thought. But first, pain relief and water.

In the end, she'd downed the aspirin, stripped where she stood, and climbed into a hot shower to try to scrub away the fog covering whatever had happened the night before. And thankfully, after a good twenty minutes, her headache was starting to ebb, and her mind was clearing a bit.

She threw on a pair of jeans and a long-sleeved shirt, then opted for her soft, house slippers before heading downstairs. But halfway down the staircase the pounding started again. This time, it was coming from the front door. Though just as she got to the door, she could hear someone putting a key in the lock. She quickly unlocked the door and pulled it open to find Alyssa and Valian on her stoop.

"Aly? What are you doing here?" she asked in confusion. "And what the hell happened to me last night?"

Seven

"Oh, my gosh! Izzy, you're here." Alyssa blurted, tugging Isabella out onto the stoop and into a bear hug. "We've been so worried!"

"Of course I'm here. Where else would I be?" Isabella pulled back and gave Alyssa a suspicious look. "And what do you mean, you've been worried? Why?"

Alyssa glance at Valian and then back at Isabella. "Maybe we should just go inside to talk about this."

Valian nodded. "There is quite a bit to talk about, Isabella."

"Alright," Isabella said slowly before turning and leading them back inside the townhouse. In the living room, she sank down into an arm chair and spread her hands wide as Alyssa and Valian settled across from her on the sofa. "Okay, so you said you were worried about me. Why is that exactly? Because I gotta tell you, I'm a bit worried myself since I woke up about an hour and a half ago feeling like I'd guzzled the local bar dry and, at first, not even sure where I was. I'm still a bit shaky even now. What did we do last night, Aly? And why can't I remember much?"

"First of all, let's start with this. What exactly do you remember of the night you came to the gallery?" Alyssa asked in a cautious tone.

Isabella frowned. *That's an odd way to put it*, she thought, and a large ball of anxiety began to unfurl in her belly. "Well, I mean, I do remember getting to the gallery and us talking about...my sleeping issues of late...but then there's not much but a jumbled mess after that." She looked back and forth between Alyssa and Valian. "What's going on, Aly? And why did you say, 'the night I came to the gallery' instead of 'last night'?"

Alyssa exchanged glances with Valian again. "Izzy, you've been missing for almost two days."

Isabella felt the blood drain from her face, and she shook her head. "No, that can't be right, Aly. No...no...I clearly remember coming to the gallery last evening. You were having the showing for that new artist."

"Sweetie, that wasn't last night. That was Wednesday evening, and today is Friday afternoon. We've been looking for you since then."

"Wait— What?" Isabella's earlier alarm began to rise again, and her breath was suddenly coming in short gulps. She leaned forward with her hands on her knees just trying to get a breath around the anxiety building inside of her like an emotional bomb about to explode.

Then Valian was there rubbing her back and murmuring to her softly. "That's it, love. Take it slow, in and out. You're hyperventilating. Don't gulp it in or you'll pass out. Breathe deep...let it out slowly."

It took a few moments but gradually she began to get herself under control. However, fear's greasy fingers still had a grip on her. She'd lost two days? Okay, she had been having lapses—lost time, but two days? How was that even possible?

"Okay, I don't understand any of this," she whispered. "You're saying that...what? I disappeared from the gallery sometime after I arrived, and I've been missing for two *days*? That just doesn't make any sense."

"It's true, Isabella," Valian said as he sat down on the ottoman. "Alyssa called me in a panic on Wednesday evening saying that you'd disappeared. I'd been in Wysteria dealing with a possible new threat to the realm, so I didn't get the message right away. But when I got here, you were already gone."

"Already gone?" Isabella asked. "Gone where?"

Alyssa shook her head. "Again, that's just it. We don't know. Your purse and coat were in the office where you'd left them—they still are—but you were just...gone."

"I can't believe this," Isabella said. "How could I just disappear and not remember *anything*?"

"Why don't we just take a breath, and like Alyssa said, go back to the start," Valian suggested. "You said that you remembered getting to the gallery and having the conversation with Alyssa about your dreams and sleeping issues, but the rest is a jumble, correct?"

"Yes. Mostly just images, colors...and..."

"And?" Valian prompted.

"It's gonna sound stupid."

"No, Izzy." Alyssa shook her head. "It won't. Trust us. We're going to help you through this. We'll figure it out."

Isabella looked back and forth at them again. "Well, images, colors, and *scents*."

"What kind of scents, Isabella?" Valian asked quietly. "Think carefully."

She chewed on her bottom lip as she tried to put it into words. "It's hard to explain, but it was like being in the middle of a field of wild flowers where everything is blooming at once. It wasn't cloying exactly but fresh and very sweet. Does that make sense?"

Valian nodded. "It does but let's put that aside for the moment. I want you to calm your mind and go back to Wednesday."

"Okay, but I don't know what good that will do," Isabella replied, her voice rising again. "Like I said, I just woke up a little over an hour ago and have no idea how I got home." She turned to Alyssa as tears filled her eyes. "Aly, I have no idea how I got *home*," she rambled on in a frantic voice. "Let alone what happened to me in the interim. I kinda freaked out at first, because I thought maybe I'd been in an accident, and clearly that's not the case, but it seems that it might be even worse than that."

"All right, yes, it's a confusing situation, but let's not panic again, okay?" Valian responded in a soothing tone. "Let's just take this one step at a time. What is the last clear thing you remember from Wednesday night?" He put up a hand. "Wait, no, let's go back a bit farther to before you left the townhouse. Tell me about how your Wednesday afternoon went. Did you have bookings or meetings for Party Poppers? Any outside meetings? Anything unusual take place?"

Isabella took a deep breath and swiped at the tears running down her face. "Poppers didn't have any bookings for the weekend, so yes, we had a couple of prep meetings about upcoming events that would be happening in the next few weeks. We did some preliminary planning, but that was about it. The day was pretty smooth. No outside appointments or meetings at all."

"And then?" Valian prompted. "What time did you get out of those prep meetings?"

This was what she needed, Isabella thought, as the logical side of her mind took control. Valian's calm, steady voice with patient, consistent questioning. If anyone could help her through this, it was most likely him. She took a deep breath and let it out slowly, working to settle her emotions and just think objectively.

"Well, I got out of the last meeting around five forty-five and headed home to shower and change for the evening, even though all I really wanted to do was put on my pajamas and pour myself a humongous glass of wine."

"Oh, Izzy—"

"No, Aly, it's no big deal. It's just that I hadn't been sleeping... well, I had been, but not well, which we discussed when I got to the gallery, right?"

Alyssa nodded. "We did. Almost as soon as you'd arrived."

"Let's not get ahead of ourselves, ladies," Valian reminded them. "One step at a time. No jumping ahead. Keep to a consistent timeline for now. So, Isabella, you went home to shower and get ready to go to the gallery. What next?"

Isabella took another breath and thought back to that night. "I spent an hour or so getting ready and then had a quick bite to eat. After that, I walked up to the corner to hail a cab."

"You took a cab to the gallery?" Valian asked.

Isabella nodded. "Yes. And that's when I had another weird lapse."

"What exactly do you mean by 'lapse'?"

Isabella looked at Valian with unease. "I don't know how to explain that either, Valian. I've been having gaps. Lost time, and it's been getting worse lately. I got into the cab, gave the driver the address for the gallery, and we pulled away from the curb. The next thing that I knew, we were parked in front of the gallery, and the cabbie was saying, 'Hey, lady, are you okay? This is where you wanted to go, right?' It was so embarrassing."

Valian took her hand. "You said that this has happened before? How long has this been going on?"

Isabella nodded, tears springing up in her eyes again. "Yes, it's been happening over the last few weeks, maybe a month or so. Like I said, it's been occurring more and more often." She took a tissue from the box on the end table, wiped her eyes, and then continued. "Anyway, that's when I got out of the taxi and felt like I was being watched. That sixth sense kind of thing, you know? Then I looked across the street and saw the woman, heard her talking to me in my head."

Valian nodded. "And what did she say? Exactly."

Isabella blinked and wiped her eyes again. "She said, *'Yes, there you are, Isabella Doyle. I see you...the time is coming, you know.'* It was like she was standing right next to me and whispering into my ear."

"Do you know what she meant by that?" Valian asked with a frown.

Isabella shook her head. "Not a clue. But I did have the weirdest sense of déjà vu, like I should've known her from...somewhere...but I had no idea where that could have been. Anyway, then a box truck went by, and when it passed, she was gone. She'd disappeared. Do you think it may be connected to what's been happening to me? To my dreams and the time loss? Or maybe even to my disappearance?"

"I don't know. Possibly, and we have some thoughts about it, but we'll come back to that later as well. Let's move on for now, get as far as you can remember in the timeline. What did you do next?"

"I went into the gallery to find Aly." Isabella paused, rubbing her forehead where the headache was resurfacing. "By the time I found her, I was getting more and more worried about all of it. The encounter with the woman on the street just about sent me over the edge. Anyway, Aly and I went back to the office so I could tell her what had been going on with me."

"Okay, good." Valian stood and walked around the living room, pausing behind the sofa where Alyssa was sitting. "So, you both are in the office and you're telling Alyssa about your dreams, the lapses, the woman on the street. Then what?" Valian persisted.

Isabella sighed. "I'm not sure."

"Think, Izzy," Alyssa urged. "Close your eyes and visualize it. We were talking about all of that. So, what happened next?"

Doing as Alyssa asked, Isabella closed her eyes and brought the interior of the gallery office into her mind. She could see it clearly. She and Alyssa sitting on the sofa, her feeling a little distressed, Aly walking her through it all, much like she and Valian were doing now. Then it suddenly flashed into her head.

I hate to bother you, but there are a couple of clients out here that want to talk to you, Aly.

Oh, and I found this on the front counter.

"Lenore!" Isabella blurted as her eyes sprang open. "Lenore came into the office because some clients were looking to buy a boatload of art and wanted to talk to Aly. And she'd also found an envelope out on the gallery counter that was addressed to me."

"Good, Izzy. Now, close your eyes again and keep going. What was in the envelope?"

Isabella closed her eyes and visualized Alyssa handing her the heavy parchment envelope with its elaborate script, could feel the apprehension she'd felt that night, just holding it in her hands. "I remember holding the envelope and thinking that it felt like something life-changing was coming. I was afraid to open it, afraid of what that something could be."

"Keep going. You're doing great," Alyssa murmured.

"I remember you talking me down off that ledge with your little pep talk, and then sliding open the envelope flap. I pulled out the note inside but..."

"But what, Isabella?" Valian asked quietly. "What happened when you pulled out the note?"

"Pink. It was...a pink, sparkly cloud. It just exploded out of the envelope. It made me sneeze."

"And?" Alyssa asked.

"And that's when the scent hit me. So sweet, so...yummy." Isabella opened her eyes. "And I was amazed that you couldn't smell it. It was so strong."

"Yes. We were both pretty confused by that, right? And how did it make you feel?" Alyssa asked.

Isabella smiled, remembering the warm, happy emotions that had rolled over her almost immediately. "It made me feel so good, happy and suddenly content, which looking back now is weird because I'd been so upset when I got there and afraid to open the envelope in the first place."

"Do you remember what the note said?" Valian asked.

Isabella frowned. "I think it was a poem of some kind with an invitation to...something. But that's when everything starts to get hazy."

Alyssa leaned forward. "Who was the note from, Izzy? Think."

With a sigh, Isabella started to say that she couldn't remember, but then a name suddenly popped into her head with a face to go along with it. "Tempest! It was signed by Tempest. She sent it to me." She got up and began to pace. "And I think I saw her. It was later, after you'd gone out into the gallery, Aly. I remember feeling wonky and lightheaded, almost tipsy. I got up to get a bottle of water out of the little fridge like you'd told me." Excited now, Isabella spun around and pointed at Alyssa. "Yes! She was there. When I turned around, she was just there...sitting on the little sofa in the same spot where I'd just been sitting. Tempest was the woman who I'd seen when I got out of the cab. She was the one who'd spoken to me in my head from across the street!"

"Are you sure, Isabella?" Valian asked.

Isabella nodded. "Absolutely positive. I vaguely remember having a conversation with her, too. I asked her what her name was, and she confirmed it." Isabella slipped back down into the chair. "Now, the bulk of that conversation is really jumbled...and full of colors, if that makes any sense. But I did remember where else that I'd seen her, or at least, I thought I had."

"Where was that?" Valian asked.

"In my dreams. She was a fae warrior in the last dream that I'd had. Anyway, I remember she said that she knew my family, and she called me *mo linbh milis.*"

Alyssa frowned. "What does that mean?"

"My sweet child," Valian murmured. "It's Irish Gaelic."

"Exactly!" Isabella shouted. "And I knew what she'd said. I don't understand how because I didn't even know what language it was, but I knew."

"And this Tempest said that she knew your family?" Alyssa asked.

"Yes. She said that she'd known my gram when she was young and had known my mom, too. She also said that she'd known about me since I was born." Isabella frowned as bits and pieces of the conversation came through the fog in her mind. "She'd visited my gram in Ireland, but that isn't where Tempest is from."

"Where is she from, Isabella?" Valian asked. "Did she say?"

She shook her head. "I don't think so, just that her homeland was very similar. At least, that's the phrase that I remember."

Isabella rubbed her temples. Her head was beginning to pound in earnest, and it was getting harder and harder to grab hold of those little bits and pieces, although she could sense those vital fragments of information hovering there in her mind just out of sight.

"All right, I think maybe that's all we should worry about for now," Valian said. "I can see that you're beginning to get a headache and could use some more rest."

"No, but there's so much more to go over," Isabella complained even though her headache was getting worse by the minute. "We have to figure this out, Valian."

"And we will, love, but your mind and body are still recovering from a traumatic experience. You need to rest for now."

"But what about the pink, sparkly stuff? I watched your face when I was explaining about the colors and the scent. You knew exactly what I was talking about. Valian, you have to tell me what you know, or what you think you know. I can't remember where I've been for two days."

"Isabella—"

"I'm not an idiot, Valian. It was some kind of drug, wasn't it?"

After a moment, Valian nodded. "We believe it was a powdered form of a substance called Faerie Bomb. Gray had a very similar experience with the liquid form this last summer." He put up a hand. "And before you ask, it's not dangerous, nor is it addictive, but it would also explain your condition when you woke up."

"But why was I the only one affected? Alyssa, you got a good dose of it as well, but couldn't smell it, and you weren't affected at all. So, why just me?"

Valian paused and glanced at Alyssa before answering her question. "Isabella, Faerie Bomb is made specifically for the fae. Only those with fae blood can smell it or have any response to the potion, for that matter."

Isabella stared at him for a full ten seconds as her poor muddled brain tried to take in what Valian was telling her. Then she smiled. Her smile spread to a grin before she started to chuckle and then to laugh out loud, until tears sprang up again and flowed down her cheeks, and her laughter turned into panicked, distraught sobs.

"Oh, no, Izzy," Alyssa cooed as she hurried over and enveloped her in a hug. "It's gonna be okay, honey. We're going to figure this out. I promise."

"How?" Isabella cried in between sobs. "What Valian just basically said was that I have faerie blood in me, right? How is that possible, Aly? How?"

"I don't know the answer to that, baby, but we're going to help you find out. You'll see."

"But how is this Tempest connected to it all? She's a faerie, right? If she's a faerie, why would she drug me like that?"

Valian came over and sat back down on the ottoman in front of them, taking her icy-cold hands in his. "Isabella, do you trust me?" he asked in soft voice.

She blinked back fresh tears, and after a moment, nodded.

"Then here's what we're going to do. You're correct, love. There is much more to this story, some of which we've yet to uncover, but we're going to get to the bottom of it all. It's just going to take some time. Unfortunately, it can't happen here in this realm." He gave her hands a gentle squeeze. "So, to that end, Alyssa is going upstairs with you now, and you're going to pack a bag. Then, after you take something for the headache and you send word to Party Poppers that you'll be out of town for several days, the three of us are going to Wysteria where we're going to go over this whole thing more thoroughly once you've gotten a bit more rest. Okay?"

Isabella swallowed and took the wad of fresh tissues that Alyssa handed her. Wiping her runny nose and her red-rimmed eyes, she nodded.

Yes, she would do as Valian asked and hold on to the notion that they would find the answers she sought in the Artemysian realm, though a little voice in the back of her mind whispered to be careful what you wish for...because it just might not be what you were expecting.

Or what you even want...

Eight

The forest was eerily silent as Gray made his way along the path through the dim, murky light. It had begun to snow again, which would add another coat to the already ankle-deep layer blanketing the trail that wound through the trees ahead. A trail of white that seemed unending.

He stopped for a moment, trying to get his bearings. He knew the terrain of his homeland very well. It was ingrained in every fiber of his being, as much a part of him as breathing with its hills and glens, its woodlands and meadows. Both Wysteria and Roseland were full of beauty and life. But this...though just as beautiful, this place was unfamiliar to him.

Figuring the best course of action was to keep moving, that something familiar was bound to crop up, he started to walk again. There had to be an end to this forest soon, as he'd already been walking for quite some time. Ten minutes later, as the path took a slight left turn, that end finally appeared as he could see light through a break in the trees up ahead, and as he approached, found that it opened onto a vast meadow of pristine snow. He stood at its edge, enjoying the beauty of its expanse, the majesty of the continuation of forest on the other side, and the grandeur of the mountainous backdrop in the distance...and felt only confusion. How was it possible that he did not know this place, those mountains in the distance?

He now had a decision to make. Did he cross the snow-covered meadow and continue on through the woodland on the far side in hopes of finding a village or town? Or turn back and retrace his steps? Turning back would take time, and he sensed that it would be dark soon. As he stood weighing his options, movement across the meadow at the edge of treeline caught his eye when a tall man in ebony robes stepped out into the light. And then two more men dress in similar attire stepped out behind him.

Curious, as he'd seen these men before, Gray took one step into the meadow and then another before being stopped by a soft female voice to his left.

"No. Do not engage, Halfling. It is not your time...yet."

Turning, he watched a tall faerie with an athletic build step out of the treeline. She was dressed in warrior's garb: leaf-green pants, a tunic trimmed in gold, and leather boots that topped her knees. She carried a long bow, and a quiver of arrows was slung over one shoulder. Her long red hair was worn in a thick braid down her back, and her finely pointed ears were adorned with jewels and an array of unique hoops.

"What do you mean, it's not my time? Who are those men?"

"Your time will come soon enough." The faerie looked back across the meadow to where the strange men stood watching. "They are a few of the elders of the Ancients."

"The ancients?" Gray frowned. "What ancients? What is this place? It's unfamiliar to me."

"Is it?" The faerie turned to him then, and her emerald-green eyes sparkled in the waning light. "We stand in the Wastelands, Halfling, on the east side of the Unwelcoming Rise. That's the Antiley mountain range in the distance. You may not know them, but I think deep down you know of those who live there. Do you not feel the pull inside of you?" She nodded toward the men at the far treeline. "Their pull?"

"I don't understand what you mean by that."

"You are the Prince of the realm and also the heir to the Winter Court, which is an impressive blend on its face, but you are so much more than that, are you not? You have more running through your veins than human or fae blood. You have an immense untapped power."

"But what difference does that make? Sure, I've seen those men before, but Isabella saw them, too."

The faerie nodded at that. "She did indeed, and considerably more, though she won't remember much for now."

"What do you mean? What more did she see?"

"Her memories will surface, and she will tell you in time. You will need to help her through the transition, as it will be incomprehensible to her at first. But she is strong. She will become."

"Become? Become what? And who are you?"

"Me?" she asked and then smiled slyly. "I would have thought you'd have worked it out by now. My name is Tempest." She nodded toward the men again. "You will meet them soon enough, as you will need them and others. For something else is coming, as well. Something dark and wicked. Go back and prepare, Halfling. Time is growing short." With that her image began to shimmer.

"No! Wait! What's coming?" Gray shouted, but Tempest was already fading along with everything else.

"Wait!" Gray shouted as he sprang up in bed. He was covered in sweat and breathing hard. It took him a minute to realize where he was before flopping back down onto the pillows and working to get his breath under control.

Well, this was going to be an interesting story to share with the others, and as soon as possible. If this latest dream was to be believed, evidently, something was already in motion, and it seemed as if they were a little late to the party.

ALEXI WAS ANGRILY SHOUTING AT VALIAN WHEN GRAY entered the war room two hours later as Alyssa, Niall, and Finvar sat at the conference table watching the exchange like some kind of weird tennis match.

"Why didn't you wake me last night when you got in? You gave me your word, Val. You said you would tag me the minute Bella was found."

Valian sighed, but there was an edge to his tone. "I told you, Alexi. Isabella was confused and distraught, and it was after midnight when we finally got here."

"You should have brought her directly to me, no matter what time it was."

"She'd just endured a dosing of Faerie Bomb and had lost two days into the fog of it. I took her to the hospital wing the minute we got here. She needed rest, Alexi, and I made an executive decision. I'm sorry if you're butt-hurt over it."

"Fuck you, Val. This has nothing to do with me having hurt feelings, and you know it." Alexi shook his head. "You know, this is so typical of how you roll."

"What the hell is that supposed to mean?"

"You just bulldoze your way along through any situation without a thought for anyone else involved. It's always Valian knows best." He gave his cousin a disgusted look, then waved a hand in the air. "Oh, don't get me wrong. I'm grateful that you found Bella and got her to Wysteria where we could take care of her, but you could have come and told me that you'd found her after you'd gotten her settled upstairs with the healers. But, of course, you didn't. You *chose* to wait until morning knowing that I was desperate to find her, desperate to know that she was all right."

"Oh, for the love of the Oracles, Alexi. I didn't think—"

"Didn't think what? Didn't think it would matter? No, Val, you just didn't think, period."

"Whoa, whoa, whoa," Gray said putting out a hand. "Let's take a step back gentlemen and breathe. This is a stressful situation for all of us. It has a lot of moving parts, and it's unfolding quickly in several directions...faster than you all know. So, let's put our emotions aside for a moment, sit down at the table, and talk about this as rationally as we can. I also have some new information that may connect. I'm just not sure how yet."

Gray watched both of them sit down at the conference table with their angry feelings swirling around the room and wondered if rational thinking would be possible at this point. "Now, for a start, someone give me a *calm*, coherent status update on Isabella's situation. I want to know how and where she was found."

Valian ran a hand through his hair and nodded. "Alyssa, Niall, and I got to New York late Thursday, so we went to the gallery first. No one had seen Isabella since the showing on Wednesday evening, and her belongings were still in the office. With the lateness of the hour, we did a quick run by her townhouse to see if perhaps she'd come home, but it was empty and there was no evidence that she'd been back. We decided to get a good night's sleep and start talking to our contacts on Friday morning." He glanced across the table. "Niall has had some of his warriors watching the gallery on a constant rotation, and we have as well. We'd hoped that at least one of those warriors had seen something that might help us with our search."

"Alright. And what did these contacts have to say?" Gray asked, looking back and forth between Valian and the High Lord.

Niall cleared his throat. "My Twilight Court warriors on duty Wednesday evening did see Isabella arrive and also noted the fae woman across the street. Not knowing what this could indicate, they kept a keen watch after Isabella went into the gallery, but they said that after the fae woman faded, they saw nothing else of note until Valian arrived much later. I spent a few hours after that checking with other sources but learned nothing further."

"It was much the same story with those lookouts we had in place," Valian added. "One did confirm that Isabella and the fae woman seemed to somehow connect for a moment before Isabella went into the gallery, but he saw nothing else, either."

"Okay, where was Bella found and when?" Alexi gritted out. "Get to the important part of the story, already."

"We went back to re-check her townhouse later Friday afternoon, Alexi," Alyssa murmured. "I pounded on the door, expecting her not to be there, but she actually answered the door as I was putting the key into the lock. It was such a relief."

"And what condition was she in when you found her?" Gray asked. "Did she remember where she'd been or what had happened to her?"

Valian shook his head. "It was very similar to your experience, Gray. She'd been up for about an hour and a half when we arrived and was still a bit shaky. She thought it was Thursday and was quite upset to hear the news that she'd lost close to two days. It was a delicate situation to have to explain, but we did our best."

As Valian went on to convey the steps they'd taken, what they'd finally learned from Isabella in the end...and what they had yet to figure out, Gray was reminded of his own experience with Faerie Bomb, and his heart went out to Isabella.

"I see," he said when Valian got to the part of the story that included Tempest and the possible link to Isabella's family in Ireland. "We still don't know exactly how Isabella is connected to Tempest but that it is, as we had guessed, possibly through her grandmother. I haven't been able to speak with Old Minerva yet, but I contacted Áine and let her know what we were looking for. She'll be here later this afternoon, so maybe she'll have something for us by then." He paused briefly before broaching the next subject.

His dream.

"On another topic that seems to be connected in a weird way, let me tell you about the dream I had this morning." Without waiting for comments or questions, he launched into an explanation of who and what he'd seen in his dream and the conversation he'd had with Tempest in it.

"So, both you and Isabella have now seen these strange men and talked to this Tempest in your dreams." Alexi looked perplexed. "That's very interesting. Do you think she's causing you to dream, maybe somehow guiding your dreams to give you information?"

Gray shook his head. "I don't know. Anything's possible, I guess."

"If so, I understand why you would be targeted. You're the Prince of the realm, but why is Bella seeing the same things? And what more could she have seen?"

"Again, that's unclear. Tempest, or whoever she is, didn't say."

Alexi pinched the bridge of his nose. "Okay, but who are these figures in black robes that she said we'll need? Did she give any indication of who they are or how they would help and with what?"

"No, like I said, Alexi, she was very cryptic." Gray thought for a moment. "Although, I will say that she seemed to think that I should know them. She asked if I could feel their 'pull'." He put up a finger. "And here's another thing. She referred to my mixed heritage, kept calling me Halfling. Now that I think about it, she said, and I quote, '*You have more running through your veins than human or fae blood. You have an immense untapped power.*'"

"Sounds like she was alluding to the Ellurian portion of your heritage," Valian murmured. "We still don't know what that will mean for you in the future, what untapped powers you will have inherited there."

"True."

Niall leaned forward. "That's, as the Field Marshal said, very interesting, but I'm a bit more concerned with the other more disturbing information that she conveyed. What is this evil, wicked 'something' that is coming as well?"

Gray nodded. "That's been worrying me, too, Niall. Unfortunately, she was free with the clues and innuendos but pretty scant on the details."

"And you didn't have any idea of where you were, your location while in this dream?" Finvar asked. "Were there no signs or familiar markings?"

"No. Nothing. This dream, like my previous nighttime excursions, took place in an unfamiliar forest, as did Isabella's, by the sound of it. If what Tempest told me in this recent dream is true, that would be because we were in the Wastelands. A place that I've never been or seen with my own eyes. She said we were on the eastern side of the Unwelcoming Rise and pointed out the Antiley mountain range in the distance."

Gray watch Valian exchange looks with Niall and Finvar.

"What?" Gray asked.

"Well, it was where Tempest was from, or so we had always thought," Valian replied.

He got up and went to the tall cabinet on the other side of the room. Rummaging around inside it until it appeared that he'd found what he was looking for in an old, rolled-up map. Coming back to the table, Valian spread it out and weighted each corner.

"This is the map of the Barrens and the Wastelands that we spoke of at our last meeting." Tapping a finger in the middle of the upper area and the clear mountainous line that seemed to divide the Wastelands in two before continuing south into the Barrens, Valian looked up at Gray. "This range is called the Unwelcoming Rise. So, if you had your conversation with Tempest—or someone purporting to be Tempest—on the eastern side of it, you would've been somewhere around here." He slid his finger to the southeast of the Rise.

"As you can see, you would have a clear view of the Antileys from there."

"The range that I saw in the distance," Gray said with a slow nod. "That would make sense."

"The Antileys are the birthplace and homeland for the Caemmeirth," Finvar added. "They could be the 'others' that she spoke of."

"That's true, Fin, but the Antileys are also said to be the homelands of the Ancients...the Ellurians," Valian murmured. "A place where they reigned for thousands of years before dying out. But, what if they didn't die out as history has taught us? What if these men in the black robes that both you and Isabella have seen in your dreams *are* the Ancients? Elders of the Ellurian race?"

"An uncomfortable thought, but that would track," Niall said quietly. He glanced at Gray. "She called them as much, did she not? Elders of the Ancients. Isn't that what she said? And she pointedly asked if you felt their 'pull.' Knew that you had something more powerful than the mix of human and fae blood running through your veins."

"You think that the men he and Bella have seen could be Gray's ancestors?" Alexi asked. "That would be...well, remarkable, right?"

"That it would, Field Marshal," Finvar replied. "That it would."

Gray nodded. "All right, as astonishing as that would be, let's not get ahead of ourselves. We don't even really know who this faerie claiming to be an honored dead warrior is for certain or if she's even real." He ran a hand over his face. This was getting more complicated by the minute. "Look, we have no proof of any of this. It's all conjecture based on dreams."

Niall raised an eyebrow. "Identical dreams that you and Isabella Christensen have had over the same period of time. I find it hard—if not impossible—to believe that this is a coincidence, especially since Tempest, real or not, has been there to impart information in both instances."

"Okay, I do see your point, but I'm going to send word to the Oracles and ask for an audience. Maybe they can shed some light on these men from my dreams. If anyone knows if the Ellurians still exist, it would be them, but why we're just finding out about it, why they would've kept something that monumental a secret is a mystery."

"But again, Niall reiterates Alexi's question of why Izzy." Alyssa had been quietly listening but finally spoke up. "How is she involved in this and why? I mean, like Alexi said, you're the Prince. You have fae blood, Ellurian blood, but why Isabella?"

Gray sighed. "I wish I knew, Alyssa." After a moment, he looked over at Niall and then to Finvar with another question forming in his mind. "Does the term 'Becoming' mean anything to either of you?"

The two High Lords exchanged looks before Niall spoke. "It is an old fae term, something that isn't spoken of much of these days. It refers to a fae or Halfling whose power hasn't awakened yet."

Finvar nodded. "To Become is to have those powers, the fae essence—dormant inside—finally begin to emerge as yours did this last summer."

"This is a term familiar in the Elven world as well, with much the same meaning," Valian added, then gave Gray a suspicious look. "Why do you ask, Gray?"

Gray leaned back in his chair as another puzzle piece slide into place. "I think we need to speak to Áine, and possibly Old Minerva as soon as possible. Because during my conversation with Tempest when we were talking about my heritage, I told her that Isabella had seen the men in the black robes as well, so what did my heritage matter. She said, *'She did indeed, and considerably more, though she won't remember much for now.'* When I asked what she meant, she just said that Isabella's memories would surface in time, but it would be hard for her, that I would have to help her with some transition. She told me that Isabella is strong...and that she would *Become*."

Nine

B y the time the meeting was winding down, Alexi was just about out of patience and anxious to get up to the hospital wing to check on Isabella before heading into Roseland to meet with several fae court patrols. Isabella, whom he'd yet to even set eyes on, thanks to his cousin's callous disregard, was all he could think about. Unfortunately, his quick exit was not to be.

"Alexi, can I have a word?" Valian called after him as he followed Alexi into the corridor, then went so far as to take hold of his arm to slow his progress. "Come on, hold up a minute."

Alexi turned with a pointed look at his cousin's hand on his arm, and then from it to Valian's face.

Valian quickly dropped the offending hand and sighed. "Look, Alexi, I'm sorry about earlier. I didn't mean to disrespect your feelings or leave you out of the loop. I really didn't," he reiterated when Alexi continued to stare at him. "I realize now that I misjudged the situation. I just got caught up in making sure Isabella was taken care of and lost track of everything else. As you said, after taking her up to the hospital wing last night, I should have eased your worry by letting you know that she'd been found."

"Yes. The bottom line? You should have kept your word, Val. If you'd have just sent someone to tell me that you'd found her and had taken her to the hospital wing, I could have met you there, been with her through the process. I could have at least seen her with my own eyes, held her in my arms." Alexi's slow burning temper flared to life again but he held onto it as best he could. "However, I don't have the time or the patience right now to relieve your guilty feelings by assuring you that what you did was okay," he said, his anger adding quiet steel to his tone. "It wasn't. And as I have nothing more to say to you at the moment, you'll have to excuse me, *cousin*. Since I haven't had the opportunity yet, I want to finally check in on Bella now before I have to head out into the field." With that, he turned on his heel and walked away, leaving Valian standing in the corridor alone.

As he climbed the wide flight of stairs to the third-floor hospital wing, Alexi worked to leave his angry feelings toward his cousin behind. If Isabella was awake, he didn't want to burden her with anything more than what she'd already had to deal with.

As he entered the medical wing, a healer checking on another patient looked up and smiled. "Good morning, Field Marshal. Are you here to see Ms. Christensen? If so, she's sleeping, has been since the Chancellor brought her in late last night. She's had a stressful few days, from what I've gathered."

Alexi nodded. "Yes. She definitely has. I just wanted to check how she was doing. I didn't get to see her when they brought her in and was only made aware this morning that she'd been found."

The healer smiled again. "Don't you worry. She'll be fine. Faerie Bomb can give one a strong hangover, especially if the faerie is not familiar with it. But as I said, she'll be right as rain by this afternoon." He pointed to the other end of the ward where Isabella was sleeping. "She's over there, second bed from the end, Field Marshal. I gave her something to replenish her strength and energy, which is also giving her the sleep that she needs, so you really won't disturb her. Go ahead and check on her. Talk softly to her, let her hear your voice. Our subconscious minds, no matter the lineage or origin, are amazing things. It will give her comfort in her slumber to hear a familiar voice."

"Good to know. Thanks. I'll do that."

As he neared her bed, Alexi couldn't help the emotions that surfaced at seeing her lying there so pale, so still. His strong, vibrant

Bella. Would their relationship change somehow now that they'd found she had fae blood? Or would their bonds grow even stronger as Valian and Tisharu's had?

He'd been with many women in his long, long life—human, fae, Elven alike—but in all those years, he'd never been one for commitment of any kind. What he'd felt for any one of them was genuine, but for the most part, usually fleeting. Then Isabella Christensen had stepped into his life with her snarky attitude, biting wit, and stunning beauty. There'd been something about her, something different that he'd felt from the moment their eyes had met. He'd been a goner and hadn't even known it until she'd taken up with Valian.

But then it was too late, or so he'd thought.

He couldn't keep the smile from his face as he remembered that evening last summer when he'd found her sitting alone in one of the palace gardens looking so sad. And just like that, everything had changed for both of them. Isabella had taken hold of his heart from that very first meeting, and now it was hers and hers alone. Always would be.

Leaning down, Alexi placed a soft kiss on Isabella's forehead and whispered in her ear. "Sleep well, *Mo chroí*. I'll see you later."

Before he decided to just pull up a chair and wait for her to wake, he turned and left her bedside. There was important business to handle, but he'd see her afterward.

"Did you wish to leave her a message with me, Field Marshal?" the healer asked when Alexi passed him on his way to the door. "I'd be glad to give it to her when she wakes. It shouldn't be but a few more hours."

Alexi started to shake his head but then stopped. "Yes, healer. Tell her that I stopped in to make sure she was all right and was much relieved to see her safe and sound. I have to go out into the field, but tell her I'll be back as soon as I can. That I..." He stopped and shook his head. "That's all. Thank you." He'd almost said what? That he loved her? Yes, he supposed that was just what he was going to say. But that was for him to tell her in person when she woke up, in his own words.

With a nod to the healer, he left the wing.

• • •

IT TOOK NO MORE THAN THIRTY MINUTES FOR ALEXI AND a squad of warriors to cross into Roseland and fade up to Queen Ayanna's Starlight Court on Roseland's northwestern coastline. The Queen met them with cordial pleasantries and a regal manner in the great hall of her court when they arrived. Tall and lean with jet black hair and eyes to match, Ayanna was usually pleasant, but always sly and watchful. She was a light wielder and could harness the energy of any light source. And she could manifest a bolt of electricity at a moment's notice. Truth be told, she gave Alexi a bit of the willies.

"Field Marshal," she crooned, holding out a hand for him to bow over. "Thank you for coming so quickly. There is much to tell you about this morning's rotation and what my lookouts stumbled across during their rounds."

Alexi straightened and nodded. "And I am anxious to hear your news. We need to get a handle on these odd tracks from whatever or whomever has been entering our kingdoms, so any solid information is vital."

"Agreed," she replied. "Having an unknown entity invading the lands surrounding my court is unacceptable. Therefore, the more rapidly this can be, as you say, *handled*, the better." She waved a bejeweled hand toward the massive oak doors to the receiving room at the end of the hall. "Come. Trevan, my lieutenant, will give you the details of his encounter."

"Excuse me?" Alexi frowned. "Did you say encounter? Am I to understand that Trevan's information is about more than just finding tracks or other signs?" Perhaps this would be just what they were looking for, something more, something solid.

"Mmm, yes. Indeed, it is," Ayanna replied with a saccharine smile. "However, I will allow him to do the telling of it."

As they reached the receiving chamber, the handful of faeries all stood as their queen entered and took her place on the twisted vines of the elaborate wooden throne at the far end of the room. Alexi followed, along with three of his Elven warriors while the rest of his entourage waited in the great hall.

"Trevan, please come and give the Field Marshal your account of what you saw in the forested land between the Starlight and Winter Courts this morning," Queen Ayanna requested.

The fae warrior came forward and gave a brief bow. "Of course, my queen." Turning to Alexi, he began. "I go out with at least one rotation a day, usually varying the times—one day in the morning, the next in the afternoon, and so on. As I am Queen Ayanna's eyes and ears in the field, I feel it's important to see these things for myself, to get the best information for my reports. However, over the last week, there's been nothing of note. The worst the patrols have run into has been a mountain troll here, a dwarf hunting party there, but as I said, nothing significant. There's been no signs of anything out of the ordinary up until today."

"Yes. Queen Ayanna did indicate that today was different. How so?"

"It was quite different. You see, I went out early today with a small group of warriors for the morning rotation, and for the first hour everything seemed quite normal."

"No tracks, no unfamiliar scents? Nothing unusual?" Alexi asked.

Trevan shook his head. "As I said, all quite normal to start."

"Yes, to start, but I'm assuming that changed?" Alexi wished the lieutenant would get to the point. He had a few more fae courts to visit regarding additional outpost rotations and wanted to get back to Wysteria before friggin' midnight.

As if sensing Alexi's impatience, Trevan smiled. "Yes. That all changed when we came out of the treeline and ran into an interesting sight. An old man standing in the middle of the snowy meadow, or so it seemed at first. However, on a closer inspection, he had short, silvery hair and eyes that shone in the morning light in that same silver and polished to a high gloss. It was a strange sight to see, even at a distance."

"Okay," Alexi said slowly. "So, that was it? You ran across a strange old man with silver hair and eyes."

The lieutenant shook his head. "No, Field Marshal, I said, *or so it seemed.* What happened next made it clear that this was not just some old man. For when he became aware of us, in that next instant he transformed into a huge, silvery-scaled dragon. It turned, and with a leap and sweep of wings, launched itself into the air. But what was most disturbing was that the dragon vanished as it took to the sky."

Alexi frowned. "Did you say vanished? Like it flew with speed? Or that it faded?"

Trevan shook his head again. "No. It was like it became invisible as it cleared the treeline, just shimmered and was gone."

A Gheori. The thought flashed across Alexi's mind as he remembered the descriptions that Niall and Finvar had given in that first meeting about the strange tracks and scents they'd encountered.

The Gheori were very calm, thoughtful, and confident. They were silver in color, like a newly minted coin, as was the fire they breathed. In dragon form, they could completely blend into their surroundings like a chameleon.

Finvar's description of the Gheori played again in Alexi's head. Trevan's similar portrayal seemed to put to bed any speculation of the continued existence of the great dragons, or whether the Caemmeirth had indeed been entering the kingdoms for some unknown reason.

"This is very interesting," Alexi murmured. "Can you take me and my warriors to the meadow where this strange event occurred? I've also encountered the tracks, the scent, but I should like to see this place as well."

"Whenever you'd like," Trevan said. "I'll gather a few of my warriors and meet you and yours outside." With that, the fae lieutenant bowed to his queen and left the receiving chamber.

Alexi followed him out ten minutes later after expressing his thanks to Queen Ayanna for her assistance and assuring her that he would keep her informed of any further developments.

The group then left the great hall, and once they were beyond the Starlight Court's boundary walls, they followed Trevan and his faeries as they began fading north toward the location of the strange morning encounter. It took them less than thirty minutes to arrive at the very spot.

This far north, the meadow in question was covered in almost a foot of snow, but they were in luck. There had been no recent precipitation, so the tracks the Gheori had made were still clear enough to see. And as Alexi walked the area, he found the exact spot where man had transformed into dragon. Footprints made by the "old man" became round, clawed impressions the size of huge dinner plates, and a large swath close to thirty feet long was an indication of where the dragon's tail had swept the snow. It was an astonishing find.

Scouring the area thoroughly, Alexi was about to turn back to the group when something shiny caught his eye. He bent down and brushed at the snow to find a large polished silver scale partially buried. Picking it up, he turned it this way and that, captivated by how it gleamed in the noonday light.

Well, no longer a myth. I guess dragons do exist, he thought as he pocketed the find and turned back to the group.

"I think that's all I need to see, Trevan. Thank you. I'll inform Queen Beatrice and Chancellor Winchester of what you witnessed and that we now have confirmation of what High Lords Niall and Finvar had suspected. Once any decisions have been made for a plan forward, I'll be in touch with Queen Ayanna as well."

Trevan nodded. "Very good, Field Marshal. If you need anything else, we'll be happy to help."

Alexi shook his head and gave the warrior a wry smile. "This will do for now. We've got a couple of other courts to meet with today, starting with the Lord Dyagmon's Winter Court, so we'll be heading farther north for now. I would encourage you and your troops to stay vigilant, though. If you have any further sightings, I would also suggest that you do not engage in any way. Just send word to the White Palace as soon as you can, and I'll come back immediately."

Once they'd said their goodbyes and went their separate ways, Alexi was skeptical that they'd find anything else quite as shocking or conclusive as Trevan's eyewitness encounter with the Gheori. However, as they met with High Lord Dyagmon and his first lieutenant, Bracken, Alexi found that he was a bit surprised.

"No, we've not seen anything as astounding as a dragon, though that scent is familiar." Bracken had muttered when they'd discussed what had happened with the Starlight warriors. "This far north, all we've seen for the most part is the occasional tracks, which are usually accompanied by that distinctive scent." He paused for a moment and then put up a finger. "But now that you've mentioned it. This morning, we did find tracks, but..."

"But what, Bracken?" Alexi asked.

"Well, we didn't *see* anything, mind you, but there was something in the air. Something other than the scent."

Alexi frowned. "What do you mean?"

"It'll probably not make much sense to you, but it was like a warmth or a heaviness in the surrounding air. I can't really explain it any better than that. And there was also an odd feeling of being watched, you know? That itch you get when you've inadvertently walked into a trap that's just about to spring, but you don't know where the trip will come? The hairs on the back of my neck stood up, and I scanned the area looking for any telltale clue of what was giving me the feeling, but there was nothing that I could see. I haven't felt anything like that since..."

"Yes? Since when?"

The old fae warrior glance up with a narrow-eyed look. "Since the Great War, Field Marshal."

"Oh, that's right. You fought in the Great War, didn't you?"

"Aye. We had dragons back then as well. The feeling I had this morning was very similar."

Alexi nodded. "High Lord Finvar said the same." He pulled the silver scale from his pocket and handed it to Bracken. "I found this in the snow at the site Trevan showed us this morning. Look familiar?"

The old warrior ran a thumb over the smooth surface of the scale and a brief smile played about his lips. "Gheori," he said in a quiet, awe-filled voice. "Trevan's account of the dragon vanishing would make sense. They could blend into their surroundings like a chameleon. Maybe the Gheori he witnessed was also here this morning during our rounds, but didn't want to be seen. Could be that's what I felt."

"Yes. Finvar did say that they had that ability."

Bracken handed the scale to Lord Dyagmon, whose surprised look told Alexi that he, too, remembered the dragons and was stunned by this find.

"This is indeed a profound development," the High Lord said. "It was thought that the Caemmeirth had gone back to their homeland, but there were those who felt the great dragons had gone extinct. This says the latter is not the case."

"Well, both Niall and Finvar were sure this is what we've been seeing with the tracks and such. This encounter confirms their suspicions, for sure. There are a couple of other courts I'd meant to check in with, but instead, I'm gonna head back to the White Palace now." Alexi took the scale back from the High Lord and re-pocketed it. "This is something that needs to be reported as soon as possible. If you run across any more tracks or have any sightings or encounters, send word immediately."

Bracken's deep laughter bounced off the stone walls. "Oh, aye, you can be certain of that. Now that I know what I'm looking for, I'll be much more vigilant."

"Yeah, well, I'll tell you what I told Trevan. If you do run across any of the Caemmeirth, don't engage. I'm told that most were not averse to human, fae, or Elven, but one breed was pretty unpredictable."

"Ah, yes, the Nyrilio. Those red bastards were that and more. Definitely a group to be wary around. Don't worry yourself about me, Field Marshal." Bracken grinned. "The Great War was a long time ago, but my memories are fair clear to this day."

Alexi grinned back at the old warrior. "Anyway, now we need to figure out where they're entering the kingdoms, how they're getting around the security wards. But most of all, why? So, give a shout the minute you have any new intel, yes?"

"I'll send word to the White Palace with anything we find," Lord Dyagmon confirmed. "And thanks for keeping us in the loop."

"You bet."

Alexi got back to the palace much earlier than he'd thought after skipping the last couple of planned stops at the other two courts on his list. He was surprised to run into Finvar as he entered the great hall. He'd figured that both Fin and Niall would have gone back to their respective courts after he'd headed out into the field.

"Hey, Fin. I see you're still here."

Finvar nodded. "Had some extra business with the Queen. I was just about to head back to court. I got word that there've been more signs or tracks of some kind found up along the northern border."

"Yeah, well, you may want to just hang out for a while longer and maybe send word to Niall to come back as well. I have some pretty astonishing news to report," Alexi said.

"No need to send word to Niall. He's still here in the palace somewhere."

"Really?"

Finvar rolled his eyes. "He was trying to get the descendant to go back to the Twilight Court with him, but she was having none of it. She's waiting for Ms. Christensen to wake up."

Alexi laughed out loud. "Like Bella, Alyssa won't be bullied into doing anything she doesn't want to do. Niall should know that by now. So, sounds like he's accepted that he'll have to wait with her. That's probably for the best, as my news is something that will be of interest to him, too. It's gonna change everything."

"Really? What news do you have, Alexi?"

Alexi shook his head. "I'm going up to see if Bella is awake first. We'll meet in the war room in thirty minutes or so, and I'll explain everything." He dug into his pocket and pulled out the silver scale. Handing it to Finvar, he grinned. "But this should hold your attention pretty well until then."

Finvar gaped at the silver scale in his hand, and then looked up in astonishment. "Is this what I think it is?"

"That's the general consensus so far."

"It can't be." The High Lord narrowed his eyes. "That means—"

"Yeah, I know how you feel." Alexi laughed at the look on the High Lord's face. "Just wait until you hear the story behind it. What's that phrase? Oh, yeah, 'Here there be dragons.'"

With that, he turned and headed up the grand staircase toward the third floor of the hospital wing.

"Aly, I told you. I feel fine. Actually, I feel better than fine," Isabella said, taking another sip of the medicinal tea that the healer had just brought for her. "My head is finally clear, and I feel so rested, almost energized. Whatever the healer gave me last night really did the trick. And this tea is really tasty." She put up a hand when Alyssa opened her mouth to protest. "And yes, the situation is a confusing mess, and I'm still pretty freaked out about it all, but we'll get to the bottom of it. At that point, I'll deal with the outcome, whatever that may be. It's all I can do because there's clearly no other choice. It is what it is."

Alyssa shook her head. "I gotta say, Izzy, you're handling this better than I did in January when I found out about my family's background with the realm and the Scepter of Fire. And I don't even have fae blood!"

Isabella laughed at the look on her friend's face. "Oh, this whole thing is definitely some kind of weirdness, all right, but as my gram always says, you can only do what you can only do. Right? One foot in front of the other, pal. That's how this works."

Watching the frown that passed across Alyssa's face, Isabella set down her cup on its saucer with a click. "What?" she asked abruptly.

"Huh?"

"You have that look, Aly. What's up?"

"What look?" Alyssa asked with raised eyebrows. "I don't have a look."

"Oh, don't give me that wide-eyed, deer-in-the-headlights stare. What's going on? I can see that there's something that you don't know how to tell me. What is it?"

Alyssa sighed and nodded. "Isabella, do you remember Áine Ó Mordha?"

Isabella rolled her eyes at that. "Please. I lost two days, Aly, not two years. I was here at the palace this last summer when she saved Tisharu's life, remember? Of course, you were off having a grand time in the Barrens with that crazy Red King, Aramond, at the time. So, yes, I remember Áine. What about her, other than she's a Halfling like Gray—and obviously, as we've now discovered—like me?"

"Okay, okay, sorry." Alyssa ran a hand through her hair and shrugged. "I guess I haven't really processed this whole thing, either. I actually just don't know how to talk to you about it. I don't want to upset you or make what you're feeling any worse than it already is."

Isabella set her tea cup and saucer down on the bedside table and took Alyssa's hand. "Look, Aly, you're my best friend in all the world. We've been besties almost since we were toddlers. I expect you to tell me straight out whatever information you come across. That's what friends do. They tell the truth, even when it's a hard truth. So, just tell me whatever it is. Trust me when I say that the only thing making this whole situation worse is the not knowing."

Alyssa smiled. "I love you, my friend. You know that?"

"Right back atcha. Now speak. What's all this about Áine?"

"Well, this might actually help with the 'not knowing' issue because she lives in Ireland, and evidently, she knows a lot of the fae living there as well. Gray contacted her and asked her to look into your family history."

"And when you say family history, you mean the Doyle side of the family, right? Because of what Tempest said about knowing my gram and my mom?"

"Yes. Tempest is fae, and she did call you Isabella Doyle at first and also 'my sweet child,' so Gray asked Áine to see if she could find a fae connection there. I mean, are you related somehow to this Tempest? We need to figure out where your fae blood comes from, Izzy, before we can move forward with anything else."

"I agree. I guess that is the best place to start." Isabella picked up her cup again but paused with it halfway to her lips. "It's just all so strange, isn't it? On New Year's Eve we find out that the realm of Artemysia exists and that you have this incredible connection to it. During that time, I remember thinking how is this possible? And why doesn't Aly's family seem to know about any of it? How could it have all been forgotten, you know?" She shook her head. "And now I find out that my butt is a little more firmly in that boat than yours is. My mom has never mentioned anything remotely connected to this whole thing. I gotta say, it's pretty surreal." She lifted her cup in a mock salute before finishing her tea.

"I know what you mean. Welcome to my world." Alyssa sighed. "Anyway, Áine's going to be here later this afternoon, and it seems like she may have found something useful."

"That sounds promising. I hope it's..."

"You hope it's what?" Alyssa asked when Isabella stopped speaking mid-sentence, then followed her friend's gaze to see Alexi striding toward them. "Ah...hey, Alexi."

"Good afternoon, Alyssa," Alexi said with a grin, but his eyes were on Isabella. He walked right up to her bedside and leaned in. "How ya doin', sweetness?"

Isabella grabbed hold of his jacket lapels and pulled him down close. "I was doing fine, but I'm doing better now," she said before he moved in for a smoldering kiss.

"Ditto," he replied when they came up for air. "Sorry I wasn't here last night when you got in. Val was supposed to tag me when they found you, but he failed in his task on an epic level. I didn't even find out that you were in the palace until this morning."

Isabella grinned. "I know. The healer gave me your message when I woke up. I'm just glad you're here now."

"Again, ditto," he repeated.

They stared at each other with dopey smiles for a few beats until the sound of a throat being cleared reminded them that Alyssa was still sitting right there.

Alexi chuckled and turned to her. "Sorry. Didn't mean to intrude and certainly didn't mean to ignore you, Alyssa. It's just—"

"That's quite all right, Alexi. And totally understandable." Alyssa stood. "As a matter of fact, I need to go see what Niall is up to. He asked me to go with him to the Twilight Court earlier but I wanted to wait for Isabella to wake up. I told him to go to court without me, but he refused. He'll probably be in a mood when I find him."

"Oh, I wouldn't worry about that," Alexi assured her. "I came back from the northwestern coast of Roseland with some very interesting information that I'm pretty sure he and Fin are discussing even as we speak. We're meeting in the war room in thirty minutes or so. I imagine Áine will be getting here in the next hour or two, as well."

Alyssa looked surprised but nodded. "Well, I'll just go see what it's all about ahead of the meeting then. Izzy, I'll see you there."

Isabella watched Alyssa walk away with a hint of a smile on her face.

"What are you smiling about?" Alexi asked as he sat down on the edge of the bed and took her hand.

"Oh...just how funny it is the way things eventually work themselves out. I mean, Aly and Niall started out at odds, to put it mildly. He was the reason that she ended up in the dungeon at the Red Palace during the whole New Year's Eve debacle. She thought he was an evil ass in the beginning. And then she found out that he was actually one of the good guys."

Alexi snorted. "Well, I'm not sure I'd go that far, but yeah, he's okay, I guess."

Isabella swatted at him. "I thought *you* were an arrogant snot when we met, and I ended up with Valian."

"Hey, well, like knows like, pal."

"Anyway, here we are. Like Aly and Niall, we found out where we needed to be."

Alexi nodded. "Took you long enough to see what a catch I am."

"Oh, brother. Says the arrogant snot." Isabella laughed. "You keep telling yourself that, buddy."

Alexi leaned. "You bet I will," he said, and then closed the distance to deliver another fiery kiss. "I've missed you, Bella," he murmured against her lips before he finally pulled back.

"I've missed you, too. The last few days—at least, what I remember of them—have been really confusing and scary."

"I know, and I'm sorry I wasn't there for you."

Isabella vigorously shook her head. "No, Alexi, it wasn't your fault. You have a very important job to do here. You can't be there to protect me every minute, and I really don't need you to be. Normally, I'm pretty capable of taking care of myself."

Alexi chuckled. "I am aware, darlin'."

"It's just that this whole mess is different. It's unknown territory for me, so it's gonna take some time for me to figure it out. I'm hoping Áine is going to at least have some clues for how to go about that."

"Well, if anyone can dig out those clues, it's Spindly."

"Spindly?" Isabella asked with a frown.

"Yeah, that's what we all used to call Áine when she was young because she was tall and skinny as a rail. I think Valian was the one to come up with that nickname. I dare say that she's filled out quite a bit since then." He laughed. "Anyway, she had a really hard time growing up as a Halfling. Her mom wanted Áine to know and understand the fae side of her heritage, to be comfortable moving between both fae and human worlds. Unfortunately, that was harder to achieve than it should have been."

"Yes, I've heard bits and pieces of that. Her father didn't want much to do with her, right?"

"Oh, man. That is an understatement. Arien was a piece of sh—" Alexi stopped abruptly and shook his head, anger flooding his features. "Sorry, but he was a worthless waste of space and oxygen. Not only did he not want anything to do with his *own child*, he thought she was tainted, an abomination. Poor kid was only eight years old, for the love of the Oracles. She had no idea why her father hated her so much. Arien would have killed her, too, if Niall hadn't been there that day and stepped in, ended him."

"Good lord, Niall killed Áine's father?"

Alexi gave a curt nod. "Yes. Arien was part of Tisharu's court, and the decades-long rift between Niall and his twin was because of what he did to save Áine's life."

"But if Arien was part of Tisharu's court, why didn't she deal with him?"

"Tisharu had reprimanded him on several occasions, as I heard it, but the fae courts can be very dicey. As queen, Tisharu is loved by her people. Though she can be quite formidable, she rules with a fair and steady hand, but with some issues she has to be cautious. There were those who sympathized with Arien, even though he'd willingly played a part in Áine's conception." Alexi sighed. "As it happened, Tisharu had gone out with a hunting party that morning, so she wasn't at court when Niall arrived to see her. It was by pure chance that he was there at all. He did what he thought was right, but no matter the right or wrong of it, Niall terminated a member of his twin's court without the Queen even being on the premises. It took them a while to get past it, but they finally did this last summer."

"And Áine? How does she feel about them?"

"Oh, she holds nothing against either of them. She loves them both, which is why she was here to help save Tisharu's life and was the one who accomplished that feat in the end. Without Áine's expertise in fae poisons, Tisharu most probably would have died." Alexi gently slipped a strand of Isabella's unruly red hair behind her ear and smiled. "Anyway, Áine is probably the perfect person to help you understand and get through the crazy transition into your new reality as a Halfling. Though I would say that it's probably best if you don't bring up her sire and the ugliness that she lived through during that time of her life."

"Yeah, no doubt. Sounds like good advice."

"Are the healers going to spring you from this place anytime soon? You really need to come to this meeting if she's going to be there, as it will be all about you. Or, at least mostly about you. My intel is going to raise some eyebrows, too, but I hope to get through all of that before Áine gets here."

"I did talk to the healer who treated me last night. He said I can go anytime I want, and Aly helped me pack a bag before we left New York, so I need to get up and get myself dressed."

"Good deal. I've got to run down to my chambers for a minute.

I'll be back in a bit and then we can move your bags down there on the way to the meeting."

With a final kiss, she watched him go with a happy heart and thought that, yes, they'd all found their way to just where they needed to be.

A LITTLE OVER AN HOUR LATER, ISABELLA AND ALEXI entered the war room to a cacophony of chatter, and for a moment it seemed to Alexi as if everyone was speaking at once. Niall was in deep conversation with Finvar discussing the silver dragon scale and what it could likely mean for the realm, while Alyssa—looking amazed—leaned in and nodded every so often. Valian was listening to the Queen and answering questions about Isabella's situation, with Gray also listening in and adding a comment here and there.

As Alexi and Isabella approached the table, all chatter came to a halt.

"Oh, Isabella, how are you, my dear?" Queen Beatrice asked with a sympathetic look. "Valian has just been filling me in on your harrowing experience."

"I'm much better today, Majesty. The healers fixed me right up," Isabella replied as Alexi followed her to a couple of unoccupied chairs at the table next to Valian and across from Niall, Alyssa, and Finvar.

"I see everyone's here, so why don't we get started?" Alexi said, pulling the chair out for Isabella. He looked around the table as he took the seat next to her. "I've just gotten back from the northwestern coast of Roseland, and there's been some fascinating developments that I need to go over with all of you."

Niall held up the silver dragon scale. "Mmm, yes. I am very interested to hear the story about this and where it was found. It's obviously a Gheori scale, and though you probably don't know of it, Gheori scales are fairly legendary on their own. It was said that to find one would bring all manner of good fortune to whomever possessed it."

"Well, that's definitely a positive thought," Alexi said and held out his hand. "So, why don't you just hand over that shiny little trinket?"

The High Lord's smile was a touch evil as he made a show of palming the large scale as best he could.

Alexi laughed. "Figures. But to satisfy your interest, let me tell you how my morning unfolded."

As Alexi went on to explain what the Starlight Court's patrol had stumbled across during their morning patrol and what they'd witnessed, he watched the faces of the two high lords closely. It was plain to see the shock and amazement that they both were feeling, especially when Alexi described the transformation from man to dragon and how—in dragon form—the Gheori had taken to the air and disappeared.

Finvar nodded at that point. "Aye, it would be just so with a Gheori. I saw that transformation on several occasions, watched as each would simply blend into their surroundings. It was as if their form shimmered and disappeared before your eyes." He took the silver scale from Niall. "And this makes clear that what Trevan and the Starlight patrol witnessed was definitely a Gheori."

Valian nodded. "Yes, that's clear. I concur. And while it's good to have that confirmation, where do we go from here? We don't know where they're entering the realm, or how, considering the security wards should be a deterrent."

"Agreed. That is a concern," Gray said. "And it sounds as if this Gheori just launched and flew out over the western sea, but then Roseland doesn't have border wards per se. At least, not on their entire border. As we all know, only the border between the kingdoms has security wards. Old Minerva put those in place around Wysteria after the Great War. However, there have been tracks that several of you have seen in the northeast of Wysteria as well...inside our borders." He shook his head and looked around the table. "How are they getting in and out? They shouldn't even be able to fly over the wards, right? I mean, there have been other flying creatures that couldn't get over them. So, that's what we need to figure out, but it looks like we're back to square one. Just watching and waiting for another possible sighting."

"Oh, don't worry your pretty head about that, young Prince," came a familiar voice from the doorway.

They all turned to find that The Witch of the Eastern Glade had appeared in the room. In the following silence, Old Minerva came forward slowly, a sly smile on her face.

Queen Beatrice got to her feet. "Good afternoon, Minerva. This is quite a surprise. Why have you come to the palace? Please, do come and sit with us."

The ancient sorceress waved the Queen back into her seat. "Do not trouble yourself, Beatrice. I've been...out of the realm for a bit and have only just received the young Prince's request for a meeting. So, I thought I'd pop by. I suppose, considering the story that the Field Marshal just told and the consternation that it has caused, my arrival is right on time."

"What do you mean by that, Old One?" Valian asked cautiously. "Are you saying that we shouldn't be worried about the Caemmeirth? Do you know how they're entering the kingdoms? How they're getting around the security wards?"

Minerva's laughter filled the room. "Don't be daft, Chancellor. I *created* the wards, did I not? Of course I know how the great dragons are entering the kingdoms."

"Would you care to enlighten us?" Niall murmured, being careful to keep any sarcasm from his tone.

Minerva turned to him slowly, her pale, gray eyes sparkling with humor. "Ah, well, well, well. The High Lord with the great stones. I do hope you have found your common sense since our last meeting, Niall."

Niall cleared his throat and looked decidedly uncomfortable. "Have no fear, Old One. I took your wise counsel to heart."

Minerva cackled at that, breaking the tension of the moment, and Alexi struggled to keep a straight face, though it was almost impossible. Niall had gone face-to-face and toe-to-toe with the witch during the summer when they'd routed the Red King in the Barrens. She'd let him off without incident but had made it clear at the time that he was walking a very treacherous line. Alexi had enjoyed that show immensely and liked to poke at the High Lord about it every so often. Niall had definitely come to his senses quickly that day, but

Alexi was certain that it was an event Niall wouldn't forget anytime soon.

"Very good. Very good, indeed. I am glad to hear it, High Lord," Minerva continued with a smirk. "Now, since you've asked so sweetly, I will do as you ask and...enlighten you all."

She moved around the table to stand between Alexi and Isabella, and Alexi felt *his* "stones" shrivel just a bit when she leaned down between them. The old sorceress turned her head and smiled at Isabella, who's eyes were as wide and round as twin moons.

"And after we chat about dragons, my dear, we'll have a long conversation about you and your news...little Halfling," the old witch murmured.

Alexi watch Isabella swallow hard, and he reached out to take her hand. Having the most powerful sorceress in the entire realm's attention—good or bad—was certainly a daunting thing in any case. He gave her hand a squeeze and winked at her when she looked up at him.

"Now, first things, first," Minerva said, straightening and getting down to business. "To your questions, Chancellor—and the High Lord's enlightenment. The wards do not affect the Caemmeirth in any way. By Oracle decree, the wards were designed to keep threats of all kinds at bay. The Caemmeirth are...brethren of a sorts. They pose no threat to this realm, indeed, live in the far northeastern mountains of the Northern Wastelands, so are technically residents and a part of this realm."

"So, the Oracles know this?" Gray asked. "That the Caemmeirth are not affected by the wards and can come and go as they please?"

Minerva turned to him with a bland look and gave a beleaguered sigh. "Young Prince, were you not just listening? The Oracles dictated how the wards were to be designed. I created them to *their* specifications."

"Then we need not worry about the great dragons at all," Queen Beatrice commented. "But if they are brethren, friends of the realm, do you know why they are now coming here from the far Wastelands, Minerva? What is it that they want?"

Minerva shook her head. "The Caemmeirth don't want anything

other than to assist and protect the kingdoms from what may possibly come."

"And what is that, Old One?" Gray asked. "I've been having dreams, seen things in them that I don't understand, which is why I wanted to meet with you and why I've also asked for an audience with the Oracles."

"Yes, I am aware, young Prince." She laid a hand on Isabella's head and ran it softly over her hair. "Both you and this one have had similar dreams, yes? Dreams of the Ancients, of a faraway land, and a warrior supposedly long dead?"

"Tempest," Isabella whispered.

Minerva dropped her hand to Isabella's shoulder and gave it a pat. "Tempest."

"Supposedly?" Valian asked. "What do you mean 'a warrior *supposedly* long dead'?"

"Tempest died in battle with Qadira," Niall insisted. "She delivered a mortal wound to the Dark Fae before she died. It was the beginning of the end of the years-long conflict. That's a documented fact, Old One."

Minerva smiled. "Is it now?"

Niall nodded emphatically. "You know that it is. There are those who saw her cut down, who swore to seeing her dead on the field after."

Finvar finally spoke up. "Are you telling us that Tempest is not dead but survived and has been alive all these many years? That the historic accounts are wrong?"

Minerva chuckled. "Yes and no. Tempest did die on that battlefield, but yet she still lives."

"But how is that possible?" Finvar asked.

Minerva shook her head at him and tsked. As she did so, Finvar's face took on an interesting shade of crimson, and he quickly looked away. Alexi felt for the High Lord. Finvar and Minerva had an uncomfortable past, and he normally avoided the witch whenever he could.

"If Tempest still lives, then where has she been since the day she was carried from the field?" Niall frowned, and after a moment, slowly leaned forward as a light of understanding began to dawn in his eyes. "Ah...I'm think I'm beginning to see."

"What is it, Niall?" Alexi asked. "See what?"

"The blood of the Ancients," Valian murmured from the other end of the table. "It was rumored that Tempest had ancient blood, that she was half fae and half Ellurian."

Niall nodded. "And the Ellurian race were Immortals. They could not die on any battlefield."

"But is being half Ellurian enough?" Gray asked. He turned to Minerva. "Was Tempest actually half fae and half Ellurian as rumored? And if so, is that the answer? Is that why she was reported as dead but then...lived?"

"It is just so," the old witch confirmed.

Gray shook his head. "But if that's true, then why isn't my mother immortal? She's half Ellurian. The blood of the Ancients flows through her veins, and mine as well."

Minerva glanced at the Queen before answering the Prince's question, and the look that passed between them held Alexi's interest. There was an intimate feel to the silent interaction. It was almost loving like a mother to a daughter. It gave Alexi pause.

After a moment, the old witch turned back to the Prince. "The Queen is half *human* and half Ellurian. It is not the same. Tempest is an immortal Halfling, an anomaly, because she's half fae and half Ellurian. And before you ask, I cannot tell you what you are or will become, Prince Graydon. You are also an anomaly and only time will tell that tale."

"But why is Tempest coming to me? She's come to me in my dreams, yes, but also in person," Isabella suddenly spoke up. She turned to the old sorceress with obvious wariness. "She said she knew my family, called me 'my sweet child.' Why me? I've only just found out that I have fae blood, and I don't even know how that's possible."

Minerva gave Isabella a gentle smile. "I will answer your questions in due time, child." She stopped and looked toward the doorway. "But first, there is someone here to give you some background that will help you to understand what I will tell you."

And they all turned to see Áine Ó Mordha as she entered the war room.

Eleven

"**G**odmother! I didn't expect to find you here," Áine exclaimed with surprise. "I went to the cabin first, but found it empty. I wanted to speak with you before coming to the palace, but then I checked your runes and saw that you were...out of the kingdom for a bit. What are you doing here?" she asked in confusion as she looked around the room at the rest of the group.

Minerva chuckled. "I've only just returned from my trip and found that the young Prince had sent word that he wished to meet with me. I thought I would drop by. We've actually been waiting for you, child. We've just now gotten around to Ms. Christensen and her new...status, shall we say? So, your arrival is perfectly timed."

"I see." Áine paused and sent Isabella a hesitant glance.

"Well, don't just stand there, girl. Come in and sit down. Tell us your news, if you have any."

Giving a stern look to Alexi and flicking her wrist toward the next chair over, Minerva indicated quite firmly that the Field Marshal should move and give her his seat. Isabella wasn't all that jazzed about sitting in such close proximity to the old witch but knew that Alexi had no choice and watched him quickly make the move.

"I do have some news," Áine murmured as she came forward and sat down in the open chair next to Gray. "It's not as detailed as I'd like, but hopefully, I can rectify that in the coming days. I haven't had a lot of time since getting Gray's message."

"I'm sure what you've found will be satisfactory," Minerva said. "She only needs some background, her family history as it pertains to the fae community is all. I will fill in the rest of the pertinent details once we have your information."

When Áine shot another uncomfortable look in Isabella's direction, Isabella shook her head and spoke up to set the Halfling's obvious discomfort aside. "It's okay, Áine. You can speak freely. Like I told Aly earlier, the not knowing is the worst part of this whole thing, so whatever you've found, I'll deal with it."

"Mmm...very brave and well said." The old witch leaned back in her chair and regarded Isabella with a narrowed look. "Of course, you really have no other choice, now do you? But an admirable attitude, all the same. Though I'm afraid you will need it."

Áine cleared her throat, and with a slight nod to Isabella, launched into the information that she'd found. "So, I've been in touch with a group of fae elders who live in and around my area in County Clare, and it seems that your family name is known to them, Isabella." She turned to Gray. "You also had asked about a fae warrior called Tempest. Unfortunately, I didn't get a whole lot more from those that I spoke to with the exception of what you'd already told me. But I can confirm that they knew the legend regarding this warrior quite well, as it had been handed down through the generations since the time of the Great War here in this realm."

Gray smiled. "No worries, Áine. As it happens, that's a question that's been put to bed just this afternoon. It seems that the legend is basically true but that Tempest is an immortal Halfling, half fae and half Ellurian. So, though she did *die* on the battlefield like the legend proclaims, she evidently didn't stay that way."

Áine looked speechless for a moment. "Yeah, now you've piqued my interest, and I want to know more about this Tempest and her larger-than-life legend. However, you can fill me in on that later." With a shake of her head, she refocused on Isabella. "Anyway, like I was saying, Isabella, though your family isn't from County Clare, the elders there were definitely aware of them. They were especially familiar with Ríona Doyle, your grandmother on the Doyle side, whom they said had been known as a healer of sorts for decades. Evidently, she's quite proficient in herbs and healing potions."

"Yes, Gram does have a huge herb garden that I used to play in as a child whenever we'd visit. And she does know quite a bit about their usage, but I don't know anything about the potions or her being a healer. Of course, we only got over to Ireland once or twice a year when I was little." Isabella glanced briefly at Minerva. "Tempest told me that she knew my family well—my gram, my mom."

"Yes. That is so," Minerva acknowledged without further comment.

Before Isabella could probe for more information, Áine interrupted her thoughts.

"How much do you remember about those visits, Isabella?" Áine asked. "Is there anything else that you can think of? Anything that stands out about your grandmother, that looking back now, seems unusual or out of character?"

Isabella thought for a few moments, childhood memories coming clearer for her in that instant than her memories of the last couple of days. "Nothing really stands out to me. Gram used to walk with me through her gardens. She'd show me the different herb plants, tell me their names and what they could be used for, but as it is with most small children, that kind of thing went in one ear and out the other, I'm afraid. What I do remember the most about those afternoons were the colors and the scents of all the plants." She smiled then as something else crossed her mind. "There is one thing, though. At some point during each visit, Gram would always make sure to tell me that I was special, and that I should never forget it, that someday I would find out just how very special I really was." She looked up at Áine, and then to Minerva. "I guess that if fae blood somehow runs in my family, that someday has finally come."

"So, it would seem," Minerva murmured with her eyes sparkling and full of secrets.

Isabella paused as that last thought struck a chord. "I guess that makes a bit more sense to me now, because when Tempest told me that she knew my gram and my mom, she also said that she'd even been aware of me since I was born. She asked me if I wanted to see where my ancestors were from."

"She did?" Alyssa asked with raised eyebrows. "You didn't tell us that, Izzy."

Isabella frowned. "I didn't remember that until just now. A few other things have been coming back to me, but none of it is very clear. Hopefully, more of my memories of those lost hours will return in the next few days. There's more there. I can feel it, but I just can't see it yet. It's like important information is just out of sight. I can't tell you how frustrating it is to not be able to get a hold of it, to pull it into the light."

"Well, I wouldn't worry too much about that, Isabella," Gray said. "In my dream this morning, Tempest told me that you'd been shown, and I quote, *considerably more*. She did say that you wouldn't remember much for now but that your memories would surface, that it would all come back to you in time, whatever that means."

"Yeah. That's not real helpful at the moment, is it?" Isabella sighed and pushed her hair back out of her face. "Anyway, Tempest did tell me that she wasn't from Ireland but that her homeland was very similar. She said that she'd visited my family in Ireland on numerous occasions. That's when she asked me if I wanted to see where my ancestors actually came from."

"Did she tell you where that was?" Áine asked. "I could do some checking in that area if we could pin it down. I mean, the elders in County Clare knew of your grandmother but didn't actually know her personally, just by reputation. That kind of thing spreads fast in the fae community, so that's not uncommon. We could dig out more information if we just knew where to dig."

"No, Tempest didn't say, but again, in my family's case, I'm pretty sure that she wasn't talking about Ireland, either," Isabella replied, a clear vision coming into her mind in a flash of Tempest reaching out a hand to her.

"How do you know that if she didn't say exactly where she was talking about?"

Isabella's eyes took on a faraway look for a brief moment. "Because she said, *Take my hand, Isabella. We'll go through the portal in the Great Park, and you can see it for yourself.* She was talking about coming to this realm, that my ancestors came from here."

"So, you went with her through the portal? To this place she was talking about?" Alexi asked, leaning forward.

"I don't know." Isabella shook her head trying to clear her thoughts. There it was again. The answer she was looking for but just out of reach. "I can't remember," she said with a frustrated growl. "But I must've, right?"

"Child, if your ancestors on your grandmother's side are from this realm, that means...that's just..." the Queen blinked several times in surprise. "Well, just extraordinary. Minerva? Can you verify this? That Isabella's family is from this realm?"

The old sorceress glanced at Isabella and then turned to the Queen. "Yes, Beatrice, I can," she said, quietly. "Actually, I can verify that and much, much more." The Old One glanced at her goddaughter. "Áine, do you have anything else to share before I begin?"

Áine laughed. "A few bits and pieces, but I'm certain that it won't hold a candle to what you can tell us. So, have at it, Godmother."

Minerva grunted and gave a succinct nod. "Well, in that case, we have quite a bit to go over, so let me start by spinning you all a very interesting yarn. We will begin with Moira Nic Corragáin, Isabella's great-grandmother. Moira is a Halfling, and like Beatrice here, is half human and half Ellurian."

"*What?*" A hysterical giggle burst out of Isabella. She slapped her hands over her mouth, and with eyes wide, she slowly shook her head.

She could literally *feel* the color drain from her face, and when she looked up at Alexi with chaotic emotions swirling around inside of her, he started to get up to come to her, but Minerva gave him a sharp look and pointed at his chair. He slowly sank down again but glared at the old witch before looking back at Isabella with his heart in his eyes.

"How can that be?" Isabella asked in a whisper. "My great-grandmother is long dead."

"No, child, she is not. Though Moira is not immortal, like Beatrice, she will live for a very long time, so she simply went home to the far Northern Wastelands to avoid the inescapable questions of aging in the human world."

Isabella looked around the room and saw that everyone seemed to be just as stunned by this news as she was. However, she attempted to breathe past the panic building inside her chest, because it seemed that Minerva wasn't quite finished.

"There's more to that piece, but we'll let it marinate a bit and move on for the moment," the old witch said. "Next is your grandmother, Ríona Nic Corragáin Doyle. Ríona is also a Halfling, but somewhat in the vein of the young Prince here. Ríona is half fae, a quarter human, and a quarter Ellurian, which is why she's known to the fae in Ireland for her herbs and potions, and as a healer. Like the Prince, she has other gifts and abilities. And who knows what she would be capable of should she use more of them, but she rarely does as she wanted a simple life in the human world."

Minerva leaned down close to Isabella and put a hand on her shoulder. "So, how's the *dealing with it* going so far?"

Anger flared in Alexi's eyes at the old witch's seemingly callous words, but though Isabella felt stunned and overwhelmed by what she'd heard so far, she took another deep breath, pushing back her panic and meeting the old witch's gaze head on. "To be honest, I'm freaking out more than a little, but don't worry about me, I'll deal," she said with a touch of defiance.

The Old One cackled at that. "Most excellent. You've got grit, little Halfling. I'll give you that. Now, where was I? Oh, yes. Next up is your mother, Marie Doyle Christensen. As you may have guessed by now, our dear Marie is also a Halfling, but like you, just a bit watered down." She smiled as she looked around the table at the gobsmacked faces before turning back to Isabella. "I won't go into all the halves and quarters of it but leave it to say that your grandfather, Patrick Doyle is a human male, and yes, Patrick knew exactly what Ríona was when he married her and they started their family. Unfortunately, it is my understanding that your mother has ignored this history as myth and nothing more, a trifling bit of hooey—which is undoubtedly why you had no idea of any of it—yet your uncles, both Rian and Sean, understand and honor their heritage."

Isabella turned wounded eyes to Alexi for a moment before

addressing the old witch. "You're correct, Old One. I knew nothing about any of this, but I am grateful for the information you've given me about my ancestry. It fills in the blanks, I guess you could say."

"And I am happy to enlighten you, child, but as I said, there is one other piece to it."

Oh, lord, what more could there be? Isabella thought. "And what is that?" she asked, hesitantly.

"While the descendant is the great-granddaughter of the great-granddaughter of the original Alice, you are the great-granddaughter of Moira Nic Corragáin."

The Old One's sentence hung in the air for a good ten to fifteen seconds, confusion hanging there alongside it, before someone snapped to what was implied in Minerva's statement.

"The magickal number of three," Valian finally murmured.

"And we have a winner." Minerva smiled. "That is correct, Chancellor."

Isabella's gaze flew to Alyssa, wild thoughts swirling in her mind. Was this the reason that she and Alyssa were best friends who'd known each other as far back as she could remember? Could this mean that their relationship was perhaps preordained somehow? She meant to voice these concerning questions to Minerva, but another memory swam into view and had Tempest's voice echoing in her mind.

The descendant would want you to know about your history, your ancestry, as she now knows hers, right?

Everyone knows of the descendant in my homeland.

Minerva nodded. "I understand the concern that I see in your eyes, child. You are just now finding out that your family's roots are here in the Artemysian realm, that you have fae and Ellurian blood running through your veins. Alyssa is the descendant. Is this just happenstance that you became friends at a young age, that your families became close early on?" She raised an eyebrow. "Or is there a deeper connection?"

"Yes. Tempest said that everyone in her homeland knows of Alyssa," Isabella replied.

"And now you are wondering if you are friends in spite of this or *because* of it? Wondering if it was not just by chance but perhaps somehow predetermined?"

Isabella glanced at Alyssa again and nodded. Both being an only child, Alyssa was the sister she'd never had, and visa-versa, or so she'd thought. That someone or something could have manipulated their lives, their feelings, had a sadness welling up inside of her.

"Unfortunately, this is something I cannot answer for either of you. That would be a question for the Oracles." Minerva shook her head. "But...in my experience, some things in this universe are just meant to be, child."

"Just so you know," Alyssa began, "I don't care what anyone says. I lean heavily toward *meant to be*, Izz."

Gray cleared his throat, cutting into the sudden silence of the emotional moment. "Isabella, like I said earlier, I've requested an audience with the Oracles to talk about our dreams, so you, me, and Alyssa? Well, we'll just ask them these questions when we're there," Gray said, then gave her a wry smile. "At this point, I think we would be smart to start making a list. My questions are piling up as well."

Isabella smiled at that and felt a bit lighter for it.

The Prince turned to Minerva then. "And pertaining to our dreams, I would like to revisit something that you said earlier, Old One. There's an important question I'd asked earlier that we kind of skipped over once we dove into the conversation about the Caemmeirth, Tempest, and then Isabella's family history."

Minerva tilted her head and studied him. "What did I say and what question did you have, young Prince?"

"You said that the Caemmeirth were coming here to assist and protect the kingdoms from what may possibly come. But you didn't say what that threat may be. What is it that's coming, Old One? In one of my recent dreams Tempest warned me of this as well. She said that *something dark and wicked* was coming. Can you tell us what that is?"

The Old One looked around the table at the anxious faces awaiting her answer and slowly shook her head. "I cannot expound on that at this time, as elements of it are yet unclear, and there are ongoing discussions being had. This is why I was out of the kingdom for a day or two. I was meeting with others who've had concerns, had seen other signs. It is the reason, as I said, that the Caemmeirth have been making regular visits to these two kingdoms."

"Other signs?" Valian asked. "Are you talking about signs like the dryad deaths that we've seen not only in the Barrens but here as well?"

"Yeah, we thought the dryad death that we ran across in the Barrens was because of the golem the Red King's sorcerer, Yulis, had conjured," Alexi added. "But after you— After Yulis' death, the golem would've been destroyed, so when we found the dryad death in this kingdom north of Willow Glen Wood at the end of spring, we didn't know what to make of it."

Gray nodded. "True. And when we went to pay our respects to the Dryad clan for their loss, young Tangy did tell us that he was sure that there had been other sprites his age that had been involved in something dark and sinister, remember?"

"Right." Alexi nodded. "Has this kind of thing been happening in other parts of the realm?"

Minerva nodded. "There have been all manner of disturbing events, but we've found no connections between most of them yet, nor has there been any clear trail to follow."

"So far, it's been only the two dryad deaths from the northeastern clan here," Valian said quietly. "But we will put out the word to all the fae courts, the dwarf clans, and everyone else in both kingdoms to keep a close eye, to stay vigilant. And to report anything they see or hear."

"That would be helpful," Minerva said. "Forewarned is forearmed."

There was another moment of silence before one last question came to Isabella. She turned to the old sorceress with a smile. "Old One, like I said, I am grateful for the information you've given me about my ancestry, though it was quite overwhelming to hear all at once. But if you don't mind, I do have one more question."

Minerva raised an eyebrow. "Only one?"

"Well, only one for now." Isabella's smile grew into a grin. "I'm fairly certain that more will flood my brain over the next days and weeks."

"What is this one question you have, child?"

"Well, why is Tempest coming to me? I mean, I get why she would come to Gray. He's the Prince of the realm, but why me? She said that she knew my family. How are we connected? Why would she want to show me where my ancestors come from, and why now?"

The old sorceress' laughter filled the room, and she shook her head. "Well, for the love of the Oracles! Dear me, did I skip over that part of the story?" Her gray eyes twinkled with amusement. "It's very simple, my dear. Tempest is your great-aunt. Your great-grandmother Moira and Tempest have the same Ellurian sire and are half-sisters."

Twelve

"How ya doing, sweetness?" Alexi murmured as he crossed the chamber's living area where Isabella sat on the sofa staring into the crackling fire. He held out a fragrant cup of tea, but when she didn't take it from him, didn't answer him or even look up, he tried again. "You look all done in, Bella, and it wrecks me. I know the session with Old Minerva had to be exhausting for you, especially with everything we learned. It would have been a lot for anyone to process. I wish you would lay down for a bit and try to get some rest...let it all go for the time being."

She tore her gaze away from the fire and looked up at him with... what? She didn't quite know what she was feeling at the moment, other than numb. Alexi was right, what they had learned about her ancestry was overwhelming, extraordinary. And yes, she did feel somewhat hollowed out by it all. Everything that she thought she'd known about her family and her life had been turned upside down in the space of a few hours, but the one thing she felt certain of was that sleep wasn't the answer. She'd already done enough of that, and no amount of slumber would change what she now knew to be true.

Isabella wasn't the sort to run and hide from her problems, to whine and complain. Never had been. And though what had just been dumped into her lap—or over her head, she thought with a heap of irony—had been enormous and mind-boggling, she sure as hell wouldn't start any of that now. No, she was determined to find a way to examine it, to digest it all and make sense of it. To find a place for it. Because something inside of her wouldn't let her do anything less, but that was for later. She didn't have the energy for it at the moment, but she also didn't quite know how to move forward, either.

Yet.

You do it one step at a time, said a voice in the back of her head. As Old Minerva had told her earlier in the day, she really had no other choice, so she'd have to be content with baby steps and hope that the way forward would present itself sooner rather than later.

Yes, overwhelming was a good word for the situation, but she wasn't going to let it beat her. She'd be damned if she'd metaphorically lay down and pull the covers over her head.

"Bella? Did you hear me?"

Alexi's deep voice cut into her dark thoughts, and she blinked up at him. "Yes, but I've slept quite enough, love. Besides, it won't help, and I worry about what dreams will come when I eventually do close my eyes. What fresh hell will I find there, you know? What will Tempest—my great-aunt—show me?"

"Aw, Bella, what can I do? I don't know how to help you. Tell me what you need. I'll do anything that I can."

Her heart melted a little at the tenderness she found in his eyes, the gentle compassion and understanding in his voice.

She shook her head and sighed. "Just come and sit with me," she told him, patting the place next to her on the sofa.

He stepped over and left her tea on the coffee table before taking a seat beside her and pulling her into his arms. His embrace was warm, comforting as she slipped her arms around him and laid her head against his chest. She listened to his strong, steady heartbeat, breathed in the woodsy scent of him, and felt her anxiety fade back just a little into the shadows of her mind, but it was enough. Then she felt him place a kiss on the top of her head, and she thought, *Yes, just enough for now.*

She didn't know how long they sat there in that way, just comforting one another with their mutual embrace, with the warmth of the fire from the hearth, but Isabella felt herself finally relaxing for the first time after the insanity of the last few days.

"Tell me a story," she whispered to him in that moment, the same way that she'd asked Valian so long ago when she'd first come to the White Palace in search of her missing friend. She listened to Alexi's deep laughter as it rumbled in his chest.

"What kind of story would you like for me to tell?"

She shrugged. "I don't care. Tell me about your family. Valian has told me some, but I want to hear it from you. I know his parents were killed in the Great War as was his brother Garrik, and that his sisters Kali and Amra live in the northeast on his family's land. I also know that his mother and yours were sisters, but I don't know anything about your side of the family. Are your parents still living? Do you have siblings?"

She felt him nod.

"As luck would have it, though my parents also fought in the war, both survived and now live in the northeast, actually very near to Kali and Amra. My mum, Tiriana Toven, practices divination, has prophetic dreams, and like your gram, has a huge herb garden. I think they would get along quite well together. Mum always has some kind of healing potions going here and there. She's a kind and patient female...and totally ruled our household without ever raising her voice for as far back as I can remember." He chuckled. "I kid you not, all she had to do was look at you with that shadow of disappointment in her eyes, and you were cooked."

Isabella found herself giggling along with him at that, even as she heard the adoration in his voice. "What about your dad? What's he like?"

"Ah, my da, Ailre Toven is a big bear of an Elven male with quite the imposing look to him. Yet he's actually a warm, jovial sort, though a solid warrior when the situation calls for it. I'm not sure I know of anyone better with a long bow, except for maybe Val. And that's only a *maybe*. I also have two sisters, Solana & Saida. They're both married with small babes of their own and also live in the northeast of Wysteria, though not as close by as Kali and Amra."

"Oh, my, Uncle Alexi?"

He laughed again. "Yeah. As they say, be afraid, be very afraid.

Solana is always threatening to put me on supervised visits so as not to teach her children any bad habits."

"So, only the two sisters?" she asked with a smile.

"Only the two sisters. I don't have any brothers, though Val has always filled that spot for me, and I think I've done the same for him since Garrik's death."

"Yes, Valian actually said as much to me at one point." She sighed. "Well, your family sounds wonderful. I'd love to meet them all someday."

Alexi kissed the top of her head again. "That can be arranged... once this immediate chaos is handled. I think that you would like them and fit right in, no matter what's in your ancestry."

After a bit, she leaned back and looked up at him. "Alexi, what do you make of all this craziness? I mean, great dragons, the ancient Ellurian race thought to have died out but maybe hasn't, something dark and evil possibly coming to destroy us all in the immediate future. Doesn't it just sound a little like everything all at once?"

He nodded. "It does indeed, love. I don't know. Gray and I are the two odd men out, so to speak. We're playing catch-up here. Val, Fin, and Niall all fought in the war, and they know about a lot of things that we don't, like the Caemmeirth, Tempest, the legends that have been buried with time. They've actually clapped eyes on some of these great dragons, spoke to them in human form."

"I get that. It's got to be frustrating for both you and Gray. Playing catch-up to keep up. Right?" she murmured.

Frowning, Alexi's eyes took on a faraway look. "It's like when we first went into the Barrens this summer following Alyssa's tracking amulet. Niall and Fin joked around about some of the horrible things, monsters really, that inhabit that desolate place—mostly just to freak me out. Then we were attacked by the very Wolvataurs that they'd just been tormenting me over." He blinked and seemed to come back to himself. "Anyway, what do I make of it all? Generally, it unnerves me, to put it mildly. Look, I've got some mean combat skills and have no problem going into battle or fighting to protect the kingdoms and those that I love, as long as I know the odds and who or what I'm fighting. I need to have the details, the pros and cons. I don't like the unknowns hanging over my head when I'm stepping into a fray."

"Agreed," she murmured and then clarified with a quick smile. "Well, not so much about going into battle, but I do agree about knowing the odds and what you're up against. That's been the worst thing for me over the last few days. The not knowing."

He pulled her close again. "We'll get through this, Bella. I promise. And once you, Gray, and Alyssa get in to see the Oracles, you may learn just what you need to help guide you to your own path."

She pulled away and looked up at him again, a bit hesitant to ask her question. "Will you come with us? Come with me?"

He went perfectly still, and she watched the wheels begin to turn in his head. She sensed that he really didn't want to say yes, but struggled with saying no as well. When he finally answered her, it warmed her heart.

"If you want me to go with you, Bella, I absolutely will."

She grinned at him. "I know you'd rather not, and I don't expect you to go in with me to meet with them. Actually, from what Aly's told me, you probably won't be allowed to go in with me, but just knowing you're somewhere near will give me the strength I think I'm gonna need."

He laughed out loud. "I don't know why. It's not like I'd be a big help if things in that inner sanctum went sideways."

She swatted at him. "You know what I mean, you big dufus."

He took her hand and brought it to his lips. "Yes. I know what you mean, sweetness. And I will brave the Temple of the Oracles if it will give you the support that you need."

"Thank you."

"You're very welcome." He looked up at the clock on the mantle. "And now, since it's about dinnertime, do you feel up to heading downstairs and having a bite to eat?"

"You know, I could eat. I just realized that I haven't eaten anything all day. Didn't hit me until just now."

"Well, you did have quite a bit on your mind today, so I'm not surprised. Would you rather I have Gryphon bring something up for you?"

The thought of dining with Alexi in the quiet of his chambers was appealing after the turmoil of the afternoon, but her earlier musings came back to her in full force. She wouldn't run and hide from anything, and definitely not from her friends and those ready to help her through this madness. Besides, she really didn't want to miss anything important. What had Minerva said earlier? Forearmed is forewarned? Well, after the events of the day, she intended to be as "forearmed" as she could be going forward.

Isabella shook her head. "No, I'll go down with you. I need to walk, get some air, do *something*."

He stood and pulled her up from the sofa. "How about we take that walk first? Maybe take a spin around the snowy courtyard gardens?"

"That sounds perfect. Give me ten minutes to make myself presentable and grab my coat, and then we can head down."

THEIR SIDE TRIP BEFORE DINNER PROVED TO BE AS perfect as it had sounded.

Though not as colorful as the courtyard gardens had been during summer's full bloom, with the pristine covering of snow glittering in the moonlight like tiny diamonds, the gardens were almost magickal. While they strolled along the cleared paths, Isabella found that her equilibrium had returned in part to the point that she was beginning to feel more like herself and less like a scared, confused child.

She hadn't realized until just that moment the toll the last few weeks had taken, not only on her body, but on her mind and spirit as well. She'd lost her positive center and had sunk into a funk that she'd been unable to disentangle herself from on her own, which was completely out of character for her. She was solutions-oriented in all things, but the revelations of the last couple of days on top of everything else that she'd been dealing with had really thrown her. Now, she was beginning to feel like she was finally getting a grip, moving forward again.

Taking a deep breath, the frosty-cold air seemed to energize her, and she smiled up at the clear, star-studded night sky. "Would you look at that sky, Alexi? What a beautiful sight."

"It is a beautiful sight, for sure. Takes my breath away," he murmured.

She turned and realized that he was looking at her and not the sky, and her pulse picked up speed.

He pulled her into his arms. "Do you remember the last time we were in this garden together at night?"

Sliding her hands up his chest and around his neck, she smiled and nodded. "I do indeed. As I recall, we were quite naughty that night."

"Well, not naughty enough, in my opinion, but it was highly satisfying *as I recall*. Of course, I wasn't entangled with someone else at the time, so I understood your need for space. Didn't mean I had to like it when you walked away."

"Please. Valian and I had already made our choices. He was still in love with Tisharu, and we both knew it almost from the start." Isabella laughed out loud. "But when I left you and went upstairs after our little make-out session and told Valian about it, he tried to make it seem like it was all your fault. Like you'd tried to take advantage of me or something."

Alexi shook his head. "Of course he did."

"Don't worry, I set him straight."

"Oh, really? And how's that?"

"I told him that you gave me a choice, and that I dove right in," she said in a sultry tone as she ran her fingers through his long, silvery-white hair. Then she nodded her head indicating the garden in which they were standing. "I also told him that if we hadn't been in this very courtyard where anyone could've seen us, it may not have stopped with just a couple of kisses."

"Huh...I guess, that was telling him." Alexi grinned.

"Yeah, well, I didn't stop there. I said that I'd been attracted to you since we'd first met on New Year's Eve."

In the moonlight, Isabella could clearly see his grin fade only to be replaced by a very surprised look.

"And what did he say to that?"

Isabella rolled her eyes. "He busted up laughing and said that he'd known, that he was pretty sure everyone in the room the night we met probably knew as well."

Alexi shook his head. "Wait, as I remember it, we only said a handful of sentences to each other."

She punched him in the shoulder. "That's what *I* said."

"So weird," he muttered, shaking his head again. "But I guess that does explain a few things."

"What do you mean? Explain what things?"

"Let's just say that Val was quite peeved at me the next morning. Practically jumped me in the hallway after the final meeting before we headed into the Barrens to find Alyssa. He was so not pleased."

"Oh, for crying out loud," Isabella huffed. "Completely unnecessary and stupid. Just another example of the male ego rearing its ugly head."

A slow, seductive smile spread across Alexi's handsome face.

"What?" she asked.

"But you admitted that you were attracted to me from the first time we met. I *knew* it!"

"Oh, brother. You did not," she grumbled and punched him again. "And maybe I was just laying it on a bit thick with him because I felt so guilty playing kissy-face with you before he and I had actually made the decision to move on."

She started to turn away but he took her arm and pulled her back up against his hard chest. "I don't really care why you said it, Bellamine. Only that you said it out loud," he murmured against her lips before scattering her thoughts with a fiery kiss.

DINNER, AS IT TURNED OUT, WAS NOT THE uncomfortable affair that Isabella had been expecting after the strained and devastating afternoon that she'd endured. It actually seemed more like an elaborate family affair, as Queen Beatrice had basically decreed that it would be so. Isabella and Alexi joined Gray, Áine, Valian, Finvar, Alyssa, and even Niall around the massive table in the dining room for the incredible evening meal that Gryphon and the kitchen staff had prepared for them.

While the conversation flowed, there was little talk of what they'd learned from the old witch earlier in the afternoon. Isabella was pretty sure that was also something that the Queen had decided upon, and she was just fine with that decision for now. However, there was a bit of disturbing news that had made its way to the palace between the end of the meeting with Minerva and the dinner they'd all just enjoyed. Valian explained what had transpired to those of the group who'd already left the palace before the news had arrived.

"We received a visit from two of the southern dwarf chieftains. They'd crossed into the Barrens during their routine patrols and were following the border north when they ran across a fairly gruesome scene. As we're just finishing up dinner, I won't go into the ugly details of it, but suffice it to say that the scene was very much as we've seen with the dryad deaths. Only this victim was not a tree sprite."

"I hesitate to ask," Alexi said. "And do I even want to know?"

Valian glanced at Alexi and then turned to the two high lords. "They found a fae warrior."

"What?" Alexi exclaimed. "In the same way? They're sure?"

Valian nodded with a dry look. "Yes, Chieftain Durnak was quite clear about that."

"What court was this warrior from?" Niall asked quietly. "Did Durnak know?"

Valian cleared his throat and nodded again. "Wysteria's Evening Court."

"Kellam," Finvar spat, then added a vicious expletive under his breath. "As you know, a group of us have been monitoring that worthless shite—" He stopped and shook his head, obviously mindful of his surroundings, and then went on. "We've been monitoring him and his court since the summer when we returned from the Barrens. High Lord Juppar has been leading the surveillance as his Starlight Court is the closest to Kellam's court, but Tisharu, Niall, and I have all been involved as well."

Gray looked at Niall and then back to Finvar. "Can you two touch base with Juppar tomorrow and let him know about this development, see if he has any new information regarding Kellam's activities? If Kellam has had a part in these deaths or has taken up with something or someone who's perpetrating them, we need to know about it. And now."

"Agreed," Finvar replied. He looked to Niall. "We could head to

Tisharu's court tomorrow morning, and if she's agreeable to it, head to the Starlight Court to meet with Juppar from there."

"We could do that." Niall spun the fork he was holding in his hand, and then laid it across his plate. "However, since Juppar's court is the closest to Kellam's, perhaps it would be wise for Juppar to meet us at my twin's court instead so as not to arouse suspicion or attention. I will contact her if you will run that by Juppar."

Finvar ran a hand down his snowy-white beard in contemplation. "I believe you're correct. That would be a better plan."

"Well, now that we've decided on that, why don't we put all else aside for now and have some dessert," Queen Beatrice said with a sharp look for Valian and the two high lords. "Let's not have more talk of death and plots at the dinner table, shall we?"

"Of course, Majesty," Valian conceded. "My apologies. It had just crossed my mind, and I only meant to bring the others up to speed."

"No worries, Chancellor," the Queen replied then turned to her chamber elf who'd magickly appeared at her side. "Now, Gryphon, what dessert delights have you conjured for us this evening?"

DESPITE THE UNSEEMLY TALK OF DEATH JUST BEFORE dessert, the evening had been a very pleasant couple of hours, but by the time Isabella and Alexi got back to his chambers, Alexi noted that she was beginning to yawn. They'd settled themselves on the sofa with a last glass of wine in front of a warm, cheerful fire which someone on the staff had rekindled while the two were at dinner. However, after less than an hour, when Alexi had to repeat himself for the third time, he simply got up from the sofa and took Isabella's wine glass from her. Then he held out his hand.

"What?" she asked, trying desperately to stifle yet another yawn.

"We're going to bed, Bella. Whether you want to admit it or not, you're exhausted. A solid night's sleep will do you good. Now, come on."

She sighed, but nodded and let him pull her up from the sofa before following him down the hall to the bedroom.

By the time they'd changed and slid beneath the covers, she was almost gone, and Alexi pulled her into his arms. "Sleep now, baby," he murmured as he waved a hand toward the lamp to douse the light.

"I'm afraid to," came her soft, sleepy response. "I'm afraid to dream, Alexi."

"Then don't, Bella. Just sleep and know that I'm right here beside you and watching over you."

"Mmm...okay..."

And then she went under, cradled in his arms.

She knew this place, this forest...yet she didn't. She was certain that she'd been here before, but she just couldn't remember when. It was a dark and foreboding place, and that was something that she did remember quite clearly.

Just on the cusp of nightfall, meager light barely filtered through the canopy above and the path forward was shrouded in mist. That would have been bad enough, but what made it even worse was the sound...or lack of it. There was nothing. It was as if the world had been entombed in a thick padding of cotton. No insects buzzing, no bird calls, no wind blowing through the trees, no sounds of any living things. It was unnatural, eerie.

She continued through the gloom along a path covered with snow and barely visible, and came upon the meadow before she'd even been aware of it. Standing there at its edge, she could barely make out the dark treeline on the far side in the impending twilight.

"I don't want to be here," she suddenly said out loud, and then shuddered at the flat sound of her own voice. Her pulse picked up speed.

"No. You do not," said a soft voice to her left.

Turning, Isabella saw Tempest looking off toward the other side of the meadow. Then her great-aunt turned and pointed back the way Isabella had just come. "But it's too late, mo linbh milis. You cannot go back."

"Why not?" Isabella asked with dread. "I don't want to go forward, either."

"Something is coming...something evil and wicked. It cannot find you here. You must go and go quickly."

Isabella's heart began to pound in her ears. "Go where? I don't know where I am. Show me the way!"

But before Tempest could answer her, the ground beneath their feet began to tremble and there was a great rumbling sound that rolled through the forest behind them. Isabella watched Tempest as she drew her sword and turned to look back along the path.

"What is it, Tempest?" Isabella asked in a voice barely audible to her own ears. Terror had a hold on her throat with its icy fingers. "What do we do?"

Following Tempest's gaze, Isabella too, looked back along the path that she'd just walked moments ago. And then she saw something. It was a black undefined shape against the darkness and the spreading mist but seemed to be rising from the forest floor. Materializing from it.

Glowing red orbs slowly took shape, and her pounding heart seemed to stop in mid-beat.

Without turning, Tempest shouted, "Go now! Run!"

And then her great-aunt charged toward the black mass with a battle cry and sword raised.

"Nooooo!" Isabella screamed and bolted up in bed.

Thirteen

Alyssa surfaced slowly in the early morning light, and feeling the heated brush of lips along her neck, tilted her head, giving those lips more space and freedom to roam. Her smile spread in satisfaction as those wandering lips complied. She'd been dreaming of him, as she often did these days, especially when they were apart for any length of time. Warm, achingly sensual dreams of Niall, High Lord of the Twilight Court.

Dark and handsome, steely and dangerous, he was an enchanting combination of everything she wanted, needed. He challenged her, encouraged her, even frightened her at times, but he had come for her in her hour of need when she was terrified and at her most vulnerable, as he had promised he always would. He was her own personal Jack of Hearts from the children's story of her family's heritage. She was the great-granddaughter of the great-grand-daughter of the original Alice. Who would've thought that after all these years, Alyssa's soulmate would have stepped right out of her ancestor's magickal tale and into her reality, stealing her breath and claiming her heart.

And yet...

That breath caught as she felt his lips continue their journey with a nip of teeth every so often along the way. She turned toward him with eyes closed as he leaned into his work in earnest. "I'll give you another hour to stop that," she murmured, then hummed her enjoyment at his deep rumble of laughter against her neck.

She smiled and opened her eyes as Niall lifted his head, and they just gazed at each other for a few moments. Feeling the familiar tightening in her belly, the acceleration of her pulse at the sultry look in his eyes, her smile spread into a grin and his lips descended, taking hers with a sudden urgency, demanding a response. And respond she did, as she always would. He was her heart, her center, her High Lord.

"*A chuisle mo chroí*," he whispered against her lips. "The pulse of my heart."

She rolled onto his chest and plunged her hands into his hair, "*Mo ghrá*." She whispered the words she'd learned from him as she took his lips with an urgency of her own. Then they were touching, tasting, exploring with fingers, with lips and tongues. His clever fingers teased her, seduced her, drove her to hunger, and when he finally took her, the joy of it had pleasure exploding through her like a whirlwind.

For moments, she could only ride the aftermath with her heart pounding in her ears, the joy of it singing in her blood.

As minutes passed, Niall finally lifted his head and gazed down at her with adoration shining in his eyes. "I have missed you over the last couple of weeks, love," he murmured.

"I've missed you, too. The preparation running up to the showing at the gallery on Wednesday took up way too much of my time. I just couldn't get away until it was finished."

He nodded solemnly. "We both have commitments that can't be avoided at times."

"Yes. The showing went well, and I'd planned to come to court the next day, but then everything happened with Izzy and it all just spiraled out of control."

He was quiet for a moment. "And how do you feel about that, about what happened with Isabella? What we learned from the old witch?"

"You mean, about Isabella being not only human but part fae and part Ellurian?" Alyssa laughed. "For God's sake, Niall. I've known her all of my life. She's my best friend, really more of a sister. I was shocked, of course, with what we learned, but she's still Isabella. She was there for me when we found out about my ancestors, my heritage, and about this other realm, so I'll be there for her now." She paused. "It's just a little strange. I think when we heard it all, she and I both had the same thoughts. Like, was our friendship contrived, our family ties manufactured? Or preordained somehow? But like Minerva said, some things in the universe are just meant to be. I agree with that."

"What?" he asked when she frowned.

"Oh, it's nothing really, not my business, but I just feel bad for Alexi, that's all."

Niall smirked. "Alexi? And why would you feel bad for the Field Marshal?"

"Because he had a right to be angry with Valian. *He's* with Isabella now, not Valian. Alexi was on pins and needles waiting for confirmation that she'd been found and was unharmed. I was so worried about Isabella at the time that I didn't think about it, but Valian knew that, had given his word that he'd let Alexi know the minute she was located. Yet, he didn't."

"Do you think Valian deliberately left Alexi out of the picture?"

She shook her head. "I don't know. Maybe not deliberately. Perhaps he just got caught up in the moment because I called him first, but I didn't know how to contact Alexi in this realm from New York. I do believe that Valian still cares for Isabella, but I think that he did overstep. At the very least, he should have let Alexi know the minute we arrived at the palace that night."

"I will admit that Valian has always been the type to take control and do things his own way, no matter how it may affect others."

"Yes, and again, Isabella is with Alexi now, and Valian is with Tisharu. That was a clear choice they made this last summer."

Niall smoothed her hair back from her face. "Well, I wouldn't worry overmuch about it now, love. If Valian steps too far out of line, I have no doubt that my twin will take care of that. And as Alexi and Valian are family, I would say that it's up to them to sort out their issues."

Alyssa sighed. "I suppose."

"Now, as we'll obviously have very little time alone together over the next few weeks until this developing chaos is resolved, I'd rather take advantage of the time we do have instead of talking about two squidges like Valian and Alexi, wouldn't you?"

Alyssa laughed at that and the pained look on his face. "I would indeed, *mo chroí*. What exactly did you have in mind?"

She was fairly certain of what he was thinking, and his grin was a bit wicked as his lips descended once again.

When they finally dressed an hour later and went down to the dining hall to have a bit of breakfast, Kassair, Niall's top general, was waiting for them there.

"My Lord," Kassair said with a short bow.

Niall nodded and narrowed his eyes. "What is it, Kassair?"

The general looked back and forth between Niall and Alyssa before responding. "We've just received word from the White Palace. The Prince has requested your presence there as soon as you are able."

"Really? Was a reason given? We were just there last evening for dinner. Has something of significance happened?"

Kassair shook his head. "No reason was given. However, I did get the feeling that something has transpired, but the messenger didn't have that information." He pulled a small, folded parchment out of the pocket of his leather vest and held it out to Niall. "He gave this to me for you."

Niall took the proffered note and cracked the royal seal. After reading it, he turned to Alyssa. "Interesting. It seems that there has been word from the Oracles."

"What did they say?" she asked. "Are they going to see us soon?"

The High Lord shook his head. "It's not disclosed in this note. I suppose we'll just have to go to the palace and find out." He put up a finger. "But first, we break our fast, yes?"

"Agreed." Alyssa grinned. "As much as I want to know what's up at the palace, we really shouldn't go anywhere on an empty stomach."

❀

"I KID YOU NOT, I LITERALLY *FELT* THE GROUND RUMBLE beneath my feet, and the friggin' roar that shook the trees scared the shit out of me! Then Tempest pulls that humongous sword of hers out of its scabbard, shouts at me to run—though where or which way was unclear—and charges *toward* whatever was coming up out of the ground in the middle of that scary-ass forest." Isabella yelled the whole thing at Valian in one breath with a wild look in her eyes. "I'm sorry, it was more than a dream, Valian!"

It had been a late night with Isabella after she'd awakened screaming from the dream—or nightmare, more like it. Alexi had heard every detail of her nightmare several times, and she'd been in this state from the moment she'd bolted awake until she'd finally run out of steam and slept again.

Only to wake up in the same mode.

Wearily, he scrubbed his hands over his face as she continued to shout at his cousin, feeling no need or desire to come to Valian's aid. *Sink or swim, cousin,* he thought as he leaned back and tried not to smile. It was probably a little petty of him, but he was still moderately pissed about how Valian had given his word but then had cut him out of the loop without a thought after finding Isabella, leaving Alexi to worry and agonize over her whereabouts. He had a satisfied feeling that the scene before him was quite the just and appropriate karma.

"Isabella," Valian began, "you've been very stressed lately. And it's no wonder why, love."

Alexi inwardly winced at his cousin's pompous tone. *Careful, Val, she will eat you alive if you patronize her,* he thought. But Valian didn't seem to notice the storm clouds brewing in Isabella's eyes.

"You've been on an emotional roller coaster over the last few weeks, to be sure, but these are just dreams. Interactive, yes. Obviously, Tempest has been trying to tell both you and Gray some very important things through these dreams, but in the end, you have to see that they're just that...dreams."

There was a very pregnant pause as Alexi watched Isabella gather the storm. He could almost feel the electricity snapping around her as her anger blossomed.

"Valian Winchester," she began in a quiet but deadly tone.

"Don't you *dare* speak to me like I'm a dimwitted child. I may have only just found out about the heritage that runs through my bloodline, may not fully understand it chapter and verse as of yet, but do I know what I saw, what I felt."

She shook her head and glared at him before he could try to placate her, and her voice grew more insistent. "And what if they're not just dreams, Valian? What if they *are* real? The first few, okay, maybe. I can give you that. Perhaps, they *were* just an interactive dream where Tempest was trying to communicate, but I'm telling you, this one was different. It *felt* different. Plus, I knew that place. I'd been there before. And not just seen it in a dream...actually *been there*."

Valian sighed. "Isabella, I don't know how that's possible."

She stared at him for a full ten seconds, and then burst into laughter. "Oh, for heaven's sake, Valian," she stammered. "Don't be obtuse. Or are you just trying to piss me off? You do realize that you live in a magickal world where just about *anything* is possible, yes? I might add that you have magickal abilities yourself, or did that slip your mind? For you to say that to me with a straight face is priceless." She put up a hand when he opened his mouth to speak. "However, if you're having a difficult time understanding it, I will explain it to you slowly. I went there with Tempest last Wednesday night. That forest was part of our little excursion to see where my ancestors were from. Is that clear enough for you?"

Valian stared at her. "I thought you said that you couldn't remember whether you went through the portal with Tempest or not," he said in a lame response.

Alexi hid a smile as Isabella growled.

"I didn't remember *then*, you big dufus. I told you, I've been remembering things here and there. I recalled our trip last night during the 'dream.' I felt that I knew the place but didn't know from when or where. It came to me right after I woke up." Isabella seemed to finally settle, her anger slowly fading, and she sighed. "Anyway, believe me or don't. I don't really give a damn. I know in my heart what I saw and felt, and when we go to meet with the Oracles, I'm going to find out just what the hell these nightly excursions really are."

"Well, it looks like you'll get that chance very soon, Isabella," Gray said, coming into the war room. "I've just received word from the Oracles that they've accepted our request."

"For all of us?" Isabella asked. "Not just you or Aly?"

Gray smiled and nodded. "Yes. For all three of us. Now, I don't know if we will be going in together or individually, and you need to prepare yourself for whatever they decide, but we should be traveling to the temple in the next few hours or so."

"That's great," Alexi said. He took Isabella's hand. "See? I'm sure we'll go and get answers for you to all the questions you've had and more, just like we talked about, okay?"

"I hope so," she replied. "I know with the recent death in the Barrens, you'll have to go and investigate that, but you're still going with me to the Oracles Temple, right?"

He could feel both Valian and Gray watching them, but didn't care. He turned, and the look he gave them dared either to deny it. Then, lifting Isabella's hand to his lips, he murmured, "Wouldn't miss it for the world, sweetness."

AN HOUR LATER, ISABELLA AND ALEXI WERE JUST COMING downstairs into the great hall when Niall and Alyssa arrived, and Isabella took the last of the stairs two at a time.

"Aly!" she shouted as she ran to give her friend a hug. "Thank heavens you're here."

Alyssa pulled back and studied Isabella's face. "What's going on, Izzy? Has something happened? The message Gray sent said to come to the palace as soon as we could, but he didn't give a reason."

Isabella nodded and thought that she might explode with the excitement in anticipation of their meeting with the Trinity. "Gray heard from the Oracles earlier. They've agreed to our request for a meeting. Evidently, we're going there this afternoon."

Alyssa's eyes went wide. "Really? So, you and Gray? That's terrific."

Isabella frowned. "No, Aly. The three of us are going. You, me, and Gray. Though, Alexi is coming with me as far as he can for moral support. Which he is just so excited about." She reached out a hand to Alexi who took it and brought it to his lips, but then gave Alyssa an exaggerated, wide-eyed look that clearly said he wasn't looking forward to the trip.

Alyssa chuckled at his antics.

"Oh, stop," Isabella told him with a roll of her eyes. "I've already told you that you don't have to come in with me, and probably won't be allowed to, anyway. All I really need you to do is wait for me in the vestibule, just so I know you're out there and nearby."

"I'm aware, darlin'," Alexi grinned and winked at Alyssa. "But I've already girded my loins...just in case."

"Oh, brother." Isabella turned back to Alyssa with a smirk. "Anyway, we're meeting Gray and Áine downstairs in the war room to go over our list and make certain we cover all of our questions. I also need to tell Gray about the friggin' nightmare that I had last night."

"You had a nightmare? What about?" Alyssa asked with a concerned look. "Was it different than the other dreams you've been having?"

"Oh, buddy, was it," Alexi said. "She woke up screaming. Scared me out of a sound sleep."

"It wasn't pretty. I'll tell you all about it, but let's wait until we get downstairs." Isabella sighed. "After the incredibly annoying time I had explaining it to Valian, who just pissed me off with his attitude, I only want to rehash the whole thing one more time. But I'll wait until we've gone over our list of questions and finished that up first."

Alyssa hesitated. "Okay, then," she said slowly.

"Wait. What's wrong?" Isabella asked. "Don't you want to get our questions answered?"

"Of course I do, Izzy. It's just that my one and only time visiting the Trinity was a scary experience, and if you'll recall, I didn't get the answers that I was looking for. And as a result, it was almost a disaster for the realm."

Niall cleared his throat. "I beg to differ, *Mo ghrá*. If memory serves, the Oracles gave you exactly what you needed, and in the end, you saved the realm."

"Well, I wouldn't say—"

"Niall's right," Alexi agreed. "And I may not be a fan of 'visiting' the Temple, but the Trinity are the wisest, most generous, and knowledgeable beings in our realm. We may not think they give us the answers we're looking for, but they will always give us the answers we need."

Isabella took Alyssa's hand and gave it a squeeze. "Look, Aly, I know that you had a hard time during the New Year's Eve debacle. I also know that you really didn't want to be the descendant, to have the fate of the realm on your shoulders and use a magickal weapon of mass destruction, but this time we all have to stand up. We don't know what's coming. Plus, we have questions that we need answered or some kind of guidance as to where those answers can be found. At least, I do." She laughed. "Anyway, whatever the Oracles deign to tell us, it will definitely be more than we know now, right?"

"Sorry. I don't mean to be a downer." Alyssa sighed and pulled Isabella in for a hug. "You are so smart, my friend, and absolutely right." She pulled back and smiled. "Then I guess we better get this party started."

Isabella nodded, and the four of them headed down to the war room where Áine and the Prince were already discussing the importance of the trip they were about to take.

"Hey, guys. Perfect timing," Gray said as they entered the room. "We were just going over my list of questions that I want to put to the Oracles. Have a seat and let's add your questions to the list and hash it all out."

"I've written mine out, so you can add them," Isabella replied and handed her list to Áine.

"Okay, my questions are basically these," Gray began, looking first at Isabella. "Number one, who are the men in the black robes in our dreams. In my last dream, Tempest indicated that they were 'elders of the Ancients,' so does that mean they are *Ellurian* elders, and if so, does it follow that the Ellurians are not the extinct race they were thought to be? Also, if they're not extinct, where have they been for the last century or two?"

Alexi nodded. "Yeah, I'd like to hear the answers to those questions myself."

"I would also be interested in those answers," Niall added. "If the

Ellurian race had been living in the realm somewhere all these years, that would be extraordinary."

"One of Isabella's questions on her list here is pertinent to both of you, Gray," Áine said, then read from Isabella's list. "Are your dreams real rather than just interactive? Or are they something else entirely?"

Gray frowned. "That's an interesting question, Isabella. Why would you think that?"

"Because the friggin' nightmare that I had last night felt different, real somehow."

"You had another dream last night?" Gray asked.

"Uh, no, she had a *nightmare*," Alexi said.

Isabella went on to explain what she'd tried to get Valian to understand earlier. When she was finished, she shook her head. "I'm telling you, I think it was more than just a dream, Gray."

"Okay, then," Gray replied. "That's good to know, and I have to say, now that you've explained your latest dream, or nightmare, I understand what you're getting at. I've felt the same way on a couple occasions, just not to that extent. And I've not yet seen any monster rising up out of the forest floor. In any case, we'll add that to the list. What else did you have?"

"Oh, just a few odds and ends, like, was Aly and my relationship preordained? Our family connection as well? How does the magickal number of three affect me? Is it different than for Aly? What do these dreams mean for me and my role in whatever's coming? Why is my heritage being revealed now?" Isabella laughed. "You know, just odds and ends."

Gray chuckled. "All good questions, for sure." He frowned then and shot a look at Alexi. "I do have one other pretty important question that I'm going to ask."

Alexi nodded. "Are the deaths we originally attributed to the golem that Yulis had conjured connected to whatever the wicked, evil thing is that may be coming?"

"Exactly. Maybe we got it all wrong in the Barrens this last summer."

"That is an unsettling thought," Niall added.

"Well, it did make sense at the time to think it was Yulis' golem's doing," Alyssa added. "Especially considering the gibberish the sylphide told Cianán and me in the Barrens. She said that there was evil ahead and behind and that neither belonged there, that both what was ahead and behind were connected." She shook her head. "I mean, what else would that suggest? It was logical to think it meant Yulis and his golem."

"For sure," Alexi agreed. "But with new deaths in the same manner so close to home, and perhaps more we haven't discovered yet? We're definitely gonna need to rethink that theory."

"Well, anyway, I think that's all I have." Gray turned to Isabella and then to Alyssa. "Either of you have anything else to add?"

"I don't," Alyssa replied. "At least, nothing more I can think of at the moment."

"Me neither," Isabella said. "I think what we have just about covers it, don't you?"

Gray smiled and looked around the table. "Then I guess we need to get a move on. The sooner we get to the temple, the sooner we get our answers."

"Oh, joy," Alexi muttered and made a face before grinning at Isabella. "Joking, sweetness. Temple of the Oracles, here we come."

Fourteen

The Temple of the Oracles was located several miles south of the White Palace, and once the group was beyond the palace's one-mile fade-restricted perimeter, the six of them faded and arrived in the blink of an eye. They stood in several inches of snow in front of the thick stone walls encircling the temple. The stone walls themselves were at least twenty feet high with notched sections every few feet around the top edge and an inset of solid wooden gates at the entrance.

Alyssa laughed out loud at the look on Isabella's face. "This shrine looks more like the entrance to a fortress or a prison rather than a holy place, right?"

Isabella stared up at the walls and nodded. "I was just thinking that. But is it to keep people out or the Trinity in?"

"Ha! And that's almost exactly what I thought when I first came here with Gray back in January. Great minds, my friend."

As the gates began to swing open seemingly of their own volition, Isabella stared at them wide-eyed and smiled. "Now, that's interesting."

Niall walked up behind them. "Ladies, it looks as if we're being invited in. Ready, love?" he asked Alyssa.

"As I'll ever be," she replied.

"Let's get this started," Gray said, as he and Áine stepped around them and took the lead.

Alyssa and Niall followed, and Alexi gave Isabella a courtly bow.

"After you, sweetness," he said with a twinkle in his eye.

Taking a deep breath, she grabbed his hand and, following Alyssa and Niall, pulled him through the open gates with her. Isabella had no idea what to expect but was stunned by the view that greeted them.

"Oh, Izzy, look! The gardens are in bloom just like they were last winter," Alyssa exclaimed.

"What the— Wow! This is amazing. There's almost six inches of snow on the ground outside the outer wall," Isabella marveled. "Yet, in this courtyard garden, there's not a trace of snow, and it feels like spring. That's just so wild."

"From what I understand, it's like this year-round," Alyssa said with a grin. "I guess the Trinity likes a milder climate and gardens full of color closer to home."

"It's really lovely."

On the far side of the garden stood the temple itself, an unremarkable, ancient stone structure adorned only with a layering of green and red ivy that again belied the idea of this being a sacred temple holding a trinity of ancient beings. In fact, the ornately carved set of enormous wooden doors at the entrance was the only indication of the mystic purpose of the temple with its intricate and varied mystical symbols.

As the group climbed the wide stone steps, those incredible doors began to open—again as if expecting them and inviting them into the vestibule.

"And so it begins."

Though whispered, Isabella heard Alyssa's words as if they were spoken directly into her head. Her pulse rate increased as they crossed the threshold, and the massive doors swung shut behind them enfolding them into the large, dimly lit antechamber, the only light coming from fiery torches in sconces along the stone walls.

Isabella's nerves had her palms suddenly damp, and she self-consciously rubbed them on her jeans, feeling a bit uneasy about what was to come.

"You okay, darlin'?" Alexi asked, leaning in close.

His voice gave her a start, but she recovered quickly and smiled. "I'll be fine. This is just all a little overwhelming, that's all."

He smiled back. "A little overwhelming? That's all? Well, I have a completely different opinion of this place—which I won't go into now—and the reason I try not to come here if I can help it."

To distract herself from her apprehension, Isabella walked over to study the walls of the vestibule. Unlike the outer walls of the temple, which were unadorned and severe, the antechamber walls were covered with more mystical symbols as well as ancient-looking petroglyphs, each seeming to Isabella more complex and foreign than anything she could've possibly imagined.

Stepping up next to Isabella and Alexi, Alyssa spoke in a low, reverent tone. "Amazing, isn't it? I would love to spend a few hours scouring these symbols, studying these petroglyphs. Gray told me during my first visit here that the temple has stood in this very place for thousands of years. A portion of the Trinity's history is etched on these walls, though evidently, no one really knows their entire story, where they came from, where their true home was, or how they even came into being."

"That's true," Alexi stated. "Outside of this temple, there are only myths and legends. Most of those are sketchy and, at best, incredibly embellished. And I'm certain that, for the most part, the lion's share of those are vastly inaccurate, anyway. No, what's on these walls are the only true records known to exist, and barely a portion of them, at that. Otherwise, nobody really knows for sure."

"Quite the ancient mystery," Isabella murmured before giving Alyssa a snarky look. "Kind of like Minerva, right? Do you think she and the Trinity are related somehow?"

Alexi snorted and then caught himself.

Alyssa pressed her lips together in an effort not to laugh out loud at Isabella's comment in this reverent place. "Who knows, but you're not wrong. Since no one has a clue where Minerva came from, either, or how old she is, I guess anything's possible."

Isabella's snarky look faded, and she again glanced up at the extraordinary engravings. "Still, these etchings, knowing that they're thousands of years old, kinda gives one pause, doesn't it? Makes you feel insignificant, almost like an afterthought of some ancient culture."

"It sure does," Alyssa agreed.

At that moment, the doors of the inner sanctum swung open and a tall, thin priest dressed in flowing white robes stepped out into the vestibule. As he came forward, Isabella's heart almost skipped a beat when the priest's eyes seemed to seek her out in the group and pin her with his sky-blue stare. She held her breath for what she was afraid was coming.

Then he spoke, and there it was.

"Isabella Doyle Christensen, the Oracles will see you now. Please follow me." He turned then and crossed back to the open doorway, stopping to wait for her to follow.

"Me first?" Isabella squeaked. "Alone?" She froze for a moment, and her anxiety ratcheted up several notches. She hadn't been all that worried about this whole idea...until this very moment. Suddenly, she had to remind herself just to breathe.

This wasn't completely unexpected. Alyssa had told her that she'd been required to see the Oracles alone in January, but Isabella was still stunned. Why her? Alyssa was the descendant, which in Isabella's mind was much more important than anything she herself could present. Why the Trinity would want to see her first was baffling.

And suddenly terrifying.

"Bella?" Alexi's soft voice penetrated her terror, and he took her arm. "Are you okay, babe?" he asked her for the second time since arriving. "Look, you don't have to do this if you don't want to. You know that. But if you still want to go through with this, I'll be right out here just like I promised."

Isabella turned into his embrace and hugged him to her like a lifeline. He held her tight, and she closed her eyes briefly, breathed in his warm, woodsy scent, and felt all the better for it. Then, with reluctance, she pulled back and nodded. "I know I don't have to do this, but I need answers, Alexi." Taking a deep, fortifying breath, she backed away from him and smiled. "But you'll be right here?"

He took her hand and kissed her palm. "I'll be right here."

With another nod, she squared her shoulders and crossed to the open doorway where the priest was patiently waiting. And then, with one last look over her shoulder at Alexi, she walked past the priest and stepped over the threshold into the inner sanctum. Turning then, she met the priest's pale eyes as he backed out of the chamber, closing the doors as he went.

Then she was alone.

Okay. What now? she thought as she listened to her heartbeat pounding in her ears.

Then came a wraithlike voice that seemed to come from everywhere at once. Or maybe it was just inside her head, but either way, Isabella just about wet herself.

"Come forward, Isabella Doyle Christensen. We have much to discuss."

She looked toward the other end of the chamber and saw that three small ethereal beings had appeared and now hovered above the altar. Even from where she stood rooted to the spot just inside the chamber, she could sense, almost *feel* the otherworldly power that radiated from them. The air was thick with it.

Isabella put a hand to her chest where she thought that her galloping heart might just leap out of her body's constraints at any moment. In her mind's eye, she could actually see it happening— almost like in an old Saturday morning cartoon—and a giggle bubbled up and out of her before she could stop it. But trying desperately to get herself under some kind of control, she took another deep, calming breath, let it out slowly, and willed her feet to move forward toward the alter...and the Trinity.

"She is fearful. Frightened of us," a singular voice said as Isabella neared the alter and stopped.

"Indeed. Still, she comes for answers in spite of her fear," another replied with an interested look.

Isabella swallowed hard. "Y-yes, I am scared. I've never spoken to a mystical being before, let alone three at once. I've never even seen one, to be honest. So, this is a first for me. But if I can get the answers to my questions about my newfound heritage, I can only hope that my apprehension will have been worth the trip."

"Mmm, yes. She has grit, and quite a strong inner force," yet

another voice murmured. *"Just as the Old One indicated. Can you not feel it?"*

"Yes. It has power, it is robust. She will need that and more for what is to come."

"Wait— You've talked to Minerva about me?" Isabella blurted before she could think better of it. "I-I mean, sorry, but why? And what do you mean 'inner force'?"

There was a brief pause as the Oracles seemed to be communicating, and then, *"You've recently learned of your magickal heritage. Is that not so?"*

"Well, I don't know about the magickal part of it, but yeah, that's one of my questions. And like, why am I just learning about my fae and Ellurian ancestry now?" Isabella asked with hesitation. "Also, I'm the great-granddaughter of Moira Nic Corragáin. The Old One said the magickal number of three also affects me but I don't know how? And since Alyssa is the descendant, does it affect her differently?"

"You embody the power of the mystical number of three as does the descendant. And though hers is multiplied by three generations and tied to the Scepter of Fire, your power is tied to your heritage. In this way, you are connected to our Trinity."

"Okay," Isabella said slowly. "But what does that mean...exactly? You say 'my power,' but I have none that I know of."

"You will find your power when you Become."

"Become? What does that—" Isabella scrubbed her hands over her face in frustration. "Still not getting you, but let's skip over that for now. So, was my relationship with the descendant preordained? Aly is my best friend, has been all my life. Our families have always been close. Was that, like, written in the stars somewhere or just a coincidence?"

"There are no coincidences. Many things in this universe are simply meant to be, Halfling. Do not question what is meant, for everything is connected."

"And nothing happens before its time."

"Okay, okay, then let's talk about these dreams that I've been having for the last few months," Isabella suggested, boldly plowing forward. "Why is Tempest coming to me in my dreams? You do know about Tempest, don't you?"

"We are the Trinity, we know all," came a combined response that echoed around the room.

"Alright, then here's another question tied to that. Are these simply interactive dreams that the Prince and I are having? Just Tempest communicating with us, showing us important things that we'll need to know? Because lately they seem like more than that. They feel like they're ramping up. Like they're somehow tangible and happening in real time." She was talking fast but took a quick breath and dove back in again before she lost her nerve. "And who are these guys we keep seeing, the men in the black robes? Tempest told the Prince that they were elders of the Ancients. Are they our ancestors? Are these guys actually Ellurians? That race was thought to be extinct. So, if they are Ellurians, where have they been all this time?"

"She has indeed come in search of answers for many questions," one Oracle said once Isabella had run out of gas. *"Where to begin?"*

"At the beginning," another voice stated.

The three paused, and their eyes suddenly rolled back in their heads. It was like something out of a horror film. Isabella didn't know quite what to make of this semi-creepy development, so she just waited, hoping that this weirdness wouldn't last long.

And it didn't. Finally, the moment passed.

"The Ellurian race...is," the Trinity voiced as one. *"It thrives on the other side of the Unwelcoming Rise...in the Antiley mountain range where the race was conceived. The Halfling warrior Tempest also resides near those mountains. The men you and Prince Graydon have seen are your ancestors."*

Isabella frowned. "If that's so, then why hasn't anyone seen them until now? I mean, from what I understand, they are an ancient race, one of the oldest in this realm, but they haven't been seen or heard from in centuries. You say they're our ancestors, but are we seeing the past in these dreams? Or are they somehow real?"

"What you see...is...or was...or will be," one being said with a serene look, as if what it said was perfectly clear to be seen.

"Yeah, that's not really helpful." Isabella sighed. Getting a straight answer from these beings, wise or not, was like pulling teeth with your bare fingers. "So, how about this. Why are they in our dreams now? And why don't they communicate with us?"

"Along with the Caemmeirth, they are waiting," another said. *"And watching."*

"Waiting and watching? For what?" Isabella asked with annoyance. Why on earth would their ancestors simply disappear for centuries? Only to reappear now? And what could they possibly be waiting for along with the great dragons?

"Everything happens in its time," said the third.

Isabella shook her head. "That really doesn't answer my question. What are they waiting for?"

"The Unclean is coming," the Oracles again voiced as one. *"The essence of that which was struck down will rise again. It is the same, yet different."*

"The unclean? Okay, that sounds pretty terrible. What's the unclean, or do I really want to know?" Isabella shuddered. Was that what she'd seen in her latest nightmare? The frightening black shape with the red glowing eyes that was rising out of the forest floor? The thing that her great-aunt charged toward right before Isabella had come awake?

"The Unclean is darkness, malevolence. The Unclean hates. The Unclean thrives on destruction and ruin," one voice said.

"The Unclean longs to reign over all. It feeds on pain and misery," another voice followed.

"As it was before, it longs to be once more," the third voice added.

"But what once was can never be again. Its essence is tainted, impure, unnatural. It must be destroyed." This last answer started out as serene as the rest but quickly grew in intensity until the last part of it was shrieked by the Trinity as one, their ethereal light also increasing until it filled the chamber and was almost blinding.

It happened so quickly that it took Isabella by surprise, and she shielded her eyes from the blast of incredible light and stumbled backward several steps, her pulse racing once more. Just as she thought to turn and run from the chamber, all became quiet again. She opened her eyes and saw that the terrifying episode had ended almost as quickly as it had begun.

Isabella blew out a breath that she hadn't even realized she'd been holding. "Okay. The Unclean is really bad news. Understood. Got that loud and clear," she said as calmly as she could manage, not wanting to anger the beings or cause another frightening outburst. However, since they were on the subject, there was one more question she thought she probably should ask.

She swallowed back her fear, and then went with her instinct. "Since we're talking about what is coming, can you tell me if the recent deaths around the realm are connected to this 'Unclean' thing? I know that everyone originally thought that the deaths were because of the golem the Red King's sorcerer had conjured, but are they wrong?"

The Oracles frowned as one. *"Everything is connected."*

"I know. You said that before, but can you just tell me if the deaths are caused by the darkness that's coming?" Isabella mentally crossed her fingers as she watched the storm clouds gather in their eyes, but then it seemed to clear.

"The deaths are a requirement. Blood is the necessity. However, what is dark cannot be made light in this fashion."

"Okay, one last question. You say that everything is connected. How am I connected to this whole thing? I have no power and have no idea how to 'Become,' if that's what it takes. Alyssa is the descendant and can wield the Scepter of Fire. Gray, Alexi, Valian, Naill and all the rest have magickal skills, weapons. What's my role in all of this?"

The three Oracles seemed to communicate among themselves for a moment, then turned back to her, each with an air of serenity. *"Your role will be clear very soon, Isabella Doyle Christensen. Look to your ancestors. You and the Prince are connected in many ways. This will be important. A saving grace,"* they finally said.

Isabella glanced over her shoulders as the doors of the inner sanctum began to open behind her. *Well, I guess this meeting is over,* she thought.

As if reading her thoughts, the Trinity spoke as one for a last time. *"There is strength in numbers. All must do their part to prevail. Now, go and be well."*

Before her eyes, the three mystical beings disappeared, leaving her alone in the inner sanctum feeling suddenly hollow and exhausted. With one last look at the altar, Isabella turned and, on wobbly legs, left the chamber.

The priest materialized out of the shadows and stepped out into the antechamber behind her with some bad news for the rest of the group.

"That will be the extent of the audience today," he said. "The Oracles wish you well." With a slight bow, he melted back into the shadows again.

"Well, that's disappointing," Gray muttered. "I didn't get to ask my questions."

Isabella shook her head. "Don't worry, Gray. I think I got answers for both of us. Though it might take all of us to decipher what they told me."

The Prince grinned. "Then I guess we'd better go back to the palace and get started."

Fifteen

fter thanking the priest for his assistance and leaving the Temple of the Oracles, the group faded from the outer wall where they'd arrived to just outside the White Palace's fade-restricted perimeter. The questions for Isabella started almost immediately as they began to walk the final stretch to the palace.

"Okay, so what did they tell you, Izzy?" Alyssa asked. "Did the Oracles answer all of your questions?"

Isabella rolled her eyes. "Hard to tell. They seem to constantly talk in riddles, and then they look at you like the answer was obvious the whole time."

"Yes!" Alyssa exclaimed. "That's exactly how it was for me. No straight answers, and the bulk of what they did tell me was so convoluted that I had no idea what they were trying to convey. It was extremely frustrating, but it seems to happen a lot around this realm. Like the sylphide Cianán and I ran across in the Barrens. She said things like 'Stay aware and vigilant, for what is ahead awaits you.'" She shook her head with an exasperated look. "I mean, *what is ahead awaits you*? Really?"

Laughing out loud, Isabella jabbed a finger at her friend. "Right! That's why I said that it would probably take all of us to decipher what the Oracles told me. Although, there were certain questions that they did answer with fairly understandable info. Like, when I asked about the magickal number of three and how it affects me, and whether it affects you differently."

"What did they say?"

"They said that I embody the power of the mystical number of three just like you do, but that your power is multiplied by three generations and tied to the Scepter of Fire. Whereas my power is evidently tied to my heritage. A pretty straight forward answer, except for the fact that I have no power that I know of, and I told them so."

Alyssa blinked at her, and then grinned. "You told them so? That was a bold move. What did they say to that?"

"Yeah, then came the convoluted part. They said, and I quote, 'You will find your power when you *become*.'" Isabella made a face. "Whatever the hell that means."

"Well, now," Gray smiled. "That is actually something several of us had a conversation about recently. I think we can help you with that, Isabella."

"Really? So, you think that you know what it means for—" Isabella stopped mid-sentence and dead in her tracks. After a moment, she turned all the way around in a very deliberate circle, trying to identify what she was feeling. She couldn't quite pinpoint the cause of the icy dread and foreboding that had suddenly poured over her. It swamped her senses, almost like being immersed in a pool of fetid water.

"Izzy? What's the matter?" Alyssa asked. "You have gone deathly pale. Are you okay?"

Isabella slowly shook her head. Deathly. Yes, that was it. Death was the one word that kept swirling around in her head. There was a foul smear of it on the air, unlike anything she'd ever experienced, filling her nostrils. It repulsed her, assaulted her with each breath, and it was all she could do to keep from gagging.

"Izzy! Talk to me," Alyssa insisted. "What is it?"

"I...don't...know. Something... Can't you smell it?"

Alyssa frowned. "Smell what?"

"Gray!" Áine cried. "What on earth?"

The rest of the group turned to find that the Prince was having a moment of his own. His eyes had gone wide and rolled back in his head so all that could be seen was a translucent white and, like Isabella, all the color had quite literally bleached from his face.

"No, don't touch him, Áine," Alexi cautioned when she'd started to do so. "I've seen him in this state before...last summer, as a matter of fact. Valian said it's an Ellurian reverie, similar to a trance but more like a prophetic vision." He stepped over to the Prince and spoke softly. "What are you seeing, Gray? Tell me."

Without blinking or turning in that direction, the Prince lifted an arm and pointed into the forest to the right of where the group now stood on the path. When he spoke, his voice had a strangely modulated, almost otherworldly tone to it. "The stench of death is in this place. Death made by the Unclean. The menace grows with each life taken. What was struck down will rise again...the same, yet different."

And then, just as quickly as it had come over him, the vision seemed to vanish. The color returned to Gray's face, leaving him blinking and looking somewhat befuddled. Realizing the entire group was staring at him, he regarded them with a wry look.

"Uh...another reverie, I take it?" he asked into the uncomfortable silence.

Alexi nodded. "Seems like. It was similar to the one this last summer. You did the pointing thing again and talked about death. So, should we be looking for another body?"

"Yes." Gray sighed and looked off toward the area that he'd pointed to during the vision. "Should be located about five hundred feet in that direction."

"Well, I suppose we'd better go and take a look," Niall said, pulling his sword from the sheath on his back.

Alexi followed suit, and then turned to Isabella. "You should probably wait here with Alyssa and Áine until we can find out what this is."

Isabella scoffed. "Yeah, that's not gonna happen, pal, so quit yammering and just lead on."

Áine laughed. "Ditto...pal!"

Niall glanced at Alyssa with a grin, and she narrowed her eyes at him. "As you know, I'm not a fan of running *toward* the unknown, but I am not standing here by myself, either," she complained. "So, let's get this over with and get back to the palace."

Alexi shook his head but relented. "Okay, but stay behind us until we know what we're looking at, okay?"

As a group, and with extreme caution, they made their way through the trees and brambles to a small clearing almost exactly the five hundred feet that the Prince had indicated. There they indeed found a body. And not a dryad or a faerie, but this time a petite pixie.

She had pale green skin and golden hair that was fanned out along the ground around her head like a halo. She looked like she was sleeping but for the dried, iridescent, green blood that had pooled beneath her body and along her slender neck. The poor creature had died in much the same way as the others.

Violet!

Isabella's first thought came with a pang of horror and nearly took her breath.

Of course, this wasn't Violet, but the look of her was similar enough to the familiar pixie that Isabella couldn't keep the terrible thought at bay. The Violet she knew had helped Alyssa escape from the Red Palace dungeon, had saved her from almost certain death. Violet's wood sprite cousin, Kaleb Pilliar was instrumental in facilitating the rescue, and Violet herself, along with Niall, had seen Alyssa to the safety of Kaleb's cabin just south of Roseland Wood. Violet was the sweetest thing, and seeing another pixie—so like her— in this terrible way made Isabella's heart hurt.

"She looks so much like Violet," Isabella whispered, subconsciously taking Alyssa's hand in hers.

Alyssa nodded. "Yes. The poor, sweet thing. What on earth would do something this vile to such a lovely being?"

"The Unclean," Isabella replied, barely audible.

"What?" the Prince asked.

"It's what you said during your vision, Gray," Alexi replied. "You said that the stench of death was here, death made by the 'Unclean.'"

"They also used that term," Isabella said quietly. She could hear the Trinity's voices ringing in her ears. "The Unclean."

"Who did, Izzy?" Alyssa asked.

"The Oracles. They said that the men in the black robes that we see in our dreams were Ellurian elders. When I asked why these elders weren't communicating with us about what was coming, especially if they were to help us in the possible fight to come, the Oracles said that they were waiting and watching." She rolled her eyes. "Again with the vague answers, but when I asked what they were waiting for, they said, 'the Unclean.'" She turned to Gray. "In your reverie, you just said that what was struck down will rise again, the same, yet different. The Trinity said almost exactly the same thing to me. They said, *The essence of that which was struck down will rise again. It is the same, yet different.*"

"Do you know what that means?" Niall asked the Prince.

"Yeah, that would be awesome," Alexi added. "Please say that you have some idea, Gray. I mean, the *unclean*, for fuck's sake? So far, this isn't sounding great."

Isabella turned to him. "Oh, it gets worse, believe me. That's not all they told me."

"Oh, goody," Alexi muttered. "There's more. Can't wait to hear."

"Unfortunately, Alexi, I haven't a clue what any of it means, so we'll have to evaluate what Isabella was told." Gray frowned. "But first, we should take this poor pixie with us back to the palace and find out where she's from, get her back to her people. Then we can dig into the information that the Trinity gave to Isabella, and hopefully, find something that may help us solve this puzzle before we run out of time."

"Uh, guys?" Áine's voice cut into their conversation. "I suggest that you hold that thought. We have company."

Áine pointed toward the treeline where a tall, slender woman stood serene and beautiful in the shadows, not forty feet away. She wore a pale gray tunic and breeches to match with knee-high black boots. Her long hair hung in silver waves nearly to her waist, and her see-through gray eyes sparkled with a silvery sheen even from forty feet away. The overall effect was stunning.

They were all so surprised that no one spoke for several

moments. Then the lovely woman filled the void by moving closer and zeroing in on Niall.

Her voice was deep and mesmerizing. "It has been a very long time, High Lord of the Twilight Court."

Niall's eyebrows shot up, and he cautiously stepped forward. "Do I know you?" he asked.

The beauty smiled. "As I said, it has been a very long time. We heard of your twin's recent dance with death over the summer, but she has recovered, yes? We hope that she is well."

Isabella watched the High Lord's face and saw the exact moment when recognition dawned.

"By the Oracles! Azzertha? Is that you?" he asked in a shocked tone. "Truly?"

She smiled and gave a slight nod. "It is."

The High Lord looked as rattled as Isabella had ever seen him, completely dumbfounded.

"Uh, Niall? You want to introduce us to your...friend?" Alexi asked in the silence that followed.

The High Lord sheathed his sword and gave his head a shake as if trying to take in what was happening. "Yes...of course. I apologize, Field Marshal. This is quite...unexpected," he replied, never taking his eyes from the woman now walking toward the group. "This is Azzertha, High Elder of the Gheori clan."

"And I see you are here with Prince Graydon, as well as the descendant," Azzertha spoke before Niall could introduce every-one. "We are aware of them, but who are the others in your party?"

"Alexi Tovin, Field Marshal," Alexi replied. "And this is Isabella Christensen."

"Ah, yes. Isabella *Doyle* Christensen. A distant relative of the fae warrior, Tempest." Azzertha turned to Áine. "And you are?"

"I'm Áine Ó Mordha."

The Gheori elder smiled broadly then. It was warm and inviting. "The Old One's goddaughter, of course. I have heard much about you. It is a pleasure to finally meet you in person."

"Wait. You know my godmother?" Áine asked in surprise.

Azzertha laughed out loud, a rich, comfortable sound that rolled over them like a warm blanket. "Child, Minerva is the oldest, most powerful sorceress in the realm. She is known to all."

"Minerva is one thing, but you seem to know everyone here," Alyssa said. "How is that?"

"We make it our business to keep an eye on all things on this side of the Unwelcoming Rise. Though all clans of the Caemmeirth reside in the Antiley mountain range, we have waited and watched for centuries. We knew that one day this would come."

"One day what would come?" Niall asked.

"Why, the return of the evil we fought in the Great War, of course. The Dark Fae was not defeated, Niall, just...detained."

"Oh, this just gets better and better, doesn't it?" Alexi muttered. "So, does someone want to give those of us with no idea what's happening a quick history lesson before this Dark Fae or Unclean or whatever the hell it is descends upon the realm?"

"I would agree, Alexi. But not here and not now," Gray replied. "As I said, we need to get this pixie back to her home before we do anything else." He turned to Azzertha. "Would you accompany us, tell us what you know of the situation?"

The Gheori elder narrowed her eyes and seemed to contemplate the Prince's request. Then she gave a brief nod. "I must meet with other elders in the Barrens, as this unfortunate pixie is not the only death found in the realm over the last few days."

"There are others?" Niall asked. "Where?"

"Yes. There was a fae death in the far north of Roseland last night, and three in the Barrens near the Wysterian border the day before, one of which was reported to you by the dwarf chieftains." She gestured to the pixie before them. "Unfortunately, this poor creature is—though not the only death found in Wysteria—the first found so close to the White Palace and the Temple of the Trinity, which is a bit more alarming."

"Uh, yeah," Alexi muttered. "Just a bit, which is why a little history for some of us would be a welcome thing."

"I understand, Field Marshal. Once I've met with the other elders, we can return tomorrow morning and give you the information you seek, if that is acceptable."

"That would be fine and greatly appreciated," Gray said. "I'll inform the Queen as soon as we get back to the palace. Thank you, Azzertha."

"Very good. In that case, I will take my leave and return in the morning." She turned to Niall. "It was good to see you again after so much time has passed, High Lord. You look fit and well. Please give Tisharu our best."

"I'll do that. Thank you. It is good to see you again as well."

With that, the Gheori elder turned and began to walk toward the treeline, but after a few steps, gave the group quite a show as she transformed into a magnificent silver dragon and took to the sky.

Silence reigned when moments later, Azzertha's image shimmered and disappeared into thin air before their eyes.

"Well, that's something you don't see every day," Alexi said in awe.

"Yeah, and not something I'll soon forget," agreed Áine.

Gray cleared his throat. "Okay, let's get a move on, people. We have a lot to do before tomorrow. Niall, will you please assist Alexi with getting the pixie back to the palace? We'll reach out to the fae community and look into finding her family when I return."

At the High Lord's quick nod, they all went their separate ways.

ISABELLA WAS HAVING A HARD TIME GETTING OVER THE amazing image of Azzertha's transformation from human to great silvery dragon and lifting gracefully into the air before their eyes, the sheen of her enormous shape against the pale light of the late afternoon sky. Even as Valian joined them and the group had settled in the war room to debrief, the image stayed with Isabella, making it difficult to concentrate. It was like nothing she could've ever imagined. And that the same great dragon actually knew who she was, knew her by name...well, it was something that Isabella didn't think she'd ever get over.

"Isabella?"

Gray's voice snapped her out of her thoughts, and she shook her head with a rueful smile. "Sorry." She chuckled, a bit embarrassed by her musings. "I'm just having trouble getting past watching a person turn into a dragon and fly away. It keeps replaying in my head. It's hard to put into words. So completely bizarre, yet so cool."

"Yes. I understand exactly what you mean. It was a pretty amazing sight. You can read about the great dragons all you want, hear the stories from those who've encountered them, but actually seeing one for yourself is an entirely different thing."

Taking a deep breath, Isabella centered herself and got down to business. "Anyway, what were you saying?"

The Prince laughed. "I asked you to take us through the questions you asked the Oracles and the answers you received. I'm hoping we can get a handle on what may be coming. Preferably before it gets here?"

Isabella nodded. "Absolutely. I've already told you the first thing we talked about. The whole magickal number of three and what it means for me, how it differs from Aly, and then the "Becoming" thing. That's where we had a hiccup. They seemed to think I should know what "Becoming" meant, and we can come back to that in a bit, but I did ask about my relationship with Aly and how close our families are, if it was a coincidence or some kind of preordained situation." She looked over at Alyssa and grinned. "Like Minerva, they said that there are no coincidences, and that many things in the universe are simply meant to be. However, they also made sure to tell me not to question what was meant because everything was connected and nothing happens before its time."

"Well, okay then," Alyssa laughed. "Guess they told us, right?"

Isabella nodded and turned to the Prince. "After that, I asked about our dreams, Gray," she said, flicking a snarky glance at Valian. "Like I told you before, my last dream was more like a nightmare and felt different, more tangible, almost like it was happening in real time."

"What did they say?" he asked.

She shook her head. "Their answer wasn't very helpful. They said that what we see in our dreams is or was or will be. So, I don't even know what to say about that."

"Yeah, that's pretty vague," Alexi grumbled. "And convoluted, if you ask me."

"But then I also asked about the men in the black robes, and if they knew about Tempest." She laughed again. "I don't think they were very happy with that question because they schooled me on it PDQ, told me that they were the Trinity, and that they knew everything."

"Oh, my." Alyssa tsked. "You little upstart. How dare you question the Trinity."

Isabella jabbed a finger at her. "Let me tell you, that's exactly what it felt like." She turned back to Gray. "Anyway, they did confirm that the men in the black robes are Ellurian elders, just as Minerva had indicated and as we'd suspected. They're our ancestors, Gray, and they are *not* extinct."

"Are you kidding?" Gray exclaimed. "I mean, I've had that thought off and on for a while now but couldn't see how it could possibly be true after all these years."

"Agreed." Niall nodded. "This is quite a surprising development. And yes, where have they been for centuries?"

"What I'm wondering is why this is only coming to light now." Valian added.

"I don't know about the why now, but evidently, they live in the Antiley mountain range where the race was born, as do the Caemmeirth. They also confirmed that Tempest—being half Ellurian—and her people live near those mountains."

"Just as we thought," Valian said.

Gray looked thoughtful. "Minerva said that the dragons wanted to help us with whatever was coming, and in my dream, Tempest told me the Ancients would be helping us as well but not to engage with them because it was not yet time. If they are going to assist us, then why aren't they communicating in our dreams? That doesn't make any sense."

Isabella nodded. "I asked that very question. The Oracles said they were 'waiting and watching.'"

"For what?" Alexi bellowed. "For fuck's sake, if you're going to help, then you don't just wait around until the eleventh hour, until the threat is at your door!"

"I know, right?" Isabella cried in exasperation. "And that's where the whole thing took the really scary turn."

"What do you mean, Izzy?" Alyssa asked.

Isabella gave Alyssa a perplexed look. "Well, when I asked what the elders were waiting for, the Oracles went kind of ballistic. Couldn't you hear them shrieking?" She looked around the table at the blank faces in surprise. "Seriously? None of you heard anything?"

"No. We didn't hear anything in the antechamber," Alexi said in confusion.

"Geez, that is so weird, because it was a pretty freaky show, I can tell you. Scared the crap right out of me. They told me the Unclean was coming, that it was darkness and thrived on destruction, fed on pain and misery. They also said this thing, whatever it is, wants to reign over everything in the realm. But mostly—and here's the kind of creepy and complicated part—it longs to be what it was but can no longer be because it's tainted and unnatural now." She gave a little shudder. "By the time they got to that point, they were shrieking like banshees and literally screamed at me that the Unclean had to be destroyed. Their light went crazy too and filled the whole chamber. It was friggin' blinding, but just when I'd decided to get the hell out of there, the tirade ended." She looked around the table again with a frown. "So, you didn't hear *any* of that?"

Gray cleared his throat. "Uh, no, not a peep."

"So weird," Isabella repeated. "Anyway, after that uproar, they calmed right down. I didn't really want to rile them up again, but I figured since we were on the subject, there was one more question that I should put out there."

"And what was that?" Valian asked.

"Well, if the recent deaths around the realm were connected to the Unclean."

"And?" Niall prompted in frustration. "What was the answer?"

"I got the same old *everything is connected* answer...at first. But then they told me something that might give us some kind of clue as to what this 'Unclean' is or was. They said, *The deaths are a requirement. Blood is the necessity. However, what is dark cannot be made light in this fashion.*" Isabella looked around the table one last time, hoping for the dawn of recognition, but was disappointed.

Gray shook his head. "I got nothin'."

"Me, neither. But I gotta say, I don't like any of this," Alexi added with a pained look.

"Yes, I'm in agreement, Alexi," Valian nodded. "This is getting more and more concerning."

"Well, I can ask Godmother," Áine said. "If anyone can tell us what it all could mean, it would probably be her."

"That's true," Niall murmured, and then grimaced. "However, I think I may have a fairly good idea of what she will say. It is a terrible thought, and I have no idea how it could be possible, but as you say, if anyone would know, it would be the Old One."

Sixteen

"So, do you want to share, Niall?" Gray asked, watching the High Lord's expression carefully. Niall could be quite cagey when it suited him, reluctant to share pertinent facts until it benefitted him—or, more accurately, his court—the most. But this was something that would not just affect the fae world but affect all of them, magickal and non-magickal alike. "Seriously, if you have a theory, we're all ears."

The High Lord narrowed his eyes and contemplated for a good twenty seconds before giving a succinct nod as if coming to a decision.

"It has to do with what Azzertha said about Qadira—the Dark Fae—not being defeated but just detained. My first thought was what does 'detained' mean? Does that mean that she's not dead? And if she's not, where was she detained all of this time? And how?" He frowned and leaned forward at the conference table. "My concern is that there were those who saw the Dark Fae die, as they did with Tempest. And Tempest had delivered that fatal blow to Qadira before succumbing to her own wounds."

"True." Valian frowned. "But there was never a confirmation about what happened to either body."

"Yes, and we now know that Tempest is half Ellurian which

makes her immortal. She can't die," Gray said. "Was the Dark Fae immortal? Do we know that?"

"That's my point," Niall said. "Qadira was an extremely powerful High Fae before she ever crossed the river into the underworld and became the Dark Fae. And like all High Fae, she would've had a very long lifespan. However, she was not immortal, therefore, if she was struck down, she could not regenerate."

"Could that trip to the underworld which made her the Dark Fae have also made Qadira immortal?" Gray asked with sudden concern.

Niall shook his head. "It did change her, strengthened her and her powers, and gave her other truly dreadful abilities. She became an abomination, but it would not have given her immortality as we know it. However, that is something else that we should talk to the Old One about. Perhaps Minerva can provide some clarification there." The High Lord thought for a moment. "I didn't connect what the Prince said in his reverie—and what the Oracles told Isabella about what was struck down rising again—with the Dark Fae until Azzertha's comment. My fear now is that Minerva will tell us that the Dark Fae is somehow still alive. Nevertheless, like I said, I don't see how that could be possible."

"I agree with the High Lord to a point," Áine said, looking around the table. "It would take some very powerful dark magicks to raise a malevolent being, especially if its essence had been tainted. I'm sure there's probably a way to do it, some kind of dark magick with which an entity could be brought back, but regardless, what was brought back would be severely and irrevocably changed."

"The same, yet different," Isabella murmured.

Áine nodded. "Exactly. If the Dark Fae is the Unclean the Oracles were talking about, that would make sense. If she was brought back, she could no longer be what she once was because her essence is now further tainted and unnatural. If Qadira was malevolent in the first place, before her change into the Dark Fae—which everything I've heard or learned about her indicates—the change or deterioration of her essence would be much, much worse."

"Which, if that's the scenario, wouldn't bode well for any of us," Valian added. "Ridding the realm of that poisonous bitch was close to impossible the first time around with thousands of lives lost in the process. It took years and, in the end, it was really all down to luck and timing."

Isabella sighed and ran a hand through her hair. "Look, I know that we're just speculating here, but if this is all true and this Qadira or Dark Fae is the Unclean, maybe she's also the monster I saw rising from the forest floor in my last dream. I mean, that terrifying black shape was coming right up out of the earth. And I think the fact that in my dream Tempest ran toward it with sword raised tells us that she knew exactly what it was as well."

"That would track," Alyssa said. "Also, here's another terrible thought. Though she didn't come right out and say it, Azzertha did allude to the recent deaths being connected to the Dark Fae."

"Yes. However, if Qadira has found a way back from whatever void or hell, or wherever she's been held after all this time, and if she's responsible for the deaths, I'd very much like to know how she's getting into the kingdoms," Valian said with a frown. "The Barrens or the Wastelands, sure, but the kingdoms? How's she getting through the security wards unseen or undetected?"

"And so close to the palace and the Temple of the Oracles," Alexi added.

"Yes, that's why I think the monster in my dream may hold the key," Isabella insisted. "What if it is Qadira? Maybe she's getting around the wards because she's not crossing through them but some-how...I don't know, coming up through the earth?"

"Like the golem did?" Alyssa looked at the others. "We all saw it. It just rose up out of the ground."

"Because it was made of earth," Alexi said, jabbing a finger at her. "Exactly."

"I'm not sure how that would be the case here. Remember, the golem was also mindless," Niall reminded them. "It was conjured from dark magick with specific instructions. It had no thought process other than what was introduced by the spell."

"That's true." Gray nodded. "So, that really doesn't fall into the what-was-struck-down-will rise-again category, does it? The golem was conjured from nothing."

"Yeah, and the Oracles did say that the deaths were required because blood was a necessity, right?" Alexi asked. "Why would a golem need blood?"

Gray leaned back and blew out a breath. "It wouldn't. But regardless, until we know more, we need to ramp up our patrols. The population of both kingdoms could be at risk. So far, the deaths have been limited to magickal beings, but are humans at risk as well?"

"Yeah, good question," Alexi said. "At least the magickal, depending on the race, have powers to protect themselves, but humans do not. So, how the hell do we get the word out? We don't want to start a panic in the non-magickal population without more concrete information to go on, right?"

"Agreed," Gray replied.

"Question?" Isabella put up a finger. "Non-magickal? Are you saying that there's a large number of us plain old humans living in this realm?"

Alexi grinned. "I hate to state the obvious, Bella, but you do know that you're not a 'plain old human,' correct?"

Isabella made a face. "You know what I mean. I just thought the population was mostly...well, others. You know? Fae and Elven, dwarves, and the rest of the magickal beings."

Alexi took her hand and gave it a squeeze. "Yes, the non-magickal —or the plain old humans—are a significant portion of the population in both kingdoms. There are hundreds of villages in both Wysteria and Roseland where humans and magickal work, play, and live side-by-side. It's kind of like your home realm where different nationalities are combined in cities and countries. It's a melting pot."

"I see."

Gray watched Isabella frown again; could almost see the wheels turning in her head. "What is it, Isabella? I can see that there's something else you're chewing over."

Isabella shrugged and nodded. "Well, what Alexi just said got me thinking about the rest of what the Oracles told me regarding the deaths, you know? Yes, they said the deaths were a requirement and the blood a necessity, but they also made clear something else. The dark can't be made light again in that way."

"Right. So, what are you getting at?"

"Well, I know that I'm new to this whole thing, but if the Dark

Fae is behind the deaths and using the blood in some kind of terrible ritual to try to rise from her own death, to become what she once was, I don't see how non-magickal beings would be at risk." She looked around the table. "I mean, seems like she would need magickal blood to do that, right?"

There was silence in the room for several moments before Áine started to chuckle.

"That is a really good point, Isabella, and I must admit, something I didn't even think about," she said. "Of course, Godmother can tell us for sure, and I'll get a hold of her as soon as possible, but it does make sense. If you're enacting dark magick to raise a dark magickal entity, I don't suppose human blood would do you much good. I think you're correct. You would need the blood of magickal beings, which may be why the deaths we've seen so far have all been from the enchanted races of the realm."

"I hope that's true," Alexi said. "Not that I wish that on anyone, but it will be much easier to spread the word throughout the magickal communities without causing too much panic."

"But that raises another issue that I've been questioning recently," Valian replied. "I've been thinking about the death of the first dryad in the Barrens. We thought it was Yulis' golem, but what if Yulis was part of the Dark Fae's plan from the start?"

"Oh, for the love of...that's a terrible theory, Val," Alexi complained. "Don't we have enough on our plates as it is? You gotta come up with more horrific crap to add?"

"I'm just saying. We have to think of every scenario as plausible until we can hone it down to what's actually relevant."

"Yeah, well, keep that list in your head, please. For my sake."

"Unfortunately, there's really no way to know for sure, as the Old One took care of that evil bastard in the mesa during our conflict with the Red King," Niall added. "And the golem would've been destroyed with Yulis' last breath, anyway."

"That's true," Valian murmured with a touch of skepticism, and then turned with a grin for his cousin. "As far as we know, that is."

"You're just such an ass at times," Alexi grumbled. "You know that?"

Gray laughed at the look on Alexi's face. "I'll tag Fin and let him know about the meeting tomorrow morning. Valian, I'm assuming that you'll be seeing Tisharu this evening?" At the Chancellor's nod, he continued. "Then you can give her the rundown and bring her to the palace for tomorrow morning's meeting if she's available. I think she may want to be here for the festivities."

Valian laughed. "Oh, that's a pretty sure bet."

Niall grinned. "I can guarantee that my twin would hate to be left out of this, especially with the Caemmeirth in attendance. Although, it would be a bit of a coup for me to hold that over her after the fact. She's very competitive, you know?"

"Yes, thank you. I'm well aware," Valian replied with a sour look.

Gray glanced at Niall. "Can you get word to Juppar? See if he would like to join our little party? Maybe he has more info on Kellum's possible part in all this by now that we can also go over."

The High Lord gave a brief nod. "We've tried to set up a meeting, but with the way things have gone over the last few days, Lord Finvar and I haven't been able to connect with Juppar yet, so I'll let him know."

"Okay. I'll talk to the Queen about our plans. She'll want to attend the meeting as well. Anyone else we need to invite?" When there were shaking heads all around, Gray closed his folder of notes. "Then I guess that's really all we can do until tomorrow morning when Azzertha returns to give us more information. So, anybody have anything else they want to add before we adjourn for now?"

When no one spoke up for that either, Isabella raised her hand.

"Yes, what is it, Isabella?" Gray asked.

"Well, if we're finished with this for the time being, can we revisit something for me? You said you could help me understand what the Oracles meant by *Becoming*."

"Oh, of course! I'm sorry," Gray apologized. "Thanks for the reminder. As I've only just gotten that information myself and, like me, your Becoming is in relation to your fae heritage, I'm going to ask Lord Niall to explain it for us." He turned to Niall with a smirk. "Niall, would you like to do the honors and give Isabella the rundown?"

Gray smiled inwardly as he watched the High Lord stiffen, watched his jaw tighten. If the High Lord of the Twilight Court was going to be part of the team, Gray felt he really needed to get more involved with the issues of said team. And Isabella Doyle Christensen, freshly minted Halfling, was definitely part of that team now.

"Niall?" Gray prompted when the High Lord had yet to say anything. He saw Alyssa lay a hand on Niall's arm, watched the High Lord take a breath and nod. He obviously wasn't happy, but he cleared his throat and complied.

"'Becoming' is an old fae term, Isabella. It's not used much these days, as it refers to a faerie or a Halfling whose power hasn't yet awakened. To 'Become' is to have those powers, your fae essence, finally begin to emerge."

Isabella blinked several times. "Oh."

"Well, 'Becoming' isn't necessarily just a fae term," Valian added. "This is also a term familiar in the Elven world where it has much the same meaning for us."

"It's all just so confusing. The Oracles told me that I would find my power when I *Become*, but I don't seem to be finding anything at all." Isabella shook her head. "Is it normal to have it happen so late? Or not at all? Or maybe they're just wrong about me."

Niall snorted. "Not likely."

"It's infrequent, but gaining one's powers later in life does occur in both races, Isabella," Valian said. "I don't know that there's much rhyme or reason to it, but it happens."

"Agreed. It does happen," Niall spoke up without taking his eyes off Isabella. "Though I disagree with you on one point, Chancellor, and will remind Isabella of what the Trinity told her to make that point. *Everything* is connected, and nothing happens before its time."

Slowly, Isabella began to smile. "Thank you for that reminder, High Lord."

"You are very welcome, little Halfling."

THE NEXT MORNING ARRIVED WITH ANTICIPATION RIDING high in the palace for the arrival of the Caemmeirth. Though there had been no announcement or discussion, word traveled quickly through the staff, and the palace was abuzz with excitement.

It had been unclear if Azzertha would be the only elder in atten-dance or if she would bring an elder or two of the other clans along with her. Gray was really hoping that the latter would turn out to be the case. Since Valian, Niall, Tisharu, Finvar, and possibly Juppar, all had some level of experience with the great dragons from fighting alongside them in the war, Gray and Alexi were a bit behind the curve, so to speak. Of course, Gray was mostly just curious and fasci-nated by the great dragons, which for all of his life he'd been taught were mythical beings. To find out that they were real was...well, it was extraordinary, incomprehensible.

"Are you about ready to meet with the Caemmeirth?" Áine asked as she approached from the direction of the dining room with a couple of steaming mugs in her hands. "I was bringing you a mug of Gryphon's amazing café mocha because it's early, and since I hadn't seen you in the dining room for breakfast yet, I figured you would need it."

Gray reached out and took the mug she offered. "Thanks. Since Azzertha didn't say exactly when they would be arriving this morn-ing, I got up early and did some prep downstairs. Time kind of got away from me, so I was just coming up to grab something." He inclined his head toward the dining room in the direction that she'd just come. "Walk with me. We can have a quick bite together. And then I've got some questions. A few things that I'd like to clear up."

They turned in tandem and walked back down the hallway to the empty dining room where the sideboards were still laden with breakfast fare.

Then he glanced at Áine. "Looks like we've got the place to ourselves. You gonna eat?"

She shook her head. "I had something earlier with the Queen and Lord Finvar, but knock yourself out."

Gray shrugged and took a plate, adding a healthy mound of scrambled eggs, four slices of crisp bacon, and two slices of toast for good measure. When he got to the table, she eyed him and his plate.

"What?" he asked.

"That's your quick bite?"

"Hey, you know what they say? Breakfast is the most important meal of the day."

She raised an eyebrow. "Is that what they say?"

"It's true," he insisted and watched her lips spread in a smile.

Gray thought, and not for the first time, how lovely Áine had become. She'd grown from that tall, lanky girl he'd first known into a poised, confident beauty. She was smart, witty, and unafraid to say exactly what she thought. He liked that about her. Though she was a Halfling like him, and Minerva's goddaughter, Áine lived and worked in Ireland. Gray hadn't seen her in too many years to count until the past summer when Tisharu had been poisoned, but now he was looking at her in a whole new light...and wondering.

"Gray?"

He gave himself a mental shake. "I'm sorry. What?"

"You said you had questions. What about?"

He sat down with his plate and mug before looking up and sharing his thoughts.

"How soon did your fae powers start to show themselves?" he asked, watching her eyebrows raise in surprise.

"Are you asking because Isabella has yet to *Become*?"

Gray took a bite of his eggs and washed them down with a few sips of his café mocha, then shook his head. "Not entirely. I mean, I had some inkling of powers early on. Healing, mending, and there were other abilities that I ignored, mostly because I was lazy."

"That's not true."

He pointed at her with his fork. "It is, and you know it. And the abilities I did use were sloppy at best because of it. Geez, Áine, after Alexi and I were ambushed last New Year's, when the Scepter of Fire was taken from us by Richter and the Red King's fae warriors, Alexi could've died on me in that forest. And he just about did. That was all down to me not honing the abilities that had already presented themselves."

Her smile was kind. "Gray, you couldn't have predicted what happened that night, and in the end, you saved Alexi's life while in the process of almost losing yours from that heinous fae poison, remember?"

He put up a hand. "Oh, trust me, I remember quite well. My point is that I had some of my powers early on—though I didn't really understand where they were coming from—but hadn't really started the process of Becoming until the Faerie Bomb incident at Minerva's cabin. I'd certainly never faded by myself before that moment. Did you...start early on? Or did it take a while for you as well?"

Áine cocked her head and pursed her lips. "My Becoming began in my early teens. I didn't really know what was happening to me, either, but I was fortunate that my mom snapped to it. Thankfully, she contacted Godmother as soon as she did. I came to live with her here for almost six months. During that time, she guided me through the process, taught me how to use my abilities, how to navigate new ones that arose from time to time. She taught me many things during those months, about potions and herbs, about fae history."

Gray pushed his plate aside and picked up his mug. "I didn't know you lived with Minerva back then."

"I think it was about the time you and Alexi went off to school in the New York realm."

"Huh." Gray watched her face—her very expressive face—before catching himself and clearing his throat. "Anyway, about Isabella, any theories on why she's just now learning about her heritage, and why she hasn't exhibited any abilities so far?"

"Well, could be a lot of reasons, but I think some more obscure abilities have actually been manifesting long before now."

Gray frowned. "What do you mean?"

"You should talk to the Queen. Evidently, she and Alyssa had a conversation about it when Isabella was still missing. There were some indications of fae abilities when she was younger."

"Really? Interesting. I'll talk to my mother and see what that entailed." Gray finished his café mocha and set his mug aside. "The other thing I was wondering is, have you spoken to Minerva about the deaths and the possibility of a dark spell being somehow used in conjunction? How that would work?"

Áine grinned. "I did."

"And?"

"*And*, she listened to everything we'd discovered, everything that the Oracles told Isabella, and all that Azzertha had told us so far, and then became quite evasive about the whole thing."

"Even with you?"

"Even with me," Áine replied. "It was weird, but not completely out of the ordinary. However, I will say that she seemed—though not worried, per se—maybe a bit uneasy when I told her about the possibility of the Dark Fae being the 'Unclean' the Oracles had spoken about."

"Minerva? Uneasy? That's not very comforting, now, is it?"

Áine leaned toward him and spoke in a whisper. "Not in the least."

Gray made a face. "Great."

"However, she was very interested about the visit today from the Caemmeirth. So, maybe she'll pop around to join us for the meeting with them."

"You think so?" Gray asked with a touch of skepticism.

"You never know. She does like to keep people guessing." Áine placed her hand over his. "Don't worry. We're going to figure this out, right?"

Gray looked into her trusting gaze and felt his own uneasiness recede just a bit. "Guess we'll give it a try." He paused. "Áine, when this is all over—"

He wasn't certain exactly what he was going to ask her, but his thoughts were interrupted by Gryphon.

"Your Grace, your visitors have arrived. They are waiting for you in the great hall."

"Thank you, Gryphon. Tell them we'll be right in."

"Very good, Sire."

When the chamber elf left the room, Gray turned back to Áine.

"What were you saying?" she asked expectantly.

He shook his head. "It can wait. I guess we better get this meeting started."

Seventeen

s Gray and Áine entered the great hall, they found the small
group awaiting them and quietly talking among themselves.
When Azzertha spotted them, she turned with a smile.

"Good morning, Prince Graydon, Áine. I hope we're not too
early...or too late. We had to make a quick stop in the Barrens on the
way here and ran into a most disturbing situation that took some
time to mitigate."

"No worries." Gray met the Gheori elder with a smile and a
shake of his head. "You're not too early or too late. Your timing is
perfect, Azzertha. Not all of our group is here yet, but should be
arriving directly. So, we can go down to the conference room and get
comfortable while we wait."

"Very good. Then let me introduce you to my companions," she
said gesturing to the three others standing with her. "This is Issai
elder, Erthos."

The muscular male with short, blue-black hair, pale blue skin,
and bright, cerulean-blue eyes stepped forward as she introduced
him. Saying nothing, he gave a brief nod and then stepped back.

Gray remembered the description Valian had given of the reti-
cent, blue-plated dragons, but wasn't prepared for their stunning
appearance in human form.

"And this is Nyrilio elder, Ridar." Azzertha gestured to the large, swarthy male sporting a bright-red buzz cut and eyes that mirrored the fiery inferno burning within him. Ridar did not step forward but gave Gray an unnerving stare.

Remembering the earlier discussion with Niall and Finvar regarding the Nyrilio breed, Gray swallowed hard, acknowledged the dragon with a quick nod, and then quickly moved on to the last of the group. However, here, he paused, astonished by the exquisite, statuesque female who held out her hand with a captivating smile.

"I am Ugharess, elder of the Airsayrth clan," she murmured.

Gray took her hand but literally lost his breath for a moment as he looked up at her sculpted face. Ugharess stood head and shoulders above everyone else in the group. She was regal, magnificent, with her long, golden hair and warm, burnished skin tone, but her iridescent eyes were what held Gray's attention. They were mesmerizing. Looking into her gaze was like falling into a vat of pure liquid gold.

"It's a pleasure to meet you, Ugharess," he murmured after a moment and forced himself to let go of her hand before he stepped back. It was all but impossible to look away from those incredible eyes, but he finally tore his gaze from hers.

"Thank you all for coming," he said, and then turned back to Azzertha to get his bearings. "You said that you ran into a disturbing situation in the Barrens. That's not surprising considering some of its inhabitants. What kind of situation? Was it related to the deaths we've been seeing around the realm?"

The Nyrilio elder grunted—a fierce sound filled with rage—and Azzertha gave him a look of warning. Turning her attention back to Gray, she smiled. "Yes. It certainly has bearing on what we're here to discuss, but perhaps we can wait until all attendees have arrived to speak of it, so as not to repeat the information."

"Of course," Gray replied, inwardly dreading what additional chaos this new information would bring.

"The Chancellor and Tisharu are already here in the palace, Graydon," Áine added. "I think they came in late last night, and Alexi and Isabella should be down shortly if they are not already waiting in the war room."

Gray hesitated a moment and was about to suggest that they head downstairs to wait when Alyssa, Niall, Finvar, and Juppar entered the hall from the outer courtyard. "Ah, good. Here are a few more of our attendees now."

Gray turned to Áine. "Can you go and find Gryphon, please? Have him inform the Queen that we'll be convening in the war room in a bit. And give Val a heads up that we're on our way there now."

"Absolutely."

He watched her go as the new arrivals joined the group.

"Azzertha," Niall said in greeting.

"Good morning, Niall." The Gheori elder turned to Finvar. "And High Lord Finvar. It has been a long time."

Finvar gave a small bow. "It has. High Lord Niall informed me of your presence yesterday. It is good to see you again after so many years."

Azzertha smiled and gestured to the other three elders. "I believe you both will remember Ridar. Also with us are Erthos and Ugharess."

Gray watched the face of the two high lords. There was caution for Ridar, intrigue for Erthos, and a sense of awe for Ugharess.

"Why don't we all go on downstairs now and get settled while we wait for the last of the group," Gray suggested. "When the Queen arrives, we can do another round of introductions and then get started."

The group agreed and followed the Prince downstairs to the war room where they found Alexi and Isabella already seated and waiting.

"Make yourselves comfortable," Gray said, gesturing toward the table. "This is Field Marshal Tovin and Isabella Christensen. Alexi, Isabella, let me present the Caemmeirth elders: Azzertha—whom you've already met, Erthos, Ridar, and Ugharess."

"Good to meet you all," Alexi acknowledged with reticence.

"Prince Graydon, regarding the pixie you found yesterday, did you find her people?" Azzertha asked.

Gray nodded. "Yes. Her family resides in the forest just to the north of the Summer Court in the southern quadrant. We returned her home yesterday afternoon. Evidently, the family had been looking for her. She was supposed to meet with her cousins farther north near the Autumn Court. Unfortunately, she never made the meeting, and when she hadn't come home by the late afternoon, they sent out search parties, but she wasn't found, probably because they were looking for her in the wrong area."

"If her family resides down near the southern horn, what was she doing north of the Temple where you found her?" Juppar asked. "That's a fair distance even from the Autumn Court's location where she should have been."

"Yes. It is." Alexi frowned. "Her parents and the elders of the family had no idea why she would've been that far north and so much closer to the border...and the Barrens. We'll definitely have to do some investigating there. Valian and I have already discussed it. It's way too similar to the dryad we found in the old growth area north of Willow Glen Wood this last summer."

"That is troubling, indeed," the Gheori elder replied.

Before they got much further, Valian and Tisharu came through the door.

"Ah, here's the Chancellor and Queen Tisharu. I believe you know both of them." Gray nodded toward the door.

"Yes. Valian," Azzertha nodded. "You are looking well."

Valian smiled. "Azzertha. Welcome to the White Palace. It's good to see you, though I wish it was under better circumstances." He eyed Ridar briefly, and then addressed Gray. "The Queen should be here directly, along with Áine."

"Tisharu, you seem recovered and quite fit after your deathly ordeal this last summer," Azzertha mused. "No lingering ill effects, I hope."

The Queen of the Twilight Court's eyebrows shot up in surprise. "You knew of my...unfortunate illness?"

The Gheori elder gave her a cryptic look. "We were aware. As we understand it, the Old One's goddaughter was key in your recovery. That was fortunate."

Tisharu lifted her chin and gave Azzertha a keen look. "It was fortunate, indeed. The Halfling saved my life, and I am extremely grateful for it."

Gray cleared his throat. "Yes, well, speaking of which, here's Áine and Queen Beatrice now."

Everyone already seated stood in deference as the Queen

approached. Once she'd taken her seat next to Gray at the head of the table, the rest of the group sat as well.

"Why don't we get the last round of introductions out of the way, and then we can move on to why we're here in the first place." Gray turned to the Queen and introduced the dragon shifters one by one.

"Though we've never met, most of us knew your father, Seanchán of the North," Ugharess murmured. "Of course, that was long ago. He was a great ruler. Kind, intelligent, and compassionate."

"He was also not one to be trifled with," Ridar added with obvious respect. "He was a formidable warrior and protector of his clans and didn't suffer fools as so many are wont to do these days."

Ugharess nodded. "His passing was a terrible loss for his people, a loss that has not been forgotten to this very day."

Queen Beatrice looked stunned for a moment but recovered quickly. "That is very kind of you to say, Ugharess, Ridar. Thank you."

Ridar grunted again. "It is but the truth."

There was a drawn-out pause as all eyes were on the red dragon who stared back almost in defiance.

"Right. Well, let's get this meeting underway then, shall we?" Gray began, breaking the silence and wanting to move things along. "But first, Azzertha, you said that your group ran across a situation in the Barrens on the way here this morning, and that it has bearing on our discussion. Could you give us a rundown of what that entailed and how it's related to what's happening around the realm?"

"I will ask Erthos to give you the details, as he was the one contacted regarding the situation in the first place," she replied, turning to the Issai elder.

Erthos leaned forward. "I have an acquaintance in the Barrens, a sand spirit who sent word that he had stumbled across something he felt that we should see, so we made a stop to check it out on the way here. One of the things we found was a dead water nymph."

"And was this nymph's death the same as the others that have been found?" Niall asked.

"It was."

"You said *one* of the things you found." Valian leaned forward, his look keen. "There was something else?"

Erthos glanced at Azzertha, and then continued. "We found the nymph when we first arrived. My contact guided us to the edge of the river where the body was located. But as we were examining the nymph, there was suddenly a terrible rumble and the earth itself began to quake. The tremors seemed to originate up river from where we were standing, so we changed back into dragon form and followed, wanting to see what was making the earth shake so."

"That sounds familiar," Alexi said, and shot a look of concern to Gray. "Like what we experienced with the golem, perhaps?"

Gray nodded. "That thought did cross my mind, especially with this happening in the Barrens."

"So, what did you find?" Alexi asked the Issai elder. "Could you locate the source?"

Erthos nodded. "About an eighth of a mile upstream, we found a darkness; a diaphanous, black shape partially enveloping a kelpie at the water's edge. The beast was struggling mightily to get free and away, but seemed unable to do so. It was a horrible sight."

Isabella gasped. "Oh, geez! A huge black shape? Just like the thing from my last nightmare. It came right up out of the ground."

"You've seen this in your dreams?" Azzertha asked with raised eyebrows.

"Sounds like what I saw. It was frightening." Isabella looked apprehensive. "Although, in my dream, it happened in the forest, and it wasn't trying to eat anything, at least I don't think it was. Anyway, Tempest was with me. She said that I shouldn't be found there and told me to run. Then she went charging toward it. That was when I woke up."

"I see."

"The kelpie's screams were pitiful, terrifying." Erthos continued. "He was a good-sized water horse, too, which are normally quite formidable, but he couldn't seem to disentangle himself from the dark entity even with his magicks."

"What did you do when you came upon the situation, Erthos?" Finvar asked. "Did the entity turn on you? Did it kill the kelpie?"

"What did we do?" Ridar ground out. "We were in dragon form, so we fried the dark entity's ass on the spot. That's what we did." The Nyrilio elder gave the High Lord a disgusted look. "We weren't just going to stand around and watch while another magickal being was slaughtered."

Erthos put up a hand to silence Ridar. "The kelpie disappeared into the river, High Lord, and the dark thing dissolved back into the earth almost immediately."

"So, you don't know what happened to the kelpie?" Alyssa asked sitting forward, worry evident in her tone. "I have a kelpie friend in the Barrens, you see, who helped me escape from the Red King and his sorcerer, Yulis, last summer when I'd been kidnapped. The chances that it was him are probably remote, but..."

Ridar's brows drew together, and he looked at Alyssa with disbelief. "You have a kelpie *friend*? That's...interesting."

"Cianán had also been imprisoned against his will, and they would have killed him when they were done with him. We made a pact. Minerva got us out of the mesa prison, but he gave his word to her that he would see me safely to the Wysterian border."

"Curious," Ridar murmured, sitting back in his seat and crossing his muscular arms. "That's a dangerous gamble, trusting a kelpie. Of course, if you give the Old One your word, to break it would be perilous, of which I'm certain this kelpie had to have been aware."

The red dragon shifter grinned at Alyssa then, and Gray was amazed at the transformation of his countenance. He looked, briefly, almost approachable.

"Regardless, you showed great courage and ingenuity in making the pact in the first place," Ridar said, grin still in place and a touch of respect coloring his tone. "I'm assuming this kelpie did as he promised?"

Alyssa smiled back at him. "He did that and more. He helped us in the fight against the Red King's forces and kept me safe while doing so."

"Curiouser and curiouser," he replied, and then shook his head. "Unfortunately, it's impossible to tell you if the kelpie we found this morning in the dark entity's deadly embrace survived or even if it had injuries. He disappeared quickly beneath the waterline, and we never saw him again."

"And you didn't see the entity again, either?" Finvar asked. "I don't suppose we could hope for its destruction."

Ridar shook his head again. "We scorched the spot where it vanished as well, just to be sure, but I don't know how much good that did. It was already gone."

"Yes, whatever it was, our fire seemed to scare it off, but it didn't destroy it," Erthos added. "Regrettably, we did also find a selkie in the area later that had not been so lucky as to get away. It was a small fresh water seal, and its death was the same as the nymph's and all the others, so this dark thing is what has been doing the killing around the realm." He looked disturbed. "And it is getting worse."

"Sounds like it," Gray murmured. "Is this the first time you've run across this dark entity?"

Azzertha nodded. "It is. There have been times when we could sense it, perhaps we'd just missed it, but we've never actually seen it until this morning."

"It seems that you and Isabella are the only ones to witness its appearance to date. That it's now being spotted can't be a good thing," Gray said. He thought for a moment. "You told us yesterday that you had been waiting and watching for centuries, that you knew this day would come because the Dark Fae hadn't been defeated but just detained. So, do you think that is what's happening, that this is the Dark Fae? The 'Unclean' the Oracles spoke of with Isabella?"

"We do. Yes," Ugharess replied.

"But how?" Niall asked impatiently. "There are those who saw her struck down. And Qadira was not immortal. Powerful, yes. Full of dark magicks acquired when she crossed into the underworld and became the Dark Fae, assuredly. But not immortal. How is it possible for her to return?"

"By those same dark magicks, High Lord," a gravelly voice came from the doorway.

All eyes turned to find the Witch of the Eastern Glade, the oldest, most powerful sorceress in the realm, standing just inside the room in all her magickal glory.

"Minerva," the Queen exclaimed. "What do you know of this?"

"The Old One is the reason that the Dark Fae has been held in check for this long," Ugharess murmured.

"Ah, yes," Minerva said as she came toward the table. "But my efforts were not enough, were they? Would never be enough. We knew it even then, knew the day would come when someone—one of her cult followers, perhaps—would find a way to break the spell I performed and let loose their monster onto the realm once again."

"Indeed, we did," Azzertha acknowledged. "However, you did all that you could at the time, Old One, and your spell has held for centuries. From that fateful day, the Caemmeirth have waited and watched as we'd promised to do. Perhaps we were not as vigilant as we should have been in the recent months, and thus, may have missed the first vital signs in midsummer of Qadira's return."

Minerva shook her head and held out a hand to the Gheori elder, who took it in her own. "There is no blame in this ugliness, Azzertha. We all knew that Qadira would find a way back...eventually. It was only a matter of time. I, myself, did not want to believe what the reports so clearly indicated, hoping they were wrong, but there it is. All we can do now is to put aside what we wished for and confront what is."

The old sorceress turned toward the group, who were watching and listening with rapt attention. "A storm is coming. At this point, that's not news to any around this table. However, most understand the consequences better than the few. Chancellor, you, the three high lords, and Queen Tisharu all fought in the Great War and know exactly what is coming."

"Yes," Valian murmured. "But if Qadira is the Unclean the Oracles spoke of with Isabella, they indicated that—even with dark magick—she may not be what she once was, she would be changed."

The old witch nodded. "That is true. However, I fear that the Dark Fae may be...more this time around."

"But being brought back with dark magicks? Wouldn't that further taint her, Godmother?" Áine asked. "Wouldn't it make the change or deterioration of her essence much worse? Perhaps she'll be weaker not stronger?"

"I suppose that would depend on the magicks used." Minerva frowned. "Yet, it is the blood that concerns me. Blood magick is one of the strongest in the dark realm of spells."

"Why is that a concern, Minerva?" Queen Beatrice asked.

"Because of how the Dark Fae died."

"Ah-ha! First, we're told that Qadira wasn't defeated, just *detained*—whatever that was supposed to mean—yet now you're saying that she *did* die, as so many others had witnessed on that battlefield." Tisharu complained in exasperation. "Make up your mind, Old One. It cannot be both." The fae Queen wrinkled her nose and gave Minerva a distrusting look. "So, did she die or not? And if she did die, it is still unclear to me—and I know, to others around this table—exactly how she could be brought back at all, blood magicks or not. She...was...not...*immortal.*"

Tisharu's last word was spat at the old witch in anger, and Minerva stared at the fae Queen with a steely gaze. Gray was stunned that Tisharu would take that tone with the most powerful being in the realm and thought she was walking a very thin line. However, she held the old witch's gaze and didn't back down an inch.

"Well, what say you, witch?" the fae Queen muttered.

By the look on Minerva's face, Gray feared she would react with her own anger, but after a few moments of silence, she relaxed and gave a weary nod. When she finally spoke, her tone was just as weary as her countenance. "Your outrage is valid, Tisharu. You deserve to know the truth of what transpired on that fateful day, a secret that has been held close for over two centuries."

"The truth of what transpired?" Valian asked. "What truth? Are you saying that our documented history is a lie? That the Dark Fae didn't perish from Tempest's mortal blows?"

The old witch shook her head. "No, Chancellor. The documented history is correct. However, it is...incomplete. Qadira did die, but history does not tell us of what came after."

Eighteen

The room erupted into a cacophony of angry questioning voices at Minerva's astounding proclamation.

"Enough!" Sparks flew as the old sorceress magickly silenced those voices with a sharp slash of her hand in the air. "I will not shout over your anger. You will hold a civil tongue or pay the consequences," she snapped. Taking a deep breath, she released it—and them—from her hold. "I will explain, but I will have order as I do so," she said in a calmer tone. "This is not a game. It is a perilous situation and cooler heads are required. There is much to tell you, much that you will need to understand before this threat can be addressed and destroyed, and our time is running short as it is."

"Minerva, what do you mean when you say that our historic records are incomplete? What don't we know?" Queen Beatrice asked. "And why was it kept secret for over two centuries?"

The old witch sighed and sat down at the table between the Queen and the Chancellor. "Toward the end of the Great War, hope was rapidly beginning to dim," the old witch began. "The entire realm had been engulfed in the conflict for decades, and in those last few months, morale was at a particularly low point for all involved."

"I'll vouch for that," Finvar said quietly. "It seemed that the battles had raged everywhere for months, years unending, and it felt as if we would gain ground one day only to lose twice as much the next...or sometimes within hours."

"Yes, Qadira's forces were dedicated from the start, but relentless and punishing toward the end," Tisharu added in a much-restrained voice. "And they didn't discriminate. They killed thousands, warrior and innocent alike. Holding the line, pushing back that line, and all the while keeping up morale among our own forces, was beginning to be an impossible task. We were losing the war, and we could all feel it."

Valian nodded. "Then we caught a break and gained some much-needed momentum."

He was thinking back now to the end of a war that had raged on for far too long, that had come close to destroying everything they'd all held dear. A war that had taken so much from each of them. He could still remember those last few weeks with vivid clarity—the sights, the sounds, the almost jubilant feel—when the tide seemed to turn. Those were heady days filled with the hope that had been all but lost.

And then Tempest had made the ultimate sacrifice. She'd given her life in an effort to end Qadira, and end the war for them all.

For over two centuries, they thought that Tempest had done just that.

"We were all so weary of war by the time the end came," he continued after a moment. "I've said it before, and it bears repeating, though it was a win that we embraced, the end that Tempest finally gave us was all just down to luck and timing."

"Luck and timing, of course, but also the immortal warrior's amazing abilities...her sacrifice," Tisharu insisted. "And, yes, though we grieved for her, we also rejoiced. The Dark Fae had been destroyed, was dead. Or so we thought."

"Well, I for one don't relish counting on good fortune in another round with an evil we all thought dead and buried," Valian replied.

"Nor do I," Niall agreed. He turned to Minerva. "So, what happened, Old One? What doesn't the historical record include? And how is it possible that after two centuries, we're having to face Qadira's threat all over again?"

Minerva stared at the far wall for a moment, and Valian knew she was remembering, could almost see it in her eyes. She was visualizing it all again in her mind, though what the Old One would recall would be far worse than anything he would remember. Of that, he was certain.

"I was on the other side of the Unwelcoming Rise when that end came for the Dark Fae," she finally began. "I'd been in a meeting in the Antiley mountains with the Ellurian elders when I got word. However, it wasn't quite what I'd expected. Yes, Qadira had been struck down, but there was a problem."

"What kind of problem?" Alexi asked, his attention, riveted.

"As Tempest was beginning to revive, some of her people came to assist her back to court where she could safely finish her regeneration. When they arrived to do so, they found that the Dark Fae's remains were also doing something quite unexpected and extraordinary. Qadira's body was...deteriorating at an accelerated rate, her blood, sinking into the earth where she'd dropped."

"Oh, no," Áine whispered.

Minerva nodded. "Yes, child. With the training I've given you, you can understand what these signs would most probably mean."

"Understand what?" Gray asked.

Áine turned to him, her look grim. "Clearly, if someone is struck down on a battlefield, their blood would soak into the earth where their body lay bleeding, but that Qadira's body itself was deteriorating quickly is a red flag for a dark spell. A death spell if I'm not mistaken."

The old sorceress smiled at her goddaughter with obvious pride. "You are not mistaken."

"Okay," Valian said. "So, what kind of death spell was this?"

"And who conjured it and when?" Tisharu asked. "Don't these kinds of spells need to be established prior to death? Aren't they more of a precaution? A safeguard or an insurance policy of sorts, yes?"

"You are correct, Tisharu. That is the main reason a death spell is usually created. There obviously were questions that needed to be addressed, but time was short. Those pertinent questions had to be set aside, as the spell had to be dealt with, negated if possible, before it was too late."

When Minerva paused with eyes closed, Valian felt a sinking feeling in the pit of his belly.

"Before it was too late?" he asked quietly. "Are you saying that there was an issue of timing with this spell?"

When the Old One opened her eyes, he could see his answer residing in their depths before she even spoke.

"Yes, as there is with all death spells. Once the victim's essence is completely absorbed into the earth...they can be resurrected with blood rituals at any time thereafter."

"But that would essentially have made Qadira an immortal waiting to happen from the moment the spell was put into place." Niall shook his head and ran a hand over his face as his grasp of the dire situation they were in solidified.

"An accurate description, High Lord. That's exactly what it would do," Áine confirmed. "You see, that's the end game of most death spells, from what I've found through my research and studies." She looked to her godmother—who gave a brief nod—before continuing. "Most basically make the individual it's created for *temporarily* immortal—usually a one-time event—because they can facilitate resurrection at a later date."

"Temporarily? *Usually* a one-time event?" Finvar shook his head. "I do not like the sound of that."

Áine sighed. "Unfortunately, the darker the spell, the worse the news gets."

"For fuck's sake, how much worse can it get?" Alexi exclaimed, then recanted. "No, never mind. I don't think I even want to know."

"I understand how you feel, Alexi," she replied. "Because depending on the incantation—and who has administered it—the spell can replicate the process over and over again into perpetuity." She leaned back in her chair and glanced at her godmother again. "Unless the death spell is invalidated by a corresponding counter spell within a certain period of time, that is."

Minerva smiled at Áine but it held little mirth. "Again, you are correct in your explanation, child."

"And?" Valian prompted, leaning forward and giving the old

witch a look of concern. Like Finvar, so far, he wasn't liking this new information either. And by the look on the Old One's face, he doubted he'd like her conclusion.

"And...I arrived too late to administer the counter spell," she murmured. "The Ellurian elders and I rushed to the field where both Qadira and the fae warrior had fallen as soon as we received the news, but the Dark Fae's body had been completely absorbed into the earth by the time we arrived. All that could be done at that point was to seal the ground that had become saturated with her essence and hope for the best."

"Hope for the *best*?" Alexi looked stricken. "What does *that* mean?"

"An incarceration spell," Áine said with a nod of understanding. "Hence the 'detained' reference."

Minerva also nodded. "Yes. As Azzertha mentioned earlier, it was the best that I could do, as the damage had been done. Someone had conjured a very dark and incredibly sophisticated death spell that had already taken form. Regrettably, an incarceration spell was the only thing left to us."

"And that's what you did?" Finvar asked. "How does this incarceration spell work?"

"These kinds of spells are a form of binding ritual. They work along with an emulsion made from powerful herbs, such as Agrimony, Asafoetida, and a healthy amount of salt." The Old One took a deep breath. "In this case, the tainted earth was doused with the powerful emulsion, and then a particularly strong binding spell was introduced, sealing the ground and preventing the entity held there from any kind of resurrection."

"Yet, it did not hold," Tisharu murmured. "Why?"

"Oh, I knew that it may not hold for an eternity, that it was possible for the incarceration spell that I put into place to be circumvented, but it was not something that just anyone with a basic grimoire or spellbook could accomplish. Someone with considerable knowledge had introduced it. As I said, the death spell was sophisticated, intricate, and strong. The incarceration spell had to be more so, which it was."

Minerva pursed her lips in thought before continuing. "In the beginning, I believed that it was Yulis' work. I believe it still, for that matter. He'd been an astute apprentice when he was younger, but he and I had parted ways in the Great War's infancy when he started to believe that he had surpassed me, knew more, was more. He let greed and the thirst for power overwhelm him, begin to diminish what he could have grown to be. Unfortunately, I could not prove his involvement in Qadira's death spell, and of course, now, I can never be sure. However, to my knowledge, he was the only one with the power and training to administer such a spell...thanks to my tutelage."

Áine shook her head. "You saw his potential, took him under your wing, and guided him. You taught him to use what was alight within him already. The fact that he turned his light toward the darkness, yearned for more power, and then used what he had for evil pursuits is not on you, Godmother." She shook her head again. "Yet, even with lofty ambitions, he was never a match for you, and never would have been."

"No. That is true," Minerva replied. "And I am aware that knowing that truth was something that ate at him. Which, I'm sorry to say, diminished him even further. He could have become a very skillful sorcerer had he listened to me, learned patience, and gained compassion for his environment. However, he lacked empathy and the understanding of humanity that was necessary for his growth. He let malice and hate, his treatment as a child, destroy him from the inside out. I tried over the years to help him out of his death spiral—for in the end, that is what it was—but he would have none of it. It gave me no joy to end him the way I did, but it was an act of mercy."

"Well, you can call it that, if you'd like, but I would call it a necessity for the well-being of the realm," Valian muttered. "Yulis was to blame for too many atrocities to count in his quest for power and control during his tenure with the Red King, so I don't find the possibility of his involvement with Qadira or her followers that much of a stretch."

When the Old One simply cocked her head and stared at him with a narrow-eyed look, Valian thought it best to change the subject. "Anyway, it sounds to me like perhaps this death spell could have been Qadira's plan all along. To effectively die at a certain point and be resurrected by her followers...resurrected as an immortal for all eternity, I might add."

Niall nodded. "That would definitely be a sound plan, if you are intent on taking over the realm and are a malevolent bitch drunk on power and ambition, that is."

"Which Qadira most certainly was," Tisharu grumbled with a look of disdain. "That and more. I agree with Valian. I can see her and Yulis working together quite easily."

"Yes. That very well could have been her strategy from the start," Minerva murmured. "With Yulis to do the honors."

"But then you sealed the ground where the Dark Fae fell, and no one could break your spell." Áine sighed. "Not even Yulis."

"Until now," Tisharu replied sharply. "Who would have the know-how, the magickal prowess to administer a blood ritual to raise the evil bitch now?"

"I can't speak to that specifically, but I may have some clues to follow," Juppar spoke up.

"Really? Do tell, High Lord," Minerva replied. "What clues have you discovered that may be relevant?"

"Before the events of this last summer, a concern had arisen for those of us residing in the north of Wysteria," Juppar began.

"A concern? What sort of concern?" Minerva asked. "Was this in addition to the underlying turmoil that was being felt and acted upon around the kingdoms in the aftermath of Aramond's defeat? The random attacks on behalf of the absent Red King?"

Juppar, looking a bit uncomfortable, shifted in his seat. "No, not necessarily separate from that unrest, connected to it. There were indications that someone in the area was possibly involved in nefarious acts, stirring up trouble in the vacuum left by the Red King's disappearance. Those random attacks that had been happening sporadically around both kingdoms were also beginning to pop up here and there in the far north." He glanced at Tisharu. "Then Queen Tisharu and her party were attacked in Willow Glen Wood, and what we found in searching the scene after that attack added more weight to our concerns."

"Yes. I was present for that confrontation." Minerva also turned to Tisharu. "Had I not been, that event would have ended much differently."

Valian felt Tisharu bristle at his side at the old witch's dig, though the look on her face remained stoney, and she held her tongue.

Minerva smiled at Valian, obviously enjoying the torment her words had caused. Turning back to Juppar, she gestured for the High Lord to continue.

Juppar took a deep breath and let it out slowly. "We found indications that the attack on Queen Tisharu's party was not a random event perpetrated by rogue fae as most of the others had been, but perhaps, instigated by someone closer to home. Then the death of a dryad in the old growth area of the forest north of Willow Glen Wood was also discovered."

"Lavender," Alexi murmured. "We found her after one of Gray's first reveries. She was so young, so innocent."

"We now know her death is connected to the others that we've seen since then. Hers was the first one found within the kingdom's borders," Tisharu added.

"Yes," Juppar said. "The discovery of the dryad seemed too close in relation to the attack on you and your warriors to be just coincidence."

"I heard of this death when I infiltrated Aramond's rogue forces and accompanied them into the Barrens where he was hiding. I had known something was afoot, but could not pinpoint it beforehand. My runes had alerted me to the eminent ambush in Willow Glen Wood, but nothing more," Minerva replied, then turned to Juppar. "Continue."

"Upon returning from the rescue mission into the Barrens and our routing of the Red King this last summer, several of us made a pact to monitor a certain...situation."

The Old One raised a questioning eyebrow, her impatience beginning to show. "And that was?"

Juppar cleared his throat. "There was a concern—"

"Oh, for the love of the Oracles, Juppar. Quit mucking about and just call it what it was," Tisharu snapped, and then turned to Minerva. "We had our *suspicions* that another high lord in the area was party to something brewing in the realm, something unseen at the time but being felt in that area and beyond. We worried that the last of the Red King's followers were beginning to coalesce, and later, that this high lord may have been involved in the dryad's demise for some reason."

"You are speaking of Kellam?" Minerva asked with a shuttered look.

"We are," Juppar confirmed. "Though it gives me no pleasure to say so, to call out another high lord."

"And why do you think that Kellam may have been covertly involved?"

"Other than the fact that he's lazy and worthless, and an embarrassment to our kind? That he cares only for himself?" Finvar muttered, then looked away from Minerva's amused but pointed stare.

"For one thing, he chose not to join the conflict last winter when the Red King attacked Wysteria, though his court could have been destroyed right along with the rest of the kingdom," Valian said. "Strange behavior for a high lord not to protect his own court. Unless there was a reason Kellam wasn't worried."

Minerva raised a gnarled finger. "But he wasn't the only Wysterian High Lord to forgo the fight. Juppar, here, did not participate, and neither did Queen Elshandra from the Summer Court, if memory serves."

"That is true, Old One," Juppar replied. "There was a conflict inside my Starlight Court that had erupted around that same time. It wasn't too serious, but I felt I could not leave until the situation was resolved. I sent word to that effect to the White Palace. We did, however, keep a vigilant eye on the battle."

"Juppar did give us a heads up that he would be unable to participate and why," Valian continued. "And though Elshandra declined without giving a reason, Kellam's answer was that he had no interest in war between the human realms, that it wasn't his Evening Court's problem. In addition, Elshandra and her warriors did join with the combined forces when we went into the Barrens to retrieve Alyssa and rout the Red King, while Kellam didn't even bother to respond to that request."

"I see," Minerva murmured. "Anything else you'd like to share, Juppar?"

The High Lord stiffened. "There is, indeed, Old One. We have been monitoring Kellam's movements and that of his lieutenants since returning from the Barrens. Someone from the Starlight Court has been meeting with a group in the Barrens almost weekly over the last two months. It's not always Kellam himself but often it is."

"And you know this how?"

"As I said, we've been watching closely and have followed discretely to observe on several occasions." Juppar shook his head. "Make no mistake, the Red King may be deposed and Yulis...well, he's no longer a threat, but there is a group in the Barrens that seems to be carrying on with what the evil pair started. Now, why and to what end? And are these meetings connected to the Dark Fae's resurrection? These are questions that have no answers...yet."

"This conversation is all well and good," Tisharu suddenly retorted. "But while it does add more weight to the few theories we already have, it doesn't answer the burning question of who would have had the knowledge and power to administer a blood ritual to raise Qadira once Yulis was no longer an option. And what this blood ritual would entail."

"Besides me?" Minerva asked in a steely tone.

"Well, obviously besides you." Tisharu rolled her eyes in a dramatic fashion. "Look, I understand that you have no interest in human squabbles, but I'm also aware that your reputation is something that you care *deeply* about. This is about the Great War, about the Dark Fae that threatened all, not just the human population. Your spell has been circumvented. And Yulis is dead. So, who else is there, Old One?"

There was silence in the room as Minerva and Tisharu glared at each other. Finally, the old witch shook her head. "There is only one other that comes to mind. Another wizard that was banished from the realm long ago...before the Great War."

"Banished for what?" Gray asked.

"Yeah, what would get someone banished from the entire realm?" Alexi chimed in.

Valian watched Minerva's face, her shuttered expression, as she looked from Alexi to Gray, and finally to Queen Beatrice, and he again felt the same sinking feeling in the pit of his stomach. But even he was unprepared for the Old One's answer.

"Trillian was banished for conjuring a rare plague that took the life of an Ellurian ruler."

Nineteen

A profound silence settled over the room as the meaning behind Minerva's words seemed to hover over the occupants like an ominous cloud. Stunned at her proclamation, Gray turned to his mother, whose face had gone as white as the snow blanketing the courtyard outside the palace walls. He had not known his grandfather, and his mother had been but a child when Seanchán of the North, though immortal, had actually succumbed to a rare plague. However, to hear that the Ellurian ruler's death from that plague had not been mere happenstance but possibly a deliberate act was contemptible.

The Queen stared at the old sorceress in disbelief and slowly shook her head. "That's just... That cannot be," she finally uttered in her shock. "Are you certain of this? This Trillian actually created the plague that killed my father?"

Minerva reached out and placed her gnarled hand over the Queen's, and the Old One's look was heartbreaking. "I'm afraid so, Beatrice."

"But...I don't understand? Renata and I were never made aware of this. From childhood, we were told that the rare plague that took our father's life was something never seen before."

"And it wasn't," Minerva assured her in a soothing voice. "When Seanchán first became ill, the healers were at a loss as to what afflicted him. They struggled to diagnose the ailment that had taken hold of him so quickly, seemingly out of the blue, assuming that it was natural-born. What they found was a virus they could not identify, a virus with magickal undertones. Unfortunately, once they discovered this, there was little time left to create a treatment or a cure, and Seanchán lost his life to the plague before a serum could be produced."

"Did my mother know the truth of how he died?"

"Yes. The Queen Mother knew."

"Who else knew the truth?" Beatrice looked to Ugharess before Minerva could answer. "You said you knew my father. Did you know this was how he died?"

The Airsayrth elder glanced at Minerva, and then back to the Queen, slowly nodding her head. "The truth of Seanchán's death is known to a very select few in our homeland, with those few being only the elders. The Caemmeirth have always had a close relationship with the Ancients, so we did what we could to assist the healers at that time." She gave Beatrice a compassionate look. "I am sorry, Queen Beatrice. As I said, Seanchán was a great ruler, revered and beloved by his people...and respected by ours as well."

Queen Beatrice turned to Minerva. "Why was the true cause of my father's death concealed from my sister and me, from his people?"

"There were extenuating circumstances, Beatrice," Minerva said. "The Ellurian empire was struggling with a bit of its own unrest at the time caused by a small, unruly faction who wished to take more of the realm for Ellurian rule...by force, if necessary. However, most of the population was loyal to Seanchán and behind his efforts to move the empire forward as a separate yet united domain and to respect the sovereignty of the minor kingdoms. Though the Ancients were the most powerful race in the realm, Seanchán had a vision of the Ellurian empire as a welcome partner and neighbor to those other kingdoms, as opposed to their conqueror.

"However, the Council of Elders was intent on easing tensions and thought that the true nature of Seanchán's death would only fan the embers of unrest to flame. They wanted to avoid a deeper conflict at all costs, so the decision was made to keep the true cause of his death restricted to a very few. Theoden, Seanchán's second in command, was quickly elected to rule in order to keep a sense of continuity, of stability, and to keep the confidence of the Ellurian people solidly in place."

"Was this about the time that the whole of the Ellurian empire was said to have vanished?" Valian asked. "Because several of us around this table who fought in the Great War were under the impression that the Ellurian race had died out completely with that plague. An impression, I might add, which has become documented history as well. It was a difficult evolution for us all to understand, but I think more so for my kind, as the Ellurian's were related to an ancient Elven race, as you well know. They are my people's distant relations."

Minerva nodded. "Theoden wanted to complete Seanchán's vision, but knew at that point in time it would be close to impossible to accomplish, as the unruly faction I spoke of were getting louder and more forceful, stirring up more and more anger around the empire. Not wanting the truth to be revealed, which Theoden felt would spark more conflict, he and the Council of Elders asked that the empire be cloaked. So, that is what a group of my magickal brethren and I did." She sighed. "I cannot say if this was a good decision or a disaster, but it is what was. However, I do understand now the angst that decision ultimately caused you and others of your race, Chancellor, and wish it could have been otherwise. We merely did what Theoden and the Council of Elders asked of us."

The old sorceress paused and took a deep breath. "Unfortunately, in spite of every decision the elders made to calm the empire, that opposing faction only continued to grow and soon became the base of Qadira's followers."

"Old One, you say a plague is what killed my grandfather, but that term denotes a wave of disease. Did anyone else die of this 'plague'?" Gray asked in a tight voice.

Minerva gave him a staid look. "No. Seanchán was the only casualty."

Righteous anger rose in Gray's throat like bile, and he leaned forward, shooting Minerva a look alive with his fury. "Then it wasn't a plague, was it? This Trillian designed and created a magickal 'virus' that killed my grandfather—and only my grandfather—at a time when, as ruler, he was trying to unite his empire. That would be treason for any empire–at the very least. So, who was this Trillian? Was he part of this disruptive faction, part of Qadira's movement? And why was he banished and not sentenced to death for his treachery?"

"Graydon," the Queen murmured, laying a hand over his on the table in an obvious attempt to temper his words.

"No, Beatrice." Minerva held up her hand. "The Prince brings up a valid question, which deserves a valid answer." The old witch turned to Gray. "There were many among us who knew the circumstances of Seanchán's death, who struggled with this very question. Trillian was a known and respected wizard in the magickal community, a wizard adept in medical research and potions. He was also one of the empire's leading epidemiologists. Unfortunately, there was no evidence to be found that he was involved with Qadira's faction in any way, though he had been working on several viral cures just before Seanchán became ill. When the Council finally held the confidential inquest after the ruler's death, Trillian testified that he'd been continuing to test several compounds. However, he swore that he didn't realize what he'd done until Seanchán became ill and the viral sample had disappeared from his laboratory. He begged for leniency, said he had no idea when the sample had disappeared, how Seanchán had been infected, or by whom."

"And the Council took his word for that?" Niall asked in a hardened tone. "You cannot be serious."

"I'm sorry to say that there was just no proof to the contrary," Minerva stated. "The ampule holding the virus sample had indeed gone missing and was never found. Trillian's quarters were thoroughly searched, as were the quarters of everyone with access to that laboratory right down to the last healer, but to no avail. By the time Seanchán died, while a close approximation of when he'd been infected could be established, there was no way to discern the how of it." She turned to Niall, and the look in her eyes was just as hard as his tone had been. "But make no mistake, High Lord. We did not just take Trillian's word for anything. Yes, his life was spared but he suffered banishment from his homeland, as by his own admission, he was the one who created the virus in the first place, whether by accident or not. He was also in charge of the laboratory, and the security of that vital space was his responsibility...and his alone."

"All right, but do we know what happened to Trillian after his banishment?" Valian asked. "To where was he banished? You say that he's the only other one you can think of who could have implemented a blood ritual for Qadira's immortal resurrection, but is it possible that he's returned to the realm somehow?"

Minerva shook her head. "I do not see how, Chancellor. The Oracles banished the wizard into an ether realm, a type of stasis."

"And when the Oracles banish you to an ether realm, it's extremely difficult to return," Ridar grumbled. "And by 'extremely difficult' I mean to say, close to impossible. The Trinity look so ethereal and innocent, but they don't mess around. They can be quite formidable when need be, and their power is unmatched." He glanced at Minerva and smiled. "Present company excepted that is."

"Duly noted, dragon shifter," the Old One replied with a narrowed look and a velvety tone to her words.

"Well, I will attest to that description of the Oracles," Isabella commented with wide eyes. "I got a pretty good dose of that yesterday. One minute they were answering my questions—albeit with somewhat confusing answers—and the next minute they were throwing out blinding light around the chamber and rattling the walls of the inner sanctuary. It was, as you said, quite formidable. Although, after being in the middle of it as it was happening, I would call it down right frightening."

Ridar chuckled and nodded.

"Yes, yes, but what of these other 'brethren' you spoke of," Tisharu ground out, her impatience coating her words like a bitter syrup. "Could not one of them have the knowledge and ability to impose this heinous blood ritual for the Dark Fae? I would assume that if they had the know-how to cloak the entire Ellurian empire, they could easily handle a blood ritual of this kind, is that not so?"

"Though a far-fetched theory, I suppose it could be possible." Minerva frowned, and it was obvious that she thought the theory lacked merit. "The knowledge and ability would obviously be there, as it is for me. Any one of them could impose a blood ritual without much trouble. However, I knew each in the group personally, and though all were extremely competent in these kinds of magicks, I cannot imagine even one of them stooping to such a catastrophic deed."

Tisharu snorted. "Just because you can't imagine it, Old One—or more likely, don't want to believe it—doesn't mean it's not possible. Just look at Qadira." The fae Queen shook her head and stared at Minerva. "I can still remember a time when her betrayal of the realm would have been unimaginable." She looked around the table. "I feel certain that the rest here today who *knew* her before the war—before her ascent to Dark Fae—would agree. Yet her greed and thirst for power turned her into a dangerous monster." She spread her arms wide. "And here we are."

"Okay, all of that aside, where do we go from here?" Valian asked. "As you said, Old One, our time seems to be running short. *Someone* has circumvented your binding spell and has obviously assisted the Dark Fae in her rise with some sort of blood ritual."

"You've also implied that there is quite the variety of death spells," Niall added. "But you've said very little about these blood rituals, nor explained how this specific ritual would be implemented. Clearly, it must have something to do with the deaths of magickal beings we've seen, but how does the damn thing work?"

Minerva nodded. "The deaths have been and continue to be what concerns me the most. As I said in the beginning, the blood is the problem."

"For the love of the Oracles," Tisharu spat, and then heaved a sigh. "And that problem would be?"

The Old One frowned at the fae Queen, and then spoke slowly, as if explaining to a child. "The blood is an indicator of the type and strength of the blood ritual, Tisharu. The more blood needed, the more power behind the ritual. Yet, the type of blood tells us even more. Though a few of these rituals need only the blood of a living being, magickal, human, or even animal, most of the more intricate rituals use only the blood of magickal beings."

"I'm assuming the raising of the Dark Fae would need strictly magickal blood and plenty of it?" Niall asked.

Minerva leaned forward, elbows on the table and entwined

fingers before turning to him. "That would be a very good assumption, High Lord. That is exactly what this particular kind of blood ritual would need. However, just as I sealed the spot of earth where Qadira's body was absorbed to keep her from rising, the blood ritual would be required to take place on that very same spot to break that incarceration spell I imposed.

"Unfortunately, though the blood is a crucial component to any such ritual, there is more to it than that. As I said, these are not spells that just anyone can create. It would take considerable magickal abilities. There are very specific incantations that go hand in hand with any blood ritual. Get it wrong, and you conjure a calamitous soup that can cause lasting destruction taking decades, sometimes centuries, to correct."

"Well, this just gets better and better, doesn't it?" Alexi scrubbed his hands over his face, then shot the old sorceress a resigned look. "Okay, then how do we begin to fight what's coming? What's our first move? How do we protect ourselves and the kingdoms, all the while fighting this threat? And more importantly, how do we win against such crazy-high odds?" He shook his head. "We definitely need a game plan, and fast."

"Those would be my questions as well," Valian said. "But first, how do we confirm if this Trillian has escaped the ether realm somehow and returned to our world, or if he was and is part of this scheme to raise the Dark Fae at all?"

"Yes, and if not him, then give us a clear-eyed view of who else we should be looking for. In other words, brethren or not," Tisharu muttered.

Minerva glared at the fae Queen again but nodded to Alexi and Valian. "These are all good questions, to be sure. I'll be meeting with the Oracles when I leave you today. They will be able to tell me if Trillian has slipped from their banishment and somehow returned, and I will find out anything else I can from them. This is our first step. In the meantime, I have some words of advice for a few here today."

She looked from one face to the next until she got to Gray. Her gaze sharpened, and Gray could almost see the thoughts swirling around behind her silvery-gray eyes. She briefly shifted her regard to Isabella, and then on to Alyssa before turning back to him.

After studying him for what seemed like an eternity, she finally spoke. "Once I get the answers that we need, there are three at this table who will play a decisive role in how this will end for all. You, Prince Graydon...our freshly minted Halfling, here," she said, indicating Isabella, before moving on to Alyssa. "And, of course, the descendant."

Gray saw a mixture of anxiety and terror flood Isabella's features as clearly as the resignation that settled over Alyssa's face, and he realized in that moment that this would be a learning curve for them all. A very steep learning curve with an extremely short period of time to get up to speed. The thought had his heart beating just a little faster.

"What do you mean, we'll play a decisive role?" Isabella sputtered. She looked back and forth from Gray to Alyssa, and her voice rose as she began to speak. "I mean, you two have amazing magickal abilities, but I don't have anything. How in all that's holy am I included in a final solution...and for everyone?" She began to shake her head. "That's just insane."

Gray watched Alexi take her hand in an effort to sooth her, but he knew it was going to take much more than that. If what Minerva said was any indication, as quickly as possible, he, Isabella, and Alyssa were going to have to step up and figure out what their roles would be in what was coming.

Isabella looked to Minerva in a full-blown panic mode. "I would no more know what to do or how to do it than I would know how to take flight without an airplane."

Minerva's next words confirmed what Gray had been thinking. "Then I suppose we better figure it out, hadn't we?"

"Here's another point that I'd like to discuss," Valian interrupted, raising a finger. "It's clear from all the reports that Qadira hasn't fully risen...yet. Isabella, you said that in your dream the Dark Fae manifested out of the ground as a dark, undefined shape, correct?"

Isabella nodded. "Yes. It didn't look like a person, just a huge, black shape coming up out of the ground. It didn't really have a specific form, which, for me, made it even more terrifying."

Valian nodded then turned to the Issai elder. "Erthos, you described what you saw this morning in the Barrens in much the same way as Isabella—as a darkness, a diaphanous black shape."

"Correct," the blue dragon elder replied. "Just as she described. It had no shape and, at times during the encounter, was almost transparent before it seemed to solidify once again. It was as if it was having a difficult time holding a distinct form."

"Yes. It did seem to struggle, like a picture coming in and out of focus," Azzertha added.

"Best guess scenario," the Chancellor said, turning to Minerva. "How much magickal blood will it take before Qadira can be fully manifested? And how much time do you think we have to prepare?"

"Also, how powerful will she be at full regeneration?" Finvar added. "I agree with what the Chancellor said earlier, I'd rather not face that evil again in my lifetime, especially if she's going to come back more powerful and be immortal, to boot."

The Old One looked between Valian and Finvar, and then shook her head. "I do understand your concerns, as I have my own as well, but I am sorry to say that I cannot answer your questions decisively until I know what blood ritual was performed and by whom." She put up a hand when Valian started to speak. "However, I can tell you this. From everything that I've seen and heard so far, and Erthos' reported state of the Dark Fae as of this morning, Qadira is regenerating faster than I would expect. This would speak to the strength of the blood ritual used. Any magickal blood that she can acquire from here forward could accelerate the speed of that regeneration exponentially."

"Meaning the more magickal lives she takes, the less time we have," Niall replied, cutting to the heart of the matter.

Minerva's look was grim and her slight smile was without humor. "Exactly. I can do nothing to stop it until I know what ritual was used, as like I said earlier, using an incorrect counter spell could bring about disastrous consequences and make the situation even worse." She looked at Isabella. "The Oracles told you about the Unclean, that it would rise, yes?"

Isabella nodded. "They did, but they said that it would come back different, that it could never be what it once was because its essence was tainted and unnatural. Since the Unclean they spoke of is Qadira, doesn't that mean that she won't be as powerful as maybe she once was, even if she rises as an immortal?"

"Perhaps." The old sorceress pursed her lips, considering Isabella's question before speaking. "The Oracles are all-knowing, so we can at least take stock in the fact that what they told you is true. But again, in reality, the outcome will depend on a few very crucial elements. Regardless, I will meet with the Trinity today and determine what else they know that we do not, and ask their advice on how to proceed. Then we can better prepare for what comes, perhaps stop the Dark Fae before she can come to full power."

"And until then?" Tisharu asked. "Do you really expect us to just sit around on our hands and wait?"

Minerva stared at the fae Queen for a beat before hooting with laughter. "Oh, no. I would never expect such mundane behavior from you, Tisharu." She sobered then, and her steely gaze swept everyone at the table. "No, no, what I expect is for all of you here to be vigilant, to combat Qadira wherever and whenever she appears. As I said, the more magickal deaths, the faster she will regenerate. Keeping her from taking more lives and absorbing more magickal blood will buy us time. And in this moment, time is what we all require."

An edgy silence hovered over the room for several moments until there was a sudden commotion at the door, and they all turned to find Gryphon with a disheveled Halifax in tow. The Cheshire Wood cat was wide-eyed and looked decidedly distressed.

"Gryphon? What is the meaning of this?" the Queen asked.

"I do apologize for the intrusion, Majesty." He pulled Halifax around and gave him a slight push forward. "But Master Halifax has some important news that you all need to hear."

"Halifax?" Gray frowned. The cat looked more frightened than Gray had ever seen him...and perhaps as if he'd been in a scuffle. "What's happened?"

The cat looked from Gray to the Queen, and finally, to the Old One. "There's been an...incident in Roseland Wood."

Twenty

"An 'incident,' you say?" Gray asked. "What are you talking about? What's happened, Halifax?"

Alexi frowned. "And what were you doing across the border in Roseland in the first place?"

Halifax seemed to forget his distress for a moment as he looked at the Field Marshal, and his face took on its normally annoyed features. "I was having brunch with Kaleb Pillar and his cousin Violet, if you must know, and we ran into the frost twins, Ligia and Drifa. We were standing there on the path talking when suddenly the ground began to shake and some kind of dark energy emerged from the earth just yards from where we all stood."

"When did this happen?" Gray asked, sitting up and focusing his attention. Like the death they'd stumbled across the day before between the White Palace and the Temple of the Oracles, an attack in Roseland Wood was definitely too close for his comfort.

There was a round of chaotic chatter as the cat now had the attention of everyone at the table. Then Minerva put up a hand and everything came to a halt. "How did this event end? Was anyone hurt, Cat?" she asked.

"No," he replied in a shaky voice. "At least, I don't think there were any injuries. We didn't know what was happening, what the dark entity was, so Kaleb, Violet, and I immediately faded back to

Kaleb's cabin—which is shielded by a protection spell—as soon as the thing began to materialize."

"Yes. I am aware of the wood sprite's protection spell," Minerva said with a raised eyebrow. "For I am the one that added that spell to his cabin in the first place, as I did with the White Palace. But what of the frost pixies?"

"That, I do not know, Old One. I assume they evaporated into ice mist and fled as soon as we faded, but I cannot be certain."

"So, as far as you know, no one was harmed...or killed?" Tisharu asked.

"Killed?" Halifax gave the fae Queen a horrified look. "No. Not as far as I know."

Minerva narrowed her eyes and turned back to the group. "I think it would be prudent to check Roseland Wood to make certain there were no magickal deaths."

"Magickal deaths?" Halifax exclaimed, color draining from his swarthy face. "What are you talking about? What was this thing we encountered? Are you saying this dark entity is what's been causing the strange deaths that have been rumored around the kingdoms?"

"Alexi and I, along with the Prince, can definitely handle a scouting trip to Roseland Wood, Old One," Valian said, ignoring the cat.

"Fine. However, I would also ask that you don't go without appropriate protection for yourselves." Minerva turned to the Caemmeirth elders. "Azzertha, can you and the other elders go with them to provide an extra layer of protection, in case it is needed?"

The Gheori elder looked to the other three, who all nodded in agreement. Turning back to Minerva, Azzertha also nodded. "We will accompany them, Old One. I, myself, would like to see this recent site."

"And I'll go back to my research," Áine said. "I'll see what else I can find to maybe give us some help."

"Excellent." Minerva stood, and with gnarled, bejeweled fingers, pulled her blood-red robes close. "Then I will go to the Temple now and speak with the Oracles. Stay vigilant...all of you." With that, the air around her shimmered, and the Witch of the Eastern Glade disappeared in a swirl of silver smoke.

Gray took a deep breath and blew it out slowly. "Alright, then. Let's get this trip organized and get on the road." He nodded to the Field Marshal. "Alexi, put together a small squad of warriors. Keep it tight. Only a handful of your best. Give them a clear rundown of where we're going and what we may run up against. Then arm yourself as well. Valian and I will do the same, and then, along with the elders, we'll meet you in the courtyard."

"Will do," Alexi acknowledged.

Gray turned to Halifax. "You will show us where this happened."

"But I—"

"That is not a request, Halifax," the Queen murmured. "I can see that this has shaken you, and that is understandable, but this is something that could very well happen in your own Cheshire Wood. Therefore, I know that you will give the group your full attention and cooperation. Yes?"

The cat swallowed hard, but nodded. "Of course, Your Majesty. I will do my best."

"Thank you." The Queen looked around the table. "Then Isabella, Alyssa, and I will leave the rest of you to your preparations, but I would also remind you all to be vigilant and stay safe," she finished, and then stood.

"But don't you think Aly and I should—" Isabella began as they all stood for the Queen, but Alexi put a hand on her arm and shook his head.

"As Minerva said, along with the Prince, the two of you will have an important role to play in bringing this terrible episode to an end," the Queen cautioned. "What that role is, as yet, we do not know, but this trip to Roseland Wood is not for you to do. You will stay here, and we will discuss what your role may look like and strategize on how to prepare for it. Now, come. We will retire to my study for now and let the rest of the group do what is needed."

With a sigh, Isabella nodded, though she didn't look happy about it. Then she and Alyssa followed the Queen from the room.

"Okay," Gray said, giving his attention back to the Caemmeirth elders as they all took their seats again. "What else can you tell us about your encounter this morning in the Barrens? So far, we've only run across the unfortunate deaths long after they've happened.

Isabella is the only one of us who's actually seen the dark entity, and that was in one of her dreams." He looked at each dragon elder. "Is there anything else you can add that may help us be more prepared in the event that we are actually confronted with the Dark Fae today?"

Ridar shook his head. "I can think of nothing that we haven't already discussed. The Dark Fae had no form and was obviously not fully regenerated at that time, but who knows what she's been up to since our encounter with her this morning."

"Or how many more magickal lives she needs to take in order to complete her rebirth," Erthos added.

"The description given by the cat seems very close to what we found in the Barrens earlier," Azzertha confirmed. "We did feel the earth shake but did not witness the Dark Fae rise. She had already partially manifested and had the kelpie in her grasp when we arrived at the scene."

Ridar nodded. "And as I said earlier, our fire seemed to deter her."

"Yes, but for how long that will be is unclear," Ugharess replied. "We can't be certain it did any lasting damage, as she disappeared very quickly back into the earth. We did burn the spot for several minutes, but I have little hope that it did much good."

"If we do run across Qadira in Roseland Wood, I would encourage you and your men to fade quickly and allow us to confront her and provide cover," Azzertha added. "There is no need to put yourselves in harm's way."

"That's all well and good, Azzertha," Niall replied. "But how do you know that you would not be at risk should you try to confront her yourselves?"

Azzertha shook her head. "I do not. For there may be a time coming soon when we will no longer be a threat to her, but we won't know that until the situation arises. However, I will remind you that, although you may be able to fade...we dragons, along with breathing fire, can fly." She grinned at him then. "In the meantime, you do bring up a good point, High Lord. None of us should take anything for granted at this juncture."

"Alright, Finvar and Niall are already armed and prepared." Gray gestured to Valian and Alexi. "But give the three of us fifteen minutes to do the same and gather the squad. Halifax, you go with the High Lords. We'll meet you all in the courtyard in twenty."

A HALF AN HOUR LATER, THE ENTOURAGE WAS ON THE move and emerged from Tarkington Forest, crossing the border between the kingdoms at the eastern edge of Roseland Wood.

Gray turned to the Cheshire Wood cat. "All right, we'll follow your lead, Halifax. Show us where the event took place."

The group moved slowly and cautiously when they entered Roseland Wood, and as they did, within moments Gray's pulse quickened, and his very skin began to tingle in a way unfamiliar to him. The hairs on his arms and the back of his neck stood on end and a hyperawareness of everything around him flooded his senses.

Well, this is something new, he thought.

The sensation was amazingly broad. It was as if everything around him had been magnified in his mind and body, and he suddenly felt connected on a fundamental level with the surrounding environment. The sights, the sounds, the scents. He could literally smell the deep, rich soil under the earthy aroma of undergrowth along the path, hear the slightest rustle of breeze through the tree canopy above, and could almost feel the very air vibrate around them as they went deeper into the forest.

But after a few moments, he realized that there was something else there, as well. Something slightly fetid and unnatural lay just beneath it all, like the shadow of a terrible odor not quite dissipated, still tainting the splendor of the forest around them.

"The spot where we saw the darkness is on this path just up ahead about twenty or thirty yards from where we are," Halifax was saying and pointing in that direction.

Gray barely registered the cat's words. An odd sound of movement, a distant shifting of earth, now held his attention. It was more of a sensation than an actual sound, much like what he'd felt in the Barrens with the golem's approach, and he could feel it rumbling within his bones as they continued along the path.

And then...

He felt it coming on before it took hold.

"Gray, are you all right?"

He heard Alexi's voice from his left as if from a great distance before the reverie seized him.

⁂

"With all due respect, Majesty. I really don't know what role I can possibly play in whatever may be coming," Isabella said. They'd settled on the sofa in the Queen's private study where they were contemplating the situation over tea. "After all, I've only just learned about my heritage, and as you know, I have no special abilities or powers. At least not yet. And we don't know when—if ever—those abilities may begin. How can we strategize about anything I may or may not be included in at this point?"

Isabella privately thought that it was impossible to know what was coming or what would happen, so how could they conceivably prepare for the unknowable?

The Queen laid a hand over Isabella's. "I know you're frightened, child. We all feel some degree of fear with what's happening and for what may come, but we must put that aside as best we can and study this situation logically."

Queen Beatrice put up a hand as Isabella shook her head and made to reply.

"And I know you are concerned that you have nothing to offer. No abilities, no special gifts. However, you have more power than you know, however dormant it may be, and I think you've had a taste of your 'abilities' for some time now."

Isabella continued to shake her head. "I don't know what you mean. I've never had any special abilities that could point to my fae or Ellurian ancestry."

"Izzy, I don't think that's exactly true," Alyssa replied.

"But Aly, you're my oldest friend. You know better than anyone that I've never had any strange powers or capabilities."

Alyssa smiled. "I didn't really snap to it until Queen Beatrice questioned me about it. She wondered if there was anything that came to mind over our long relationship and asked me to really think about it. My first instinct was to say that I'd never noticed anything out of the ordinary. But then I did stop, did really think about it." She leaned forward and turned, looking Isabella in the eye. "And do you know what I found?"

Isabella frowned. "No. What?"

"I remembered a couple of little things that, when examining them, didn't seem so little after all."

"Really? Like what?"

Alyssa sat back and set her cup on the side table. "Well, for one thing, from the time we were children, whenever I misplaced something, you were the one person that could always tell me what I was looking for and where to find it."

Isabella snorted. "Oh, come on. That's not much of a special power."

"It might not seem like it on the surface, but, Izzy, it *is*. When we were young, it was usually something like where I'd left a specific sweater or favorite toy, and it didn't matter if you'd been around when I'd laid it down or lost it. As we got older, it pertained to more substantial things. Where I'd left my keys or my phone, where I'd left my coat or my handbag. And you were never around when any of those things went missing, either."

"But Aly—"

"Izzy, sometimes even before I'd asked, you would tell me what I was thinking about and where I could find it. You'd just mention it out of the blue, almost as if you were reading my mind. And when I asked you how you knew where to look for these things, do you remember what you always told me?"

Isabella was starting to get an uneasy feeling. "That I could see it in my mind," she whispered.

"That's right. That you could see it clearly in your mind, as if it was the most common thing in the world. It was confusing for me in the beginning because my child's mind didn't know how something like that was possible. I certainly didn't have that ability. But your answer was always the same, so I quit asking, and like with most childhood concerns, forgot about it after a time. I think I just accepted it at face value and moved on."

"Okay," Isabella murmured, trying to breathe around the weird anxiety rising in her chest. "I guess I can see that as a bit strange, but—"

"And do you remember us kids playing hide and go seek in the big house your parents had in Connecticut back then?"

"Well, sure."

"You were the best at that game, Izz. You always won. You were the last one standing every single time. When you hid, no one could ever find you, remember?"

"So? I was good at hiding. What does that have to do with anything?"

"I'll tell you. When I really thought about it, what I remembered was watching you hide, knowing exactly *where* you were hiding, and then watching whoever was 'it' looking in that spot...and not finding you there."

"Yeah, but—"

"*And,* when the 'all free' was called at the end, you would pop up from that very spot. Don't you remember me always asking you where you went when the others were looking for you?"

Isabella frowned. She did remember that, but she'd never understood why Alyssa had asked her that question time and again. She'd never gone anywhere. She'd always stayed in the spot where she'd originally hidden.

"So, what are you saying, Aly? You think I disappeared or became invisible or something?"

"I don't know, Izz. Could be. Maybe, like Gray, you've had powers from the beginning, and we just didn't know it."

"Isabella, think back," the Queen said softly. "Let's start with this. You said that you could always see in your mind what Alyssa was searching for and where to locate whatever it was, correct?"

"Yes," Isabella replied slowly. "It would just pop into my mind at a certain point, so I'd tell her when it did. Looking at it now, that does seem sort of weird, but back then, I didn't even question it."

"Alright, now think about the game. When you hid, what were you thinking about?"

"With all due respect, Majesty, how should I know? We were children playing a stupid game," Isabella's voice rose slightly along with her increasing anxiety.

"Izzy, take a breath and really think. When you were hiding, were you thinking about lunch, playing the next game, how bored you were, what we would do next?" Alyssa asked. "Or were you hoping not to be found?"

Isabella opened and closed her mouth a couple of times, a denial on her lips, but then stopped. She blinked several times as the memory of those games came sharp into her mind's eye. And she realized that Alyssa had hit on exactly what had gone through her mind each and every time. She *had* hoped not to be found.

"I made myself invisible?" she murmured with wide eyes. "Oh, my gosh, Aly. I'd hoped not to be found, and so I wasn't."

Alyssa laughed and clapped her hands together in glee. "I wonder what other fae or Ellurian gifts you've subtly used over your lifetime that we had no idea about. This is so cool, Izzy!"

Isabella grinned back at her but wasn't really sure how she felt about the whole thing. It was one thing to be told you had a magickal ancestry you knew nothing about, and quite another to see the evidence of that as far back as childhood. Her grin faded slowly as a disturbing thought crossed her mind.

"Izz? What's the matter? Does this upset you?" Alyssa asked with concern. "Because it's part of what makes you so special. I find it amazing."

"No. No, it's not that. I was just wondering if my parents knew about my abilities, saw these things happening, and just decided not to explain it to me."

"That a good question, Isabella," the Queen murmured. "And entirely plausible considering that they knew about your family's ancestry and told you none of it."

"True." Isabella shook her head. "I mean, Minerva did say that my uncles embraced their ancestry, but that my mom thought of her magickal heritage as a ridiculous myth. Mom turned her back on it. So, did she see these abilities cropping up in her daughter and just ignored what was happening? And why did my uncles say nothing?"

"Perhaps your parents warned them not to speak of it," Queen Beatrice replied. "Do you remember your mother or father ever addressing a situation where you might have been using a magickal ability? Being told it was inappropriate or given an alternate explanation?"

"No. I don't remember either of them ever contradicting me or telling me that I was imagining things. But I wonder if maybe they looked at each other from time to time and worried about it. Maybe they hoped that if they ignored these episodes, that perhaps they would all just go away after a while."

"What are you going to do now, Izz? Will you broach the subject with them, ask them what they've known and why they haven't explained anything to you?" Alyssa asked.

Isabella gave a fierce nod. "Oh, yeah. We're gonna have a come-to-Jesus meeting when all of this is said and done. In the meantime, I think we need to..."

"Izzy, what is it? Are you okay?"

A strange sensation started to build in Isabella's chest, and she took a deep breath as the room began to fade and a soft, white light slowly filled her vision. She could hear Alyssa's voice, as if from far away, calling her name...

Before the reverie took her.

Twenty-One

"Isabella!" Alyssa exclaimed.

Her friend's eyes had rolled back in her head. The color had also drained from Isabella's face, and though Alyssa knew what was probably happening, she was still stunned by this turn of events. Isabella was having a reverie, a trance-like state. Alyssa had seen this very thing first-hand with the Prince the day before on their way back from the Temple of the Oracles. She knew that Gray had been experiencing these reveries since the summer, but though strange dreams and time-lapses had been plaguing Isabella for a couple of months, this was something new. Isabella's Ellurian heritage was beginning to show.

"What should we do, Majesty?" Alyssa asked the Queen, concern for Isabella rising in her chest.

"Is this the first time that you've seen Isabella have one of these spells?" the Queen asked.

Alyssa nodded. "Yes. She's had lapses in time over the last couple of months, but I don't think that she's had a reverie like Gray's until now. Of course, she may have been having these as well and just hadn't realized it."

The Queen cleared her throat and spoke softly to Isabella. "What are you seeing, Isabella? Can you tell us?"

When Isabella spoke, her voice sounded strange to Alyssa, oddly robotic and stilted, but the message she conveyed was alarming.

"The Unclean grows stronger. Its essence moves through the earth searching...searching," Isabella murmured.

"What does Qadira search for, Isabella?" Queen Beatrice asked.

"Life blood of the magickal. Death is near, yet more is looming." Isabella lifted her arm and pointed off to her right.

"Oh, no." Alyssa looked to the Queen. "Do you think that she's seeing what's happening in Roseland Wood? Or maybe this is closer to the palace?"

"I don't know, but as Minerva said, the palace has a protection spell in place, so even if this is happening close by, we'll be safe here." The Queen shook her head. "And if this is taking place in Roseland Wood, there's nothing we can do about it now, but I'm certain the team will proceed with the appropriate caution."

They stared at Isabella, as an odd humming sound emanated from her throat. Then she spoke again. "Jeopardy for all. The Unclean returns for more...more. Stay vigilant, move quickly."

Isabella blinked several times as the color rushed back into her face, and she looked around, met the stares of Alyssa and the Queen. "What are you guys looking at? Did I just have another lapse in time or something?"

"No, Izzy. It was a little more than a time lapse. You had one of those Ellurian reveries that Gray's been having," Alyssa told her.

Isabella looked back and forth, eyes wide, between Alyssa and the Queen. "I did? *Seriously?*"

"Yes. You did. Do you remember any of it?"

Isabella started to shake her head, but then stopped. "It's...all jumbled, but I think there was another death somewhere."

"In Roseland Wood?" the Queen asked.

"I'm not sure. Maybe. I do remember now the scent of evergreen trees, a forest...and yes, there was a winding path. I think the death was magickal, maybe a faerie...just off the path somewhere."

"What else do you remember, Izz?" Alyssa prodded.

For a moment, Isabella's eyes took on a faraway look. "It's weird. I could hear...no, not really hear. It was more of a sensation of something moving or tunneling. Like, maybe through the earth?" She shook her head and turned to Alyssa. "That's all I remember. It all seemed so far away, so remote, and yet...not. And that doesn't make much sense at all, does it?"

"It actually does make sense, Isabella," the Queen replied. "I've had these Ellurian reveries from time to time. I know how disorienting they can be."

"So, what do you think it all means, Majesty?" Alyssa asked. "What if the scouting party is in the middle of this scenario and doesn't know what's coming?"

"This is disturbing, to be sure, but we don't know anything for certain, Alyssa. This could be happening anywhere in the realm. Or Isabella could have simply been seeing what has already happened. In any case, all we can do is pray for the group's safe return and hope for the best."

VALIAN STEPPED UP NEXT TO THE PRINCE AND LEANED IN close. The Prince's eyes were rolled back in his head showing only an opaque white, and his skin had gone pale as well.

"Gray?" Valian spoke quietly. "What is it? What are you seeing?"

"The Unclean grows stronger. Its essence moves through the earth searching...searching," the Prince said in the rhythmic inflection of an Ellurian reverie. "Life blood of the magickal. Death is near, yet more is looming." He lifted his arm and pointed to the thick vegetation off the path to his right.

"Well, I guess we better check it out." Alexi said. Gathering a few warriors, they stepped off the path in that direction, making their way through the brush and disappearing. After several moments, Alexi returned alone, nodding. "There is a dead wood sprite about a hundred yards in that direction. I left the three warriors with the body to keep watch for the time being, just in case."

"A dead wood sprite?" Halifax blanched. "It wasn't Kaleb, was it? I saw him safely to his cabin before I rushed to the palace with the news of what had happened."

Alexi shook his head. "Not Kaleb, no."

Standing beside Valian, the Prince emitted a strange humming sound, and then said, "Jeopardy for all. The Unclean returns for more...more. Stay vigilant, move quickly."

"Okay, I don't like the sound of that," Alexi muttered. "Maybe we should pick up the pace here."

"Agreed," Valian replied. "Have those warriors get the wood sprite back to the palace now, and then let's get moving."

"On it," Alexi said and vanished back into the brush.

Gray blinked and looked around. His color had returned and his eyes showed his confusion but were clear. "That was interesting," he said with raised eyebrows. "And anxiety ridden. Another death?"

"Yes. What do you remember?" Valian asked.

"That's pretty much it. But before the reverie started, I was sensing something strange. I would say it was an odd sound, but it was more than that."

"What do you mean?" Niall asked.

"It's hard to describe. It *was* a sound but almost more of a sensation that I could feel in my bones. Practically a rumbling, like something moving through the earth." Gray cocked his head. "I can still sort of feel it, but it doesn't seem as loud...or as strong."

"We could sense it as well," Ugharess said.

"Still can," Ridar added as he searched the path stretching into the forest before them.

Finvar turned to Erthos. "You said that the ground shook this morning in the Barrens and led you to the Dark Fae attacking that kelpie. Could what you all have sensed here be the Dark Fae moving away as we arrived?" he asked. "Since there's a dead wood sprite in the brush just off the path, we may have barely missed her."

"That would make sense, as her decaying odor is still prevalent in the air here," Erthos replied, wrinkling his nose.

"Yes, it is the same as what we discovered in the Barrens," Azzertha confirmed. "There was more than the smell of death in the air, as there is here. It is the terrible odor of her deterioration."

Alexi reappeared from the brush at that point and stepped back onto the path. "I gave the warriors detailed instructions. They took the wood sprite's body and faded back to the Wysterian border. Are we ready to move out?"

"I do believe so." Valian looked around at the rest of the group who all seemed in agreement. "Gray?"

"Yes. Let's continue, but do it cautiously. The rumbling I've felt, though it's distant at the moment, is still there. We need to be alert."

"Absolutely," Ridar stated. "From what we've seen, Qadira may not be entirely regenerated, but so far, she moves very quickly. We don't know how that will change with each magickal life she takes or the closer she gets to completing the process, but we don't want to get caught unaware. To underestimate her would be perilous."

"I wholeheartedly agree with Ridar," Tisharu said. "Those of you who can sense this rumbling of her movement need to be watchful for any changes and let the rest of us know immediately."

"Yes, that can't be overstated," a voice came from the left, as to everyone's surprise, Tempest stepped out into view. "That Dark Fae bitch was always wily and unpredictable before, but with the erosion of her essence, she's incredibly unstable now, to boot."

Silence reigned for a moment as the group stared at the new arrival, before Gray found his voice and stepped forward. "Tempest. It's good to finally meet you face-to-face instead of in a dream."

"And you, Prince Graydon." The immortal warrior's gaze scanned the group, before stopping on the fae Queen. She grinned. "Tisharu. It's been a while."

"A *while*?" Tisharu asked with an incredulous look. "We all thought you were dead and buried, you crazy wench. And now we find out that you're not only alive but immortal as well?" She shook her head. "I'm not certain if I'm relieved or annoyed."

Tempest's rich laughter rang out. "You've obviously not changed much through the years, old friend. And I see your twin is here. Greetings to you, Niall, and to you as well, Finvar. It is good to see you both after so much time has passed." The Immortal's gaze then swung to Valian and her smile became a touch sultry, her voice taking on a suggestive tone. "Ah, and Chancellor Winchester. I see you're still looking...fine."

Valian was aware of the storm clouds brewing in Tisharu's eyes, but his grin for Tempest was easy, and he nodded. "You're not looking too bad yourself, Tempest, for a dead fae warrior, that is." In that moment, he felt the decades fall away as memories of the war, fighting side-by-side with this exceptional warrior for a common cause, and their comradery in doing so, rose up in his mind. "You know, I was skeptical at first when Old Minerva told us that you lived after your final battle with Qadira, that you were an Immortal, but I am exceedingly glad to see it confirmed with my own eyes."

Tisharu hissed as the immortal fae warrior winked at Valian.

Tempest laughed again and turned to the Caemmeirth elders. "I see that the group has brought in the heat for backup. I'm glad for it. I had thought to contact you a week or so ago to discuss it, Azzertha, but got distracted. We may need all the help we can get before this is all said and done."

"Yes, after the event in the Barrens this morning, we could see that the Dark Fae is getting stronger," Ugharess replied.

"Event?" Tempest's smile faded, and she moved closer to the group. "You encountered Qadira this morning?"

"We did," Azzertha said, and went on to describe what they'd seen. "The Dark Fae's form was still fairly diaphanous and without a distinctive shape, and our fire seemed to discourage her for now, but she is definitely getting stronger with each magickal death."

Tempest nodded. "Yes, I have had a few of those encounters with Qadira over the last month or so and have seen the growth with each life she's taken in that time."

The look on the dragon elder's face was grim. "I'm not certain how much time we have left before she becomes fully regenerated and takes a substantial form. At that point, there might be nothing left to deter her. And destroying her may become...problematic."

"That's why we need to hunt her down and destroy her before it gets worse," Ridar added. "Unless the Old One can come up with something in her meeting with the Trinity, once Qadira is fully restored it might be too late. We may not get a better chance at her."

"What you say is true, Ridar." Tempest considered. "However, we must use caution as well, and for just that reason. The Trinity say that she will not be 'what she once was,' but we don't know exactly what that means. Will she be stronger than she was or weakened with the deterioration of her essence? Regardless, what we do know is that she'll be immortal, which poses its own issues."

"Just so," Ridar replied. "We could kill her over and over and never be rid of her for good. And that's an unacceptable outcome for everyone."

Tempest took a deep breath and let it out slowly. "You have my agreement on that. We've been at a disadvantage so far, trailing her movements, always a step behind as we've run across the bodies she's left in her wake."

Ridar nodded. "All the more reason to step up our game and hunt her down."

"I may be wrong, but don't we have that opportunity right now?" Niall asked with a raised eyebrow. "Both Gray and you elders have sensed her movement, can sense her still. This is the best chance we've had to take an offensive position. Maybe destroy her and end this before it truly begins."

The Prince turned to Finvar. "What do you think, Fin? Do we wait until we've heard back from Minerva, maybe lose the chance to act? Or do we pursue Qadira now, not knowing how far she's progressed in her regeneration and risk finding that out at an inopportune moment?"

Finvar's look was steely. "That is the question. I lean toward the latter. We pursue the evil bitch now, but with the utmost care. As Ridar says, we may not get another chance."

"And you, Val?" Gray asked. "What do you say?"

Valian narrowed his eyes and considered. He wasn't sure they really had a choice. They needed to cut off the head of the snake if they had the chance, and he had no stomach for another long, drawn-out war with a nearly insurmountable evil entity if they failed. After a moment, he nodded. "I'm with Fin and Ridar. We take a shot now. Can you still feel her movement? Will you be able to track Qadira?"

"Yes. The reverberation of her movement is distant but I can still feel it." Gray turned to the dragon elders. "Can you all still sense it, too?"

"As you say, it's a distant thrum but we can track it," Ridar confirmed. "Unfortunately, we dragons should probably do it from the air, which will make sensing her movement through the earth harder, but you'll be here on the ground as well, so it should be a fairly easy task."

"Fairly easy task for whom? We'll be the ones directly in her path when we catch up to her." Tisharu muttered, then hissed again when Ridar grinned at her.

"Yes, targeting her from the air if and when she materializes will be easier, for sure," Erthos agreed. "However, *sensing* her from the air will not be a fairly easy task, my Nyrilian brother, and you know it. That will be a dicey state of affairs that will put the others at risk while we circle above."

Ridar shook his head. "Not if the Immortal warrior can keep us informed with mental messages." He raised an eyebrow at Tempest, then narrowed his eyes when she stared back at him with a bland look and said nothing. Huffing a bit of steam, he turned to the group. "In any case, we should quit dallying and get moving now before we lose her altogether."

"All right. Everyone else in agreement?" Valian asked.

The other Caemmeirth elders nodded, along with the rest of the team.

But Halifax cleared his throat and put up a finger before voicing his concern. "Do I really need to be a part of this insanity, Chancellor? I've shown you where our earlier encounter happened and have gotten you within striking distance. Plus, I would like to go to the palace to see about this unfortunate wood sprite, maybe contact the family, if possible. I know quite a few sprite communities in this area, so I may be able to find the family quickly."

Valian wasn't all that sure that the cat's implied altruistic reasoning was actually behind his request. Halifax wasn't known for playing well with others or putting himself in harm's way, but Valian wasn't going to put anyone outside of their core group in danger. "No, you're right, Halifax. You've done what was asked of you. It would be appreciated if you would take care of the family notification. That is, if you can find out who the family is and where they're located."

An almost imperceptible sigh of relief escaped the Cheshire Wood cat before he turned to the Prince and gave a short bow. "Safe hunting to you and the team, Your Grace," he said before vanishing.

Valian's gaze swept the group. "Okay, then let's move like we have a purpose, people."

Tempest turned to the dragon elders. "There's a clearing about a quarter of a mile ahead where the four of you will have ample room to easily transform and take flight."

"Good," Azzertha murmured with a nod of thanks.

With that, the group fell into step and began to walk deeper into the forest. It seemed an unspoken decision that Gray and Tempest would take the lead with the Caemmeirth elders right behind them. This made perfect sense to Valian, since they were the ones who could hear and feel the Dark Fae's movements and relay that information to the rest of the team. Nevertheless, he would be sure to keep his wits about him, just in case. As they walked along, he could sense that the rest of the group was probably thinking the same thing. Everyone was alert and watchful, and there was very little chit-chat among them.

When they reached the small clearing that Tempest had spoken of, the four Caemmeirth elders shifted into dragon form and launched in the blink of an eye. No matter how many times Valian had witnessed that transformation—and those, he could count on one hand—it never ceased to amaze him. He stood watching in awe with the others before finally turning away.

With a vision of the dragons taking so gracefully to the sky replaying in all of their heads, the rest of the group finally walked to the treeline on the far side of the clearing and re-entered the forest. Once again, Valian could sense the tension rising in the warriors who followed behind the team. He couldn't blame them. It was the same edgy apprehension that he felt in his own gut. He thought it was probably a good sign, and hoped it meant everyone was looking sharp. They couldn't afford to let down their guards.

They'd continued on for another ten minutes or so when the forest finally receded a bit, and they came upon a cluster of houses on the outskirts of a small village. It was oddly quiet for the midday hour with virtually no activity to be seen or heard anywhere.

Where is everyone? Valian thought when they walked past the houses and into the heart of the little hamlet. Even here, there was silence. He was getting a very bad feeling.

Then there was movement to their right. A twitch of a curtain in a bakery window. It was gone as quickly as it occurred, but Valian called out to Gray and made a detour in that direction with Tisharu close on their heels. He tried the door and found it locked, though the sign in the window said that the bakery was open. Glancing at Gray and Tisharu, he knocked softly. With his Elven hearing, he could just discern faint voices whispering from inside, but not what was being said. Still, no one opened the door. So, he tried again, this time calling to whoever was obviously hiding within the establishment.

"We're very sorry to disturb you, and we don't want to frighten anyone. I'm Chancellor Winchester here from the White Palace. We would very much like to speak with you, if you are so inclined."

It took a few moments and more frantic whispering from inside the bakery before the locks clicked and the door opened a crack. A dwarf peered out at them, and Valian could almost taste the fear rolling off of him in waves. "You-you're the Chancellor, you say?"

"Yes, sir. I am." Valian gestured to Gray and Tisharu. "And this is Prince Graydon, along with Queen Tisharu from Wysteria's Twilight Court."

The door opened further then and some of the dwarf's fear seemed to recede.

"Oh, thank the Oracles," a high-pitched voice from behind the dwarf cried, and a small pixie stepped into view in the doorway next to him. "Chancellor Winchester? Prince Graydon? Is it really you?"

Valian smiled when he recognized Kaleb Pilliar's cousin. "Violet. Hello. I'm very happy to see that you are here and unharmed. Halifax told us about your earlier encounter with the dark entity. We've come to search the area. May we come in?"

Violet's wings fluttered, and she bobbed her head. Her golden hair, braided haphazardly, bounced from side-to-side, shimmering with magical iridescence in the mid-afternoon light. "Yes, yes, please do. It is such a relief to see you as well."

They entered the bakery as the rest of the team spread out to check on other residences in the village. Once they'd taken the seats offered at a table next to the bakery counter, Violet sighed and popped up out of her chair again. "Oh my. Where are my manners? This is Osseal," she said, gesturing to the dwarf next to her. "We run the bakery together."

"It's a pleasure to meet you, Osseal," the Prince said.

"Can I get you something to drink? Tea or—" Violet stammered.

"No, no, Violet. Please don't trouble yourself. We can't stay long." Gray waved her back into her seat. "We're tracking this dark entity you encountered this morning. Halifax told us what happened, but could you give us your version?"

"Absolutely. Though, if the cat relayed the story, I don't know what else I could add."

"It's not that we question Halifax, Violet," Valian assured her. "It's just that we want to have all the information we can get. You may have seen or can remember something crucial that he failed to cover when we spoke."

"I see." Violet chewed on her bottom lip. "Well, then let me start at the beginning. My cousin, Kaleb, and I were to meet up with Halifax in Roseland Wood mid-morning for brunch here in the village, and as we arrived, we ran into Drifa and Ligia." The pixie then gave them a clear—albeit frightening—account of what had transpired next, ending with how she, Kaleb, and Halifax had faded to Kaleb's cabin right after the Dark Fae had appeared.

"It was a terrifying sight. The dark thing was like nothing that I've ever seen before, and it gave off a horrible odor." She leaned in, her lavender eyes darkening to a deep purple, and whispered, "It smelled of death and decay. Plus, there was the sound that it made."

"Sound?" Tisharu asked. "What sound?"

Violet leaned back, tilting her head and pursing her lips in thought. "It was a guttural sound, as if it was trying to speak but couldn't make words properly. Then there was a dreadful screech as the three of us grabbed hands and faded," she finished with a shudder.

"And did you see what happened with the frost twins?" Tisharu asked. "Halifax did not."

"Oh yes, I did. I saw them both evaporate. Their ice mist had dissipated just before we faded." The pixie turned to Valian. "We stayed with Kaleb for over an hour. The Old One had cast a protection spell on his cabin, so we knew that we would be safe there. But after a while, Halifax thought he should go to the palace and tell you what happened, and I began to worry about Osseal and my family here in the village. I mean, what if that dark thing came here after we'd faded? After Halifax left for the White Palace, Kaleb tried to talk me out of leaving but I came anyway." She turned wide eyes to Gray. "What was that thing, Prince Graydon?"

"It was the Dark Fae, Violet. She's been taking the lives of magickal beings to regenerate, so you were right to fade quickly when she appeared. Have you seen any evidence that she was here in the village after you encountered her in the forest?"

Violet shook her head. "Not since I've been here. Osseal? Tell them."

The dwarf blinked several times and then nodded. "This Dark Fae did not materialize here, but the ground shook at one point quite violently. It was almost like an earthquake but for the terrible odor that Violet spoke of. Then it was gone. When Violet showed up and told us what they had witnessed, we figured the entity bypassed our village, but we've all stayed inside since then. We weren't sure what else to do."

"That was probably the smartest thing you could do," Gray acknowledged. "Until we can find her and destroy her, we all need to be—"

"Gray, what is it?" Valian asked, watching the Prince tilt his head, his eyes briefly taking on a faraway look as if keenly listening to something.

"The sound of her movement is getting louder," Gray said, his eyes snapping to Valian's. "She's moving. We need to go."

Before they could get up from the table, the bakery door flew open, and Tempest shouted, "She's coming! We have to go now."

＃ Twenty-Two

"Violet, you and Osseal stay inside. This is a dangerous situation, and I don't want you to get caught in the middle of it. We'll let you know when the danger has passed," Gray said before hurrying out of the bakery after Valian and Tisharu to meet with the others in the village square.

The rumbling sensation of Qadira's movement was getting stronger by the minute, and Gray's heart began to pound in his chest. The ground trembled under his feet and the thunderous sound of the Dark Fae's approach rang in his ears.

"We don't know how many other lives she's taken since she was last seen in the forest. She's had a good couple of hours," Tempest shouted over the increasing din. "Everyone needs to expect the unexpected. Stay sharp and focused. Do not underestimate her."

"What about the Caemmeirth?" Finvar shouted back. "Do they know what's happening?"

"Yes. And they're almost here." Tempest pointed to the eastern sky where, flying in an impressive formation, the dragons were just coming into view over the trees on the horizon. "Everyone spread out, but not too thinly, and be ready."

What had been only a slight vibration in the ground moments before had quickly increased to a jarring quake making just standing still difficult.

"Here she *comes!*" Tempest yelled.

And in the next moment, a dark shape began to emerge from the earth at the edge of the forest toward the far end of the lane. Though not complete, Qadira had indeed progressed in her regeneration, making Gray wonder how many more bodies they were going to find before the day's end. The Dark Fae's silhouette was no longer transparent—though her features were not completely defined—and gave the appearance of a person, which Gray found disturbing. The guttural cry Qadira uttered, along with what sounded like an awkward attempt at speech, had the hairs on his arms and the back of his neck standing on end.

The Dark Fae then began a deceptively slow progression toward them, which almost felt like a predator stalking its prey, and Gray glanced uneasily toward Tempest. The immortal warrior was rubbing her hands together in a brisk fashion where sparks were beginning to fly. To Gray's surprise, as she pulled her palms slightly apart, she had generated a mini lightning storm between them.

Gray's fascination with Tempest's activity was cut short when the Dark Fae gave another scream, and Gray turned back to see that Qadira's slow movement forward had turned into an accelerated rush toward them. Sword at the ready, he steeled himself and faced her advancing form. But before Qadira could get close enough to engage, Tempest shoved her hands forward, palms out, and twin bolts of bright-white lightning shot out. The barrage struck the Dark Fae squarely in the upper torso, sending her flying backward. Qadira screamed again as the bolts pierced her chest, knocking her to the ground where her shape wavered as if her form wasn't quite as solid as it seemed.

But Qadira wasn't down for long.

Gray and Tempest started forward, and Niall, Finvar, and Alexi advanced around from the right, while Valian and Tisharu moved toward the dark entity from the left. As they began to converge on Qadira from three sides, she seemed to absorb the electric energy that Tempest had shot at her. Rising up, she continued to grow in stature until she was standing at twice the height that she'd been just moments ago. Her displeasure was evident in the guttural roar that she uttered, and she moved with blazing speed, shooting electrified energy at them in several blasts.

Valian and Tisharu dove out of the way in the nick of time, and Finvar countered quickly with an explosion of ice that met those blasts head on and coated Qadira from head to toe in a hardened, icy shell. It stopped her only momentarily before she broke free and surged forward.

Tempest threw her hands out in front of her, and on instinct, Gray did the same, feeling a rush of power quickly grow inside his chest and burst its way out of him. Their dual effort seemed to build an invisible field of energy that succeeded in holding the Dark Fae back temporarily, but Qadira pivoted just as quickly as she'd advanced. Turning with amazing speed, she attacked a small cluster of fae warriors who had circled around and were now approaching her from behind. Their battle cries as they began their attack rapidly turned to cries of terror and agony as the Dark Fae enveloped three of them at once, draining them of their lifeblood in record time and seeming to grow in height and build with each life she took. The rest of the group fled but not before she could pick off two more of the retreating warriors before they could get out of her range.

She's so incredibly fast, Gray thought as he watched what had played out in a matter of seconds.

As the Dark Fae turned back to face the team, he wondered if they were indeed too late in pursuing her, if she had regenerated to the point that nothing they could do would stop her now. As these thoughts went through his mind—in a sudden, blinding flash of light—fire rained down in four powerful streams from above, encasing the Dark Fae in its molten onslaught.

The Caemmeirth had arrived.

The Dark Fae's high-pitched screams shredded the air as she seemed to be completely consumed by the firestorm the great dragons spewed at her. But within moments, her cries waned, and she grew still. As the barrage of dragon-fire dissipated, nothing stood on the spot but blackened earth where Qadira had been only moments before.

Silence reigned as they waited, unsure of what had happened, or what would happen next.

"Is it done?" Tisharu's words hung in the hushed moment. "Did the fire destroy her? It couldn't have been that easy, could it?"

"I can no longer feel her or sense her movement," Tempest said, but then shook her head as she walked toward the smoldering, blackened spot where the Dark Fae had stood. "But no. I don't think she's destroyed or that we did any lasting damage to her."

"Yeah, I can't sense her, either," Gray said. "But I'm with you. I don't think we made much of a dent. From what we just witnessed, I'm gonna say that she's progressed beyond that in her regeneration."

"The dragons' fire seemed to again have deterred her and may have caused her pain, but no, it didn't destroy her," Tempest agreed. "I think you're correct, Prince Graydon. She's gotten too strong for that. The Caemmeirth may still be able to frighten her away for the moment, but I'm afraid that will not be for long." She turned to the group. "We all saw how quickly and easily she consumed those five warriors and how she grew with each life she took."

"I'm with you on that," Valian said. "She'll take a bit of time to lick her wounds from our confrontation, but she'll soon be back... and probably stronger than ever. We did nothing here but piss her off."

"Yeah, that was a lightning round of a shit-show for sure," Alexi grumbled. "Man, that is one fast bitch."

"Yes. It does look like we've waited too long to go on the offensive," Niall said. "But that can't be helped now."

"To be fair, we had no idea what was happening in the beginning," Finvar replied with a shake of his head. "But I also admit that we were a bit too slow in snapping to it."

Tempest gazed down at the blackened earth before looking up at Gray. "Qadira is close to full regeneration. And at that point, she will be not only immortal but possibly invincible as well."

There was a sudden burst of wind as the group turned and watched the Caemmeirth land one by one, in the village square, each transforming into human form.

"That was incredibly unsatisfying," Ridar grumbled as the four dragon elders approached. "Obviously, the dark bitch has progressed, gotten stronger."

"Yes. We were just talking about that. We're definitely going to have to come up with a new strategy," Valian replied. "This confrontation did very little other than to anger her, which does not bode well for whatever response she'll have."

"I'm afraid that is true, Chancellor," Azzertha murmured. "Hopefully, the Old One will have some good news when she returns from the Temple of the Oracles. I fear that we are now at a crossroads and, I think, at a terrible disadvantage."

"I'm going to check in with the Ellurian elders," Tempest said. "I'll see what help—if any—they may have for us, and I'll return as soon as I can." She looked around at the group for one last fleeting moment. "In the meantime, stay safe...and frosty."

At that, the immortal warrior disappeared in a shimmer of light.

With a disgusted look, Tisharu shook her head. "Showoff," she muttered.

Gray smiled at the offended look on the fae Queen's face before returning to the tasks at hand. "Okay. Val, let's go touch base with Violet and Osseal, let them know that the coast is clear for now, but that they need to stay, as Tempest just said, frosty. Then we'll clean up here, gather our dead, and head back to the palace. Maybe Minerva is back with that good news, and we can get a new strategy sketched out."

"Sounds like a plan," Valian replied.

"We'll get started on the clean-up," Alexi said. "I'll have the dead warriors transported home and meet you at the palace as soon as we get back."

"Lord Finvar and I will accompany you and the rest of your squad, Field Marshal," Niall confirmed.

Ugharess stepped forward. "We have a few...issues that we need to re-check in the Barrens, so will take our leave as well. We'll return as soon as we can to see what new information the Old One may have for us."

"Thank you all for your assistance," Gray acknowledged, and then watched the dragons shift and take flight.

Then the rest of the team went their separate ways.

As a frequent visitor to the Temple of the Oracles, and being almost as old as the temple itself, the Witch of the Eastern Glade rarely had to wait for an audience with the Trinity. And so, she was a bit surprised and annoyed when she'd been greeted—and made to wait for over twenty minutes in the vestibule—by a priest she had not seen before. A priest that had a vague note of concern prickling at the back of her mind.

Curious, she thought. *What is this?*

Although, it wasn't completely out of the ordinary to find a new face serving in the temple from time to time, it was bewildering to Minerva. She'd visited the temple often and found that these kinds of changes were extremely few and far between. Joining the Order was a calling—serving the Trinity, an honor. And though priests of the Order moved on to other posts in the realm on occasion or passed on into the ether, which necessitated replacement, it was exceedingly rare. Serving at the Temple of the Oracles was the supreme privilege, the pinnacle of the priesthood.

Minerva studied the new priest as he came back to show her into the inner sanctum. He was tall and lean in his pristine white robes, with pale skin and piercing sky-blue eyes. She wasn't sure why, but there was something about him that was starting to bother her.

That prickling feeling was getting stronger.

It wasn't anything specific about his appearance that troubled her, for he had a similar look to the other priests who served the Trinity here in the temple. Other than the fact that he would not hold her gaze and looked everywhere but directly at her, his behavior was no different, either. Yet, there was...something. She couldn't quite put her finger on it, but whatever it was, it was very close to the surface now, and getting closer by the minute.

The people who came to the temple for an audience with the Oracles tended to be nervous and skittish. After all, the Trinity could be quite imposing. Most of the priests who served at the temple were gentle and accommodating. They had a way about them that put visitors at ease, helped them to prepare for entering the inner sanctum and facing the Oracles with their requests or inquiries. However, this priest was himself skittish and nervous and seemed to be perspiring overmuch, which added to Minerva's unease.

What did he have to be nervous about?

Minerva frowned as the odd feeling persisted, tickling her senses like a tiny alarm, but she followed him into the inner sanctum. She scrutinized him when he backed out of the chamber and closed the doors behind him without ever looking up at her or bowing toward the Oracles, as was the norm.

Curiouser and curiouser, she thought before turning back to the Trinity hovering above the altar at the other end of the chamber.

"Come closer, Old One," the Trinity chorused as one. *"Tell us what troubles you so. For we feel there is much you wish to discuss."*

"Indeed there is," Minerva called out as she began to move down the aisle toward them, but halfway there, she paused, looking back over her shoulder toward the closed doors for a moment before continuing to the altar. "However, before we get started with why I'm here," she began, raising a bejeweled finger. "Can we first discuss the new face here in the temple?" She hooked a thumb toward the door behind her. "May I ask who he is, this new priest? Where he comes from and how long he's been serving here in the temple?"

"Brother Arana came to us at the end of summer from a monastery in the northeastern region of the Unwelcoming Rise as a replacement for Brother Gooden who passed into the ether at midsummer. The request for appointment was sent from the Abbot there. Why do you ask?" an ethereal voice murmured.

"Brother Arana?" Minerva frowned and felt the first possible crux of her concern drop into place. This was quite unexpected...and even more disturbing than she'd thought. Was this the reason for the alarm she was feeling? "As in *Trillian* Arana? Surely not."

The Trinity nodded as one, spoke as one. *"He is a distant descendant of the banished wizard Trillian Arana, yes."*

Minerva could not believe her ears. "Why would you have one of Trillian's descendants here in the temple? You, yourselves, banished Trillian for creating the virus that killed the Ellurian ruler, Seanchán of the North."

"Trillian Arana was banished long before Brother Arana was born centuries later. Brother Arana had no contact with Trillian Arana. Prior Namreal accepted the request from the Abbot, verifying all information, before passing it on to us for confirmation."

Minerva gave a beleaguered sigh and her voice rose as she spoke. "But what does this priest know of that time? Of his own ancestry? How much of what happened with Trillian is he aware of? What was he told?"

She shook her head, took a moment to breathe and lower her voice again before continuing. "As you are aware, *someone* spun a death spell to raise the Dark Fae, a death spell that very few had the capability to create. You also know that both Yulis and Trillian were two of those few. Add to it, now someone has circumvented the incredibly sophisticated incarceration spell that I, myself, put in place to keep Qadira from rising again. Yulis—the perpetrator of the original death spell—is himself, dead. And this very ethereal body banished Trillian for his part in Seanchán's death centuries ago. I know of no one else in the realm who would have the ability to circumvent the kind of incarceration spell that I implemented and used to seal the ground where Qadira perished, not to mention to create and administer a blood ritual to raise her as well." She paused meaningfully. "Except perhaps a descendant of those who could?"

"This is a disturbing accusation," the Trinity intoned.

"Mmm, yes, it is." Minerva narrowed her eyes. "What kind of verification did Prior Namreal perform? Did he research Brother Arana's history and possible abilities, his personal activities? Did he check to see how Brother Arana's immediate family felt about the accusations and ultimate banishment of their ancestor?"

Minerva began to pace, shaking her head, then she stopped and faced the Trinity again. "We are, *all of us*, at a perilous moment in time, my holy Trinity. We must quickly find the culprit who administered that blood ritual to raise Qadira. I must have the exact spell used in order to counter it and reverse that damage. If not, I fear the Dark Fae will prevail, which would surely mean death and destruction to the entire realm. She is already regenerating at an accelerated speed. This was precisely the reason that I came to you today. And to find a descendant of Trillian's here in your holy temple? Well, that gives me much consternation, indeed."

"You are correct, Old One. This is most alarming that this realm may be on the verge of possible annihilation, that our temple may be compromised in this way. We must deliberate and substantiate."

With that, the three ethereal beings' eyes went opaque and glassy, and a deep humming sound filled the chamber. Although frustrated by their answer, Minerva had no choice but to wait. Yet, she was satisfied that she had given them the impetus to look at Brother Arana more closely. Hopefully, they would find that Prior Namreal's verification was thorough and held none of the concerns running through her mind at the moment.

After almost ten long minutes, the Oracles blinked in unison, and their eyes cleared. The doors of the inner sanctum burst open, and Brother Arana was propelled down the aisle toward them, two larger priests on either side of him. Prior Namreal followed. When they got to the altar, the two escorting priests silently pushed Brother Arana forward, indicating that he should kneel before the Trinity, and then they moved to each side as the prior, himself, stepped forward between them.

"We have brought Brother Arana as requested, my holy Trinity," Prior Namreal stated with head bowed.

He was an elderly priest of Elven ancestry who'd been prior for over a century. Minerva knew he would be well aware of Trillian's banishment and the reasons why. She also knew him to be an honest, caring, and compassionate individual, but wondered if his compassion had clouded his vision where Brother Arana was concerned. She recognized through many previous conversations with the prior that he was a believer in second chances and rehabilitation. Had he failed to do a thorough background verification of the young priest's activities, wanting not to project Trillian's crimes onto a distant relative? The prior's next statement made that clear.

"I apologize for turning a blind eye to the possibility of inappropriate activities Brother Arana may have enacted before coming to us here at the temple after Brother Gooden's passing. I should have been more thorough, should have given his connection to Trillian Arana more weight in my consideration." Prior Namreal hung his head. "I've failed in my duties in this matter. I let my empathy for his background color my decisions."

"Thank you, Prior Namreal," the Trinity intoned as one. *"We appreciate your candor and honesty in this matter."*

"Brother Arana, tell us what you have done," an Oracle

commanded in a disapproving tone as the priest had knelt in silence before them during the exchange with Prior Namreal.

"I-I don't understand," Brother Arana mumbled. "I don't know what you mean?"

"Ah, he feigns ignorance," another Oracle mused.

"I've done nothing wrong."

"And he lies even as we have seen his treachery in our minds' eyes," a third Oracle added.

"I have done nothing," he repeated. "I don't—"

Before Brother Arana could finish another denial he was lifted into the air in front of the altar. His eyes went wide and terrified as he flailed his arms and cried out.

"Tell us what you've DONE!" The Trinity's sudden roared command filled the space and shook the chamber like an earthquake.

Brother Arana cried out again, and then went silent and slack as the Trinity took him over, body and mind.

Then he began to speak.

Twenty-Three

The late afternoon light had waned in the western sky by the time most of the group met back up at the palace after their confrontation with the Dark Fae. Valian, Tisharu, and the Prince had stayed behind to speak with Violet, Osseal, and several of the other families in the village before they'd left the area. They'd wanted to make certain the village inhabitants knew that, though Qadira had moved on for the moment, all would need to stay alert for any possible indications of her return until the she could be neutralized.

However, after the day's earlier debacle, Valian wasn't feeling hopeful about any of it.

After they left the village, he and Tisharu had made an appearance at her Twilight Court before heading to the White Palace. The fae Queen had wanted to update her most trusted lieutenant, Raef, on what had occurred, and give him instructions accordingly for the evening ahead and the morning to come.

Once they'd arrived at the palace, they retired to Valian's chambers for a much-needed respite ahead of the dinner hour. Valian was certain that the evening meal would most probably include a lengthy deliberation regarding their encounter with the Dark Fae and possible strategies for moving forward, if the Queen would allow it. Her Royal Highness tended to prohibit such conversation at the dinner table, but either way, after the day they'd had, it would undoubtedly be a topic of discussion at some point and another late night for them all.

"You are looking tired, *mo chroí*," Tisharu murmured as she slipped her arms around him. "And worried."

Valian sighed and enfolded her into his arms, kissing the top of her head. "There is much to consider...and worry about, I'd say."

"After today's encounter, I would tend to agree. Yet, we must be patient and wait to learn what the Old One has discovered, if anything. I will give the ancient hag due credit. She has a way of coming through with pertinent information and workable solutions just when one begins to lose hope. However, more often than not, her assistance does not come until the eleventh hour." Tisharu gave him a pained look. "It is most frustrating, especially coming from one so powerful as her."

Valian laughed at the look on Tisharu's face and her accompanying tone. "And you have a way of cutting through to the heart of the matter, *mo ghrá*. But what you say is true. We'll need to wait and pray to the Oracles that, once again, Old Minerva has a solution for us this time. I for one, do not relish another long, drawn-out fight with Qadira. The first time around was plenty for me. She was powerful before her trip to the underworld where she became the Dark Fae, but we don't know how the terrible powers she garnered from her time there will change and evolve with her rising. And, of course, once fully regenerated, she'll be immortal as well."

"Yes, but Áine said that if Qadira was brought back, she could no longer be what she once was because her essence is now tainted and unnatural from her time in that dark realm. Also, that the change or deterioration of her essence would be much worse."

"True, but I fear that is just guesswork, love. And remember what Minerva told us then, that it would depend on the dark magicks used. The blood spell is the crux of the matter. It's possible —depending on the spell used—that Qadira may not only be immortal now, but that her powers could've been enhanced not diminished. What we saw today was troubling, and may be evidence of that, particularly since Qadira has not yet completely regenerated.

What might she become, what of her powers may be heightened exponentially when that regeneration is complete?"

Tisharu leaned back and tilted her head, giving him a speculative look. "It's not like you to go to a 'doom and gloom' outlook so quickly, *mo chroí*."

"And I'm not now," he replied with a shake of his head. "I'm just being realistic, considering all the facts." He smiled wryly. "And I will admit that I'm feeling a bit tired, so there's that, too."

She reached up and laid her hand on his cheek. "We will take what comes together, yes? We will prevail in the end. Of that I am certain."

Valian raised an eyebrow. "Have you seen the end in your visions? That would truly set my mind at ease."

Tisharu shook her head. "I do not need my visions to tell me what I know in my heart to be true."

Valian took her hand from his cheek, placed a kiss in her palm, and murmured, "*Grá mo chroí thú.*"

"Yes. As you are the love of my heart, as well," she whispered back. "We are perfectly matched, are we not, *a ghrá?* If this fight with the Dark Fae is our end, then we go together into the ether."

"Together." Valian framed her beautiful face with both hands before sliding his fingers into her fiery-red curls. He smiled seductively. "Now, since we have a little time to kill until dinner, I have some thoughts on a delightful way to spend it."

She narrowed her eyes. "Do you, now?"

"I do," he replied as his lips came down to claim hers.

DINNER TURNED OUT TO BE A SURPRISINGLY PLEASANT affair, with Gryphon serving a salad of roasted pears, watercress, and toasted pecans, followed by poached cod, baked pheasant with cherry chutney, glazed carrots, and roasted potatoes. A dessert of cherry meringue mousse topped off the elegant meal and was served with coffee or tea.

Besides the Queen, Gray, Alyssa, Isabella, Alexi, Áine, Valian, and Tisharu, both High Lords, Niall and Finvar, had also stayed for the evening meal rounding out the dinner party. As Valian had surmised, at the start of the meal, Queen Beatrice had shut down any attempt to discuss the Dark Fae or the team's earlier encounter with her, so it did take some of the tension out of the air for a time.

The delicious dinner concluded with all attendees sated, fortified, and finally ready to move on to darker topics. Just as the conversation took the turn in that direction, there was an unexpected eddy of silver smoke at the doorway, and the Witch of the Eastern Glade appeared.

"Oh, Minerva! Good evening," the Queen greeted the sorceress. "Your timing is perfect as we have just finished dinner. Have you come with news?"

Though the Old One's face was passive, Valian could see by the look in her eyes that Minerva did, indeed, have news. He could also sense that her news was not all good.

The witch looked to Queen Beatrice at the head of the table. "There is much to discuss, Beatrice."

"Will you sit with us, maybe have something to eat or drink as you tell us what you know? I can have Gryphon bring you whatever you would like."

"I will sit with you and tell you all, but you need not trouble yourself or Gryphon further," Minerva said as she took the open seat at the other end of the dining room table. For a moment, she was silent, perusing the faces awaiting her news. Then she took a breath and began. "I have just come from a lengthy meeting with the Trinity. There have been several disturbing revelations that we must discuss, and I am glad to see all the necessary parties are here at this table."

The previously enjoyable dinner atmosphere dissolved in a flash at her words and became increasingly troubled as she began to tell them what had happened at the temple.

"Brother *Arana*?" Niall exclaimed with a disbelieving look when the witch had gotten to that part of the tale. "You cannot be serious."

"Yes," Valian agreed. "That does seem exceedingly unwise and dangerous to have a descendant of Trillian Arana serving in the temple, especially since the Oracles were the ones to banish the wizard in the first place."

"*Unwise*?" Niall sputtered. "It's insanity, is what it is. Where was the vetting? Was the Trinity not made aware?" He ran a hand over his face, and the resignation was evident in his voice, his manner. "Of course they were aware. They are all-knowing. How could they not be?"

Minerva nodded. "You are both correct in your assumptions. Prior Namreal was the one who received the request for appointment from the Abbot at the monastery where Brother Arana was originally serving. The prior knew of the connection. However, because Brother Arana hadn't yet been born when Trillian was banished, Namreal let his compassion overrule any possible concerns." She nodded again. "And yes, the Trinity is all-knowing, so they were aware but they also seemed unconcerned about the connection. However, that is water under the bridge at this point. Though Brother Arana was only transferred to the temple at the end of summer, the damage is already done."

"What do you mean, Godmother?" Áine asked, trepidation coloring her tone. "What damage?"

"When I questioned the priest's appointment to fill the vacancy Brother Gooden's passing had created, pointed out that little was known about Brother Arana's family and what he'd been told about his ancestor, the Oracles became quite unsettled. The young priest was brought into the chamber and questioned. Of course, by that time, the Trinity had already thoroughly scanned his mind, seen his treachery."

"Treachery?" Tisharu asked. "What did he do? Get to the point, Old One."

The old sorceress turned narrowed eyes to the fae Queen, and power radiated from her even as her tone was chilly. "Your impatience is not a virtue, faerie. Hold your tongue. I'm getting to that."

Tisharu paled slightly but defiantly held the old witch's gaze.

Turning back to the group, Minerva continued. "It seems that from early childhood, Brother Arana had been regaled with stories about his infamous ancestor. Stories that, unfortunately, painted Trillian in a much different light."

"Let me guess," Alexi muttered. "He was characterized as a martyr, unfairly judged and banished."

The Old One's smile was grim. "Correct, Field Marshal. Down

through the years, that was the feeling held by a small faction in Trillian's immediate family and is the story they passed onto the Arana generations who followed in those family lines." She put up a hand. "Now, granted, as I said, it was a small bloc of the condemned wizard's family, but as in most uprisings they were, collectively, a very loud voice. And most of them were followers of Qadira in the early days, as well." She took a deep breath and seemed to calm herself. "Brother Arana, regrettably, was spawned from one of those factions."

"And I'm assuming, much like in any cult, he was indoctrinated, groomed...and ultimately activated," Valian murmured. He had a thousand questions but knew better than to ask a single one. Old Minerva would get to the core of the issue in her own time. But then again, time was running thin.

"Correct, Chancellor. Brother Arana's indoctrination began at a very young age, and by the time of Brother Gooden's passing in midsummer, Brother Arana was ready to heed the call that had been instilled in him for several decades." Minerva stared at Valian. "Revenge for an ancestor wrongly accused and banished from his homeland, his people, and their cause."

"I'm assuming this played a part in him wanting to serve at the temple," Queen Beatrice said. "But how would that have played into his scheme of revenge? It would be complete and utter insanity to try to exact any type of revenge on the Trinity for Trillian's banishment. They are the most powerful beings in this realm and would have detected that kind of threat almost immediately."

"Well, I do wonder at that now, as they didn't seem to snap to his deception in the first place until the Old One here pointed it out to them," Tisharu muttered.

Minerva ignored the fae Queen's sarcasm and shook her head slowly. "Actually, it was much more insidious than exacting revenge on the Oracles, Beatrice. He wished to acquire Trillian's grimoire, which had been seized during the official investigation of Seanchán's death. The book of spells had been turned over to the Oracles after the wizard's banishment," Minerva replied. "As it turns out, our Brother Arana is quite the adept wizardly apprentice."

"Seriously?" Alexi looked stunned. "He's a priest...and a wizard? Is that even allowed?"

"Don't be obtuse, Field Marshal," Tisharu admonished. "No, that's not allowed, which is the bloody point."

Minerva sighed. "Evidently, when it was discovered in his childhood years that he had an aptitude for magicks, he was trained in the magickal science arts—like his martyred ancestor before him—by certain members of his family. This was done under a veil of secrecy while he was still in short pants and completed long before he joined the priesthood." The sorceress turned to Alexi. "But Tisharu is correct. Serving in the priesthood and practicing wizardly magicks is strictly prohibited. However, that is exactly what he was doing, what he was taught to do. From what I could discern, he was very careful with his magicks, so he was taught well. Once he entered the priesthood, he did so with a specific goal in mind."

"To somehow retrieve Trillian's grimoire," Áine murmured.

"Yes, child, that was always his goal." The old witch nodded. "For that is what held the ultimate weapon for his plan. You see, he was looking for an acceptable blood ritual, one that would circumvent the incarceration spell that I enacted to prevent Qadira from rising. A blood ritual that would also reactivate the death spell that Yulis had originally administered."

"Cementing her immortality, and possibly that of her invincibility to boot," Valian said. The situation had been increasingly dangerous, but this was a dire complication. It added to his earlier fear that there may not be a way to rid themselves of the Dark Fae once and for all.

"I don't understand. Are you saying that this shit-stain of a priest is responsible for the Dark Fae's rise, that he may have condemned us all by invoking the blood ritual required? How is that even possible?" Finvar blurted, sending a chilling mist into the air of the dining room along with his anger.

"Unfortunately, yes, High Lord. Brother Arana is responsible...in a roundabout way."

"What do you mean, in a roundabout way? You said that Yulis and Trillian were the only two you could think of who had the ability to enact a blood ritual of this kind. Was this something the young priest was capable of as well?"

Minerva shook her head. "You misunderstand, High Lord. Brother Arana acquired access to the temple library where Trillian's grimoire was being stored and used it to find a blood ritual. He couldn't remove the grimoire from the library, as that would surely have sent up the alarm, so he spent time over the summer perusing, copying, and secreting away several different blood rituals that he found there."

Gray frowned. "Okay, I'm confused. Did he implement the blood ritual or not? And if he did, how'd he do it? I mean, wouldn't it have to be done on the spot where Qadira perished and you initially administered the incarceration spell?"

"Indeed it would, young Prince."

"But it was my understanding that the priests serving the temple —like those serving any other monastery—are not allowed to leave the premises."

"That is true. However, Brother Arana did not leave the premises, nor did he enact the ritual himself. He put the instructions for the blood rituals that he'd selected from the grimoire along with his notes into an envelope and handed it to one of his co-conspirators through one of the notched sections at the top of the outer wall. That is what I meant by being responsible in a roundabout way. Without his placement in the temple, the ritual wouldn't have been found or implemented in the first place."

"Is this priest mentally deficient?" Finvar spat. "He had to know that enacting the blood ritual—whoever actually did it—would doom the entire realm, him and his family included. He couldn't possibly think that Qadira would spare him or any of her miserable followers once she was regenerated."

Minerva laughed out loud. "Oh, High Lord, that is exactly what her followers all think. That no matter what heinous acts they perform, as long as they're serving the Dark Fae, they will be spared and the rest of the realm will be destroyed."

"But that's...it's delusional." Finvar huffed and shook his head, a dumbfounded look on his face.

"Agreed," Minerva replied. "Now, you can see why I usually

prefer to avoid conflicts between humans. There is no rhyme nor reason to their thought process."

"But these are not just humans," Tisharu insisted. "These are magickal beings as well. Fae, Elven, dwarves. All sorts of beings who are brainwashed by Qadira."

Minerva stared impassively at the fae Queen for a moment before speaking. "And your point is?"

"Okay, if Arana handed the instructions off, then who administered the blood ritual?" Valian asked before Tisharu got herself into trouble by responding to the old witch's implied comment. "Do we know this?"

"No, Chancellor, that is unclear as of yet," Minerva replied. "However, I think it will be of interest to you and several at this table as to where the information went when it was retrieved from the temple."

"And where would that be, Old One?" Niall asked with restrained impatience.

"It was taken to the Wysteria's Evening Court and handed over to none other than—"

"Kellam!" Finvar exclaimed with derision. "I knew he was somehow involved with the Dark Fae's return. The fucking traitor." He shot Minerva a steely look. "Please tell me that you will take him to the Oracles for his treasonous acts like you did the Red King. It is nothing less than he deserves for betraying us all."

Minerva smile was scary. "Do not trouble yourself, High Lord. That has already been taken care of. Unfortunately, Kellam and his reckoning is the least of our problems."

"What does that mean, Minerva?" Queen Beatrice asked. "If you know the blood ritual information that this priest extracted from Trillian's grimoire, I assume that then you can counter the ritual and send Qadira back to her grave. Is that not so?"

"In a perfect world, that would be correct, Beatrice," Minerva replied with a heavy sigh and a shake of her head. "But you and I both know, that is not how these things usually work out."

"Wait. You said that you knew what information Arana had slipped to the Evening Court. Why isn't it a matter of simple countering the ritual used?" Tisharu asked.

The old witch looked weary for a brief moment before straightening in her seat. "Because, as I said before, Brother Arana copied down several blood rituals along with his notes. Since he did not enact the ritual himself but handed the information off, he does not know which of the rituals he selected was chosen by whoever eventually administered the blood ritual."

"And since we don't actually know who did, we're pretty much screwed," Valian added. "Right?"

"Perhaps, Chancellor," Minerva said with a smile. "And then again, perhaps not."

Twenty-Four

"Perhaps not? What does that mean?" Alexi asked Minerva. "If you don't know what blood ritual was administered or even by whom, seems to me that Val's right. We're screwed. If we can't stop Qadira from completing her regeneration, she'll be virtually unstoppable."

The Old One turned her steely gaze on him, and Alexi could have sworn he saw her eyes twinkle before she smiled—and a bit evilly, he thought—at him. He actually felt a chill run down his spine.

That's just so not right, he thought. *And really disturbing.*

"As I said," Minerva began. "Brother Arana had selected several blood rituals from Trillian's grimoire and handed the information over to a co-conspirator in an envelope. As it happens, I have a copy of that list in my possession, Field Marshal." She tilted her head and narrowed her sparkling gray eyes. "Now, it is true, I don't know who did the casting of the blood ritual...*yet*. And I may not know which of the rituals listed was ultimately chosen...*yet*. However, I do know the name of the co-conspirator to which Brother Arana handed that envelope."

"Okay then," Alexi said with a nod. "So, we squeeze this co-conspirator until he tells us who did the deed, and then we do the same with the perpetrator until they give up the ritual that was used." He looked around the room and then back at Minerva. "Right?"

"Mmm, yes. The 'squeezing' of the co-conspirator, as you say, is being done by the Trinity as we speak," Minerva told him. "I don't suppose I need to tell you what that will entail?"

Alexi shook his head and felt another shudder skitter down his back. "Uh...no. I don't think I want that information taking up space in my brain, but thanks."

Nope, he thought. *No thank you, ma'am, you can just keep that shit to yourself.*

"I thought not," Minerva replied with an amused look.

That look, coupled with her gleeful tone, had Alexi worrying for a moment that he may have voiced his thoughts out loud, or that the old witch had actually read his mind, which he figured she was perfectly capable of doing. But then Minerva turned back to the group, and he let out a breath that he hadn't realized he'd been holding.

"Unfortunately, the process of running down the specific blood ritual used is going to take some time. Time I am not certain that we have." The Old One looked at the Prince, Isabella, and Alyssa in turn. "You three are going to be crucial. I've already spoken to Tempest and the Ellurian elders. You will meet with them tomorrow."

"Wait— What?" Gray stammered, his next volley of questions coming rapid-fire. "We're meeting with the Ellurians? Where? And why? How is that going to help us now? Do they know how to destroy the Dark Fae? And if so, why don't they just do it themselves?"

Minerva put up a hand, interrupting the Prince's onslaught. "Take a breath, young Prince. All will become clear in due time. Tempest will come to retrieve the three of you mid-morning for the trip to Daidoria, the capitol city of the cloaked Ellurian empire. There you will meet with your ancestors at the Temple of Ahshara. As to the why of it, well, it is time to see what you are made of, boy." Minerva stood and glanced at Isabella. "And in light of earlier events, it is also time for the new Halfling to begin spreading her own wings."

And with that parting shot, the Witch of the Eastern Glade vanished in a swirl of silver smoke.

"Well, that was fun," Alexi muttered into the silence that followed Minerva's departure. "Not."

"What did she mean by time to 'spread my own wings'?" Isabella asked no one in particular.

"What happened here this afternoon?" Gray asked. "Or was she talking about our dust-up with the Dark Fae in Roseland Wood?"

"Oh, my gosh, Izzy," Alyssa exclaimed. "Maybe she was talking about your reverie."

Valian's head snapped up. "I beg your pardon." He looked back and forth between Alyssa and Isabella. "Reverie? What reverie?"

Isabella sighed and gave him a resigned look. "I told you that I'd been losing time, so I thought that's what happened, but evidently, I had one of those vision thingies that Gray's been having. It was weird."

"What?" Feeling slightly dumbfounded, Alexi stared at Isabella. "You had a reverie, Bella? Why didn't you tell me?"

Isabella shrugged and blinked at him with a sheepish look. "I meant to tell you, I really did, but when you got back to the palace and told me about your encounter with the Dark Fae...well, it was just so frightening and crazy that I got caught up in it all. Plus, for me, the reverie was kinda like losing time again, because I didn't really remember much of it when it first happened, still don't. Then, I guess...I just...forgot. I'm sorry. Like I said, I meant to tell you."

"Look, don't feel bad, Alexi. It truly came out of the blue," Alyssa added. "She and I were sitting and talking with Queen Beatrice, and suddenly Isabella's eyes just rolled back in her head."

"But you're sure it was a reverie? And not just another loss of time?" Valian asked.

"Yes," Alyssa assured him. "When the Queen asked her what she was seeing, Izzy started speaking in a really strange voice. It was pretty surreal."

"It was definitely a reverie, Chancellor," the Queen confirmed. "As you know, I've had them myself from time to time, so I know what to look for and how they play out."

"What did she say during her trance?" Valian asked, as Isabella squirmed in her chair.

Alyssa glanced at her friend. "She said that the Unclean was growing stronger, which we already knew, and then something about the Dark Fae's essence was moving through the earth...searching."

"Searching for what?" Áine asked.

"The life blood of the magickal," Gray murmured.

"Yes! That's exactly what she said," Alyssa cried, pointing at the Prince. "But how did you know that?"

"Gray had a vision when we got to Roseland Wood," Valian responded. "What else did Isabella say in her reverie, Alyssa? What were her exact words?"

"Well...it's...hard to give you an exact quote, but there was something about death being near, and maybe more to come." She tilted her head, considering. "Then she said...there was jeopardy for all and the *Unclean* was returning for more. Wait, why do you want to know her exact words?"

"Because it appears that she was seeing the same thing I was seeing, used the exact wording that I did while in my own reverie." Gray replied. "Perhaps, at the very same time. That's interesting...and significant, I think."

"What?" Áine looked astonished. "Both of you having the same reverie at the same time?" She studied both of them for a moment. "That would be the Ellurian part of each of you connecting in a *joint* vision simultaneously. Now, that *is* interesting. And yes, Gray, I think you're right. It may be very significant."

"Uh, yeah," Alexi agreed, turning to Isabella and taking her hand. "You've been wondering how you fit into this whole thing. Maybe this trip to meet with the Ellurian elders will unlock more of your abilities, Bella. It could be a good thing and help you understand not only your place in the bigger scheme but also how it all works."

Isabella nodded slowly. "I suppose you're right. And if I'm gonna have this weird stuff popping up, it would be nice to get a handle on it beforehand."

"But why am *I* going on this little excursion?" Alyssa asked.

"That's what I don't understand. I don't have any magickal abilities, nor do I have anything to do with the Ellurians."

"Well, the Old One did say that the end of this nightmare may come down to you three," Niall reminded her. "She said you would all be crucial, remember?"

"Do you think it may have something to do with the Scepter of Fire?" Isabella mused. "Maybe Aly will need to use the scepter in conjunction with whatever it is that Gray and I will have to do."

Niall glanced at Alyssa. "That could very well be. However, you won't know until you go and meet with the Ellurian elders."

"You mean, until *we* meet with them," Alyssa said. "I'm not going without you."

"You may not have a choice, Alyssa," the Queen replied quietly. "We will ask Tempest when she arrives tomorrow, but the three of you may be the only ones allowed to go to the Ellurian empire." The Queen put up a hand when Alyssa made to argue. "There is no help for it, child. It's not our call, and we must abide by the Ellurians' wishes no matter what they decide. In the meantime, we will just have to wait until Tempest arrives tomorrow morning to find out."

"Nevertheless, it sounds to me as if Old Minerva knew about your reverie, Isabella," Valian said. "And correct me if I'm wrong, Gray, but didn't you have a new experience with your abilities during our skirmish today with Qadira?"

The Prince looked briefly surprised, but nodded. "You're right. I did. I was watching Tempest and had what I can only describe as a strong instinct to follow her lead. It felt almost like the precursor to a blood storm or the energy wave that came to me in the Barrens that I used to strike down the golem. It was a powerful force building inside my chest, but this time when it burst out of me it seemed to be an invisible shield instead of a killing wave."

"Yes. I thought so." Valian nodded. "I suspect that the Old One knew exactly what happened today for both you and Isabella. Hence, her cryptic remarks and this meeting that's been arranged with the Ellurian elders. After all, these are Ellurian abilities we're talking about."

Alexi leaned back in his chair. "Okay, so while these three go to find out what the Ellurians have to say and what help they can be, what do the rest of us do in the meantime? I mean, we can't just continue to sit around on our hands and wait for something to happen. Like Old Minerva said, we're running out of time. We need to make a better plan, be more proactive. And we need to do it now."

"I agree with the Field Marshal. That has been my opinion from the start," Niall murmured, pinning Valian with a hard look. "As you know, I am a fan of going on the offensive instead of reacting to events, which is where we've been. I am of a mind that we have less time than we think, and we're dawdling behind Qadira like inexperienced children."

"A little harsh, but unfortunately, true," Valian replied. "However, the hour is getting late and there's not much more we can do tonight. We'll meet first thing tomorrow morning before Tempest arrives and start the process of drafting that plan." He nodded to both High Lords and then to Tisharu. "Can you three be here early for that meeting?"

Both Finvar and Niall nodded.

"I'll be here," Finvar replied. "But I'll need to update and ready my troops first, as I'm sure Lord Niall and Queen Tisharu will want to do."

"Agreed," Niall confirmed with a nod.

"I concur with both my twin and the Field Marshal. It's time for us to take decisive action," Tisharu added. "I, for one, am done with waiting around to see where that dark bitch will strike next. Therefore, after discussing this with my lieutenant and preparing my own warriors for what may be coming, I'll be back tomorrow morning as well."

"Good." Gray cleared his throat. "We'll need to speak to all the other Queens and High Lords from the courts of both kingdoms once we get rolling with a concrete plan. This is going to involve the entire realm, so we'll need a solid, unified front from both kingdoms when we ultimately have to face Qadira. But until then, maybe one of you can tag Juppar and any others you think prudent at this point?"

"I can contact Juppar," Finvar said. "I know he'll want his Starlight Court to be represented, since he was the tip of the spear with Kellam's recent...removal from the Evening Court. He's also mentoring High Lord Quinn, Kellam's replacement, so he can keep the Evening Court in the loop."

Niall pushed his empty dessert plate back and leaned forward. "I've kept several of my brethren from Roseland's courts up to date on what we've been doing so far, so I'll see if Ayanna or Dyagmon will want to attend. Maybe even Luminox from the Daylight Court can be persuaded."

"Dyagmon? Really? His previous involvement with the Red King does not inspire trust and does give me some pause." Queen Beatrice said.

"Yes, that is understandable, Your Majesty. However, Dyagmon has seen the error of that choice since Aramond's downfall," Niall assured her. "Also, he and his court did not fight with the Red King. He wisely avoided that conflict. We have discussed the matter at length. Like most of the fae rulers of the Roseland courts, he was but trying to keep his Winter Court from harm's way during that unfortunate time period."

"That's true, Majesty," Alexi confirmed. "I have met with High Lord Dyagmon and his lieutenant Bracken recently. He was quite engaged and accommodating. He does, indeed, understand the urgency of the situation with the Dark Fae, and he seemed to be willing to help in any way."

"Thank you both. That does set my mind more at ease," the Queen replied.

"In addition to those mentioned here, I can tag Citron," Tisharu said. "We've also had several conversations about the recent events that have occurred here in Wysteria. He may want *his* Daylight Court to be involved as well."

"Good," Gray said with a nod. "Okay. Then if that's all for now, I suggest that everyone get some sleep. The morning will come all too soon, and I have a feeling that tomorrow is gonna be jam-packed."

THE FOLLOWING MORNING DAWNED COLD AND CLEAR. The late fall cloud cover had been replaced by blue skies and bright sunlight that did little to warm up the brisk air or melt the snow already layering the ground. The scheduled meeting Valian called for the previous night had gotten underway early. Queen Ayanna and High Lords Dyagmon and Luminox from Roseland's courts, as well as High Lords Juppar and Citron from Wysteria's courts, had joined the core group in the war room. Isabella and Alyssa had attended, but there hadn't been much for them to do or add, so they'd sat wide-eyed as a battle plan had been hashed out and specific duties had been assigned.

Tempest had arrived at the palace toward the end of the meeting, and confirmed that only Isabella, Alyssa, and Gray would be permitted to enter the Ellurian empire. This did not sit well with Alyssa, but as the Queen had stated the night before, it was not their call, and they'd have to abide by the wishes of the Ellurian elders.

As Alyssa had lingered in the Great Hall with Niall for her good-byes, Alexi had walked Isabella out to the main gates where he'd pulled her up close and kissed her senseless. He'd only just released her and stepped back when Tempest had loudly cleared her throat as she passed them. Once Alyssa finally joined them, they'd set off on foot toward Larkspur Meadow and the end of the mile fade-restriction barrier. When Isabella had looked back over her shoulder just before they'd entered the treeline at the edge of Cheshire Wood, Alexi had still been standing at the gate watching them.

Once they'd crossed the fade-restriction barrier, they began to fade in short hops. Alyssa traveled with Gray, who'd taken to fading —as if by second nature—after his Faerie Bomb episode during the summer. Isabella traveled with Tempest. There were periods of walking along the way as well. During that time, Isabella tried to concentrate on the beauty of the wintry landscape as they made their way to the Ellurian empire and not the apprehension of what they'd possibly find when they arrived.

"I sense your unease about this trip, *mo linbh milis*," Tempest stated as they'd passed through the security wards and crossed into the southern end of the Northern Wastelands. "You have nothing to be worried about. It is your ancient homeland. You have Ellurian blood running through your veins."

"And fae blood," Isabella replied.

"Yes. And fae blood."

"But I just discovered all of this, would never have known any of it if you hadn't sent me that invitation laced with Faerie Bomb. It was a lot. Still is." Isabella glanced at Tempest and marveled again at the fact that this tall, fae warrior was her great aunt. "Why did you do that? Dose me with Faerie Bomb? Why not just tell me all of this?"

Tempest's throaty laughter rang out. "Would you have believed me? Yes, you knew about this world through the descendant, had even been...close with Valian Winchester. Knew who and what he was, but would you have believed me had I just showed up and told you all?"

Isabella considered for a moment and then smiled. "I suppose that's fair, although, I did believe Valian when he told me that he was Elven and a chancellor in an alternate realm. But that's neither here nor there now, as we'll never know."

Tempest gave her a sidelong look, studying her until Isabella began to feel self-conscious.

Then the warrior grinned. "You have no idea how much you remind me of me, Isabella. Your great-grandmother will be annoyed over that, I can tell you. But Moira will also be quite proud of how you are accepting your newfound heritage and quickly adapting to it, as she was a bit disappointed with your mother, Marie."

Isabella shook her head. "This is very surreal, I gotta tell you. I was just getting used to Aly being the descendant, the magick of this place, being in a relationship with an elf." She rolled her eyes and shook her head. "And, geez, saying that out loud isn't weird or anything. But then I find out that my heritage is mixed up in it all, that part of my family is actually *from* here? It's just bizarre and really hard to wrap my mind around."

Tempest put an arm around Isabella's shoulders and gave her a quick squeeze. "As I said, you remind me of me, and that's how I know that you're going to be just fine. You're strong and courageous, *mo linbh milis.* You will do well."

Tempest turned to Gray and Alyssa who were walking a few yards behind. "All right, Your Grace, we're all going to have to hold hands for our next fade because you've never been here before. Except, of course, in dreams, but that won't count for much for fading, and I don't want to lose anyone. We're going to hop to my family court, the Court of the Eastern Rise, where we're going to pick up some help. Moira Nic Corragáin will accompany us to Daidoria and help me to get you all there safely."

"My great-grandmother is coming with us?" Isabella sputtered. "Really?"

Tempest laughed. "Yes, child. Moira is awaiting our arrival." She held out a hand. "Are you ready to meet her?"

Isabella took Tempest's hand, and then looked back at Alyssa and reached out with her free hand. "Come on, descendant. Let's go meet my great-grandmother."

Alyssa beamed. "Heck yeah!"

As Gray took his place on the other side of the immortal warrior, Tempest looked at each in turn. "Hold on, me lovelies. We're off to faerie land."

With that, they faded as one.

<h1 style="text-align:center">Twenty-Five</h1>

I t didn't take long for them to arrive at the Court of the Eastern Rise, which sat in the foothills at the eastern base of the mountain range it was named for. The Unwelcoming Rise rose up before them like a dark omen, its immense span, lofty height, and craggy cliffs imposing as well as ominous. It was just another mountain range, but for some reason just standing in its shadow made Isabella uneasy.

The Rise divided the Northern Wastelands into two very different regions. The western side of the range had a desolate landscape much like the Barrens. Flat-topped mesas were scattered across the terrain amid sand, rock, and desert scrub. The eastern side of the mountains looked and felt like a different world. The landscape here was lush and green, and Isabella marveled at the beauty that surrounded them as they stood at the court's outer stone wall.

Moira Nic Corragáin was indeed waiting for them as they entered the court's great hall. Isabella couldn't help but stare at this woman—her great-grandmother—who, like Queen Beatrice, was half human and half Ellurian. She looked exactly like the framed black and white photos Isabella's mother had hung along with the photos of other family members on the gallery wall in their Connecticut home. Photos from decades past.

Moira stepped forward, a warm smile on her lovely face. She

didn't look a day over fifty with smooth barely-lined skin, sharp green eyes, and wild red hair that she'd made an attempt to tame into a tight coil at the back of her head. It wasn't hard to see where Isabella had gotten her coloring, both in hair and eyes.

"Oh, Isabella, *mo chailín milis,*" Moira gushed as she crushed Isabella to her ample bosom in a grandmotherly hug and spoke softly into her ear. "My sweet, sweet baby girl. How I have waited for this moment." Holding Isabella close a bit longer, Moira finally pulled back, tears sparkling in her eyes. "I promised myself that I wouldn't cry when I finally got to meet you, see you with my own eyes, but alas, I can't help myself."

Isabella felt her eyes fill as well, and she blinked back her own tears. "This is just...so surreal. I've seen pictures of you, heard stories from Gram, but—"

Moira laughed out loud. "Oh, I can well guess at which stories Ríona may have told you. I was quite infamous in my youth, what the kids today would probably call a wild child."

"I loved those stories. Every single one of them," Isabella whispered as a lone tear broke free and coursed down her cheek.

Her great-grandmother reached out and wiped it away. "Oh, now, *a stór,*" Moira murmured, hugging Isabella close again. "Tears of joy, yes?"

"Yes. Joy. Absolutely." Isabella sniffed. Leaning back, she gazed up into her great-grandmother's eyes so like her own. "Meeting you just fills me up with it."

Moira looked over at Gray and Alyssa, and then to Tempest. "So, Sister, you've not only brought me one of my great-grandbabies, you've also brought me the descendant, and a prince, no less."

"I have," Tempest replied. "And I've warned them all good and proper about you and your wild ways."

Moira laughed again. "Did you now?" She leaned toward Gray and Alyssa and spoke in a conspiratorial whisper. "You know, you can't believe a thing this one says...well, what she says about me, anyway. She's always been just a wee bit jealous of me."

Tempest snorted, but grinned at that. Then her smile faded. "I'm sorry to put a rush on this, Moira, especially since you and Isabella have just met, but we do need to move this along. The elders will be waiting at the temple in Daidoria. And we are running out of time with the fecking Dark Fae."

"Yes, yes, of course." Moira smiled at Isabella. "We'll have a chance to get better acquainted and spend some time together later, but Tempest is right. There is much to do and time is short. Let me just grab my coat and gloves, and then we can be on our way."

It didn't take long before they were again standing outside the court's main gates with Tempest giving them some instructions for the trip.

"Since the Ellurian Empire has been cloaked for over a century, we'll be unable to fade into the capitol city. So, Prince Graydon, you and the descendant—"

"Alyssa. My name is Alyssa Montague," Alyssa interrupted. "Just saying..."

"And please, call me Gray," the Prince quickly insisted. "Titles carry no weight in what we're about today."

"As you wish." Tempest nodded to them both. "Gray, you and Alyssa will fade with me again, and Isabella will fade with Moria. We'll do this in longer hops. It should only take two or three fades for this stretch of the journey. Moira and I are frequent visitors to the empire and have done this many times. However, we will be forced to walk a bit further when we get closer to our destination because the fade restriction for the empire is double that of the White Palace."

"Wow. It's a two-mile restriction zone? That's crazy," Isabella said. "What happens if someone tries to fade into the empire? Do they hit an invisible wall or something?"

"No, no. Nothing that shocking," Moira replied. "Like with the fade restriction for the palace, the perpetrators would pass right through and find themselves on the other side of the empire without even knowing it."

"Pass right through? But how is that possible?" Alyssa asked, then stopped herself. She smiled and shook her head. "And that was a ridiculous thing to ask in a realm where magick reigns."

"Yes, 'tis all done with magick," Tempest said with a grin of her own. "Old Minerva brims with it, doncha know? In order to get into the empire, you must first live there, have business there, or otherwise have permission to enter the gates. And fading isn't allowed in the capitol city at all."

"Crazy," Isabella repeated in a hushed tone. "But I guess it's that way for security concerns, right?"

"It is," Tempest replied, then sighed. "All right, then. Is everyone ready? We need to be on our way so we don't keep the elders waiting."

Almost before Isabella could give a reply, they'd faded, and in the next instant, were materializing again in a wide, snow-covered meadow. The morning sunlight sparkled like diamonds over the snowy vista, but Isabella barely had time to take it all in, breathe in the crisp air, before they were on the move again. Two more fade sprints, and they arrived in yet another field just on the outskirts of the restriction zone for the Ellurian Empire.

"Okay, we walk from here. Stay close and keep your wits about you," Tempest warned. "The landscape here is verdant and beautiful, even peaceful, but it is deceiving. Like the rest of the Wastelands, all manner of beasties live and hunt here as well. And though most of them hunt after the sun goes down, there are those who prowl the daylight hours."

"Well, that's good to know," Gray murmured as they began to cross the snowy field. "A bit of a harsh reality check, but a good reminder."

"Yeah, I'd rather not run into any of those beasties, thank you very much," Alyssa replied. "My time in the Barrens last summer was a good lesson, for sure."

"I can't even imagine," Isabella agreed. "It's bad enough seeing some of those frightening creatures in my dreams. I don't need to see them up close and personal in reality."

Isabella perused the landscape when they'd gotten halfway across the meadow, and she began to have the strangest sense of déjà vu. Thinking back over her dreams, she knew that she'd seen this place before. As she looked across to the other side of the field, bits and pieces of those dreams began to surface again. She had a clear image of the men dressed in black robes standing sentinel-like along the treeline...watching.

A shiver made its way down her spine.

Then Gray came alongside her and took her hand, giving her a start. He nodded toward the treeline. "That's where I saw them, too."

Isabella frowned. "How did you...?"

The Prince shook his head. "The image just sprang up in my mind. The men in black robes. That's who you were thinking about, wasn't it?"

Isabella nodded. "I saw them in my dreams several times. Tempest told me not to engage them."

Gray glanced at the warrior walking on the other side of Alyssa. "She told me the same in one of my dreams, said it wasn't my time yet. Guess she was right. Looks like now it may be. We'll be seeing them today."

They walked on in silence for another thirty minutes through a large swath of forested land where the tree canopy was so dense it was like walking through the woodland in the dead of night.

"I sure wouldn't want to be making this trip alone," Alyssa said in almost a whisper.

"I agree. It's a beautiful forest, but it does kinda give me the willies," Isabella replied. "Though I can't put my finger on just why."

"It makes me think of my escape from the Red Palace. Violet and I moving through the dark of Roseland Wood with terror flooding my senses at every little noise. Then being chased by that mountain troll." She gave an exaggerated shudder. "Horrible. And not something I'd ever want to repeat."

Tempest gave her a sidelong glance. "You had a run in with a mountain troll and lived to tell about it?"

"Yes, well, I lived to tell about it, thanks to Niall. He came looking for us and found us at just the right time. That troll took off like he was on fire the minute he set eyes on the High Lord of Roseland's Twilight Court coming at him with that humongous sword he wields."

"Mmm, yes. I would imagine. Niall does have a dangerous air about him."

"That he does," Alyssa murmured with a smile.

Isabella laughed out loud. "That's just one of the many things Aly loves about him. Right, pal?"

Alyssa flushed but laughed along with Isabella. "I can't deny that, Izz. There is something attractive about a handsome, dangerous male. I'm sure you know what I mean. Alexi Tovan is no slouch in that area."

"No he is not."

"Interesting," Tempest murmured. She considered Alyssa for a moment. "The High Lord and the descendant. That would make a good story. Sort of like Beauty and the Beast, or maybe an addendum to little Alice's original tale."

Alyssa shook her head. "Considering that Niall is not a fan of how he was depicted in those children's stories, I'm certain he would not be amused with either."

"The Knave of Hearts? Come on, Aly. He is a bit of a scoundrel, so Alice's description does fit him pretty well," Isabella said. "Though I can see how he would be annoyed with it all."

"Ah, well, it is an interesting thought, nonetheless." Tempest turned to Isabella then with a quizzical look. "Then there's the Halfling and the Elven warrior. Could be another interesting story there, yes?" she asked.

But before Isabella could respond, Tempest's attention snapped backed to the path ahead, and she slowed her steps. Coming to an abrupt halt, the fae immortal raised a closed fist, indicating that they should all stop walking as well.

"Yes," Moira said. "I felt it, too, Sister. Someone is approaching... with stealth."

Both Tempest and Moira stepped in front of the others. The immortal warrior pulled her lethal sword from its sheath on her back, and Moira magickly conjured her own. Isabella could almost taste the tension that charged the air. They all waited for several anxious moments before a handful of Elven warriors emerged from the brush onto the path ahead of them.

"Well, well, what do we have here? An immortal fae warrior, her sister, and who else?" The leader of the group stepped closer.

"Good morning to you, Aubron," Tempest called, lowering her sword and then returning it to its sheath. "What are you doing lurking here in Louranby Wood? Do you have nothing better to do?"

Aubron chuckled. "We've been patrolling while you lollygag

about in the western kingdoms." Then the elf sobered and came closer. "We had a run in earlier with a group of Qadira's followers farther north, Tempest."

The fae warrior frowned. "So close to the cloaked empire? That's disturbing."

Aubron nodded. "It's getting worse, too. Their movement is growing again now that the Dark Fae has risen."

"Yes. I'm aware of that."

"Did you also know that there have been groups moving south in the last few weeks? We've been hearing rumblings of a coalition, an alliance mounting in the Barrens."

Tempest sighed. "No, I had not heard that, but I'm not surprised. Qadira's followers didn't just have a change of heart and fade away when we beat her down at the end of the war." She ran a hand over her face. "This is good information, Aubron. I will pass it along to the Caemmeirth as well as Queen Beatrice in the western kingdoms." She gestured to the others standing behind her and her sister. "Moira and I are actually escorting Prince Graydon, Alyssa Montague, the descendant, and Moira's great-granddaughter, Isabella Doyle Christensen to the temple in Daidoria to meet with the elders as we speak."

The Elven warrior's face showed his surprise but he quickly recovered and nodded. "Yes, well, look sharp and watch your back with a cautious eye. That group of rebels came out of nowhere, so just be mindful."

"We're almost to the empire's border now," Moira said, flicking her magically conjured sword away. "But thank you for the warning, Aubron. We'll keep an eye out. Now, you stay out of trouble, do you hear?"

"Ah, now, Moira, where is the fun in that?" the elf quipped with a grin. "Safe travels to you all."

With that, the group of Elven warriors melted back into the brush and disappeared as quickly as they'd arrived.

"Let's get a move on," Tempest suggested. "We've less than a quarter mile to go."

"Yes," Moira agreed. "I'll breathe easier once we're inside the empire's boundary. Easier still, once we're within the walls of Daidoria."

Ten minutes later, they emerged from the treeline into yet another large snow-covered pasture where both Tempest and Moira stopped walking and turned to them.

"In order to enter the cloaked empire, we will all need to hold hands," Moira stated. "Tempest and I have permission to enter, so we're your way in as well."

She and Tempest intermingled themselves between the other three—Moira between Alyssa and Isabella, and Tempest between Isabella and Gray.

"Alright. Hold on," Tempest said with a grin. "Here we go."

The group started walking forward hand in hand into the field in a line of five. Isabella wondered what they were supposed to see. Where was this empire? Would it just appear before them? But then about a hundred yards or so in, it was like walking into a wall of thick fog. The next thing she knew, they'd stepped out of the haze, and her entire field of vision had changed. She caught sight of the impressive walls of an ancient-looking city spread out before them with another beautiful, rugged mountain range—one she remembered from her dreams—covered in snow in the distance.

It was a stunning sight indeed. The group dropped hands, and all Isabella could do was gape at the city's vast size and circumference. From where they stood, the walls seemed enormous with ramparts running along the top perimeter of the thick stone in both directions.

"Welcome to the Ellurian Empire and the capitol city of Daidoria, child," Moira whispered into her ear. "This is an important part of your heritage, Isabella."

"This is amazing, is what it is" Isabella whispered. "I've never been here, but somehow it feels—"

"Familiar?" Gray finished for her. "Yeah, I kind of feel the same way."

Tempest chuckled. "Well, come on, then. Let's go meet some of your distant relatives."

It was another ten-minute walk to Daidoria's gates and then on into the city itself. Isabella thought that this must be what tourists feel like when visiting New York City for the first time, though this was in more of an old-world sort of way. She imagined that cities around her home world would have looked much the same as this in centuries past. She knew that she was gawking at everything and everyone as they walked into the heart of the city, but she couldn't help herself. The restaurants, the shops full of all manner of magickal wares, the horse-drawn carts. It was a melding of the old and the magickal. And it was fascinating, like something out of a fairy tale, which she figured was an apt correlation.

When they'd reached the other end of the thoroughfare, Tempest paused on a corner and pointed to the mysterious, gothic-like structure on a hill overlooking this part of the city.

"Our destination. The Temple of Ashara," she said.

They continued up the incline, and though Isabella thought of herself as fit, she was breathing hard by the time they got to the top of the hill. She was relieved to finally be standing at the temple gates. Taking a moment to get her breath under control, she studied the temple's massive outer walls.

Unlike the austere look and feel of the Temple of the Oracles, the Temple of Ashara was more like what she'd expected a sanctuary or shrine to be. The outer stone walls were topped with ornate ironwork, the gates adorned with intricate carvings and mystical symbols. Where the Temple of the Oracles felt more like a fortress or prison, this was a towering, awe-inspiring cathedral shrouded in mystery.

It wasn't long before a small door next to the massive gates opened, and a priest in dark robes beckoned them inside. Looking around at Gray and Alyssa with wide eyes, Isabella's heart began to pound. What would they find within these walls? What would be expected of them?

Moira stepped close and put an arm around Isabella's shoulders. "Just breathe, *a stór*. There is nothing to be frightened of here. This is your destiny, Isabella."

That's what worries me, Isabella thought. "But what if I don't measure up? Look, I have no fae or Ellurian abilities," she said aloud, then frowned. "Well, I did have a reverie yesterday, but other than that, I'm woefully unequipped for any of this. I'm just as ordinary as they come in magickal terms. I mean, I plan parties and events for a living, for crying out loud." She turned to Moira. "I just don't want to let everyone down."

"Don't be ridiculous," Tempest said, stepping up beside them. "Never gonna happen. And you are far from ordinary, Isabella Doyle. You come from a long line of extraordinary warriors and conjurers. You are destined for great things. This is merely the beginning."

"Tempest, you're not helping," Moira admonished, and then turned Isabella around to face her. "Now, you listen to me, *mo linbh milis*. The one thing my sister is correct about is that there is nothing ordinary about you. Your time of Becoming will be here sooner than you think. The elders in this very temple will guide you and help you through it. And you could never let anyone down, least of all me." She stood up straight and gave a succinct nod. "So, close your eyes, take a deep breath, and let it out slowly. Do it now."

Isabella swallowed hard and then did as she was told...and was amazed to feel her anxiety begin to slip away. When she opened her eyes, she looked up at Moira in surprise. "Did you do that?"

Moira smiled and tapped the end of Isabella's nose. "No, child. You did. Now, come. We're keeping the nice priest waiting."

With another quick breath, Isabella and the others stepped through the side door and into the courtyard of the temple as they prepared to greet their entwined destinies.

Twenty-Six

Though both the Temple of the Oracles and the Temple of Ahshara each gave off a very different vibe on the outside, Isabella found that on the inside, they had a similar reverent, almost hallowed feel. Like the temple that housed the Trinity, the vestibule walls here were covered with much the same kinds of mystical symbols, but in this temple, the Ellurian history was told not only through hieroglyphics but through ancient Ellurian script as well.

There were also noticeable differences in not only appearance but in the number of those who served in the Temple of Ahshara. Just within fifteen minutes of entering the vestibule, Isabella had noticed not just one, but had counted eight priests going about their daily tasks, all dressed in the same burgundy robes, including the priest who'd met them at the outer gates and stood with them now.

After a hushed discussion had taken place between Tempest and the priest, the immortal warrior turned to the group. "I'll be going in first to give the elders an update of what we learned earlier from Aubron, and then I'm heading back to the White Palace to pass that information on to Queen Beatrice and Chancellor Winchester while you three have your meeting with the elders. I'm hoping they've done some appropriate planning for what may come. I'm also going to speak with the Old One while I'm there, if I can." She turned and took Isabella's hand, giving it a brief squeeze. "You will do well here, *mo chailín milis*. Of that, Moira and I have no doubt. Follow the voice inside you, for it will show you the way. And above all, remember who you are and who you've come from."

Isabella took a deep breath and nodded.

The immortal warrior then turned and followed the priest into the sanctuary.

While they waited for Tempest's return, the rest of the group spent their time milling about the vestibule. As they'd done at the Temple of the Oracles on Sunday afternoon, they studied the ancient writing and intricate symbols that covered the walls depicting Ellurian history. Surprisingly, they had only about fifteen minutes to wait before Tempest returned, and after a whispered conversation with Moira, the two grasped forearms and shared a brief hug.

"As Aubron advised, watch your back, Sister," Moira said. "And, as always, safe travels."

Tempest nodded. "And you as well, Sister. Take care of *The Three* while I'm gone. We are on the countdown and time grows short. We have no room for error now." Then she spun on her heel and was gone without a backward glance.

The priest stepped up at that point and spoke to Moira in a hushed tone, who then gestured for Isabella, Alyssa, and Gray to follow, and they were finally led into the sanctuary. There, they were met by four imposing figures, one of which held a long staff of some kind made of twisted wood and topped with a fist-sized crystal of clear, azure-blue.

The elders.

Though Isabella had only seen them from a distance, these were the tall men from her dreams, wearing the same black robes and standing like sentinels at the other end of the sanctuary in front of an elaborate altar.

"Come forward," the elder holding the staff called in a deep, baritone voice. "Do not be timid. There is much to discuss...and to learn about each of you."

"And much required knowledge to impart before you leave this temple," said another.

"Time grows short," added a third.

And so it begins, Isabella thought then willed her feet to move forward along with the others.

As the group approached the elders, Isabella got a better look at the four men and was surprised by their youthful countenance. She'd expected ancient beings to appear old and timeworn. Of course, just about everyone in the Artemysian realm was much older than they appeared, so there was no telling how old the elders really were.

"I am Aleksander, senior elder of Ahshara. Moira Nic Corragáin, you will go with Elder Garin now." He gestured to one of the other elders. "He has questions for you and a few issues to review." Then turning back, Aleksander studied Isabella, Gray, and Alyssa with narrowed eyes before—obviously satisfied by what he'd seen— dismissing them and nodding at Moira. "*The Three* will follow me."

"Very good, Elder Aleksander," Moira replied, then winked at Isabella.

Isabella exchanged wary glances with Alyssa and Gray and could see that they, too, were uneasy about what was to come. Her anxiety rose but she took several deep breaths and tried to remember what both her great-grandmother and Tempest had told her. If this was what she was meant to do, no matter how surreal or scary it seemed, she'd made up her mind to see it through.

With a last fleeting glance at Moira's retreating back, Isabella followed Elder Aleksander along with Alyssa and Gray. The two remaining elders trailed behind them. The senior elder guided them around the ornate altar to the back of the chamber where he pressed his palm to the smooth, dark stone. There was a deep rumble from somewhere inside the structure and an opening slowly appeared in the wall. As the door swung inward, a stone staircase curving down- ward from the landing into the darkness was revealed. The stairwell was lit only with what Isabella considered faerie lights around the base perimeter of the landing and on the wall next to each step. And then there was Elder Aleksander's staff. Its azure crystal was now glowing and splashing bright-blue light around the close confines of the area.

In silence, they followed the elder through the doorway and started down the steps. It was like something out of a fantasy or a medieval movie, and Isabella reminded herself to be cautious. Here there were no handrails or banisters of any kind, just wide stone steps and smooth walls disappearing into the gloom. There was no telling how far down they were going, and a misstep here could be disastrous.

As they descended, the air was cool and a bit damp on Isabella's face. Cooler still, the deeper they went, making her glad that she'd worn a good winter coat and a warm pair of gloves for the trip. She pulled the gloves out of her pocket where she'd put them when they'd arrived and drew them back on when the light puffs of her own breath hung in the air.

They passed two landings as they continued down into the bowels of the cathedral, each with a door leading out of the stairwell, but to where? Another room? A hallway to another area of the cathedral? Isabella had lost all sense of direction and couldn't even imagine how far beneath the hallowed space the staircase went.

She did, however, wonder how much deeper into this labyrinth they would go before reaching their destination or if this was some kind of weird test. But on the heels of that thought, they reached yet another landing, and this time, Elder Aleksander placed a hand on the stone next to the landing door, and there was a mechanical 'click.' To Isabella's relief, the door swung open and they all followed him out of the stairwell and into a large—and thankfully warmer—chamber.

Once they crossed the threshold, the large space was illuminated by pinpricks of light—reminiscent of bright stars—scattered across the ceiling. It gave the chamber an almost otherworldly feel. But the broadest and strongest beam of light bore down on the very center of the room where the largest crystal orb that Isabella had ever seen sat atop a square stone pillar nearly four feet in height. Raised stone benches framed the pillar on three of the four sides.

Elder Aleksander stopped next to the crystal orb and gestured for them to take a seat, which they did. And with the warmth of the chamber, they all removed their winter garb.

"Alyssa Montague, you are the descendant. I sense that you are wondering why you are here," he said. "Is this not so?"

Alyssa cleared her throat and nodded. "Um, yes, I suppose so. I have no relationship to the Ellurian Empire. And with the exception of the Scepter of Fire, I don't have much of a relationship to either of the kingdoms. So...why *am* I here?"

"You are here because of the scepter. You alone can wield the Scepter of Fire that the Oracles designed for your ancestor to use to protect this realm. You will be needed to do so again." He glanced at each of them in turn. "You are *The Three*."

"The three? As in, the magickal number of three?" Gray asked with a frown.

The elder nodded. "Correct. The descendant is the great-granddaughter of the great-granddaughter of the original Alice. Isabella Doyle Christensen is the great-granddaughter of Moira Nic Corragáin. And you, Prince Graydon—while not governed by the magickal number of three—are the son of the High Lord of Wysteria's Winter Court, as well as the grandson of Seanchán of the North. You and Isabella Doyle Christensen are Halflings in a similar manner. You both have human, fae, and Ellurian blood. You also each have more power residing within you than you know, which is why we are here today."

"Look, I don't mean to be contrary, or anything, but I don't have any powers from either of those birthrights," Isabella said. "Well, not much, anyway. What I do have is pretty pitiful, and I seriously don't know how I can be of any help here, but I'll do whatever you think necessary. Both Tempest and my great-grandmother think that this is my destiny." She shrugged. "So, I guess I'm all in."

The elder tilted his head and studied her for so long that Isabella began to squirm. Then he beckoned to both her and Gray. "The two of you come here and stand next to the Crystal of Ahshara."

When they both did so, he continued. "Prince Graydon, we shall start with you, as you have experienced more of your magickal abilities and in a more consistent manner. Place both of your hands on crystal, please."

Gray looked at Isabella with raised eyebrows but complied. Within moments, the crystal lit up with a bright light and all color drain from the Prince's face. As they had during his reverie on Sunday afternoon, his eyes went wide, rolling back in his head so that all that could be seen was a translucent white.

"Can you hear me, Prince Graydon?" Elder Aleksander asked.

"Yes," Gray answered.

His voice was calm and low, unlike the monotoned responses Isabella had witnessed during the Prince's previous reverie.

"Good. It is time for you to take control of your combined Ellurian and fae abilities, the immense power that lingers within you. I want you to look deep, find the core of that power where it awaits you. Can you see it?"

Gray's eyebrows lowered for a moment, but then he nodded. "Yes. I see it. It pulses."

"Can you feel the power emanating there? Hear the thrum of it, feel it in your bones?"

"Yes."

"I want you to reach out with your mind and take hold of that kernel, that core of power. Feel it in your hands, as it spreads up your arms, as it infuses your entire being. Do it now."

Gray's whole body stiffened and then also began to glow and pulse with an ethereal light. It was mesmerizing...and a little bit disturbing. What was he feeling? Did he know what was happening to him?

And even more disturbing, am I next? Isabella thought.

After several minutes, the light radiating from the Prince began to ebb, and then winked out altogether. The Prince blinked several times and then glanced at Isabella, a grin spreading across his handsome face. He looked as he always had, though Isabella could sense that something fundamental in him had changed.

He was almost gleeful with it.

"Okay. Now, that was quite the rush," he said, dropping his hands from the crystal and running them through his hair. "I mean... wow!"

"Prince Graydon, pay attention, please. Can you still feel the core of your power? Can you access it at will?" Elder Aleksander asked with a stern look.

Gray closed his eyes for a moment, and his grin settled into a pleasurable smile. He lifted his hands, palms up, and fire leapt in both. Opening his eyes, he laughed out loud as the flames continued to dance in his palms. "That would be a yes, Elder Aleksander. I can see it, feel it where it now resides with complete clarity. It's amazing."

Gray closed his hands into fists and the flames died away. "The power I've felt up to this point has always been scattered, unfocused, and at times even non-existent. This...this is something else, and I feel certain that I can access it...well, whenever I wish."

"Excellent. Then please take your seat next to the descendant."

Elder Aleksander gestured toward the bench where Alyssa sat watching, but when Isabella meant to follow, the elder shook his head. "No. Not you, Isabella Doyle Christensen."

Isabella's breath backed up in her chest, and her heart began to pound in her ears, but she turned and stepped back into place at the pillar. "I guess this means that it's my turn," she whispered.

"Indeed," the elder replied, and the twinkle in his eye surprised Isabella. "It is now your turn. Place your hands on the crystal, please."

Isabella took a deep breath around the lump of fear in her chest and blew it out slowly. Then, she placed both of her palms onto the crystal orb.

This was much different than anything else she'd experienced. She'd remembered nothing from the time lapses she'd endured, remembered very little of the reverie that she'd had just the day before, but now she felt everything. She no longer saw the chamber or the crystal, but could feel the orb under her fingertips. Her field of vision was now a warm, comforting glow—her guide, the soothing tone of Elder Aleksander's voice.

"Can you hear me, Isabella?" his voice asked.

"Yes," she answered.

"Good. As with the Prince, it is now your time to take control of your combined abilities, both fae and Ellurian. You also have an immense power sleeping inside you, and we're going to awaken it. Look deeper now, child. Find your core of power where it slumbers. Can you do that?"

At first, Isabella struggled. There was suddenly so much here, so many strange and wonderful images dancing before her eyes. Then something extraordinary emerged from the disorder, piercing the clutter and taking her breath. A golden sphere with a pulsing light of its own came into view. It seemed so close that Isabella itched to reach out and touch it.

"Isabella? Can you see the core of your power?" the elder asked.

"Yes," she replied in a voice gone breathless. "I've found it. It's... beautiful."

"Can you feel its pulse?"

"Yes. Like a heartbeat."

"Now, reach out and grasp it, feel its power permeate your being. Do it now."

As Isabella reached out in her mind and took hold of the golden core, her body went rigid as an intense electric energy shot through her from head to toe. Her vision was again filled with golden light, and a deep thrumming echoed the pulsing of that light. It was as awe-inspiring as it was overwhelming. After several moments, it all settled down into a familiar hum that seemed to inhabit her very bones. She opened her eyes, blinking a few times, and removed her hands from the crystal orb.

Glancing at Gray, she laughed out loud. "Boy, you weren't kidding, were you? That really was a rush. Kinda still is."

"Isabella, I need you to focus, as you are not finished," Elder Aleksander said in a severe tone. "This is crucial. Can you still feel your core of power? Can you also access it?"

Isabella blinked again, and then nodded. "I think so. I mean, I can still see it in my mind and feel it pulsing, like, in my bones. It's pretty strange."

The elder narrowed his eyes. "Strange or not, it is a good first step. However, since you haven't used your power in any meaningful form, we'll need to do some testing. And, of course, some training. We'll start with something simple—generating energy. This is a basic function of all of your abilities. Hold your hands out in front of you, palms facing each other. Like this."

Elder Aleksander demonstrated, and then Isabella followed.

"Now, close your eyes and take command of your core. Think about electric energy, the feel of it. Visualize it arcing and snapping between your palms. Can you see that?"

Isabella nodded. "I do see it. It's like a mini-lightning storm." She opened her eyes and saw that the tickling in both of her palms was caused by the miniature storm snapping between them. There was no pain with it, but she wondered what would happen if she flung that electrical energy at something or someone.

"Very good," Elder Aleksander commended. "You should never feel pain of any kind from this energy no matter what you conjure it for. However, use caution, as it can be quite destructive when used as a weapon."

Isabella wondered if he'd read her mind or was just giving instruction. Either way, his warning gave her pause.

"As I said, this energy is the foundation of all your abilities. It's how you wish to use this energy that determines the outcome. Now, try another. This time, with your eyes open. Think of the fire that Prince Graydon exhibited."

Isabella blinked and the mini-lightning storm ceased. She turned her palms upward and found that she had but to cast a single thought to fire, and the flames leapt in her palms.

"This is..." She giggled. "Well, I just have no words for this." She turned to the elder with an astonished look. "All of this was buried down inside me? I just don't understand why it took so long to come to light. I mean, why now after all this time?"

"Perhaps, you didn't need it before. However, I would imagine that some of your ability has seeped out of you here and there over the years, but was ignored or explained away."

"We talked about that. Remember, Izzy?" Alyssa said from where she was sitting on the stone bench next to Gray and listening intently. "How you could always tell me what I was looking for and where to find it. Also, that you seemed to disappear during games of hide-and-go-seek."

The twinkle was back in the elder's eyes. "You must understand that destiny is written in a different way for each of us, Isabella. It shows itself and blossoms when the time is right, and not before. Your time has come. Do not squander it." He turned to Gray. "Now, let's try a few more things for both of you."

THE THREE SPENT ANOTHER TWO AND A HALF HOURS with Elder Aleksander in the crystal chamber before Gray and

Isabella began to feel more confident with their powers, and the elder was satisfied with this first level of their command of it. Gray knew that Isabella was still shaky about her abilities and how to use them, but he had to admit that he was pretty impressed with how she'd taken to something so foreign to her in such a short amount of time.

Alyssa had gotten some time in with them as well. Elder Aleksander seemed adamant that she would need to wield the Scepter of Fire before this nightmare with the Dark Fae was finally over, and that it would be in conjunction with the abilities both Gray and Isabella now held.

Unfortunately, Gray was beginning to have his doubts that they would ever be free of Qadira's threat. If her followers had indeed been uniting in the Barrens over the last few weeks, he was afraid that another all-out war was on the horizon. Since they'd just divested themselves of Aramond, the Red King, over the summer after years of struggle, Gray wasn't pleased with the prospect of another long, drawn-out conflict. Especially with a nearly unstoppable, dark immortal and her followers.

He tried to put those disturbing thoughts aside as they climbed back up from the dark recesses of the cathedral and emerged into the sanctuary where Moira was waiting for them. But something was beginning to nag at him, an uneasy feeling inside that was getting stronger by the minute. He wasn't certain what it was, but starting out of the vestibule into the waning light of the late afternoon, Isabella took his arm. When he met her eyes, he knew she was feeling his uneasiness, too.

"Something's wrong," Isabella said. "Can you feel it?"

"I've been feeling the same. How about we try looking at it together?"

She nodded, linking hands with his as Moira and Alyssa joined them.

"What's happening here?" Moira asked.

"Gray and I are sensing something...off. We're just going to check it out," Isabella said.

"Check it out?" Alyssa asked. "How are you going to do that?"

Looking into Gray's eyes, Isabella smiled. "Easy-peasy."

And just like that, they stepped into a reverie together, and this time, they both knew exactly what they were doing.

Twenty-Seven

When Tempest left the Temple of Ahshara, her first intended destination was the White Palace to apprise the Queen and Valian of what she and Moira had learned from Aubron. After that, she'd planned a visit to Old Minerva's cabin. If things were heating up in the Barrens with Qadira's follow-ers, Tempest needed to touch base with the old sorceress to see what progress had been made in the search for the blood ritual used to raise the Dark Fae. If the correct ritual wasn't found soon, their only hope would be laid at the feet of the three unlikely saviors that she'd just helped Moira deliver to the temple. Elder Aleksander had been adamant that *The Three*—as he called them—would ultimately be the ones to put an end to Qadira.

But would they be ready to face that challenge when it arrived?

Tempest didn't know the answer to that question. However, they'd deal with that if and when it was required. In the meantime, she was going to put into place as many fail-safes as she could manage to give them all time—whatever time they had left—to prepare for any possible outcomes.

She'd left the Ellurian Empire behind with Aubron's earlier warnings looming large in her mind, and as she faded from point to point, caution was her constant traveling companion. She would be unwise to take those warnings for granted with rebel forces now popping up when least expected.

As she materialized at the Wastelands-Barrens boundary just shy of the security wards along Wysteria's northeastern border, she paused to scan her surroundings. She was always vigilant when traveling anywhere near the Barrens, even on a good day. However, these were uncertain times, to say the least, and she would breathe a bit easier once she'd left the Barrens behind, if only just for a few hours.

Tempest took another quick scan of the terrain before she walked the last five hundred yards or so and crossed through the wards into the kingdom of Wysteria just north of Willow Glen Wood. She'd entered the Wood and was about to fade south to the White Palace's fade-restriction zone when her senses began to tingle. She was not alone in the Wood. Someone or something was near.

And watching her.

With slow and careful movement, Tempest reached for the sword at her back, pulling it from its sheath. Then she walked in a tight circle, scanning the path and the immediate underbrush.

"I see your skills of detection are still in working order, warrior."

The voice, followed by a rusty cackle, seemed to come from everywhere at once, but Tempest relaxed when she recognized, if not the voice, the sound of the laughter.

"Why you insist on this ornery behavior is beyond my ken and not the least bit amusing, Old One," she said, sheathing her sword. "Now, come out and show yourself. Tell me why you're lurking in the gloom and quit wasting my time. I'm on a mission."

In a sudden swirl of gray smoke, the Witch of the Eastern Glade appeared on the path before her. "You have a smart mouth, Tempest. Always have had," she grumbled.

Tempest crossed her arms and narrowed her eyes. "And your point would be what? I did learn all that my smart mouth has to offer from the very best."

The old witch cackled again, her pale, gray eyes sparkling with mirth. "Flattery will get you nowhere, you immortal imp." Minerva tilted her head and studied her. "What mission is it then? What are you about in Willow Glen Wood? You're a long way from the Court of the Rise."

Shaking her head, Tempest sighed. "Please. I suspect you know exactly why I'm here. I'm on my way to the palace, aren't I? Moira and I spoke with Aubron this morning on our way to Daidoria with *The Three* in tow. He gave us some disturbing news, and I was on my way to pass it along to the Queen. Do I really need to tell you what news I'm carrying?"

Minerva's smile faded and those gray eyes, so full of mirth moments before, went hard and dark. "No," she said. "I am well aware of what you've heard, of what's happening in the Barrens...and elsewhere."

"What do you mean 'elsewhere?' Are Qadira's forces growing somewhere else as well?" Tempest stepped closer, lowering her voice. "And where are we with the search for the blood ritual? We're running out of time, Minerva."

The Old One shook her head. "No, child, we're not running out of time. We *are* out of time. The Dark Fae has fully regenerated. Qadira is now immortal. And yes, her forces are growing not only in the Barrens, but in pockets here in both kingdoms as well. And she'll be on the move within hours, I fear."

"Then we are lost," Tempest whispered. "That monstrous bitch will destroy everything she touches, and we'll not be able to stop her now. *The Three* are not ready, Old One. Not a match for what Qadira has become."

A slow smile spread across the old sorceress' face.

"What are you smiling about now, you old crone?" Tempest cried. "Have you finally lost all your faculties? This is disastrous news."

Minerva waved a hand in the air. "Oh, for the love of the Oracles, don't be so dramatic. Or so dim."

Tempest blinked at the old witch, then frowned. "Tell me you have a plan," she demanded.

"I have a plan." Minerva smirked. "There. Feel better? You won't like it much, as it may require a sacrifice on your part, but you are correct. *The Three* are not quite ready for this, so we must do something to buy them some time. Come. These woods have ears. We'll adjourn to the cabin and discuss the details before you carry on to the palace."

"WELL, GEE, KIDS, IT LOOKS LIKE WE'RE ALL IN A boatload of trouble here," Alexi stated with a cheeky smile. "Any suggestions on how we bail ourselves out of this sinking ship? If so, now would be the perfect time to throw any ideas you have out onto the table."

Valian agreed with Alexi, and though his cousin's flippant tone belied the seriousness of the situation, Alexi's face told a different story. They were indeed in a boatload of trouble. Old Minerva had made an emergency visit to the palace two hours ago, relaying the latest news about the Dark Fae.

That news was not good.

The fact that sixteen of the eighteen leaders of both kingdoms' fae courts had answered the call in record time and were now here seated around the war room conference table attested to how dire the situation actually was. Only two of Roseland's fae leaders, Queen Mabry of the Evening Court, and High Lord Balzar of the Autumn Court, had refused to attend. Though that was not much of a surprise since they were both allies of the Red King during that conflict. No matter the outcome now with Qadira, this would end poorly for both of them.

Valian cleared his throat and spoke into the uncomfortable silence. "Just so there's no misunderstanding and we're all on the same page, I'm going to recap in the simplest terms what the Field Marshal has just explained to you. The information that Old Minerva passed on to us is that the Dark Fae is completely regenerated and is now also immortal. Which means that any offensive plans we'd drawn up earlier are now obsolete. At this point, defending the kingdoms must be the priority."

"This is truly catastrophic news, Chancellor, but it's actually worse than that, isn't it?" Quinn, Kellam's replacement as High Lord of Wysteria's Evening Court countered.

"What do you mean, Quinn?" Alexi asked.

"Well, the Dark Fae's followers have been uniting in the Barrens over the last few months. That process has increased in the past three weeks. I know this because Kellam was part of that treachery, though I had no power at the time to stop him."

Valian nodded. "That is true. We've suspected that this may be occurring but have only just found out in the last week or so how quickly that alliance has grown and the extent of the coalition's numbers."

"Then we are out of time," Olivia, Queen of Roseland's Spring Court exclaimed. Her cornflower blue eyes snapped with her anger in contrast to her sweet appearance, and she ran a hand through her pixie-short, frosty-pink hair. "What do we do now? It seems that the bulk of the Dark Fae's followers have been joining forces in the Barrens, and I realize that this is more of a daunting prospect for those Wysterian courts located along the eastern border of the kingdom. However, there have also been pockets of dissidence in Roseland, those who followed Aramond in the past and who would follow Qadira now." She put up a hand and shook her head. "Now, I am more than willing to gather my warriors and lead them into battle alongside this coalition, but in doing so, I will not leave my court unprotected."

"And nor should you have to," Niall said before turning to the others. "Several of us in Roseland's northland have also seen this threat rise, our people attacked and killed by the Dark Fae. Olivia is correct to be concerned for her court should she join our forces to defend the eastern border of Wysteria from an offensive launched from the Barrens. Balzar's Autumn Court is not far from hers in the south of Roseland. In addition to that, Mabry's Evening court in the north is near to several fae courts represented here at this table, my court included."

There was nodding around the table followed by an uproar of chatter and grumbling.

"Enough whining and yammering!" Niall finally shouted into the din, pounding the table with a fist. After a moment, the room quieted. "I've not told you anything you don't already know in your hearts. Neither Mabry nor Balzar can be trusted at this juncture after their participation in the Red King's crusade for revenge and power." He leaned forward and looked into the eyes of the tense faces around the table. "Having acknowledged that, it is imperative that the border between Wysteria and the Barrens not be breached. No court in either kingdom will be safe from the

Dark Fae should she prevail, not to mention all the other communities that would also be at risk. She's caused enough harm in the kingdoms already, but one can only imagine the devastation, the death and destruction that she'll bring to bear should she get the chance."

"And we cannot give her that chance," Finvar agreed.

"Then what do you propose, Niall?" Alexi asked. "It's going to take all of us and probably more to fend off Qadira if that's even possible at this point. She's immortal, yes, but we still have no idea what kind of dark powers she now possesses from her time in the underworld or how her immortality will impact those powers."

"I agree, Field Marshal," Niall replied. "I propose that we divide and conquer. We design—and with all due haste, I might add—two formidable fronts. The larger of the two will engage any assault in an effort to protect the Wysterian-Barrens border. The other force will convene at the Red Palace and keep watch over Roseland, putting down any pockets of resistance there, but also, to be ready to deploy to the border between the kingdoms in the event that becomes necessary."

There was silence for several moments as the High Lord's proposal was digested by the group. Soon there were more nods, and this time, murmurs of approval.

Valian and Niall stared at each other for several moments before both began to smile.

"Good plan, old friend," Valian said.

Niall tipped his head. "I do come up with them from time to time, remember?"

Valian chuckled. "That I do."

The two had been close at one time. Brothers in arms during the Great War. Valian thought about the many situations he and Niall had been through together over the decades, each always having the other's back. Then Valian's breakup with Tisharu had come close to destroying all of it. Since he and Tisharu had finally found their way back to each other, the tension between Valian and Niall was easing. Would they ever return to the friendship they'd one enjoyed? Valian didn't know the answer to that question, but for now, this feeling of truce was enough.

"Alrighty then, who's gonna draw up that special team chart?" Alexi asked, looking around the room. "Any volunteers?"

"I think the Chancellor and I can take care of that. What do you think, Valian?" Niall replied with a smirk.

Valian shook his head and sighed. "Yes. I suppose we're the ones to do it." He made a few notes on the pad in front of him, and then looked up. "However, it will be a fast and furious process. We have a lot to do, troops to prepare, and very little time left to execute this plan. Everyone here will need to be on board with whatever we come up with. No questions, no complaining. I'll have a quick show of hands. All in favor of me and the High Lord designing this plan?"

Though it took a few moments, Valian was pleased to see that all hands around the table went up in the end, but he went through the motion anyway. "All opposed? No one? Very good. Give us an hour and we'll meet back here for the final implementation. Until then, I suggest everyone do as much prep as you can in the time you have. Once we start rolling with this, deployment will be immediate, and there won't be a minute to spare."

As the fae leadership rose and filtered from the room, Valian motioned Alexi over and spoke quietly. "How long would it take you to meet with the dwarven leadership in the southern quadrant?"

Alexi blew out a breath. "I don't know, an hour and a half maybe. That's if they're in their dwarvenholds and not out hunting or patrolling. You know how they can be. Sometimes they're gone for days just traipsing around the realm."

Valian nodded. "Okay. Take a few warriors with you. Find Durnak specifically, explain to him what we need. He can touch base with the other chieftains. Then get back here as soon as you can."

"Will do."

Alexi turned to go, but turned back when Valian called his name.

"And Alexi? Stay sharp and watch your back."

"Always do, cousin."

Valian watched him go, and then he and Niall got to work.

THE HOUR WENT BY IN A FLURRY OF ACTIVITY ON ALL sides. The fae leaders began filtering back into the war room, and within a short time they had all regained their places at the table. Valian passed around copies of the plan he and Niall had hammered out in the short time they'd been given, and he was pleasantly surprised that there was little discussion or complaining about what they'd come up with. The only real requested change came from Ilapho, the High Lord of Roseland's Dawn Court, who wished to be assigned to the Roseland detail due to location logistics. The change was made quickly and without issue, as Luminox wished his Daylight troops to deploy at the Barrens border instead.

Alexi returned from the southern quadrant with news from the border just as the fae leaders bound for the Barrens were readying their troops and Valian and Niall were finishing up with the two fae leaders.

"First of all, I got lucky," Alexi said, shaking his head. "I caught Durnak as he and his dwarf battalion were gearing up."

"Gearing up for what?" Valian asked. "Had he already heard what was happening here at the palace?"

Alexi shook his head. "No. He'd taken a small patrol out earlier just over the border into the Barrens like he usually does once or twice a week. They cross just south of here and patrol the Barrens-side of the border north before crossing back into Wysteria at Tark-ington Forest."

"Yes, I'm aware that they do that."

"Anyway, he said that as they were moving north they almost ran straight into a good-sized army marching toward the Wysterian border. And, Val, they were heading toward the border just to the north of here between the Eastern Glade and Tarkington Forest."

"How long ago was this?" Niall asked.

"Couple of hours, three at the most." Alexi ran a hand over his face. "My guess is that they'll start by testing the wards."

"And troops only? Did Durnak say anything about Qadira?" Niall asked.

Alexi shook his head. "No. But that doesn't mean she wasn't with them. Either way, she's coming. But if she's with them, who knows how long it will take before she gets them through the wards. We need to get our troops on the move. Now!"

"Agreed." Valian replied. "And Durnak? What's his status? Is he going to contact the other chieftains in the southern quadrant?"

"Yes. And I told him once he had, to finish gearing up and head this way. Shouldn't be long before they arrive. He was pretty anxious to get moving."

"Good deal. Go see to your battalions, Field Marshal. We'll be right along." Valian watched him go and then turned to Niall. "Ready, old friend? Let's get the party started."

As they grabbed their battle gear and headed upstairs and out of the Great Hall, they met Tempest coming through the courtyard toward them.

"What's happening here, Chancellor?" she demanded to know. "I've come to give you news about Qadira but it seems there's something else going on here."

"Qadira's army is on the move," Niall told her. "One of the dwarf chieftains was on patrol a few hours ago and ran into the mass moving toward Wysteria. With the Dark Fae fully regenerated, we're deploying our troops along the border as well as in Roseland."

"Then it has begun," Tempest acknowledged.

"Yes. Any word from Gray?" Valian asked. "Are they still in Daidoria?"

"As far as I know." She gave him a troubled look. "They are not ready for this."

Valian nodded. "We'll just have to meet this threat head on. There's nothing else that we can do. I'll not lie down and let that evil bitch stomp all over us."

"Yes, well, I've just come from meeting with old Minerva. We have a plan, Chancellor. Get your army on the move, and then I'll quickly fill you two in before we follow."

LIGHT. WARM AND GOLDEN. HE WAS SATURATED IN IT. His, hers. It was the most interesting sensation, this combined reverie, the first where Gray actually was cognizant of what was happening to him, around him.

He was aware of the cathedral looming at his back, could feel the stone of the cathedral steps under his feet, the chill in the air around them as the afternoon waned. He could sense Moira and Alyssa close by and their apprehension as they stood watching.

And finally, there was Isabella, her hands gripping his, her heart beating in time with his own. He wasn't alone, and it was oddly comforting. She was with him, experiencing this other world that only they could see.

"It's coming," she said.

He heard her voice in his head and nodded. "It is...*she* is."

Isabella's face swam into view in his mind as she spoke.

"The Dark Fae has finished regeneration. The Unclean is fully risen, but what once was can never be again," she said.

"Yes. The same, yet different," he agreed.

"Hundreds come before her. They are at the door and searching for a way in."

Gray saw it all in his mind. "She will sacrifice many. In her craving for power, she will destroy what she most desires. If she is not stopped, the realm will burn."

"It has begun," Isabella murmured. "*The Three* must now rise."

"We are two of *The Three*," they intoned together.

Then Gray blinked and the vision passed. He looked into Isabella's eyes, saw them clear and then widen.

"Dear God! Qadira's forces are at the Wysterian border," Isabella cried in a panicked voice. "Gray, they don't know what's coming." She turned to Moira. "We have to go. Now!"

"We have no time, *a stór*," Moira said, shaking her head. "There's nothing we can do from here."

"No! We have to do *something*." Grabbing Gray's coat sleeve, she pleaded with him. "Please, Gray."

"Moira's right, Isabella. We'd never get back in time, even if we were ready to meet Qadira head on, which you know that we aren't. You, me, and Alyssa? It's the three of us. We still need the Scepter of Fire for Alyssa, and it's not even in this realm," Gray said. "You know what I'm saying is true."

Tears filled Isabella's eyes and spilled down her cheeks. "But we can't just abandon our friends, those that we love."

Gray took her into his arms and held her close. "And we won't. I promise you that. But for now, we have to believe that they'll meet this challenge, hold the line until we can get there." He pulled back and wiped the tears from her cheeks. "Remember, Old Minerva is with them. There ain't nothing that old witch can't do. Qadira is no match for the Old One, right?"

Isabella sniffed and then nodded with a choked laugh. "She's something all right."

"You bet." Gray pulled her close again and his eyes met Alyssa's over Isabella's shoulder. In the descendant's eyes he saw the fear that had come alive inside him. He'd seen what was happening, seen the possible outcomes. He thought of all their friends and family members, the innocent people with no way to protect themselves from what was coming. Yes, he knew what was at stake, and his most ardent hope was that what he'd just said to Isabella was the truth, but in his heart, doubt had taken up residence. There didn't seem to be anything they could do at this point but watch it all from afar. They'd come here because supposedly, they were *The Three*. The only ones to possibly stop the Dark Fae, rid the realm of her evil for good.

But he could see no hope of that outcome now.

Moira stepped closer then, and her voice was calm and firm. "Where is the scepter, Gray?"

"What?"

"Where is the Scepter of Fire located right now?" Moira repeated.

"I-I don't know exactly," he stammered. "I mean, it's in the New York realm, but..." He blinked, and then turned to Alyssa. "You know, don't you?"

Alyssa, eyes big and round, nodded.

Moira took Alyssa's arm. "Can you get to it now? If we were to go this very minute?" she asked, urgency beginning to color her tone.

Alyssa looked from Moira to Isabella to Gray, and back to Moira. "Yes. I can...I suppose."

"Don't suppose, child. Tell me true. Can you get to it if we go to collect it now?"

"I can," Alyssa confirmed.

Gray frowned. "But Moira—"

"There's an old portal here in the bowels of the cathedral," Moira said, interrupting the Prince. "I can't say what condition it's in or when it was last used, but Elder Aleksander will know."

When the three of them stared at her with blank looks, Moira growled in exasperation. "Well, do you want to try to do this or don't you?"

"Yes!" they shouted as one.

"Absolutely!" Isabella cried, and gave her great-grandmother a tight hug. "Thank you," she whispered into Moira's ear.

Moira pulled back and tenderly slipped a wayward strand of hair behind Isabella's ear. "Don't thank me yet, *a stór*. We've a long way to go and little time left. Now, come. Let's go find Elder Aleksander."

Twenty-Eight

Even though the basic plan Valian and Niall had devised for deploying the troops had been perfectly executed, things were beginning to deteriorate at the Barrens border by the time all of the designated groups were in play. The security wards that Old Minerva had put in place decades ago had been under constant attack for several hours at that point and were now stressed to the max from the continuous pressure brought to bear by the rebel forces.

After Minerva had relayed the information on the Dark Fae earlier, she'd promised to contact the Caemmeirth for their assistance with what was certainly to come. Though Tisharu and several of the other fae leaders had been itching to cross into the Barrens and engage, Valian had held the troops in place along the Wysterian side of the border for the better part of an hour now. He'd hoped that the great dragons would at least give them an edge and provide some backup for the fae courts, but so far they'd yet to make an appearance. He knew that they couldn't wait any longer and, along with Niall, had made the decision to move now.

Alexi voiced his concern as he came hurrying over.

"This waiting game isn't working, Val," the Field Marshal shouted over the din of Qadira's troops still struggling to get through the wards just a hundred yards or so away. "We've managed to pick off a large number of the rebel forces from this side without many casualties ourselves, but we can't wait for the dragons any longer. We need to push into the Barrens and engage on that side of the border or the wards are eventually going to fail. Once they do, Qadira's rebels will flood unchecked into the kingdom, and we won't be able to hold the line."

Valian nodded. "I know. Niall is spreading the word in both directions as we speak. When he gives me the signal, the first wave crosses, so get to your battalion and make sure that you're ready."

Alexi turned and sprinted up the line to the north. As he did, Valian surveyed the situation. Qadira had yet to show herself, either, but he was certain that she wasn't far away. She wouldn't care how many of her rebels were taken out. They were pawns, a distraction meant to draw out the fight, fatigue their defending forces. She'd appear when they'd least expect it, and then the real fight would begin. The most precarious part: finally facing the Dark Fae herself.

The weather was another issue adding to Valian's concern. It was taking a turn for the worse as twilight inched closer. He could already see his breath and the breath of those around him frosting the air, feel the cold edging its way under his armor. The temperature was dropping rapidly, and scanning the cloud-covered sky, he could all but smell the fresh snow showers on their way to add another few inches to the four or so already covering the ground.

But the real problem would come after nightfall, which was fast approaching. He estimated that they had another three, possibly four hours before they'd lose the light and be fighting in the dark. In any battle, the cover of darkness was considered an advantage for stealth and concealment. However, in a hostile terrain with a solid cloud cover and no moon to light their surroundings, a battle like this could be all the more complicated.

And all the more deadly.

On the heels of that thought, Tempest pushed through the mass of warriors and made her way to him. "The southern line is ready and just waiting for the signal," she told him. "Remember, keep an eye out for the Dark Fae. The minute she's spotted, I'll need someone to punch a hole. Hopefully, that will be the Caemmeirth. They'll be able to burn a path through the crowded field and conceal my approach to that heinous bitch better than anyone else could. For this to work, I must get right up close before she senses that I'm there. Their fire will be the perfect cover."

"I've been keeping an eye out for the dragons but they're not here yet." Valian shook his head. "Unfortunately, we can't wait for them any longer. The wards are already showing signs of instability. We can't afford to let them fail."

Tempest looked out toward the wild landscape just over the border and nodded.

"We have to push into the Barrens now, Tempest, before the weather and darkness make it even more perilous."

"You're right, of course. We have no choice and will just have to pray to the Oracles that the Caemmeirth arrive in time." She turned to him with a resolute look in her eyes. "And that Minerva's plan can be executed with faultless timing. For now, it is our only hope."

Valian frowned. "Tempest, are you sure you want to do this? Do you think this scheme will actually work, or are you putting yourself at risk for a maybe?"

The Immortal's face was serene as she looked toward the seething clusters of warriors just on the other side of the border. A mass all struggling to cross into the kingdom to wreak their havoc on behalf of the Dark Fae, a mass fueled by the hate and lies that Qadira had begun spreading over a century ago.

"I suppose if I had my druthers, I'd rather be puttering in my winter garden with Moira," she murmured. "Or enjoying the cool evening sipping a glass of faerie mead on my porch or in front of a cozy fire."

When she turned back to him again, Valian could read the tenacity in her piercing gaze.

"But those aren't my options tonight, now are they?" she said. "If *The Three* are the only ones to rid us of the Dark Fae once and for all, and this plan will give them the time they need to prepare, then so be it. Any possible sacrifice that I must make will be worth the price." A devilish grin eased across her face. "Besides, we're talking about a plan devised by the Old One. There's no *maybe* about it when that batty, old crone is conjuring. And no questioning, for that matter. You should know that by now, Valian."

The Immortal warrior held out her arm, and he clasped it without hesitation.

"May the Trinity watch over you and keep you safe," she said.

"And you as well," Valian replied.

Tempest's eyes gleamed. "This has a familiar feel, does it not?"

"It does indeed. Though it's distant and...unwelcome."

"Ha! Yes, it is at that. Hold the line, Chancellor. See you on the other side." Then she turned and melted into the throng.

Valian watched her go and wondered how long they could do what she'd demanded.

Hold the line.

He didn't have long to ponder that question, as Niall gave the signal, and the first wave of their combined armies poured over the border into the Barrens, meeting the crush of rebels head-on. They fought with weapons of both steel and magick, pushing back Qadira's forces, making more and more room for the next wave and the next after that.

Taking a deep breath of the frigid air, Valian followed them across and into the fray between the second and third wave. With both his sword and his bow and quiver strapped to his back, he sprinted between and around the clashing bodies. He dodged and spun, slicing his way through the horde with his Elven fighting daggers and cutting a bloody path as he moved further and further into the Barrens with its clusters of small pines and scrub grounded in half a foot of hardened snow.

To his right, Valian caught sight of Juppar and a handful of his warriors through the warring mass in the process of fending off a group of rebel fae. Blocking a fae warrior to his right, Juppar missed the lesser fae at his back who buried a dagger into the High Lord's arm just below his shoulder armor. Knowing he couldn't get to the Juppar in time to be of any use, Valian let two of his daggers fly, both of which easily found their marks, and the attacking fae went down where he stood.

Valian's blades were a blur of motion as he whirled and slashed his way toward the group, watching two of Juppar's warriors cut down as he approached. He buried one of his knives to the hilt in a faerie's chest to his left before jerking it free, flipping it in his hand,

and launching it at yet another warrior hurtling toward him. The charging faerie went down as quickly as the last.

Retrieving his weapons, Valian took out several mortal soldiers when he rushed past them like a blur on his way to join Juppar's group where he helped them take control of the fight. It didn't end well for the few lesser fae warriors left who were now outnumbered with no comrades to come to their defense. The main front of the battle had been pushed back further into the Barrens where the scrub had thinned to wide swaths of snow-covered sand. All that was left there were pockets of small skirmishes.

"That looks painful," Valian said as Juppar winced and pulled the fae's dagger from his arm.

"I've had worse," the High Lord replied. "But it does sting just a mite. I got distracted. Didn't see that fae rebel with this dagger until it was almost too late."

Valian nodded and scanned the area. "Have you seen any dragons yet, Juppar? They were supposed to be here by now. And I've lost sight of Tempest."

"The dragons? I haven't, no, nor Tempest, but then, like you, I've been a bit busy." The High Lord grinned. "Haven't seen hide nor hair of the Dark Fae yet, either. That makes me a bit jittery, I don't mind telling you."

"I know. But she's close by. I guarantee that. It's a sure bet that she'll appear when we least expect it, so watch your back."

"Aye, of that there's no doubt." He shoved the fae dagger he'd taken from his arm into an empty sheath on his armored vest and blew out a breath as he wrapped the wound with a scrap of cloth. "Thanks for the assist, and good hunting, Chancellor."

They clasped forearms briefly. "May the Oracles protect you," they said together, then turned in opposite directions and melted back into the melee.

"I CAN'T RECALL THE LAST TIME ANYONE HAS USED OUR gateway for any reason," Elder Aleksander said as he led the group down the same stone stairwell that they'd previously used. "I, myself, haven't used it in several decades, but then, I've had no reason to go through the portal."

As they reached the crystal chamber's landing, they continued past its doorway and descended lower still to yet another floor. By Isabella's count, the ancient portal lay four levels beneath the Temple of Ahshara, and reminded her a little of the one under the White Palace that she and Valian had used back in January. However, where the old portal below the palace was rarely used, its tunnels were kept clear. This one was in pretty sad condition with cobwebs and all manner of debris—some of which, Isabella didn't want to scrutinize too closely—just about everywhere you turned.

"Now, this thing still works, right?" Isabella asked, giving the gateway a skeptical look. "I mean, it doesn't seem like it has any juice."

"Yeah, the vortex of the old portal in Central Park is always live. This one looks dark and...silent," Alyssa agreed, though Isabella thought it was more like "dark and dead."

"Don't you worry. Portals never die," Moira replied as if she'd read Isabella's thoughts. "As long as its gateway still stands, that is. And as you can plainly see, though a bit worse for wear, this one is still standing strong."

She stepped up next to the portal's facade and placed a hand on its surrounding stonework. After a moment, there were several snaps and crackles, like energy of some kind beginning to connect. It took a few more beats before a hum commenced and quickly grew as if an electrical motor was coming alive. Then there was a soft *whoosh*, and the old portal's vortex with its swirling light and colors sprang to life.

Moira turned with a grin. "There. What did I tell you? Ready?"

Isabella swallowed hard. "Okay, the last time I went through one of these with Aly, we got separated. And that was a total cluster, if you know what I'm saying, so I'm not sure about this. I mean, I want to go...we *need* to go, but—"

"Now, you stop right there," Moira said. "You'll be fine, but if you'd like to do this in baby steps, take my hand, and we'll go together. Gray and Alyssa can follow. All right?"

Isabella took a deep breath and nodded. Stepping forward, she took her great-grandmother's warm hand in a firm grip, and together, they stepped through the portal.

❋

THIS WHOLE THING IS GOING SIDEWAYS FAST, Alexi thought.

Just when they were making headway, had pushed Qadira's forces further and further into the Barrens, another wave seemed to have come out of nowhere, and now they were losing ground. The violent conflict had been going on for close to two hours now. And adding to the misery, about an hour in, the sky had started to spit an icy snow which was piling up and beginning to freeze, making fighting—hell, even just keeping your feet under you—that much more difficult.

And of course, dusk was coming. Another hour, maybe an hour and a half, and darkness would fall. And wouldn't that just be fun?

They'd been fighting for close to two hours straight already, and Alexi was starting to lose steam. He'd be bruised and sore in the morning, but now, he just needed a second wind, or possibly a third. Taking a quick breath, he sensed movement to his left and turned just in time to raise his sword, catching the force of the attacking soldier's metal in a clang of steel. Even though his attacker was mortal, he was a large, burly man, almost a head taller than Alexi with a brawny build and thick, muscular limbs. The vibration from his strike raced up Alexi's fatigued arms, but he had a death-grip on his sword, his sodden, leather gloves holding fast.

The two warriors continued to thrust and parry, dodging and advancing over the muddy, icy ground, slipping and sliding, with feet continually looking for purchase. And then, in the midst of an advance, the big man tripped over a broken tree root partially concealed by snow cover that—by the grace of the Trinity—Alexi had just missed. He wasted no time. Digging deep, Alexi spun, and with a backward motion, sliced the soldier's midsection wide open with help of the man's forward momentum as he fell. Turning, he then plunged his sword into a fae warrior charging him from the side.

With incredible effort, Alexi pulled his sword free and, stumbling, went to his knees. He prayed to the Oracles that he was clear for the moment, because he wasn't sure he had enough strength left to haul himself up just yet, let alone defend himself. There was blood running down one arm but he had no idea if it was his or the soldier's he'd gutted. He knelt where he was, there in the freezing, muddy snow, leaning on his sword and just trying to breathe.

"Alexi!" a voice called over the discord of battle.

Covered in blood, gore, and a healthy amount of half-frozen mud, Alexi wiped some of the grime from his face and turned toward the shout. Relief flooded through him. Valian was sprinting in his direction.

"Alexi, are you hurt?" Valian shouted as he skidded to a halt in the slush next to where Alexi knelt.

"Hey, Val. Good to see you're still vertical," he replied with a lopsided grin.

Valian frowned. "I said, are you hurt? You're covered in blood."

"I heard you, cousin. And it's not the first time that I've been covered in blood and gore during a battle, Val. But to answer your question, no, I'm not hurt. Well, no more than one normally is when fighting in the middle of a warring mass for a couple hours. But don't worry, very little of the blood I'm wearing is mine." Alexi held out his arm. "Now, quit glowering at me, and help me up."

The glowering didn't stop but Valian did help him to his feet, and Alexi did his damnedest not to wobble once there, although it was a dicey thing.

"Have you seen Tempest?" Valian asked.

At the urgent tone of his cousin's question, Alexi nodded. "I did. About ten minutes ago." He nodded toward the main body of the conflict deeper in the Barrens. "She was moving fast in that direction. Why?"

"Several things have happened at once, Alexi, and shit's about to spiral. Qadira has finally shown herself. She's on the other side of that main conflict and moving this way. The Caemmeirth have also arrived. We need to find Tempest now. We only have another hour or so before dark, and our window of opportunity is pretty tight."

"Window of opportunity for what?"

"Tempest and Minerva hatched a plan, and it's already unfolding, but the timing has to be flawless. Do me a favor, cousin. Keep your wits about you for the next hour or so and stay clear of the dragon fire when it begins."

Alexi gaped at him. "Dragon fire? Seriously? What are you talking about?"

"There's no time to explain. Just do as I say." Valian put a hand on Alexi's shoulder. "Now, are you good to go?"

"I'm good. Guess I'll just follow your lead."

Valian nodded. "I'll try to give you the pertinent details on the way. Come on. Finding Tempest now is imperative."

They turned and headed toward the fighting at the other end of the field.

TEMPEST HAD SPENT THE FIRST HOUR OF THE CONFLICT moving through the fighting mass with its tangled limbs, crashing weaponry, and blasts of magick, cutting her own swath of ruin as she went. The cacophony of explosions and clashing swords mingled with the terrible cries of the wounded and dying, filling the air with the horror that came with any kind of war. Arrows rained down from above intermittently, and strikes of electric energy lit up the sky like fireworks. She dodged small brush fires as she sprinted through the ravaged landscape, though there was little vegetation this far into the Barrens. But it seemed what little there was of it was burning here and there—most probably started by those magickal blasts— even with the saturation of the ground from the inclement weather.

She fought hard alongside fae, Elven, and dwarven warriors, yet always keeping a keen eye toward the skies above for the familiar silhouette of dragon wings. Until at last, she'd finally caught sight of their formation on the horizon. And though her pulse sped up thinking about what was to come, the tightness in her chest eased just a bit. Unfortunately, that easing didn't last long when ten minutes later, she felt the other. Like a putrid insult, a greasy coating at the back of the throat, she sensed her.

Qadira had made her presence known.

Tempest and the Dark Fae were bound together by death from centuries past, but only Tempest should have risen. Now, it was up to her to begin the rectification, to use what the Old One had given her to take back what was illegitimately acquired.

She laid a hand over the pocket of her battle armor where the instrument of that beginning was secreted away...waiting. With the arrival of the Dark Fae, the Old One's plan would now commence.

Tempest heard her name called and turned to see Valian and Alexi running toward her.

"The Dark Fae has arrived," Valian shouted over the sounds of the battle. "She's at the far end of the main front and moving this direction."

Tempest nodded. "I know. I sensed her when she first appeared. The dragons are also here. We've agreed on the timing as well as the path."

"What's happening?" Alexi yelled. "What timing? What path?"

"I'm sorry," Tempest said, shaking her head. "There's no time for explanation. The Dark Fae is advancing rapidly. She's laying waste to everything in her path without care for either side of the conflict." She looked at Valian. "Ridar's run is about to begin. I'll hitch a ride, but when we get near enough, I'll be on my own. Clear the way as best you can. Ridar won't be able the make a distinction between forces from the air."

"We'll do what we can," Valian replied. "Niall, Finvar, and Luminox are already spreading the word."

"We have but minutes left before it starts." Tempest held out her arm as she had before. "May the Oracles protect us all."

Valian grasped her arm. "May the Oracles protect us all," he and Alexi repeated together.

"And may you kick her bloody ass," Alexi added.

With a grin, Tempest looked to the sky where the red dragon could be seen making a final sweeping turn to begin his run up the field at the Dark Fae. They would have to time this just right. She would ride with Ridar as he laid down his wall of fire until she was right on top of Qadira.

As Ridar retracted his massive wings and began to dive, Tempest pulled the enchanted dagger Minerva had given her from a sheath in her armor and started her run as well. As she dodged small skirmishes and leapt over scattered, decimated bodies, the great dragon snatched her up, sweeping her along with him as his fire scorched the landscape and all in his path below. The heat was intense, searing her lungs. It was like flying into the middle of an inferno, even though Ridar did his best to shield her within his grasp. Through slitted eyes, she watched the terrain blackened by Ridar's red-hot blaze. And somewhere up ahead, she knew Qadira also watched, unaware of what was hidden behind the dragon's firestorm.

"Get ready!" Ridar growled between blasts before he plunged toward the ground.

Just as he released her from his grasp, a bright light exploded around them and the great dragon roared as the Dark Fae's blast of energy tore through his left wing. Ridar's massive body pinwheeled to the right as he struggled to gain altitude, and Tempest tumbled to the ground just yards from where Qadira stood. She immediately rolled to her feet, and in a blur of motion, flew at the Dark Fae. With a triumphant battle cry, Tempest buried the enchanted dagger she held into Qadira's chest to the hilt before the Dark Fae knew what was happening.

Twenty-Nine

"What's up with you?" Isabella asked, eyeing Alyssa as they followed Gray and Moira along the path toward the old portal deep in Central Park.

Retrieving the Scepter of Fire hadn't been a problem and had taken less time than Isabella had feared, but what was left of daylight was sitting along the horizon and slipping toward the edge at a good clip. Now, the consternation on Alyssa's face as they trudged along the path had Isabella wondering what was causing her friend's distress—other than worrying about what they were on their way to do and how little time they had left to do it.

"What do you mean?" Alyssa finally asked with a sidelong glance. "There's nothing—"

"Come on, Aly. How long have we known each other? Something definitely has you twisted up. What is it?"

Alyssa rolled her eyes. "You mean other than the fact that we're about to go head-to-head with an evil immortal fae who we may or may not be able to destroy but could possibly destroy us and the entire Artemysian realm instead?"

"Yeah. Other than that." Isabella grinned. But her grin faded at the look of true fear in her friend's eyes. "*Is* that what this is about, Aly?"

Alyssa sighed and took Isabella's arm, pulling her up close as they continued to walk, her voice low. "Izz, I'm scared. No, I'm beyond that. I'm terrified."

"Well, of course you are. I am too. You'd be an idiot if you weren't afraid of what's coming, and you're not an idiot, my friend. It's a terrifying situation, but at least you've had some hands-on experience with this kind of thing in recent months. I've only been a spectator up until now. I don't really know what kind of power I actually have or even how to use it. I may not be any help at all. But we're *The Three*, Aly. We're the realm's last best hope if you believe Elder Aleksander, or Minerva, for that matter. Without us, Qadira wins. She'll shatter the lives of so many innocent people. She'll decimate this realm. You know that. And after destroying Artemysia, what would stop her from looking to our home realm?"

"I know, but that's exactly what I'm talking about, Izzy. I-I..."

"What, Aly? Talk to me."

"Well...this is ultimately gonna come down to me and the scepter, right? I mean, yes, we're *The Three*, and I can't do what I have to do without you and Gray, but what if...what if I can't make the scepter work this time around?"

Isabella frowned. "Of course you can make the scepter work. You're the only one who can. You're the descendant, remember?"

"I'm aware of that, but look what happened with the scepter that first time when Niall brought it to the palace. It fired right up when I took it from him, but then it just died. I couldn't get it to work no matter how hard I tried. I mean, it was a crapshoot right up to the very end when we went up to the top of the ramparts during the battle. I didn't know if I would be able to use it or not."

"Yes, but then you did. Brilliantly, I might add."

"But what if that happens again, Izzy? I've only actually used it that one time. What if I can't make it work again, especially when we need it the most?"

Isabella pulled Alyssa to a stop and turned her around. "Aly, listen to yourself. You're doing exactly what you did before."

"What are you saying?"

"You're doubting yourself, talking yourself right out onto that ledge again. You're letting what's here..." Isabella said, tapping Alyssa's forehead. "screw up what's in here..." she finished, tapping

Alyssa on the chest. "In your heart, you know that this is what you were destined to do."

Isabella put up a hand when Alyssa began to shake her head. "Look, pal, let me ask you a question. When you were having these very same thoughts that day, right before the battle began, what did Niall say to you before he left for the field? Do you remember his words?"

Alyssa slowly nodded. "Of course I remember. He told me that the Oracles were right, that I had everything I needed inside of me." A poignant smile crossed Alyssa's face at the memory. "He also told me to never doubt myself, to hold the scepter in my hands, step up to the wall, and change my destiny."

"Hmm, and what do you think he would say to you now?"

Alyssa's smile widened. "He'd say the same, only he'd probably add 'what are you waiting for, descendant of Alice?'" She laughed out loud. "Then, if I was lucky, he'd kiss me senseless again like he's done a thousand times since that first kiss."

"Exactly. And what did the little voice in your head say to you up on that snowy rampart in January? Come on. Say it out loud."

"Send the light to push back the darkness...become the light. Become the reckoning," Alyssa whispered.

Isabella nodded and took both of Alyssa's hands in her own. "Aly, Niall is out there right now. So are Alexi and Valian and Tisharu and Finvar, and a host of others who are at risk. Not to mention the Queen and Áine and Gryphon and Halifax. Violet and Kaleb. So many people that we love and care about. We can't let them down. We just can't."

"Hey! What are you two doing?" Gray shouted from where he and Moira stood waiting at the portal. "Come on. Get a move on. We're losing the light fast."

Isabella smiled at Alyssa. "He's so pushy. You'd think he was prince of the realm or something."

Alyssa laughed. "Yeah, but unfortunately, he's right. Time's a wastin'." She jerked her head toward the portal. "So, let's go kick some Dark Fae ass."

"There you are." Isabella winked. "I was afraid that I'd lost you for a minute."

They turned and caught up with Moira and the Prince, and taking hands, they all walked together into the swirling vortex of the portal.

TIME SLOWED TO A CRAWL AS TEMPEST AND QADIRA SPUN in a deathly embrace before the ground shook and another blast of magickal energy exploded between them. The Dark Fae's anguished, ear-splitting scream tore through the receding light as the two were thrown a fair distance apart. Tempest gave her head a shake and rolled to her feet, raising her sword and readying herself for whatever would come now.

Across the field, Qadira lay motionless in a pool of greasy, black liquid, the dagger still embedded—a stake through the heart.

As minutes passed, and not knowing quite what to expect, Tempest took one cautious step and then another before pausing. She stood, rooted to the spot, eyes sharp, watching the Dark Fae for any subtle movement, any indication of life.

One last time.

And then, after several tense moments, there it was.

Qadira's body jerked like a frenzied marionette. Once, twice, a third time. And she began to wheeze and hack, the thick, black liquid spewing from her mouth with each heaving breath. Finally, she rolled, pushing up to her knees, and with another shriek of agony, tugged at the enchanted dagger buried in her chest.

"You will pay dearly for this," Qadira ground out, her eyes watering and lips twisted, her face a mask of pain. The Dark Fae struggled, slowly gaining her feet and, with one mighty yank, jerked the dagger free.

"Excuse me, but why is that evil bitch still standing?" a voice asked from Tempest's right.

"Yeah, doesn't look like that dagger did much good after all," came another voice from her left.

To Tempest's surprise, Niall and Queen Ayanna stood at her right shoulder, with Finvar and Luminox on her left. They'd arrived, ready to stand with her against the Dark Fae.

"Yes, well, that dagger may be small, but it carries a mighty punch," she told them.

"What kind of punch?" Luminox asked as the Dark Fae flung the dagger away. "Better be substantial or we're in deep trouble."

"Mmm, wait for it," Tempest replied, her eyes never leaving Qadira's.

"You do know that I'm immortal now, right? You stupid Halfling," Qadira yelled, her smile for Tempest, malevolent. "You can't defeat me now. I've waited an eternity for this, and I'll relish devouring this realm and everything in it. This time around, I'm going to destroy you all."

"Do you think so?" Tempest shouted back. "I'm not so sure."

Qadira ran her fingers through the nasty gore over the wound in her chest, and her smile began to fade. It was replaced by a frown of concern.

"Yes," Tempest nodded, taking a step forward. "Can you feel it? The wound to your chest healing, closing over? The Old One's spell is now sealed inside of you, spreading through your rotted essence."

"What is this?" Wiping more black liquid from her face with the back of her hand, Qadira grimaced with pain and bent at the waist, clutching at her chest. "What have you *done*?" she shrieked.

"It's a simple correction," Tempest said. "You *were* immortal, Qadira...briefly. I'm afraid it was but a temporary thing." She shook her head and gave the Dark Fae a pitying look. "You are an abomination, tainted. Your immortality was illegitimately bestowed in the first place. It has been rescinded."

The blood ritual that had raised Qadira had also gifted her with perpetual immortality. The Old One had found a way to circumvent that gift. Her spell had ended Qadira's everlasting immortality. With the dagger, Tempest had delivered not only Minerva's spell, but a last death-blow to the Dark Fae's heart. This one rebirth was now all that she would ever get.

Shock and disbelief, followed by fury filled the Dark Fae's bitter countenance. "*No!* This cannot be!"

"Oh, but I assure you, it can," Tempest said. "Though old Minerva has yet to discover the exact blood ritual that was used to raise you, my dagger was imbued with a very specific spell to alter the immortality given with your resurrection. What was done, has been undone. This time when we end you, there will be no coming back from it."

"You cannot *do this!*" Qadira cried. "It won't be *allowed!*"

In the next moment, the group was taken by surprise when Qadira screamed her fury and flung out her arms. They had little time to prepare and the wave of raw energy that exploded from the Dark Fae blew through the five warriors like a hurricane, scattering them in every direction. Tempest was thrown a good twenty yards where she landed on her back with the wind knock from her body. She knew they had no time to spare and lost precious moments as she struggled just to drag in a breath, to refill her lungs.

Fortunately, Luminox was the first to recover and tried to put up his powerful shields to give them some protection, but his effort was weak and ineffectual. His abilities were powered by the sun, which the cloud cover had hampered.

The sun that had also just slipped over the horizon.

Nightfall.

However, Queen Ayanna came to their rescue. The light wielder distracted Qadira with a barrage of lightning just long enough for the others to recover and take up defensive positions. They all knew that it was now or never. The Old One's spell had taken Qadira's immortality, but without *The Three*, they had little chance of destroying the Dark Fae on their own. The best that they could do was to buy more time.

Niall did what he could with his powers of twilight to help them all blend into the night as they approached the Dark Fae from several different directions, and Finvar sent an avalanche of ice and wind barreling toward her. But though Qadira was now mortal, the terrible powers she'd acquired while in the underworld were not affected. She was more lethal now than ever before.

Adding to the dire situation, the burned and blackened path that Ridar had scorched on his earlier run at the Dark Fae had filled in with more fighting, and Qadira's rebels were inching toward them. Soon they would be outflanked and outnumbered, having to watch their backs as well as protect themselves from the Dark Fae.

From the look of it, Niall and Ayanna were already at that point, surrounded by warring combatants and fighting back-to-back. But on the other side of the field, Finvar and Luminox were holding their own and pushing back with vigor. Unfortunately, Tempest's attention was snagged just a little too long by what was happening around her.

She felt the strike before she could react, and everything went into slow motion as she was lifted off her feet and went, for a second time in ten minutes, airborne. She landed hard, and this time came close to losing consciousness. Disoriented with ears ringing, she struggled against darkness that had nothing to do with the nightfall around her.

"So, what was that you were saying about ending me, Halfling? I'm really going to enjoy this."

Tempest opened her eyes and groped for the sword that was no longer within reach.

The Dark Fae stood over her with hunger in her eyes and a cruel smile on her face. In her hand, she held a long, lethal-looking blade.

GRAY HAD BROUGHT THEM BACK INTO THE REALM VIA A portal at the north end of Willow Glen Wood that neither Isabella nor Alyssa had ever seen. He'd aimed to get them as close to the Barrens border and the fighting as he could, as both he and Isabella had been sure that's what they'd seen in a second joint reverie they'd had before leaving New York.

Alyssa still wasn't sure how this whole thing was going to play out, but now that she had the scepter in its velvet drawstring bag slung over one shoulder, she considered it. As they'd traveled back to Artemysia, her first use of the scepter played on a loop in her head. Looking at it objectively, she now knew that her issues the first time around had been mostly of her own making. As Isabella had suggested, once she'd let go of her fears and insecurities, the scepter had worked just fine. And Alyssa had to admit, it had been an amazing experience. She was praying that this time around would be the same—without all the worries, doubts, or panic.

"Okay, let's stop here and regroup a bit," Gray said as they stepped out of the vortex just inside the northern edge of Willow Glen Wood. He looked at Isabella. "Maybe we should just check to see if there's anything else we should know before going any further."

Isabella nodded. And, facing each other, within seconds their eyes had rolled back in their heads and all color had drained from their faces. Alyssa wasn't sure she would ever get used to watching these reveries. However, Isabella had taken to them like she'd been having them all of her life, which Alyssa now wondered if she had.

"The fiery path begins," Gray spoke up. "The immortal warrior flies with it."

"Other warriors will follow but time is short," Isabella murmured. "So much death, yet she still hovers, thirsting for more."

"And more she will find," Gray added.

"So much already lost. *The Three* must make haste or lose all," they intoned together.

Then they both blinked and the short reverie ended.

"Okay, that sounded really terrible," Alyssa said.

"Tell us what you saw," Moira implored. "What does it all mean?"

Gray ran a hand through his hair. "The fighting is still ongoing. The dragons are there, but so is Qadira. I don't think that it's going well for either side. Which will probably work just fine for that evil bitch."

"And 'the immortal flies?' What did that mean?" Alyssa asked.

"Tempest," Moira said. "She's the immortal, right?"

Isabella nodded. "I think so. I'm not sure what they've done, but I do know that it wasn't enough. It's up to us now. It may already be too late. We have to go."

The group faded then to the south, to the Eastern Glade where a chaotic scene greeted them on arrival. The security wards had held, but only just, and only because the kingdom's troops had surged over the border into the Barrens where the bulk of the fighting was still taking place.

They met Juppar as he was coming back across the border with an injured Quinn.

"Juppar!" Gray hailed the High Lord. "How goes the fight?"

The High Lord shook his head as he handed Quinn off to a

group of healers. "We were pushing the rebel forces back in the beginning, but over the last hour we've lost ground and troops."

"And the Dark Fae?"

"The great dragons arrived a while back. One of them made a run at her with Tempest in tow. I'm not sure what happened with that, but there's been a surge in rebel troops and magicks lighting up the sky since then." He gestured to the east where that light show could still be seen against the darkening sky. "We've only minutes until sundown, and then, I fear all may be lost."

"Gray!"

The Prince turned toward the shout. Valian and Alexi were just crossing the border.

"Thank the Oracles," Gray said, giving both friends a half-hug. "We were afraid that we would be too late. What do you know?"

The look on the Chancellor's face said it all. Things were dire.

"Tempest and Old One came up with a plan," Valian said. "Minerva has yet to find a spell to counter the blood ritual that raised Qadira, but she did the next best thing. She gave Tempest a dagger imbued with a spell to counter Qadira's immortality, but it had to be plunged directly into the Dark Fae's heart. Unfortunately, there was also a snag in the plan. Evidently, Minerva wasn't certain whether or not it would affect Tempest as well."

"What? Surely you can't mean that it would not only take Qadira's immortality but my sister's as well?" Moira said in disbelief.

"Yes. That's exactly what I mean. Look, Tempest knew the risk but was willing to take that chance. She hitched a ride with Ridar as he burned a path to Qadira's location in hopes of completing that mission. The outcome is still unclear, but Niall, Finvar, Luminox, and Ayanna went to provide backup about ten or fifteen minutes ago."

"No one's come back yet, and you can see for yourselves the magicks in the distance," Alexi added. "If you're going to do something, it better be soon."

"Can you two go with us? Provide some distraction if we need it?"

"Absolutely," Valian said. "What's the plan?"

"The plan is ridding the realm of the Dark Fae for good," the

Prince replied, then turned to his traveling companions. "Are you three ready to get this party started?"

"I'm ready," Moira stated.

"Now or never," Isabella said with a nod.

"I don't know about starting the party, but I'm ready to end it with a bang," Alyssa added, pulling the scepter free from its velvet cover. "Let's do this."

"I'm going with you," Juppar said. "May the Oracles protect us all and keep us safe."

Valian, Alexi, Moira, and Juppar took the lead, and with a last deep breath, Alyssa held the scepter tight to her chest and followed with Isabella and Gray close on each side. They faded as far as they dared and then began to run toward the explosions of light against the now completely dark sky.

Those in the lead did their best to clear the way but running full out in a foot of snow with no moonlight to show the way was hazardous on its own. They got glimpses of the ground from small fires here and there, dodged bloody, ruined bodies, small skirmishes, and battled their way through active fighting. Alyssa almost lost her footing as she slipped and slid through an area where the heavy fighting had turned the snow cover into icy, muddy slush. Just as she'd gotten herself under control, the ground suddenly lurched violently under her feet, and she almost went down. Gray grabbed her arm, steadying her.

"What was that?" she yelled. "Did you see that blast of light up ahead?"

"Yeah. Unfortunately, I think that's where we're headed," Gray shouted back.

"Oh, goody."

A few minutes later, there was another explosion of light. It lit up a large swath of fighting for several moments, enough time to see Tempest hurling through the air and landing poorly.

"Tempest!" Moira cried, and the group started in that direction at a run.

But the Dark Fae got to the immortal warrior first. "So, what was that you were saying about ending me, Halfling?" she asked Tempest. "I'm really going to enjoy this."

With those terrible words, Qadira raised a long blade and plunged it into Tempest's chest. With a primal scream, she pulled it out and raised it again.

"*No!*" Moira cried and sprinted forward calling Tempest's name.

"Moira! Stop!" Gray shouted.

Though Moira didn't acknowledge his shout, the Dark Fae did. Her head snapped up, and with a sharp thrust of her hand, a wave of violent energy swatted Moira aside like she was nothing but an annoying insect. Then Qadira turned toward the approaching group. With blood and gore covering her face and hands and a look of madness in her eyes, the Dark Fae looked every inch the evil entity she was purported to be.

Like that day in January in the tower when they'd raced to the top of the ramparts, Alyssa was again reminded of the little girl from Kansas who'd saved the day on her trip to Oz, who'd faced down the wicked witch and won. Well, this was a wicked witch, if she'd ever seen one. And she intended to face her down and win.

"Well, well, what have we here?" Qadira crooned. "A group of weak, pathetic fae come to rescue an equally pathetic comrade? You do realize that you're too late. Tempest may have taken my immortality, but I will have hers as well once I remove her heart. Either way, she'll never rise, and you'll never defeat me now, either." She paused and zeroed in on Alyssa. "Ah, an added bonus. You've brought me the descendant as well. This will surely be a triumphant day."

Before anyone could speak, a hum filled the air. Both Gray and Isabella were holding their hands out palms up...and were both glowing with light.

"What is this foolishness?" Qadira asked. She stepped forward and away from where Tempest lay unmoving. "You have no power to best me." She again threw out a hand and sent a blast of energy at them, but it hit some sort of invisible wall and exploded in a shower of light and thunder.

Gray and Isabella had conjured a protective barrier around the group...around Alyssa.

It was her time.

She held the scepter in both hands and closed her eyes blocking out the heinous view before her. A strange tranquility settled over her, warm and pure. Her pulse slowed and her heartbeat quieted. Like before, the sounds of battle vanished, replaced by the soft thrum of power and energy flowing through her. She could feel the strength of the scepter unfurling, beginning to move inside her, like a beautiful, numinous creature waking and stretching.

And as before, there was incredible light, a starburst of it behind her eyelids. Alyssa remembered the childlike voice she'd heard on the rampart. *Feel the light, become the light*, the voice had whispered to her. *Send the light to push back the darkness...become the light. Become the reckoning.*

In her mind, Alyssa was again everywhere at once, wherever there was conflict in this place. And front and center was the Dark Fae.

"I am the light," Alyssa murmured. "I am the reckoning..."

Like standing on that rampart in the January snowfall, a final blast of massive energy and light speared out in all directions, its dazzling rays searing the rebel forces where they stood, turning darkness to ash. And along with those turned to ash was Qadira, the Dark Fae.

The Scepter of Fire went silent then, and Alyssa dropped where she stood.

Epilogue

Isabella hurried up the wide staircase to the third floor, where the White Palace's hospital wing was located. When she'd left her vigil earlier, she'd only intended to catch a quick nap, but she'd slept for over three hours. She was anxious now about what she would find when she got back to the ward. It had been almost thirty-six hours since they'd faced the Dark Fae. Thirty-six hours of worrying, waiting, of hoping and praying.

Alyssa had again wielded the Scepter of Fire brilliantly. But in the light of day, the death and destruction had been incomprehensible to Isabella. Hundreds of bodies littered the muddy, icy slush in all directions along with the piles of ash of those rebel combatants who'd still been fighting when the scepter had sent out its cleansing light.

Just across the border, the healers had been overwhelmed with the injured and dying. Her heart had just about stopped when they'd found Alexi covered in blood and gore lying on a makeshift cot with a healer bending over him and Valian looking on. He'd taken an arrow through his shoulder, but it was not life-threatening. And though he'd lost some blood, to her relief, most of the blood that covered him had not been his own.

Surprisingly, the rest of the group who'd faced Qadira in the end had come through that final fight with little injury. Niall and Finvar had cuts and bruises, Juppar had been treated for his earlier stab wound, and both Tisharu and Ayanna seemed to be unscathed and were crowing about their battle prowess.

As before, Alyssa had passed out cold where she'd stood after the scepter had done its job. And though she was still in the hospital wing, she would recover completely and be ready to go home in another day or so.

But Isabella's fear was not for the group or her oldest friend.

Seeing her great-grandmother, hurled through the air like a paper doll and her great-aunt stabbed through the heart before they could stop Qadira's rampage had traumatized Isabella. In the hours after the battle had ended, she'd ridden an emotional roller coaster. Moira, though alive, had been unconscious for almost twelve hours before she'd finally rallied. She had a concussion, a broken arm, and three broken ribs, but thank the Oracles and her Ellurian ancestry, she would heal quickly.

Tempest, however, was another story. Her status was, as of yet, undetermined.

After the battle, they'd found her body cold and deathly still in the snow where she'd fallen. They'd brought her back to the palace with Moira and the others in hopes that she'd soon resurrect. But as of three hours ago, when Isabella had left to take a short break, there'd been no change.

It was still uncertain whether Tempest would revive at all. Valian had explained that Old Minerva had imbued a dagger with a spell to rescind Qadira's immortality, a dagger which Tempest had plunged into the Dark Fae's heart, completing that mission. The problem was that Minerva couldn't be sure if Tempest's immortality would be affected by the spell or not. Tempest had been immortal from birth because of her heritage and not because of a blood ritual, so in theory, she would be immune to the spell. But Minerva was reluctant to make a prediction.

So, now they waited. If Tempest didn't awaken soon, she never would.

"Izzy! There you are," Alyssa exclaimed when Isabella entered the hospital ward. "It just started!"

Isabella frowned. "What jus—"

"It's Tempest, Izz." Alyssa pointed to the other end of the ward where several healers were gathered around Tempest's bed. "They think she may be waking up."

"What?" Isabella hurried to the other end of the room. "What's happening?" she asked one of the healers. "Please tell me that Tempest is regenerating."

The Elven healer turned with a cautious smile. "Her condition does look promising. She now has a faint pulse and her temperature is beginning to rise, but we can't jump to conclusions," he warned. "She's been...lifeless for longer than usual, so hopefully there is no permanent damage."

"Now that she has vital signs, however faint, we've given her an infusion of a regenerative potion that should help with the process," another healer added. "But again, only time will tell."

"Isabella?" a soft voice came from the next bed over.

Isabella turned and rushed to Moira's bedside. "Great-gram, you're awake. How are you feeling?"

Moira cleared her throat. "Like I've been run over by a bus," she murmured in a rusty voice. "But I'll live. How is Tempest?"

"Up until this morning there had been no change, but in the last couple of hours it seems that there may be hope at last. She has a pulse, Gram. And her temperature is rising, so that's good news, right?"

"Indeed," Moira said with a yawn, then she winked. "She always was a slowpoke. Lollygagging along."

Isabella laughed. "Well, don't you worry. You just close your eyes and get some rest. Everything is going to be fine."

"Such a good girl you are," Moira murmured as her eyes slipped shut, and she was asleep in moments.

OVER THE NEXT TWO DAYS THERE WAS A FLURRY OF activity, and Isabella's world was finally beginning to right itself. Moira was healing with amazing speed and grumbling about going home. But the most joyous news was that Tempest had almost completely regenerated, and though she was still a bit weak, she'd at least regained her snark.

"Quit your bitchin', sister. A concussion and a few broken

bones? Bah!" she told Moira. "Don't be such a wuss. You're not the one who died, you know?"

"Oh, like that's something new for you?" Moira countered with a tsk. "For all the many times that you've died, you certainly took your sweet time coming back this time. Isabella was out of her mind with worry. You should be ashamed."

Isabella shook her head. "Okay, you two. Aly and I were going to head back to New York in an hour or so, but if this is how you're going to act, maybe I should stay and give the healers some backup."

"Oh, now, darlin' that's not necessary," Moira waved a hand and grinned. "We're just fussing, like we always do. I'm going to see the dead one here home tomorrow morning, so you go on and say your goodbyes to your handsome Elven Field Marshal. We'll see you soon enough."

"Yes, ma'am. I'll be back in a few weeks just as soon as I get caught up on my business schedule."

"And have a conversation with Marie, I'm imagining?" Moira asked with a knowing look.

Isabella nodded. "Oh, yeah. Mom and I are going to have a really in-depth conversation, for sure." She gave them each a careful hug and then stood for a moment just looking at them both. "Now, you two have a safe trip home and stay out of trouble. I'll see you soon." Isabella turned away, but then turned back with a grin. "Oh...and I love you both very much."

She made her way downstairs to find Alexi waiting in the great hall with Alyssa, Niall, and Queen Beatrice.

"Did you say your goodbyes to Moira and Tempest?" the Queen asked.

"I did. I think they're both ready to go home as well, but won't be heading that way until sometime tomorrow. I kinda hate leaving them so soon after...well, you know." Isabella paused and looked around the great hall. "It feels odd leaving the realm at all after learning so much about my heritage."

"You'll be back in a few weeks, Bella," Alexi reminded her. "The realm isn't going anywhere and neither are they. I wouldn't be surprised if they come to see you in New York, especially after you have your 'talk' with your mom."

"True. I just worry about Tempest. We still don't know if her immortality was affected by Minerva's spell or not. And I know that Qadira was destroyed by the scepter along with the rebel forces, but something feels...unresolved to me, though I can't really put my finger on what."

"Geez, don't put that out there, Izzy," Alyssa cried. "You know the universe is snarky that way. The next thing you know, something nasty will be rearing its ugly head. I mean, come on. You all saw Qadira's ashes, right?"

"We did," Niall agreed. "The power of three seemed to have done the trick."

"I know, I know." Isabella laughed. "It's probably just that I haven't been able to get the whole episode out of my head yet."

"You're not the only one, babe," Alexi said with a grimace.

"Well, I have a meeting with my advisory council, so I'll wish you both a safe trip home, and we'll see you soon," the Queen said, pulling first Isabella and then Alyssa in for goodbye hugs.

"Are we ready to go?" Alexi asked as the Queen walked away.

"I am *sooo* ready," Alyssa exclaimed, and then at Niall's narrowed eyes, qualified the remark. "I just meant that I've got a lot to do when I get back. We have another new artist showing to prepare for at the gallery next week."

"Mmm," Niall grunted.

"And you know that you could always come into New York for that. Alexi could come too, for that matter. We could all have dinner in the city."

"That would be awesome," Isabella agreed.

"We'll see," the High Lord murmured giving the Field Marshal a side-eye.

Isabella swung her backpack over her shoulder as Alexi grabbed her duffel back. "As Gray's fond of saying, let's get this party started."

Gray and Áine were just coming through the outer gates as the group headed out into the courtyard. It didn't escape Isabella's notice that the two were actually holding hands, which made her smile. There had been possible "new relationship" vibes between the two for the last couple of months, but this was a new step.

"Hey, you two. Where've you been?" she asked with a pointed look. "And what have you been up to?"

Áine grinned. "We've been walking in the fresh snow. It was cold but energizing."

"We actually went to talk to Minerva earlier. Now that Tempest has regenerated, we'd hoped it meant that her immortality had not been affected by the spell used on Qadira, but Minerva is still undecided."

"She said that Tempest shouldn't take any chances...just in case," Áine added. "Tempest's immortality may be unaffected, but like Qadira, she may have only gotten the one last regeneration."

"And there's only one way to find out, right?" Isabella asked, knowing the answer.

"You got it," Gray said. "If she dies and doesn't come back, you'll know."

Áine punched him and gave him a surprised look.

"What?"

"Or she dies and does come back?"

The Prince frowned. "Well, yeah, that's a given, right?"

"You could have led with the positive side," Áine said with a roll of her eyes, then turned with a grin. "My Prince, such tact, such sensitivity."

"Hey!" Gray said. "I've got plenty of tact and sensitivity."

"*Anyway*, are you guys heading out?" Áine asked. "Want some company to the portal? Mr. Tact and Sensitivity and I would love to join you."

Isabella laughed at the look on the Prince's face. She had a feeling that these two Halflings were easing into a whole different relationship than they'd ever had before. She found it endearing.

"Sure," Alexi said looking around at the others. "I'd say, the more the merrier, right?"

"Absolutely," said Isabella.

As the three couples started off toward the treeline and the end of the fade-restriction zone, Isabella looked back at the palace, and for a split second, that feeling of something unsettled was there just out of reach. Then it was gone.

With a sigh, Isabella Doyle Christensen took her Elven Field Marshal's hand and turned toward home.

WRITTEN AS JONI SAUER-FOLGER

Hidden Treasures, a romantic suspense novel

About the Author

A native of Oregon, Joni Sauer-Folger spent twenty-two years with an airline traveling and moving around the country before settling down near the beautiful Pacific Ocean with her three very spoiled cats. When she's not spending quality time with the characters she creates, she enjoys gardening, crafting, and working in local theater.

For more information, visit:
www.jonisauerfolger.com

A small press bound by the belief that every voice matters.

Sign up for our newsletter to learn about new releases and more.
https://oliver-heberbooks.com/subscribe/

Follow us on social media:

facebook.com/oliverheberbooks

instagram.com/oliverheberbooks

amazon.com/oliverheberbooks

youtube.com/@OliverHeberBooksPublisher